Children of Decay

A NOVEL BY

GOPI BAIN

Content Warning: This book contains a few instances of strong language as well as a few scenes of violence and gore. The story explores dark and sensitive themes around religious discrimination, socioeconomic disparity and social isolation. The characters include social pariahs and people with physical and mental disability and illness.

The characters and events of this book are fictional and any resemblance to actual events or persons (living or dead) is purely confidential.

No part of this book may be reproduced or transmitted in any form or by any means, electronic or mechanical, including photocopying, recording or by any information storage and retrieval system, except for limited quotations for reviewing-purpose.

Copyright © 2022 Gopi Bain

All rights reserved.

ISBN: 978-0-646-86625-3

DEDICATION

To my Nanu and Nana who inspired me to embrace who I am
and to my loving wife, who reminded me who I am when I
had lost my way

CONTENTS

Book 1: The Decay   11
- 1 AN UNEXPECTED HOST   13
- 2 A FISHING STORY   15
- 3 A RUMOR OF MURDER   19
- 4 A FISH-GOD   23
- 5 AN OLD AND VIOLENT GRAVEYARD   27
- 6 A PRETTY FACE WITH A BOTTLE   30
- 7 A TANGLE OF WATERLILIES   33
- 8 A ROOF THAT FELL   37
- 9 TIMES THAT WERE QUIET   43
- 10 A POND FULL OF BLOOD   45
- 11 BISHNU TELLS GHOST STORIES   47
- 12 A TREE OF SANCTITY   52
- 13 AN INTERMISSION OF REFLECTION   60
- 14 AN UNFINISHED STORY   63
- 15 AN ADVENTURE BEGINS   67
- 16 A TALE OF MADNESS   70

Book 2: The Gathering   75
- 17 A NIGHT OF MISCHIEF   77
- 18 AN ESTATE ON THE CURVE   80
- 19 A DREAM OF A NESTLING   83
- 20 A CHEST FULL OF IDEAS   91
- 21 A GRACIOUS WEAKLING   98
- 22 OF GODS AND WORSHIPS   104
- 23 A SUPERSTITION ABOUT INEVITABILITY   110
- 24 A DRUNKEN MALFEASANCE   115
- 25 ANOTHER FISHING STORY   119
- 26 AN EXILE FOR TEMPORARY PEACE   126
- 27 A TREASURE OF MISFORTUNE   130

Book 3: The Capture   137
- 28 A PREMONITION   139
- 29 A NIGHT OF CHAOS   141
- 30 A DISPLACEMENT OF AMBIGUITY   144
- 31 A CHILD OF REDEMPTION   148
- 32 A GUARDED SWAMPLAND   153
- 33 A PLAUSIBLE INVITATION   156
- 34 A RIGHTFUL MADNESS   160
- 35 A TEST OF HUMANITY   164
- 36 A SECRET CARRIER   166
- 37 THOUGHTS AND DEEDS OF UNWANTED CHILDREN   169
- 38 ASHRAF UL MAKHLUQAT   176
- 39 A SHIMMER OF LIGHT FROM THE OUTSIDE   182
- 40 A GARDEN OF INNOCENCE   185
- 41 A GAME AMONG CHILDREN   189
- 42 A FUNERAL, AN INEVITABILITY   193
- 43 A FATEFUL IMPRISONMENT   198

Book 4: The Release — **205**
- 44 KOMLA BIBI — 207
- 45 RIGHTEOUS OLD LOVERS — 212
- 46 A TUG OF THE LEASH — 215
- 47 A WHISPER IN THE WIND — 220
- 48 A SLAYING OF DEMONS — 227
- 49 PIPALI — 229
- 50 A CRUELTY IN MOTHERHOOD — 232
- 51 A CARRIAGE OF MOURNING — 237
- 52 AN ABANDONED TREASURE — 241
- 53 A JOURNEY THROUGH DECAY — 245
- 54 A STORM OF CHANGE — 249
- 55 A SECRET INTERMISSION — 252
- 56 WHAT MAKES A MONSTER — 254
- 57 'O-BROMHON, NOHO TUMI TATO' — 258
- 58 A BUCKET FULL OF BLOOD — 264
- 59 A WARM PLACE — 267
- 60 A PROMISE OF REBIRTH — 273

CHILDREN OF DECAY

ACKNOWLEDGMENTS

Children of Decay wouldn't have been possible without the contributions of the many beta readers and editors. So, I'd like to extend my gratitude to all the great people from Fiverr and Scribophile who helped me shape it into being.

From that brilliant community, a very special thanks goes to Andreea Padurean who provided me excellent structural editorial feedback and encouragement on Fiverr that was fit for the genre I wrote in.

From Fiverr community, I'd also like to thank Connie H. Her copy edit was pivotal in vastly improving the readability of my book and making it publishable.

I wouldn't have been able to write this book without the guidance and encouragement of many indie writers and authors on social media.

From that amazing community, I'd like to extend my appreciation for Barbara Avon—a brilliant, multi-genre, independent author—for her guidance and advice at different steps in publishing Children of Decay.

I'd also like to thank Eva Leppard—a talented independent writer—who offered me her valuable advice and guidance as well.

I extend my deepest appreciation to all my friends and family who encouraged me to write my book: Nazneen, Joseph, Kerry, Iftakher, Nabil, Josh and Rachel. I'd like to give special thanks to Vanessa Costabile for helping me develop the book cover.

Lastly, I would like to send my warm regards to the people of villages all across Bangladesh, particularly in the district of Brahmanbaria. Despite being born in a city, due to personal and professional circumstances, I had to spend a notable amount of my life in those places where I had gained the inspiration for the characters for my book. Their views, beliefs, stories, myths and friendships taught me to look beyond all the materialism around me and be inspired to write Children of Decay.

Book 1: The Decay

CHILDREN OF DECAY

1 AN UNEXPECTED HOST

A part of me was hoping not to find the old man in that dark room. So, when I discovered the inconspicuous human shape sitting at the table near the window, it unnerved me. I questioned the wisdom behind my decision to even come here. The single, contorted little hut was the only sign of habitation at the edge of an empty moor. Right behind it, a small, bare hillock rose up into the early morning mist.

I took a step forward, keeping my eyes on the old man, thinking of the terrible tales people had yarned about him. A throbbing pang of dread pressed against my heart. I glanced back at the boy who brought me here—the only one in the village who assured me that the old man was harmless. Looking at his smoky silhouette sitting on the ground in the distance gave me some confidence.

When I turned around, I felt like I was seeing something completely different. Nothing in the scenery had changed and the old man hadn't yet noticed me. He sat at the edge of the bed, working on something on the table near the window. Only this time, I saw him in a different light. The outline of his body seemed like a fragile and delicate part of its surroundings—not to be disturbed or interrupted. Suddenly, my pre-existing dread turned into intruder's guilt.

As I thought about retreating and took a step backward, my foot scuffed the dusty ground. The old man sensed me and looked up towards the door. I felt my heart skip a beat. The old man got up and started making his way noiselessly towards me. He was definitely an aged person, as evident by his general appearance. Yet he didn't have broken jaws or blazed-out complexion—features old men typically have in this area. Just a simple, plain face. A short, white beard covered the jaw and the cheeks gracefully. Perhaps the only feature that revealed his true age was his eyes—perplexed, detached, yet pacifying—sitting over high, lightly wrinkled cheekbones.

"Are you Arup Sai?" I asked cautiously.

The old man stared in my direction. Yet it felt like he wasn't looking at me at all. In his eyes, for a few moments, I saw a perplexed emptiness that I couldn't explain back then. *Is he blind?* I thought to myself. But then his eyes focused on me.

"I heard about a boy who has a special interest in one of the things that I do." I was startled by his gruff voice. "Are you that boy?"

"I... I came here to see your flutes, sir... and how you make them."

"And what would you gain from learning about my flute-making?"

"I intend to film it, sir." I took a gulp. "You see, I'm trying to—"

"Please, come in," he interrupted. "Why are you standing over there like a stranger?" A broad smile made his white beard sparkle and right at that moment, all my fear, guilt and edginess, disappeared like feathers in the wind.

2 A FISHING STORY

"Ever heard of the evergreen fish?"

That was the last thing the boy whispered before he snapped into action. Like a statue, he stood for about a minute, eyeing a large catfish close to the surface of the shallow water. Then, as if animated by electricity, he drove the spear-like weapon into the water-covered, shallow jute-field. A flicker of blood splashed out of the water and onto the dry land where we stood, kissing the side of my left toe and painting half of his right foot crimson.

"Wow, didn't expect it to get this bloody," he said with a sideways grin. "Must have caught that one right in the heart. It's good that it died without a struggle. It's sad to see fish struggle to death. It stays with you when you cook and eat them."

He pulled his spear out and at the end of it was a large bloody catfish, about one and a half feet long. Its body shone like a black diamond in the sun on one side and gleamed white as a sheet of paper on the other. On the dark side, close to its head, the unforgiving, sharp end of the spear had gone in and come out the other side. Thick blood gushed out relentlessly.

"Just what I thought," he said, still grinning, until he saw the horror in my eyes. "It's okay. It's only this bloody because it's bleeding from the heart. Other ones won't bleed as much. You'll see."

The boy standing in front of me with a face full of murderous grin was Bishnu, a Hindu boy who took care of Dadima[i] and her farming lands. He was a Hindu boy in the Muslim part of the village and the story of how he got here is quite fascinating.

His appearance had all the hallmarks of a fairly good-looking villager: lean body, carved out by pure physical labor, all the tight features jammed into a small frame that wasn't more than five feet, four inches tall. His dark complexion suggested long hours spent in the hot tropical sun, yet his body had an indescribable glow to it. He had silky, long hair that came down to his neck—unlike other villagers, who worked hard in the fields and preferred their haircuts as short as possible. On his chin, he had a sliver of a goatee, which made his grin seem mischievous. His eyes were dark brown and full of boyish wonder. It was clear that he enjoyed fishing deeply.

The rainy season was in full flow, but it was that time in the day when the sky cleared up and the heat of the sun made its way into the watery world as a reminder of the harsh tropical summer that had just passed. Bishnu put the bloody catfish into a large aluminum bowl and started getting into the water-drenched jute-field.

"The evergreen fish, you say?" I said as I started to follow him.

"Hey, be careful!" he shouted out. "Take off your shoes. Mud-water eats away at the lifespan of shoes faster than fire."

I had already taken one step into the jute-field and felt the hot mud slither into the sole of my shoe.

"You might want to clean that up when you get home," he said. "Take it off if you want to come in."

I followed his instruction and strode barefoot into the mud. For a moment, I thought I had stepped into lava. But at the very next moment, I felt the grasp of the ice-cold mud underneath the scorching top layer.

"Never walked into a wet jute-field, eh?" he said, observing me with a smile of smug curiosity. "Careful of the little catfish stings," he said. "They are not as venomous as snake bites, but they hurt just as much. It's an off chance, though. They won't sting you unless you hunt them. Very intelligent creatures, these little buggers! They recognize hunters as soon as one approaches their territory and tend to stay away. They will flock around you, but stay clear of me. The only way to catch them is to get your hands dirty."

Following his own advice, he knelt down on the water covered field. The water around him made almost no ripple as he deftly and noiselessly guided his slick body into the water. I watched him in quiet admiration as he began eying the mud underneath the water with a focused frown. After about thirty seconds, he raised his right hand from his lap and kept it still and poised about a foot above the water surface. And then, with the same kind of electric jolt with which he had hurled his weapon at the catfish earlier, he plunged his hand into the water. But it came up empty.

"So close," he murmured, ever so softly. Only a few seconds later, his hand flickered into action again. This time, it came out of the water holding a catfish by the head. Like a small black snake, it twisted and turned, trying to be free of Bishnu's grip.

Bishnu quickly opened the small, bamboo-woven canister hanging by his waist, plunged the fish into it and closed the lid. He went on. The more catfish he caught, the more violently the bamboo storage shook at his waist.

I focused my attention on the mud, where he was hunting them down one by one.

"They make tiny little caves like this in the mud," Bishnu explained, with excitement in his eyes. "They put their entire body in there and stick their head out close to the surface of the water, where it's easier to breathe." He glanced at me and grinned. "That's where we come in. We stick our hands in there and grab them right by their heads." He shifted his gaze back on the water. "But they are very clever creatures. The moment they see you, they flip their heads back into the cave and stick their tails out. You have to catch them when they are not looking."

"Then why not just grab them by their tails?" I asked.

Bishnu grinned lightly, still observing the water. "Oh, you don't want to do that," he said without explanation and went right back to his work.

Quite frankly, I was expecting a more satisfactory answer to my question. But I didn't bother asking again, as he seemed quite engrossed in his work. I started observing him attentively. He was right: every time the fish sensed danger, they instantly flipped their heads back into the watery caves, popping out their tails. The slithery tails seemed easier to catch than the heads and still, Bishnu would simply let the opportunity go, saying things like, 'Oh no, it sensed me,' or 'Nope, too clever,' before moving onto the next one.

Eventually, my curiosity got the better of me and I knelt down on the mud. I tried to make as little disturbance as possible, just like him. But I made a lot more ripple on the water than he did and I felt movement around me underneath the water. The catfishes around me had sensed my presence. Bishnu looked at me and grinned.

"Just stay still for a minute," he said as he brought his gaze back to the muddy water. "They will come back to you. They are clever creatures, but not very wise. They have very little memory. So, they will eventually come back and flock around you again. They have come here to breed in the shallow, fresh rainwater. It's good for them, but there isn't a lot of room here as there are in the much larger water bodies where they came from." His hand jolted into the water again, coming up with another catfish. He smiled at me as he put it into his canister. "So, just stay where you are and make as little movement as possible."

I took his advice and started to take stock of my surroundings to kill time. It wasn't raining as heavily as it had in the morning, but it was still silently drizzling and my clothes were already wet. In the distance, I could see the swampland across the crop fields and within the gaps of the trees, a glimpse of Dadima's household where I was residing as a guest. A tin-shed establishment with a yellow rooftop.

The catfishes had come back, so I started to follow Bishnu's procedure. He glanced at me with a faint grin and went back to work. I shadowed his technique and tried to catch a few but came up empty. At times, I would feel their slippery heads in my fingers, but when I would bring my fist out of the water, it would be holding onto nothingness. The next thing I would see was their tails sticking out, waving at me. Mocking my failure.

"You just need practice," Bishnu whispered with a grin.

I grinned back, but it was still not clear to me why we were not allowed to grab them by their tails. Eventually, both our eyes fixated on a couple of big ones in two closely adjacent caves.

"Wow. Big ones, those buggers," Bishnu whispered in excitement. "You might want to give them a try. Big ones are easy to grab."

I took a deep breath and approached as noiselessly as I could. But as I got closer, my movement created the weakest little water waves and that was enough. To my utter despair, they sensed my presence and, as expected, flipped their heads into the cave.

"Ah, that's unfortunate," Bishnu muttered, as he touched my shoulder. "Don't worry. Keep trying. It gets better, trust me."

I sighed in exasperation. They were probably the biggest ones I had seen so far. Their tails were still skimming the surface of the water. I was too frustrated to let this go. So, without any warning, I pinched into their tails. Remarkably, my index finger and thumb closed perfectly around the two tails and I flicked them out of the water with a broad smile. But my joy of accomplishment lasted less than two seconds as the two fishes jolted back towards the two sides of my palm and bit into it. A powerful, blunt pain burst out from the center of my hand. I screamed, lost my balance and fell back into the mud.

With mud and water in my eyes, I caught blurry glimpses of Bishnu laughing while he pulled me onto dry land. I looked at my hand. The two catfish were still clamped onto it as if their lives depended on it. I had let go of their tails a long time ago. Their jerky movements subsided. My hand went numb with pain as it lay deadweight on the ground along with the two catfish.

"Congratulations," Bishnu said, catching his breath. "You caught your first catfish."

3 A RUMOUR OF MURDER

To the east of the quaint little rural community, I had come to visit lies a bustling, sprawling village-market named Choubazaar. The place gave economic value to the crops of this fertile land. On both sides of a wide concrete road stood crop-merchants' warehouses. They got their supplies from farmers, who brought the yields of their hard work on their shoulders, or on oxen-pulled wooden carts if they could afford it. Monstrous trucks full of crops stood near the warehouses, ready to carry the produce to the capital. In between these warehouses were bamboo-shed confectioneries, with seats for sipping tea and biting into shingaras[ii].

"Fresh fish shoppers are impulse shoppers," Bishnu told me, once we had put our containers down on the side of the road. "They never plan on buying the fish when they come to Choubazaar, but they do come with luxury on their minds. And the most profitable kind of luxury is necessary luxury."

"Necessary luxury?" I asked.

"Yes," he answered, smiling. "The luxury for a guest who holds the key to improvement of the host's social position. Someone from a wealthier family, considering the host's daughter's hand in marriage for their prospective young heir. A visitor from the capital, such as yourself, thinking about taking a housekeeper, leaving the host with one less mouth to feed. A landowner looking for new recruits to farm his fields." Bishnu nodded. "The general villager needs to appease these types of people. When they visit, it becomes a matter of utmost importance to treat them to a hearty, expensive meal. So, the man of the host family breaks out some of his life savings, puts on some clean, presentable clothing and comes right here to Choubazaar to buy quality rations for his wife at home, who is preparing the meal. They usually have their mind settled on a good rooster, some beef shank pieces, kalijira rice[iii] and some aromatic spices."

"So, what makes buy your fish instead?"

"Just the mere sight and sound of it!" Bishnu proclaimed with pride in his eyes. "The moment they hear the clinking of metal containers, they turn to me. Nothing expresses hearty hospitality like freshly-caught fish of the season. I once sold fishes to the same landlord whose empty farmland I had caught them from and he bought them at a premium, with a smile on his face. You don't need to stay in the bazaar for too long with these."

To prove his words right, our fish sold within minutes. A neatly-dressed man bought them and walked away with a victorious smile on his face.

"What he just paid us is four times the price he would have paid for the same fish from a typical fish-grocer," commented Bishnu with a grin, as soon as the man left. "That's the price of freshly caught fish, still alive and kicking."

I sat down on a bench in front of a confectionery store while Bishnu went to clean himself up. A raised platform nearby housed a tube-well for public use. He pumped it a few times until it produced red, iron-tinted stream of water that washed the mud off his legs. He then untangled the folds of his lungi[iv], letting it fall from above his knees to his ankles. Hidden within the folds was a sky-blue shirt, which he put back on. He then splashed some water on his face and hair.

after he was done, he looked nothing like someone who had been in the mud all day. Water drops glistened on his dark hair and the thin goatee. Despite his sun-blazed skin, his complexion wasn't the same pitch dark that the farmer class in this area usually had.

"Huh, look at you. You need a bath." Bishnu chuckled. "I was going to ask you to clean up here, but I don't think that will achieve anything."

I joined him and laughed at myself. My clothes were painted with dried-up mud, constantly reminding me of its cold, rough presence.

"I wasn't planning on getting into the mud, but I don't regret it," I said. "Don't worry, I will make better arrangements next time."

"You don't have to come fishing with me again. I only took you fishing because Dadima asked me to."

"And I enjoyed it and will do it again. Mud and bruises don't scare me."

"In all honesty, I never anticipated you to jump into the mud with me. How is your hand? Do you still feel the sting?"

I looked at my right hand. I had almost forgotten that I had gotten stung by two catfish at the same time. One of the two sting marks was slightly off-center, on the lower right of my palm. The other was on the opposite side, just under the knuckles of my index and middle fingers. That one had hurt more and still gave me a tingle when I touched it.

"It felt like acid being injected into my hand when I got stung, but the pain went away pretty quickly," I replied.

"Yeah, catfish stings heal pretty fast. The best antidote for catfish venom is water. It dilutes the venom to the point where it's no longer painful. Therefore, the best remedy for catfish stings during fishing is to simply continue fishing."

With a deep breath, he looked at me with a speculative frown on his still-smiling face.

"So, tell me, what do you want from Arup Sai?"

"Huh?" I wasn't prepared at all for the question. "Did Dadima tell you about this?"

"Yes," Bishnu replied, in a cautious tone. "She tasked me to take you to him."

"Oh, I see. Well... you see, one of Dadima's nieces is married to a cousin of mine, who told me about him and his craft."

"What kind of craft?"

"His flutes, of course."

"Oh, so that's what this is about," Bishnu responded with a sigh of relief.

"Yeah. My cousin told me fascinating things about him," I continued. "He told me that he doesn't make flutes from bamboos like other flute-makers, but from tree branches, by hollowing them out from the inside somehow."

"Yeah, he does that."

"That's fascinating."

"Hmm. Well, not that fascinating when you see how he does it."

"You know how he does it?"

Instead of answering my question, Bishnu quickly surveyed his surroundings, turned to me and asked, "So, you want to see how he makes them?"

"Yes. But also film it—might be good material if I want to write about it someday."

"So, you are a writer?"

"Oh, no, no." I chuckled. "I have never written for pleasure in my life. But if I ever want to, this will be good source material."

"Hmm...why would you want to write about it?"

"I don't know. Posterity, perhaps? Reminding the future generations of a dying craft. My cousin told me that the old man is the only one who does this. Is that right?"

"Yes," Bishnu confirmed. Breathing in, he gazed into the distance. "I think we could do better reminding ourselves of what we could save, rather than what we will inevitably lose. But that's just my opinion."

we sat together in silence for a while. "Dadima never told me you were the one who would take me to him," I said finally.

"Then how did you expect to get to him?"

"I... I thought I would just ask around and people would help me out."

Bishnu broke into a quiet laughter. He steadied himself and surveyed the surroundings again. "So, you are telling me that you can just ask people everywhere where Arup Sai is and they will tell you?"

"Won't they?" I asked, confused.

Bishnu shook his head. "Look. First of all, the man is a hermit. No one here talks to him. The only time you will see him is when he shows up here to buy his necessities. And even then, the shopkeepers keep the interactions at a minimum."

"Why?"

"Why? What do you mean why? They fear him. Quite profoundly, in fact. They avoid his gaze, give him what he comes for and look away until he leaves."

"Oh, but...why?" I asked. "Why would people be afraid of a solitary old man making flutes?"

Bishnu narrowed his eyes and stared at me for a few seconds. "Oh, you...you really don't know?" he muttered. "Your cousin never told you?"

"Told me what?"

Bishnu drew closed to me and uttered in a low voice, "People are afraid of him because they believe he murdered his own wife and children."

4 A FISH-GOD

"You haven't yet told me about the evergreen fish."

Bishnu grinned at my question as he sat near the edge of my bed. It was a few hours after sundown. We had just come back to settle into my room in Dadima's house, after gorging hungrily on the supper she had prepared for us. The fragrant vegetables, with tender small koi fish and soft brown rice, had taken our fatigue away almost instantly.

"You haven't forgotten about it, have you?" chuckled Bishnu.

"What is it? A fish that lives forever?"

"You can say that if you want to put it simply. It's a myth, a legend."

"What kind of legend?"

Bishnu breathed in and gazed contemplatively out the window. The night had settled in and in the swamp that lay beyond, crickets chirped loudly. In the distance, the swishing and swirling rhythm of the sea of crops portrayed an odd maddening serenity. Rainy season's cold, slithering gusts cut through the heavy, humid air. The world was chaotic, yet calming.

"Some people believe that some fish are immortal," Bishnu explained, "That they only face death when we catch them or when other predators eat them. But unless they meet an unnatural death, they will live forever."

"Do you actually believe in such a thing?"

"Well, fishermen have caught fish four times the size they were supposed to be. I know a fisherman who once made a scar in a fish's mouth while catching it. When he was about to put it in his container, it slipped away and escaped. Seventeen years later, he caught the same fish again. It was six times bigger and bore the same scar in its gums."

"So, what did he do to the fish?"

"He let it go."

"He let it go? Why?"

"It's ill-advised to kill an evergreen fish with the knowledge that it is evergreen. It brings ill fate. You should respect them, especially as a fisherman. If you kill an evergreen fish, no fish will flock around you again."

"So, who are they? Some kind of fish gods?"

"Maybe, maybe not. But it is a belief, nevertheless. A fisherman's code, if you will. I never caught one yet. But I know people who have. Some people even worship them."

"Worship them?"

"Yes," answered Bishnu. "People say that there is a place across to the north of The Great Green Lake where one of them lived for centuries, swimming around a small, round, sacred island. People in that area worship that fish as a god."

"Have you been there?" I asked.

"A few times, yes," he answered.

"Have you seen that fish?" I asked, with anticipation in my voice. Bishnu grinned, with mischief in his eyes. "Come on now, tell me,"

Bishnu gazed out of the window again. After a brief windy pause, it had started to rain again. If you listened carefully, you could hear watery droplets falling from leaves and branches of the trees into the watery swamp. As rain picked up more, I could hear it hitting the tin rooftops in metallic rhythm.

"No, I haven't," Bishnu finally said, with a smile, which, to my surprise, hid some indescribable pain. "I have never seen the fish."

Is he unhappy that, as a fisherman, he has never seen an evergreen fish? Is it important for a fisherman to meet one?

"How can you believe in something that you haven't seen?" I asked.

"I don't necessarily believe in a fish god that lives forever."

"You…don't?"

"No. But I like the tenacity of the concept."

"The tenacity?"

"Yes, the tenacity," he said with a sigh as he brought his gaze back to me. "The idea that a fish has avoided being caught by its natural predators to the point where it lived long enough to see us treat it as a god is… quite a god-like achievement."

"An unusual way of seeing gods," I scoffed.

"Is it? Is it really?"

"What do you mean?"

"Isn't that the base concept of every religion? Think about it. All the legends about Prophets and Abatars[v]. What is the one common theme among them? The tenacity of *escape*. Flawless characters, chased by people trying to harm them and the ideologies they represent. And in that process of escape and survival, they elevate themselves to levels higher than mere humans. So, I don't think it's unusual for people to believe in an idea like the evergreen fish. It comes from the very same part of us that makes us put simple people on divine pedestals."

"So godly incarnations are essentially escapists?"

"Essentially. Yeah."

We both fell silent. Bishnu sat at the edge of my bed with his knees to his chest and I with my back to the wall. I concentrated on the maddening rhythm of rain falling on the tin rooftop. It felt cathartic.

"Well, I am no God or any of His incarnations, so I cannot escape the life I've left behind anymore," I proclaimed, breaking the silence. "It's been a pleasure to get to know you. It really has. But I guess if I cannot film Arup Sai's flute-making, there's no point in –"

"You don't want to go to Arup Sai anymore?"

"Well, you said he murdered his own wife and children."

"I said *people say* he murdered his wife and children."

"He…didn't?"

Bishnu broke into jolly laughter. "No, of course not. He is harmless."

"How do you know?"

"Trust me, I know. He wouldn't step on a dung beetle if he could help it."

"How can you be so sure?"

"Because I am perhaps the only person in this village that interacts with him on a regular basis…Well, whatever you can call *interaction* with that hermit medicine-man. That's the reason why Dadima has tasked me with the responsibility of taking you to him."

"So, if he barely interacts with anybody, why does he interact with you?"

"Because I am his only way of earning a living."

"What do you mean?"

"Who do you think sells his flutes? I am his middle man."

"Oh…fascinating. That makes a lot of sense, now," I said with a rising smile. The thought that I would finally get to meet Arup Sai gave me a sense of optimism. "So. What kind of buyers do the flutes attract? Collectors?" I chuckled. "I hardly feel you can find collectors of artistic paraphernalia by an alleged murderer in this modest rural land."

"You think this village is full of poor people, don't you?"

I didn't know how to answer the question, so I smiled back at him awkwardly.

Bishnu went on. "There are some pretty rich people in this part of the world and they are eccentric too!"

"Really?"

Bishnu gave me a furtive grin. "Ever heard of the Bhairabs?"

"Bhairabs?"

"Yes. The wealthiest family in this district."

"You told me that this is the wealthier part of the village and I haven't seen any house here better-looking than the one we're in right now."

"The Bhairabs do not live in this part of the village," Bishnu said, smirking. "They don't live in the south, either."

"That's the whole village, isn't it?" I asked, perplexed.

Bishnu kept smiling. "You are forgetting the Hindupara to the west, along the shores of the Great Green Lake."

"Oh, I see. So, they live there?"

"Not quite. They live further away from Hindupara, on an island they own."

"Oh, now you're just telling me fairy tales, Bishnu," I scoffed.

"It's not a fairy tale. It's real."

"Well, then why don't you take me there?"

"Hmm…well," he went on. "The Bhairabs are quite private in their affairs—"

"See, now you are just trying to get out of—"

"—but I will see how I can arrange something for you," he finished.

I squinted my eyes with playful skepticism. "So, they are real?"

"As real as the very air you breathe."

"And you can take me to them."

"I think I can, but for now, let's bring our ambition down to meeting just one of them. What do you say?"

"Meeting here? In this part of the village?"

Bishnu nodded.

"Sure, why not?" I said. "When can I meet this person?"

"Let's get you to Arup Sai, first. Then we can get to the Bhairabs."

"Sure."

A sudden flapping of wings startled us. Through the window, we saw a spotted dove fly away from its hiding place in one of the bushes in the swamp. The rain had stopped and the world felt stunted for a few seconds before the night came alive again.

5 AN OLD AND VIOLENT GRAVEYARD

"From the burning pyre of the old, the new come to life. But the real tragedy is when the old are too stubborn to let go, so the new have to be sacrificed in their place."

My video camera was rolling and I had no idea what the old man was talking about. I stared at Arup Sai with a confused expression that said, "What do you mean?"

"Well," Arup Sai said, smiling at my camera. "I am a stubborn old man and you are young and new, sacrificing your time to understand my stubborn little craft."

"Are you trying to tell me that this project I'm doing is a waste of time?"

"Absolutely not. On the contrary, I think it is very necessary."

"Why so?"

"You will see, in time," said the old man, carefully combing his snow-white beard.

As my video camera rolled, I started thinking about Arup Sai's strange habitation. Outside, there wasn't a blade of grass in sight. The ground that seemed solid from a distance broke apart under my feet with a subtle, lingering dampness. Bishnu made me wear a pair of tattered old slippers from Dadima's house instead of my normal footwear. "You don't want to go there with your fancy capital-dwelling shoes, trust me," he explained.

On my first day, Bishnu came with me but left me to myself a few hundred meters from the old man's house.

"You're not going to introduce me?" I had asked him.

"He doesn't like too many visitors. He was told you would come and I can bet that he is only expecting one person and that's you," he responded. "Now, go on. Don't be afraid. When you see him, you will realize he wouldn't be able to harm you, even if he wanted to."

I had been warned by many about this man. Some had outright advised me not to go if I cared for my life. To be honest, I would have listened to them had I not met Bishnu.

The thumping sound of a wooden box being put on the table startled me. The old man was smiling at me. *Did he do that to get my attention?* On the table, a toolbox laid wide open, with metal instruments of different sizes. From that assortment, he picked up what seemed like a little hammer. Giving me one last glance, he proceeded towards the door. I was not prepared to go outdoors, but my camera was rolling. I struggled with the heavy equipment as I followed him.

His house was situated in front of a small, bare hillock that rose up in a steep slope. It was quite an effort to keep pace with him up the incline with the heavy camera, but I managed. After a minute of climbing, the hillock started to slope down at a more comfortable angle and I had the opportunity to get my breath back. But what I saw in front of me took my breath away.

I was standing in front of what can only be described as a carnage of a broken-down forest. Large, wide chunks of dead tree trunks scattered over a large area, simmering under the thick fog. The whole area felt like a surreal, abandoned battlefield. The ground was laid bare, without a shred of grass.

The old man started towards one of the trunks. I followed. *If that's where he gets his material from, then it's quite an inventory!* As I got closer to him, he gave me an amused smile.

"The most important part of making a good flute is picking out the right branch." He started talking. "There are many factors involved. The branch has to be the right thickness and age."

He examined the branches of several trunks. Every so often, he would tap on a branch with his little hammer. If he became more interested, he would bend down, bring his ear closer to the branch and give it a couple more solid taps.

"Why are you tapping these branches?" I asked with anticipation.

"To see how ready they are," the old man muttered. "As you can see, all these trees here are dead and termites are eating away at their insides. So, when a branch is hollow enough for me to make a flute, that's when I take them out. I leave the rest to get more hollowed-out until they are ready."

"That's why you're tapping on them with that small hammer," I said, riding on the gratification of satisfied curiosity.

"Yes." The old man kept working.

"That's... amazing."

The old man wasn't listening to me. He stared at one branch for a few seconds after examining it fully. "This will do," he muttered.

He gripped the branch firmly, close to where it connected to the tree trunk and pulled downwards. It clipped right off, releasing a puff of sawdust.

"Why do you do this?" I whispered.

Arup Sai glanced towards me. There was a sign of aggravation on his face as if me asking that question had somehow offended him.

"This is the only way I know how to give them a purpose," He got up and looked down at the branch in his hand. "We got what we need. Let's head back."

Back in the hut, the old man sat down at his table near the window. The misty morning light illuminated his workspace. From his toolbox, he took out a knife with a long, thin blade and started to curve the inside of the branch. Shaved-off white particles came off easily and fell on the table. Gradually, the hollow inside got bigger and more consistently round.

After performing his craft with silent precision, Arup Sai glanced up at me and grinned. "How good your flute becomes depends entirely on how well you smooth out the surface inside."

He went on and on about his work, talking about it and doing it at the same time. At one point, he looked as if he wasn't talking to me at all, but only to himself. As he was working, slowly but surely, the mask lifted from his face. I started to see a completely different person, one with a face full of childish wonder.

6 A PRETTY FACE WITH A BOTTLE

"So, you must be Bishnuda's friend."

A soft, ringing voice in the middle of a sea of crops broke my train of thought. It was the end of the rainy season when the soil was rich with fertility. The crops were of a wide spectrum of green, red and grey. Hidden among these fields of crops were the occasional tiny bits of bare land—each with a hut in the middle.

These huts were not for the poor. They belonged to landlords who lived far away and could afford a spare piece of land for themselves to stay in when they came to inspect their crops. I was sitting in one of those bare lands in front of one of those huts, annoyed at Bishnu. He had brought me here, knocked lightly on the door, said, "Hmm… not sure if anyone is in yet," and disappeared into the crops, without giving me a chance to respond. After waiting for a while, I was considering trying my luck at making it back to Dadima's house through the jig-jagging alleyways among the crop-fields until I heard that ringing voice.

The girl standing in front of me was wearing an old salwar kameez with faded red workings, with an orna[vi] wrapped around her upper body and shoulders. She had simple features that might have been drawn by someone who had only just learned to draw a basic human face. Her hair was jet-black, parted in the middle, glistening with the earthy smell of coconut oil. She had proportionately placed nose, lips and eyebrows. None of those features announced themselves too vividly.

"Oh, yes. Yes, I am," I responded to her question.

She picked up a couple of foldable wooden chairs leaning on the walls of the hut, set them up and indicated that I take a seat, which I obliged. She sat in front of me and smiled and for the first time, I was introduced to the most distinct feature of her face. Her wide eyes, with large, licorice-black pupils were a sharp contrast to the simplicity of her other features.

"Namaskaar," she said, clasping her hands together and bowing slightly. "My name is Nondi. Bishnuda told me a lot about you."

"I hope not too much," I said with a polite smile.

"He told me that you like to hear his stories and ponder over whether ghosts are real," she said to which I nodded in affirmation. "You don't have to believe everything he says, you know?" She chuckled. "Bishnuda doesn't lie, but his senses are… let's say, more open to imagination than others."

"I gathered that."

"Bishnuda told me that you're eager to meet someone from the Bhairab family."

"I wouldn't call it eager. I just didn't want to believe him when he said there is a wealthy family that lives on a far-away island. So, he told me he'll introduce me to someone from the family who's coming here."

"And that someone is…" Nondi glanced back worriedly towards the hut. "Taking a nap, right now," she said with an uncomfortable laugh. "Hopefully, he'll be up soon."

"Oh," I said. "So, you aren't—"

"Oh no, I am not a Bhairab, not by far," said the girl, breaking out into a graceful laugh. "I'm only their housemaid. They adopted me when I was a child. I am…nobody. So please, don't be so polite."

"Oh," I said, taken aback by the bluntness of her response. "but Bishnu never told me about—"

The girl broke into full-blown laughter this time, which lit up the already bright environment with a warm ambiance.

"Bishnuda doesn't say a lot of things," she went on. "Partly because they don't fit in with his stories and partly because there are aspects of his life he prefers to keep to himself." She drew a deep breath. "What else did he say about the Bhairabs?"

"Well," I said thoughtfully. "He said that they are from a secluded island that they own and prefer keeping to themselves."

"That's a half-truth. The Bhairabs have business far and wide. Gone are the days when they could live in isolation. Many generations ago, their wealth and prestige, combined with their secretive ways, gave them a mysterious aura. But now they've become much more open to the world."

"Hmm," I responded. "And what's the true half?"

"Well," Nondi said. "Even though they have business everywhere, they prefer to live within their own community. They don't make connections outside their locality if it isn't necessary."

"Sounds the same as any rich farming family," I commented.

"In a way, I suppose," she answered

Our conversation was interrupted by a sleepy, boyish voice from inside the hut, followed by a loud crash of metal tableware that startled me.

"Nondi, take me home. My work is done."

After a few thumping noises, out came one of the most beautiful people I had ever laid eyes on. The first time I met Babu Bhairab is crystal clear in my memory. The fading sun behind him limned his body as he stepped out of the hut and tumbled closer. He had a sharp jaw, a fair face with blood-red lips, raven-dark curly hair, milky-white arms and a short, lean body. He was holding a bottle. As he wrung his eyes full of sleep, he opened them properly to look at us, revealing jet-black pupils. He was wearing a grey blanket and a white dhuti[vii], with vibrant red and dark blue needlework. His attire was wrinkled and would have looked untidy on anyone else, but seemed perfectly fine on him.

"What work have you done, Babuda?" Nondi said. "You have been slumped all day in there. Babaji[viii] wanted you to go out and see the crops. He gave you tasks to—"

"I have done my work," he said in a raised voice with great effort. It was pretty obvious that he was heavily inebriated. He turned to me and stared in wonder for a while. I smiled nervously, but he turned back to Nondi, ignoring me and said, "And now, I've had my rest."

"What work have you done, Babuda?" Nondi repeated. "You were out 'til late last night in Choubazaar. Babaji sent you here to see if his crops are coming out well, if his farmers are not stealing from him. You were to make sure that all the fields are ready to harvest, as—"

"The farmers and the crops are doing fine. I...I know it. You know it. We all know it," Babu Bhairab interrupted, raising his hand. His voice was still broken and inconsistent. "No farmer would ever dare steal a grain from the Bhairabs. Checking on these farmers isn't the reason why Babaji sent me here. He...he sent me here so that I'm off the island, so he and Meghabda can conduct their *real* business."

He mumbled something unintelligible under his breath before taking a swig out of the bottle in his hand. The transparent, golden-red liquid came down an inch. He wiped his mouth with his other arm and turned to walk back to the hut. But after only a couple of steps, he turned around quite sharply, which made him almost lose his footing.

"Wait a minute!" He pointed his bottle-holding hand towards me. "Who...who is this man? Seems like town-folk. Is..." He frowned. "Is he—"

"Yes, he is my friend you wanted to meet," Bishnu proclaimed, appearing from the crops. A piece of cloth in his hand was wrapped around a few green watery vines. "You invited him here yourself. You said that you have an interesting proposition for him. Remember?"

Babu Bhairab stared at Bishnu with a blank expression. Then, without uttering a word, he went back into the hut, in uneven steps. Another crashing sound came, followed by loud snores.

7 A TANGLE OF WATERLILIES

To the south of the village lay a sea of crops, owned by the wealthier farmers of the north. Right beside the crop fields, the south-eastern side of the village belonged to the landless laborer farmers. While the northern locality was wooded and quaint, the south-eastern locality was vast and swampy. On the shores of the small water bodies stood lined-up shacks of mud, bamboo and hay-covered thatches, with large, shared front yards. Most of these houses' doors were open, with the inhabitants resting on bamboo mats, enjoying the afternoon breeze. They stared in wonderment as I, accompanied by Bishnu and Nondi, passed them by.

The laid-back atmosphere was inviting. Children were jumping into water bodies, having swimming races, catching snails and mussels to feed the poultry. At the bank of some of the ponds, thick tree trunks leaned forward into the water, which the children used as ledges to jump off. The adults were busy cleaning their clothes on the stone slabs on the shores.

"Another day, another drunken disappointment with Babuda." Bishnu's melancholic voice broke my train of thought.

"You are too easy to disappoint, Bishnuda," commented Nondi, in a tired voice.

"Am I now?" Bishnu said. "He was the one who wanted to meet my friend and then when the time came, what does he do? Comes out of the hut with a bottle, drunk out of his wits."

"I have explained this to you before, Bishnuda," Nondi responded. "He is not really having a good time at home lately."

"Well, I know a lot is going on at his home, but what I fail to understand is how it affects him. He has no responsibility in any of it," Bishnu said.

Nondi gave Bishnu a pain-filled stare. "You'll understand if you reach out to him."   "And how exactly do you suppose I can do that?" Bishnu's reply came instantly. "Have you seen him lately? Even the briefest of interactions ends up with him aggravating me. And the company he keeps?" He scoffed. "He is impossible to be with these days."

"All I expect from you, Bishnuda, is some compassion for your friend. You, of all people, should understand that," Nondi said in a calm voice. She turned to me and smiled. "I apologize on both of our behalf. You came here to meet Babuda, but instead, you got this argument among friends."

"Hey, I don't mind," I said. "You two both seem to care for Babu Bhairab in your own way. There's nothing wrong with that. You two sound like parents arguing about their problem child."

I managed to get a chuckle out of them with that comment. But, the sting of the argument they just had still lingered as they walked silently with their heads down.

The marshy landscape started to turn into greener patches, with the odd large tree here and there. The gatherings of thatched huts reduced in density and the noise of human habitation was replaced by the sounds of chirping birds and active forest critters. Waterbodies began to be surrounded by patches of trees rather than homes.

"You catch the best fish in those," commented Bishnu, breaking the silence, seeing me observing the waterbodies. "Fish live in larger schools there due to fewer disruptions. But you have to be patient and in the late, quiet evenings and nights, you have to be aware of *them*." He gave me a mysterious smile.

"Them?" I asked, confused.

"Oh, here we go," Nondi joined the conversation, giggling. "Another of your ghost stories."

"Believe it or not, Nondi, but they exist," said Bishnu, calmly. "I've seen them."

"You see a lot of things that others don't, Bishnuda," Nondi said. "Yet when it comes to seeing the obvious, you remain blissfully unaware."

"What is that supposed to mean?" asked Bishnu.

"That's enough, you two. Don't start again," I interfered.

Up ahead we saw the outline of a dense forest. We went past the last sign of visible habitation, where a skeletal old woman in a shari[ix] without a blouse[x] sat in her front yard. Her eyes carried an indescribable, maddening pain.

We entered a small patch of light woodland with tall trees and thick, colorful bushes. A few hundred meters ahead, I saw a large pond. Its water sparkled in the sunlight. As we walked further in, at the southwestern corner of the woodland, a single hut near a coconut tree became visible. To the west of the hut was the edge of the sea of crop fields that ran parallel to the southern village. Both the crop fields and the hut stood as the last frontier of civilization before a dense, bushy forest developed abruptly to the far-south.

"This is where you live?" I asked, pointing towards the hut.

"Yes," said Bishnu, with enthusiasm.

We got to the large pond. Lush green plants swayed under transparent waters. Bishnu dipped his sandaled feet to clean his feet and we followed. When we walked into the small front yard of Bishnu's hut, he smiled at me with pride and pointed towards the crop fields right next it.

"From here, most of the lands you see belong to Dadima," he said. "Dadima has been insisting I take you to see her lands. Well, here they are."

I followed his gaze. Right at the edge of the crop fields where the forest started, a wall of netting went up high.

"I put them up," Bishnu explained. "Crops this close to the forest get attacked by critters. Dadaji[xi] used to bring me here as a child and taught me all I know about being a farmer. I used to play around that pond." He pointed towards the waterbody we had just passed by. "This is where I first started fishing."

"Why don't you tell him about the fish hag you see here so often, Bishnuda?"

We both turned to Nondi as we heard her voice. She carried a furtive one-sided grin.

"Fish hag?" I asked. "What's that?"

Nondi broke into a giggle.

Bishnu glanced at her with playful disdain. "Don't listen to her," he said. "Wait here."

Nondi looked on as Bishnu went into the hut. The grin that she was holding faded, as she exhaled with a worried look. But as soon as she noticed me, she turned away. I peeked into the hut.

There were only two pieces of furniture: a bed and a table. The table held a large, silver steel jug, a few glasses and a steel trunk in the corner. Bishnu kneeled down, reached under the bed and brought out a rolled-up bamboo mat. He grabbed three glasses from the table. He rolled the bamboo mat on his small front yard and gestured us to sit on it. As we followed his cue, he put the glasses on top of the mat in front of us.

"Hold on," he said and launched himself onto one of the coconut trees.

Hugging the trunk tightly, he balanced his entire body on its tall trunk and climbed with proficiency. Within the time it took me to absorb all this, he was already halfway up. In the next minute, he was at the top, where he collected three green coconuts, tied them around his waist with a piece of cotton towel and slid down swiftly. At the bottom, he pulled out a sharp kachi[xii] that stuck out on the ground and chopped off the top of the coconuts. He made little holes on their flat, white heads and brought them to us, grinning at the bewildered expression on my face.

"That was impressive," I acknowledged.

"Been climbing these trees since I was a child," Bishnu responded. "They were my favorite places to hide when Dadima or Dadaji got mad at me." He poured the liquid from the green coconuts into the glasses. The semitransparent liquid smelt earthy and tasted sweet with a bit of zing in it. Instantly, a cool, relaxed sensation took over my body.

"You had to hide from them often?" I said, grinning back.

To my surprise, Bishnu's face tightened in response. He didn't seem to have taken the question as lightly, as it was meant. "I was, in the beginning," he said looking away. "I was… hesitant. I…wasn't convinced of what they were planning to do with me. I didn't trust them."

"You had trouble trusting people at such an early age?" I asked.

I heard an anxious exhale. Nondi was observing Bishnu intently and I followed suit, but Bishnu avoided both of our glares, playing with his drink.

"Over here, most parents barely make enough to feed their children," he said. "Many abandon them or send them off to the capital. The quicker you can be rid of your children, the less mouths to feed." He looked up, finally. "So, you can see why I found it difficult to accept the fact that an old man who had just found me in tattered clothes would take me into his care with no selfish intentions."

"That's fair," I commented.

"It is," he said. "But then, as I grew up, I learned that he really did care for me and loved me like a son." His voice shook a bit as he finished that sentence.

"That he did," I said, realizing this boy carried a lot in his heart.

Bishnu took a deep breath and smiled at us. He got up and went back into his hut and came out with the bag he'd been carrying all the way from the crop fields. He sat in front of us, reached into the bag and pulled out a large, tangled clump of earthy black roots and watery green vines, which held three shaplas[xiii] with petals—pink on the outside and rosy white on the inside.

"This," he said, "will make Kuberda very happy. He loves shaluks[xiv] very much, yet he doesn't get to have them much." He glanced at Nondi, who smirked back, resting her chin on her hand. "What?" asked Bishnu.

Nondi shook her head without answering.

"Anyway, take this to Kuberda. I scoured all over the crop fields for this," he said, handing the tangle of waterlilies to Nondi, who carefully slid the flowers back into the bag with the rest. "You can also cook the vines. They're well-developed and should be delicious. God knows when you will be crossing the river again."

"Thank you," Nondi said, getting up. "Let's head back. It's getting dark."

8 A ROOF THAT FELL

"I'll arrange another get-together with Babuda," Nondi abruptly said as she stepped into the little hut in the middle of the crop fields.

She closed the door with a discontent glance at Bishnu. Bishnu frowned back, without exchanging any words. It was clear that their argument about Babu Bhairab hadn't left either of them in a good mood, even though our conversations had changed topic since.

Bishnu guided me out of the crop fields and we went back into the northern locality. I left him to process his thoughts. We walked into a narrow alleyway, shaded by bamboo-tree clumps and large, tin-shed houses. The piercing Magreeb Azan[xv] made me look back to see the sun setting behind us as it stretched out our own shadows in front of us. The rainy season was almost over—no more swirls of wind or occasional drizzles. But signs of the season still persisted. A light breeze was making the bamboo clumps sizzle and even though it wasn't raining, a few large, cold drops of water occasionally fell on me. They were residues of rain from earlier in the day that the leaves had held on to.

"Bishnu, oi Bishnu! Where are you heading?" A high-pitched male voice broke our awkward silence. A short, stout man came out from one of the tin-shed houses and joined us.

"Where have you been, my friend? Haven't seen you for ages," he said, smiling toothily. "I've been looking for you all over the village and Choubazaar. I need some patchwork on the covering underneath the roof of my house[xvi]." He said. "Made that covering with a lot of love. My little brother brought his new bride home. So, I had to liven up the house. I had the old covering replaced with a new one by an expensive carpenter. That bastard charged me a price and a half, but I got it done with decorated bamboo strings. You know the type? The one that bends around the stitching?"

"I know what you are talking about, Battiji," Bishnu said calmly. "It's not easy."

"But I know you can do it, Bishnu. I've seen you doing tougher work," the man said, with desperate confidence. "That carpenter made the foundation around the edges with bad wood that mites just ate away. It looked pretty, so he knew he could get away with doing substandard work. Son of a pig, that one!" He spat violently on the ground as he walked with us, completely ignoring me. "Last Friday, when all the men in the house were at Jumma[xvii], it fell on our new bride and nearly killed my little nephew of two months."

Bishnu exhaled irritably, still avoiding the man's gaze. "I will come at dawn tomorrow. But I cannot promise anything."

"That is all I need, Bishnu," the man said happily, slapping Bishnu's back. Then he looked at me furtively. "So, you got another pretty rich friend here, eh?" He chuckled, surveying me. "Hmm…soft, glary eyes. All polite and proper. You are from the capital, aren't you?"

"Huh?" I asked. I hadn't realized that he had directed the conversation towards me. "Oh, yes. Yes, I am."

He started laughing and to his surprise, I joined him, which stunted his laughter a bit. I didn't feel embarrassed by the judgment in what he said. Instead, I saw the humor in it. I did seem quite out of place. I was also pondering on how awful he must be feeling right now, with the damage to his house. I wondered how his brother's wife must be feeling, seeing her nest break down. It felt strange not to feel uncomfortable despite being looked down upon by someone and instead empathize with his situation. I had never been so altruistic.

Bishnu, on the other hand, didn't seem too thrilled by his remark. "I will see you tomorrow, after Fazr[xviii] Battiji. Will that work?"

"Of course, Bishnu. That will be lovely. Bring your town-friend, too. Tonni, my brother's wife, will take care of you. I'll pay you well, Bishnu. You're a lifesaver." He left promptly, giving me a quick glance—this time, with a touch of amicability.

"No, you won't! You will barely pay me to cover the cost of the materials," Bishnu muttered as the man's footsteps quickly disappeared in the houses behind us.

"How do you know?" I inquired. "He seems genuinely thankful."

"Oh, he is definitely thankful, no doubt about that," Bishnu answered. "But he also had to finance his brother's wedding and he needs to invest in sowing and ploughing his land to get a good harvest later in the year. This is not a good time for people like him to throw money everywhere."

"But he *said* that he will pay you well."

Bishnu broke into a warm smile. "You don't know how things work around here, do you?" he commented. "People here don't pay when they are trying to save money. This time of the year, the soil is fertile and farmers are planning to sow the seeds for the harvest in late autumn, they are not keen to spend money on anything else."

"On top of that, you have to understand that he just organized a wedding for his brother. People put their best financial resources into weddings, which means he is *really* not intending to spend a lot of money at this moment."

"So why did he say that he would pay you well?"

"Look, payment here can be many things," Bishnu said. "It can be money, it can be a favor, or it can simply mean a nice gesture of hospitality…which is probably the case, this time." He smiled serenely at my puzzled face. "Remember, he invited you as well?"

"Yes?"

"This means his brother's wife will probably organize some breakfast for us and after I'm done inspecting the damage, she will invite us to have breakfast with her. That will be my payment."

"Huh, so there actually won't be any monetary transaction?"

"Only enough to cover the costs of the materials and he will know the cost of the materials, trust me. He will head to Choubazaar today to check the prices."

I chuckled in wonderment. "So then, why did you accept his offer?"

"For two reasons." Bishnu sighed. "Firstly, helping him now will spread a good name for me across the village, so when people have money in their hands in late autumn, they will ask me to mend their house, in return of monetary payment, of course."

"Interesting. Is this what you do for a living?"

"I don't really do much for a living. I already have a roof over my head. I look after Dadima and her farmlands and she provides for me," he said contentedly. "But, when I have free time, I do a few things here and there to save some money."

"Like?"

"Like this." He pointed to the empty containers in my hand. "I catch fish and sell it to people in Choubazaar. And in other seasons, I mend houses."

"Is that a good source of income?"

"It is, in the right seasons. You see, the houses in this area are mostly made of mud, bamboo and wood and for people like Battiji, who is a little better off, tin-shed. Being built with such materials makes the houses susceptible to weather damage throughout the year. In summer, mud floors and walls crack without moisture. Winter mornings wet the hay-covered roof with heavy dew, making the houses colder than outside. Then comes the rainy season and water starts seeping in, weakening the bases. Autumn and late autumn bring no harm to the houses. It is the time for harvest and people finally have the financial means to mend their houses enough to survive the rest of the year. That is why they need someone good with tools to fix their homes."

"Where did you learn all this?"

"Learn what?"

"Fishing and mending houses. Who taught you?"

Bishnu chuckled out. "Nobody taught me anything. I learned from observing other people."

"How so? How did you learn to fish, for instance?"

As we spoke, we had come out of the alleyway between tin-shed houses and bamboo patches and into a woodland with tall trees and serene bird calls in the distance.

"Hmm," Bishnu said pensively. "These things came to me through different stages of my life, I guess. Dadaji used to take me to work on his crop fields. We used to get up at the earliest hours of the morning and start our work." I saw a glimmer of nostalgia in his eyes. "When it wasn't the season to work on the fields, we would still go out to gather tall grass for the cattle."

"Dadima and Dadaji had cattle back then?" I asked, surprised. I hadn't seen any stable in Dadima's house.

"Yes, they did," said Bishnu, smiling. "Back when they were younger and had the energy to take care of them. As Dadaji got older, we started to sell off our cattle. Over time, we had none."

"I see."

"It was in the north-western corner, right by the window, behind the bed."

I pictured the house I was staying in as a guest. There indeed was a vacant spot in that area, full of unkempt shrubs.

"Anyway," Bishnu continued. "It was on those trips with Dadaji that I discovered the joy of fishing. The crop fields are full of small swamplands where fishermen catch fish with their nets and spears. When Dadaji was busy at work and didn't need my hand, I would wander off to work with them. Their work fascinated me."

We were still walking through the woodland. The environment had quietened down significantly. There was barely any sound, except for the occasional bird-calls. If I hadn't been with Bishnu, I would have been a little afraid.

"Did we come through on this path?" I inquired.

"Oh, no, no," Bishnu chuckled. "We went to Choubazaar on the crop field side. We didn't take this route. This way is quicker." Seeing my agitated face, he put his hand on my shoulder. "It's just harmless woodland. No monsters or ghouls," he assured me. "You might find a pack of foxes if you come here at night. That's about it."

"Remind me to never come here at night, then."

Bishnu laughed out loud, which echoed. "Don't be afraid," he said. "Scary things don't live here. If you want to find scary things, go to swamps and shores of water bodies. But even in those places, they won't bother you. They have their own lives and agendas." He smiled at me. "If you let them do what they are doing, they won't bother you."

"Wow, you actually believe in these things."

"Of course. These entities are all around us," he said. I examined his face, but he was serious.

"Why don't to tell me about these things?" I wasn't sure why I felt this curiosity despite the fear I felt.

"You sure?" Bishnu chuckled, glancing towards me.

"I am," I said, nodding back.

"Ok. I'll come to Dadima's house tonight and tell you some of my stories. I just have a few things to take care of in Choubazar and then I will come right back. I'll stay with you tonight, so I can wake you up early to go to Battiji's house."

"Good plan," I said. "You have to go back to Choubazaar again?"

"I do. I have a few errands to run."

"You are a busy man, aren't you?"

As we traversed through the woodland, I felt my fear dissipate. I started to rather appreciate the environment. If I concentrated, I could hear light wind gliding through the trees in a serene melody.

"You still want to know how I learned to fix houses?"

I was taken aback by Bishnu's question. "What do you mean?"

"You wanted to know how I learned to fish and mend houses. I've only told you how I learned fishing."

"Oh, right. I almost forgot about my own question." I scoffed.

"That happens," Bishnu assured me. "When we tell stories, conversations get sidetracked. That's the nature of all stories, I feel. It's what makes them enjoyable. What's the point of stories if everything goes to plan?" Bishnu caressed his goatee, gazing pensively ahead. "I learned to mend houses by building my own house."

"You built your own house?"

"Yes, I did. From the foundation to the roof. I made the foundation, smoothed the earthy floor, wove the bamboo walls, put together the tin-shed roof. All by myself," he said, with pride in his voice. "Dadaji took me in when I was little. As I grew up, I wanted to live close to the crops as that's where I spent most of my time. So, I started observing carpenters and menders everywhere. Tried to do the things they do. Trial and error. Heh. Gradually, I picked up the trade."

"Dadaji was a great influence on you, wasn't he?"

"He was there for me when I was abandoned and left to nothingness," he said. "So, yes, he was."

We went on walking quietly side by side for a while. The woodland was coming to an end as a few houses started to appear around us.

"That's admirable, you know?" I said, finally breaking the lingering silence.

"What's admirable?"

"That you have learned all this by yourself."

"I had to. In hindsight, it was Dadaji who encouraged me to build my own house. He always wanted me to be my own person and not depend on everyone around me. He knew that nobody would tend to my house. Nobody here would touch a Hindu household. So, he wanted me to learn it myself."

"That's funny. They won't fix your house, but they don't have a problem asking you to mend theirs?"

"I do it cheap and I do it well. That's what counts. People forget their differences when it comes to necessity."

I looked at Bishnu with wonderment, but he didn't seem to notice. In this land of poverty and backbreaking labor, people had always approached me with an understandable, pragmatic curiosity. The glamour they had seen on the television about living in the capital made them aspire to be a part of that world. But I hadn't seen that behavior from Bishnu. He seemed quite comfortable with what and where he was. His personality, which was a strange mixture of day-dreamer and observational wisdom, fascinated me. I felt, at that time, that he was less burdened with reality than the rest of the villagers. I realize now that I couldn't have been more wrong.

"Let me make a guess. You colored those roofs," I said as I spotted Dadima's yellow-topped house in the distance.

"That I did," replied Bishnu, smiling. "You like it?"

"I do." I said as we entered the yard of the house, "You still haven't told me the other reason."

"What other reason?" Bishnu asked.

"You said you have two reasons why you decided to help out Battiji, despite him not giving you anything monetary in return. You only told me one. What is the other?"

"Oh." Bishnu said. "The other reason is that I am not someone who chooses to leave people behind when they come to me for help."

9 TIMES THAT WERE QUIET

"Want to go fishing in the crop fields?"

The first time I heard about Bishnu was from Dadima, about six months after arriving at her home as a guest.

"I am pretty sure plants don't grow fish, Dadima." I chuckled.

"You are not going to harvest fish from the plants, my naat[xix]," Dadima said smiling. "You will catch them from the flooded crop fields. You see, In the rainy season, the water spills from ponds into the crop fields and fish swim into these fields because they breathe better in shallow waters. Many varieties of fish that would be hard to find in other seasons can easily be caught from the flooded crop fields in this season."

"What makes you think I would go fishing? Do I look like a fisherman, Dadima?" I said with a giggle.

"No, but you can try. You can go out there, get some fresh air and fish with Bishnu."

"Bishnu?" I asked. "Is he that caretaker-boy who brings you groceries?"

Dadima stared at my confused face and shrugged. "You haven't talked with him yet, have you?"

"No."

"How odd is it that you have been here for six months and you haven't even talked with Bishnu?"

I kept silent for a while, figuring out how to answer that question. "Well, I can now," I said, finally.

"Well, you should. Being antisocial isn't good for your mind."

"All right, then. I will. 'Bishnu' sounds like a Hindu name."

"It is. I'm guessing you are wondering how he ended up living in a Muslim locality?"

"That I am."

"Alright then, get ready for a story of heartbreak!"

"I am all ears."

"At the edge of the village, on the shores of the Great Green Lake, lives a Hindu community. During the English colony, the English divided the continent into several lands under the names of landlords called 'jamidaars,' who were biased towards their own religion. If a Hindu jamidaar ruled a land, he would discriminate against the Muslims, to the point where most of them would leave their lands and live elsewhere. Our locality was ruled by a Muslim jamidaar, who did the same to the Hindu population here. So, they had to move to the shores of the Great Green Lake. Times have changed. Hindus and Muslims have learned to tolerate each other. But the Hindus never came back from where they went and today, that community is known as 'Hindupara.'"

"Interesting history," I commented. "Is this where Bishnu came from?"

"Patience, naat! This is what happens when you become antisocial," said Dadima, in response. "One day, your Dadaji brought a boy home. He had taken him in as a caretaker of our house and lands. I had never seen the boy in the village before. His clothes were torn up and he didn't seem like he had taken a shower for weeks.

"When I asked your Dadaji where he found the boy, he told me that he was a stray child from Hindupara, whose parents had abandoned him. He couldn't find a job in Hindupara because he came from a lower caste, so he came over to the mainland. He was walking around in Choubazaar, looking for work. But people were not comfortable giving him any work. Although the colonial times were far gone, people are still skeptical of Hindu folk.

"Since your Dadaji was considered a murubbi[xx], people came to him about the matter. Your Dadaji went to the boy, sat him down at a tea-stall and talked to him. The boy called himself 'Bishnu.' Your Dadaji realized that, given the boy's circumstances, if there was anyone in the mainland who could take care of him without facing judgement, it was himself. So, he brought the boy home. When Bishnu grew up a bit more, we gave him a place to stay near our crop fields and that's where he lives now."

Dadima then placed a hand on my shoulder and smiled affectionately. "You should go and talk to him. He is a very decent boy," she went on, "He takes care after himself. He does some house-mending work for people in the village. I like that about him. He is saving up for his future. He is responsible and reliable. I find peace in having that conviction."

10 A POND FULL OF BLOOD

"Want to see something horribly beautiful?"

In the middle of one of our light conversations after a day of filming, Arup Sai asked me this curious question. The rainy season had just finished and the sky was much clearer. The sun was just a pale white orb, about to set in the western horizon.

"How can something be horrible, but also beautiful?" I asked.

"It's something beautiful," he said with a crooked smile. "For a horrible reason."

"Interesting," I said. "Show me then. Should I bring my camera?"

"No," said old man, in a stern voice. "Come with me."

He got up and started walking east, up the slope and through the swathe of broken tree trunks. For a faint moment, I remembered all the warnings people had given me about the old man, but I chose to discard them and followed him.

I had never gone this deep into the landscape before; it was bigger than I thought. An enormous landscape of dead trees, without any sign of life, felt unnerving.

"Is this the horribly beautiful thing you were talking about?" I asked. "It's not beautiful, not to me."

"Keep going," came the reply.

The crooked hut was a faint speck in the distance. The hint of dampness on my feet was gradually becoming more prominent and with it, the soil was getting darker. Eventually, it became blackened and almost muddy. Something didn't feel right. We reached an incline. I was familiar with such inclines. It indicated a water body up ahead. The old man was standing at the top, ushering me to come. As I got closer, an oddly familiar smell hit me. Something inside of me churned. I hurried up and reached where the old man stood.

It was a large pond, a dead pond. The water was shallow and still. But what struck me was its color—a deep crimson red, with white froth around the edges of the shore. Within the pitch-dark shoreline around it, the still water glistened like a blood-red ruby in the middle of a coal mine. The familiar, intensifying odor broke my heart.

"Beautiful, isn't it?" the old man said.

"What in God's name is this?" I whispered.

"Civilization, my friend. Progress."

"What caused this?" I corrected my question.

The old man pointed towards the other side of the lake. "That."

I had been so occupied with what was in front of me, I hadn't actually registered what was ahead. So, I gazed towards the horizon and there it lay, in the diminishing glow of early evening: an entire locality—small concrete establishments of various sizes and shapes scattered about.

In the background of all these formations stood a monstrous factory building, menacing and dark in the fading light. A dense swirl of white smoke rose to the sky from a single thick smokestack made of bricks. The smoke seemed lifeless and moved upwards with no intention of leaving the atmosphere. I looked on as the old man observed me intently. The Magreeb Azan from a distant mosque, filled the void of our stunted silence.

11 BISHNU TELLS GHOST STORIES

The rainy season was over. Torrential rain had damaged a lot of houses, but people's financial capacity to mend them was scarce. Bishnu took on contracts. Some of them barely paid for the materials he needed. Most of them had no payment.

When asked, he would say, "The work I am doing now will spread good words and in late autumn, when people have more money, I will get a surplus of well-paid fix-jobs."

But I knew that wasn't the truth. On many occasions, he voluntarily went to people's houses to provide his service. Most of these houses were meagre accommodations of impoverished farmers, who neither could afford a fix-job (even at Bishnu's cheap rate), nor had the social standing to spread a good name for Bishnu. But their hay-covered thatches were virtually depleted and the muddy walls about to split open and I thanked the heavens Bishnu had the heart to repair them.

By then, the water from the crop fields had depleted, but our fishing adventures weren't over. On days when Bishnu didn't have mending jobs, we fished at water bodies across the village.

These fishing trips were not as easy as the ones in the crop fields, as the fish, with more space to spread out to, were harder to catch. It required patience. While we waited for the fish to take our baits, darkness prevailed in the closing hours of the day in swampy atmospheres. In those environments, Bishnu told me ghost stories. As I listened, sudden splashes of waves would startle me, much to Bishnu's enjoyment. Something inside me expected the entities from Bishnu's tales to appear at any point.

But over time, to my surprise, I started to enjoy my own fear. The rush of alertness made me more sensitive to changes in the environment. I learned to listen to the quiet sounds coming from the waters to determine which side the fish had gone to and find good spots. Soon, our trips got longer, lasting hours after sunset. I started to become more of a partner to Bishnu's fishing craft than his apprentice. As our fishing trips got longer, Bishnu's stories about how he had encountered the paranormal got more elaborate.

"As a child, I had an unnatural fear of the dark. Other children didn't fear it as much as I. I never liked being outside in the darkness. I didn't even like being in the house with Dadima when Dadaji was gone for Magreeb prayer. As the sun would start to melt in the horizon and darkness would fall, with Dadaji gone, I always felt that something dark with ill intent would materialize and cause us harm.

"It is a common practice here to send the youngest of the house to get groceries from Choubazaar in late evenings since that is usually the time when the elders would realize what they are running out of in the kitchen while making dinner. I was perhaps the only one who didn't want to do that for years. Fortunately, Dadaji loved taking long walks to Choubazaar and didn't mind doing it with me. Walking with him helped me get over my fear. He showed me there was nothing to fear after dark and the village is just the same as it is during the daytime.

"At nights, I slept beside Dadaji. Sometimes, I woke up in the heart of the night, terrified. But he was always right beside me to tell me there was nothing to be afraid of. 'One day I won't be here, Bishnu. And you have to be brave enough to protect your Dadima from whatever you fear,' he told me.

"One day I was coming back from Choubazaar and the daylight was fading. Dadaji wasn't with me, so naturally, I was hurrying my steps. My gaze shifted towards the small swamp right next to the house. The place always had a deviously creepy way of presenting itself in the dark. For a moment, I felt that some entity was drawing close to me and there was nothing I could do. My feet froze. But then, the fear passed through me and for some unexplained reason, I shouted out, 'Hey, whoever is out there, show yourself!'

"That's the moment when my fear of the dark turned into a strong urge to understand—to see what's out there. Often Dadaji would wake up for his morning prayers to an empty bed and discover that I'd been playing around some bushes all night. I would lay awake at the depth of the night and whenever I heard strange noises from somewhere out there, I slipped silently out of my bed to find its source. I learned that most of the time, the sounds came from owls. Owls are quite proficient in making strange noises. But, on occasion, when the source of the noise remained unknown, it excited me.

"One night, I was playing with my Dadaji's torch, flashing its beam on different things from the window. Dadaji was observing me without intervention. But the moment I flashed at the top of a mango tree that was standing at the end of our yard, he snatched the torchlight from my hand and said, 'You better not flash the light on things in the darkness, my naat. You might just see things you are not supposed to.'

"I stared at him in wonderment and asked, 'What's up on the mango tree?'

"Dadaji sighed and said, 'You are a curious little boy, aren't you? You don't have to know everything about the world. Some things are better off unknown.'

"I wasn't satisfied with the answer. So, at midnight, I tiptoed past the sleeping Dadaji, slid his torch into my pocket, went out into the yard and flashed the light across different parts of the tree for several minutes. I wanted to see what was lurking there and what it would do if I illuminated it. To my disappointment, all I saw were lots of bats and owls. Yet I wondered what exactly Dadaji was warning me against. So, I went to the only person that I believed would give me an answer: Dadima.

"'Why did you go about shining light on treetops like that, child?' Dadima's rough tone surprised me. I was expecting her to be softer and more accepting of my audacities than Dadaji. 'You want to bring misery and death to your family?'

"She went on to explain to me about a frightening mythical bird called 'Jom Kuli,' which in simple terms means 'carrier of death.' It looks like a very ugly owl and if you happen to come across one of these ill-fated creatures, you or a member of your family will die pretty soon.

"After that, my young mind was burdened with guilt. I had seen many owls that night, but I couldn't quite recall if I had seen any that was particularly gruesome-looking. I couldn't flesh out the details of every single one of them and that terrified me. After a few days of anxiety, I started feeling feverish.

"'It's okay, Dadima,' I said, laying on my back with my head sticking out from under a blanket while she poured cold water over my forehead[xxi]. 'I will die, so you or Dadaji don't have to.'

"'What in God's name are you muttering about?' Dadima exclaimed.

"'I...I think I saw a Jom Kuli at the top of the Mango tree that night when I shone Dadaji's torch on it,' I said as my body shivered. 'But since I am dying now, you or Dadaji don't have to.'

"Dadima nearly fell off her sitting stool, laughing as I stared in confusion. 'You didn't see any Jom Kuli, Bishnu,' she said. 'If you had ever seen one, you would know.'

"It turned out that I had developed the fever from anxiety because I thought I had put the only two people in my life in mortal danger."

"That was lovely, Bishnu," I commented.

"Thank you," Bishnu responded.

"However, if I remember correctly, you told me that you would tell me stories about actual ghosts. Ones you've seen for real," I said.

"... and not the fearful imagination of a child of five? I understand." Bishnu chuckled. "I just wanted to tell you how I developed my interest about paranormal things." He paused to take a deep breath. "As I got older, I realized that things like that do exist and fishermen like me run into them quite often."

"Hmm...I'm confused," I admitted. "So, ghosts like fishermen?"

"Absolutely not. The idea of ghosts liking us couldn't be further from the truth. They hate us, in fact."

"Why?"

"Because we tend to be in their way. Like them, we also seek quiet places with water bodies not disturbed by children splashing on them and adults washing their laundry. And that's where these entities prefer to tread as well. I wouldn't be able to count how many times I have come across a fish hag while quietly fishing in a swampy pond."

"Fish hag? Is that the one Nondi was talking about?"

Bishnu sniggered. "Nondi thinks my stories are ridiculous."

"And do you mind?"

"Not really. People like me, who do believe in these things, learn to accept the fact that most people don't. Besides, Nondi doesn't have the luxury of believing in these things."

"What do you mean?"

"Well, you saw how much of a handful Babuda is and you haven't even met the whole family yet. She simply doesn't have the time anymore to venture into quiet places at night to encounter fish hags." Bishnu sighed. "Come to think of it, she doesn't have time for anything these days."

"You feel concerned about her?"

"She just feels...lost these days. You know?" Bishnu stared blankly at the empty waters. "I feel that the friend I have known since childhood isn't there anymore."

"Maybe it's just part of growing up. Maybe she is becoming her own, mature person."

We sat for a while in silence.

"So, fish hags," I said finally. "Tell me about them."

"What would you like to know?" Bishnu asked.

"What are they and when did you first see one?"

Bishnu grinned at the anticipation in my eyes. "They are pretty much what their name suggests. They are otherworldly entities, always searching for fish to eat. Some localities tend to worship them out of fear, but in my opinion, they are not very intelligent. They are just very strange animals who are eager for their desired diet.

"They usually stay away from people, but sometimes, when they get no fish, they can get aggressive. In those cases, they tend to attack people's homes and go through their kitchens for fish. Some even attack fish merchants in Choubazaar. In some localities, people leave out fish in buckets near the shores of water bodies at night to keep them satisfied."

"And you have seen them?"

"Yes. Quite often, actually. The first time I saw one was in the pond near my house. I have seen him many times since. I don't mind him now, but it was quite terrifying when I first saw him. It was about five…maybe six years ago. I was quietly sitting near my pond, waiting for a fish to take the bait when I heard splashing on the other side to the right.

"I looked up and there he was. A humanoid creature. Pitch black skin, no hair on his head and a pale white beard covering his face. He was walking in a part of the pond that could easily drown a fully-grown man. He had long, bony legs and was gazing intently into the water. I gasped only a little bit and that was enough for him to detect me.

"My eyes met with his, which flashed like bright, white torchlights in the dying light of the late afternoon. Terrified, I threw my fishing rod into the water and ran for my life. I dived into my hut and locked the door. I peered out of the window, hoping that maybe I saw a twisted figment of my imagination. But there he was. He didn't chase after me but simply continued his hunt. Since then, I've seen him regularly. We mind our own business and stay out of each other's way. He's harmless, really."

12 A TREE OF SANCTITY

"Why don't you stay with me for a while? I'm sure Dadima wouldn't mind."

I frowned furtively at Bishnu. Following our routine, I was about to leave Bishnu to his business at Choubazaar after selling off the couple of snakehead fish we caught that day. What Bishnu had just suggested would break that routine.

"You want me to stay with you?" I asked.

"Yes. Nights are when Choubazaar gets more interesting. You'll meet colorful folk you wouldn't meet in daylight."

"Any colorful folk in particular you'd like me to meet?"

With a mischievous smirk, he went to the nearby tube-well to clean himself. After he finished, he said, smiling, "Let's go."

I followed him down the brick road into the uncharted northern territory of the market. We went past grocery establishments made of connected bamboo walls. As gaps appeared between shops, I saw an open moor to the east that seemed to go on forever. To the west, the river, which people called the Great Green Lake, rippled with a wide spectrum of colors in the red setting sun, housing shadowy silhouettes of small islands and fishing boats.

As we went further to the north, the market shifted from crop warehouses, groceries and confectionery stores to sawmills and forges. But soon, these shops, too, became few and far between, making the barren, open moor and the vast river on both sides more noticeable. *Where is Bishnu taking me?*

We came to a cluster of large, tin-shed restaurants. Bishnu finally stopped, at the very last of them. It stood a good fifty paces away from the rest and seemed a little rundown. A couple of dim bulbs provided very minimal ambiance for the empty benches and tables. It stood on bamboo and wooden foundations coming out of the shallow waters at the curve of the Great Green Lake. Near the foundations, stood a boat-line illuminated by a few much brighter bulbs wired around to the foundation-pillars. Within the gaps of the pillars, in the shadows, were a few wooden carts with jute blankets covering what I assumed to be inventory.

"You going to stand over there forever?" Bishnu's voice broke me out of my trance.

I smiled at him and we walked into the restaurant.

"You brought in a new nobleman today," a gruff voice greeted us. Sitting at the counter at the front of the shop was a large, rotund man with thinning hairline and long, thick greying beard from which a dirty grin peeked out.

"Can I interest you gentlemen with any of these?" The man motioned towards the cabinet behind him full of bottles of colorful drinks, which made me realize why the shop was at the fringes of Choubazaar. In a village of strong Muslim-influence, liquor was contraband.

"I sincerely hope not," Bishnu replied. "My friend here is from the capital and is not here for a drink."

To this, the rotund, bearded man finally looked at me, with wonder in his eyes. "A capital-folk. That's a first. Are the Bangla mods[xxii] here too cheap for you, sir?" he asked, with heavy irony in his voice.

"No, I just belong to the part of the population that doesn't drink," I replied, calmly.

To this, he gasped. "So, a Muslim. God Almighty, I am seeing all sorts today!" He chuckled. "Are you here to burn down my shop, sir?"

"He is here just for some of your delicious sweets," said Bishnu, breaking the exchange. He leaned over the rotund man's counter and locked eyes with him. "Why do you have to pick a fight with everybody, Ustadji? Hmm? If you want your store to survive, you need to stop picking fights. Now, we're going to take a seat and would like it very much if you bring us a couple of roshgullas[xxiii]."

I observed Bishnu in wonder. Hidden within this friendly, day-dreaming fisherman boy, I felt the presence of a pragmatic, mature man. Something told me he really didn't want me to have any qualms with the bearded, rotund shopkeeper and the stunted eyes of the rotund man told me that he understood it, too.

We sat in one of the seats facing the door, near a window, which gave me a glance outside. Further to the north were dense woodlands, marking the end of the river to the west, the open moor to the east and Choubazaar in the middle.

The rotund man came and put down two small plates that had two tennis-ball shaped balls of sweet dessert dipped in clear syrup. He gave me a quick glance and left.

I took stock of the interior. The dimly lit back portion of the restaurant had bamboo-lined floorings. Posters of low-budget movies aimed at the local population decorated the walls.

"So, where are the *colorful folk* you spoke about? All I see around here is just us." I chuckled, but Bishnu's didn't seem to have registered it as I caught him worriedly looking over my shoulder.

"Is everything okay, Bishnu?" I asked.

Bishnu was squinting his eyes, trying to trace something in the distance through the window. I followed his gaze. On the wooded bank of the river, a number of silhouettes started to appear. As they walked around the northwestern bend of the Great Green Lake, I managed to trace the figures more clearly. A large group was approaching the boatshed. When the light illuminated them, I instantly identified its leader, Babu Bhairab.

His fair skin glowed among his dark-skinned entourage and his raven black curly hair was unmistakably recognizable. The group that he was leading appeared to be strange and unsavory. There were four masculine-looking women wearing colorful, decorated sharis and blouses. A couple of men walked beside him, laughing. They had thick moustaches and were obviously far older than Babu Bhairab. But they were barely two-thirds of his height. That was just the front of the congregation, followed by a larger mob. There were a few boys of Babu Bhairab's height and age, some of them missing a limb; a man and a woman walking together, the man holding a round, large bamboo container, while the woman held a stick of bamboo as tall as she was, with a cloth-bag tied at the top; a number of men and women walking along supported by staffs, many of them dressed in vibrant colors.

Among these people, Babu Bhairab seemed out of place; yet somehow, he didn't. He was giggling and walking in springy steps with a bottle in each hand. Suddenly, he skipped and turned towards the group. He walked backward and craftily swayed his hips side to side, causing the group to giggle louder. He was clearly in a playful mood, in contrast to the girl walking quietly beside him with her face covered by her orna. It was Nondi. The group walked up the stairs of the boatshed, into the restaurant.

"You are not going to burn some goat meat this time, Babuda?" A moustachioed man slapped Babu Bhairab's shoulder, grinning. "I could gather a few men, dig up a hole, fill it up with bricks and—"

"Not sure it will happen this time around, Nituda. I'm here for business, not pleasure," Babu Bhairab responded, grinning, eying me. The rest of the group followed his gaze.

"Pretty lad from the capital, I see," one of the masculine women proclaimed, approaching me. "Tell me, how can we get to know you better?"

The three other women like her started giggling.

"Oh, leave him be, Nasrin. He is confused as it is, being so far away from home," Babu Bhairab said. "And besides…" He glanced at Bishnu. "He is Bishnu's new, esteemed, capital-dwelling friend. We shouldn't be disrespecting him here now, should we?"

Bishnu stared back at Babu Bhairab with an irritable look.

"Nituda, why don't you take your people to their businesses?" Nondi's firm voice came as she entered the restaurant, exchanging a stare-down with the man. "The more time you waste, the less money you make."

"That's true," the man named Nitu nodded. "Come now, boys and girls. Let's go," he said, giving me one last glance. The others followed him out.

Babu Bhairab gave a playful, sideward glance at Nondi and walked towards us. He turned his head towards the counter and said, "Ustadji, why don't you—"

"Babuda, I'd like to remind you of the promise you made to me about how you would conduct yourself with Bishnuda's friend," Nondi interrupted, extending her hand towards Babu Bhairab. "You promised," she reinforced.

"—give us two more roshgullas," Babu Bhairab finished. "That's all I was about to ask for," he said, looking at Nondi, who didn't retract her hand.

Babu Bhairab scoffed. "Babaji put you up to this, didn't he?"

"No, he didn't. Babaji barely tells me anything about how to deal with you and you know that," came the instant reply. "But you gave me your word that you won't conduct yourself the way you did last time. So, I suggest you keep your word."

Babu Bhairab glanced up at her. "Ok, fine," he said, finally, handing over his bottles to Nondi.

Upon taking them, she walked over to our table and took a seat opposite us. Babu Bhairab took the seat beside her. Ustadji came and quietly placed two more plates of roshgulla down. He exchanged a quick glance with Bishnu before heading back to his counter.

"You, my dear guest, will be a contractor," Babu Bhairab's abrupt statement made me stare at him in confusion for a few moments.

"A contractor?" I asked.

"Yes, a contractor," replied Babu Bhairab. "You will be Bishnu's manager and he will do some decorative work on our house for the event."

"I don't think Bishnu needs managing," I said, chuckling.

"He doesn't?" Babu Bhairab chuckled along with me. "I hear villagers say that you are always there when Bishnu goes on his fix-jobs."

By then, I had gotten pretty tired of his games. "Look, I'm glad that I have managed to become a source of entertainment for you, I really am," I said. "But does any of this have a point, or are you just here to waste our time?" Babu Bhairab didn't give a reply to my inquiry as he only offered a wicked grin. "If there's nothing more to talk about, I will make myself scarce."

Babu Bhairab, eying me with furtive confusion, turned to Bishnu. "He doesn't know?"

"No, of course, he doesn't," responded Bishnu. "Why would I just give him this information myself? It needs to come from you."

"Bah," Babu Bhairab said. He waved arrogantly. "You know I don't care about all this secrecy. Just tell him."

"You don't care, but I do," came Nondi's stern response. "I care about you and Bishnuda's safety. I also care about the Bhairab family's name."

"You talk of us Bhairabs as if they are your family," said Babu Bhairab.

"Bhairabs are the only family I—"

"They are not your family, Nondi," Babu Bhairab said in a nonchalant voice. "At some point, you must accept it and find your own. If you keep trusting them, one day, they will turn on you. Bhairabs tend to do that. That's the price you will pay for all your loyalty. So, I suggest you act smart and take care of yourself."

Nondi had a staring contest with Babu Bhairab for a few seconds before he waved his hand again.

"Okay, okay." He sank back into his seat and looked at me. "Alright, then, what would you like to know?"

"From what I have observed so far," I responded. "I'll start with why you want me to come to your house as a contractor."

"Because I couldn't get you in any other way."

"Why do you want me there in the first place?"

"Well… I thought bringing a town-folk into the mix would liven up the party."

"It's not a party, Babuda. It's an important family event." Nondi said.

"It *is* a party, Nondi," Babu Bhairab responded with a wry smile. "It's a meet-and-greet. People will be fed, entertained, made happy and sent home. Just like a party."

After a few more moments of having another staring contest with Nondi, he turned to me. "Okay, let me explain to you the simple things first," Babuu Bhairab said. "You are invited to the Bhairab household to stay with us for a while. You are invited because you are a contractor who will be responsible for fixing a very ancient house."

"For the thousandth time, I am not a contractor," I said in a dry voice.

"I know that. You just have to pretend to be one," said Babu Bhairab, irritably. "Bishnu will do the work and you will oversee the project as his manager. That's how I have sold this to Babaji."

"And this Babaji is…?" I asked.

"Raghab Bhairab, the head of the Bhairab household," Babu Bhairab said in a commanding voice with a heavy dose of mockery. "Raghab Bhairab is known throughout the village as Babaji, which means 'father.' And he is treated across the island with the same level of respect. People look up to him as their protector. He has the last say in all the affairs of the island. People consider him wise. Knower of all the answers."

Babu Bhairab paused, grinning furtively. He turned to Nondi. This time, he slowly placed his hand on the neck of one of the bottles she was holding on her lap and started to pull it towards him. After a few seconds of resistance, Nondi let it go. Babu Bhairab unscrewed the bottle and poured the golden liquid into the glass in front of him. He only filled it about a quarter. Then he screwed the bottle cap back on and gave the bottle back to her with an approving nod. Nondi eyed him with clear disenchantment in her eyes.

Babu Bhairab leaned forward and finished the drink in one swift swig, putting the glass down with a loud bang. Then he continued, "And he also happens to be my father. Not in the way he is father to every other villager on the island, but you know—" He waved his hand in a form of gesture. "—hereditarily."

"Yeah, I gathered that," I shrugged. "Your name gave it away."

"A jester, I see!" Babu Bhairab chuckled. He then glanced at Bishnu, pointing at me. "This one will be an interesting company."

"As interesting a companion as I might make," I said, calmly, "I am still not sure what kind of event I am going to or what my purpose is there."

"To answer your second question," Babu Bhairab said, leaning towards me. "I wanted to see how things turn up if a high-born fellow from the capital, like you, joins the event."

"So, that's what I am to you?" I asked. "Just a curious addition?"

Babu Bhairab grinned as he sank back into his chair. "Don't take this as disrespect," he said. "I am curious. You are bored and want to explore new places. Why don't we help each other out?"

"Our guest hasn't consented to go yet, Babuda," Nondi interjected.

"Oh, he will definitely come...after I tell him what all this is about," said Babu Bhairab, mysteriously.

"Alright then," I said, maintaining disinterest on my face. "Tell me what this is about."

He went on to tell me a strange, fantastical story which, while captivating me greatly, overwhelmed me with disbelief as well.

"You see, Bhairabs have a lineage that goes back hundreds of years," Babu Bhairab said, "and we have protected this lineage with great discretion. We went through war, colonization, divide and cultural change, but we have always protected ourselves from all that. And we have gone to great lengths to do so. This event you are going to is an example of what great lengths we will go to in order to protect our name.

"In our house, we have a large, ancient, underground cellar, locked shut by an iron gate that hasn't been opened for hundreds of years. This room was built an unknown number of years ago by one of our family's forgotten ancestors and in that room lies a sacred family secret. This ancestor of ours took our family's pride and fortune very seriously. He thought that at some point in the future, there would be a time when our family name would be in threat of extinction.

"So, he kept something, locked away in that room, which would restore the Bhairab name. The key to that room has been passed down from generation to generation and the room is only to be opened when the Bhairab name starts showing signs of being forgotten." He paused to take a deep breath.

"Now, you might be thinking: how exactly does a family name show signs of being forgotten?" His eyes carried curious tenacity, but despite being fascinated by the story so far, I kept a calm demeanor.

He continued. "In the backyard of our house, there's a large banyan tree which has lived for hundreds of years. Some say the tree was first planted by the same ancestor who built the room, but that is not confirmed. What is confirmed is that the tree represents the strength of the Bhairab name. When the tree starts to show signs of decay, that will signify the start of erosion of the family name. And therefore, that will be the time to open the cellar."

He paused and frowned pensively for a while. "But the tree never rotted," he continued. "We were quite proud of that because the tree being alive signified the strength and sacredness of our family name. However, that pride has finally taken a fall. We have found signs of decay at the tree's roots. We discovered it about a week ago. From what we know from our forefathers, after the decay is discovered, the next full moon should be the day the gate is opened by the key passed down to us through generations. And that is going to happen in about three weeks."

Babu Bhairab looked at us again. "Since the Bhairabs are a prestigious family, this prophecy is known throughout the district and people are curious about it. When people are curious about something, they spread rumors if their curiosity isn't satisfied. Therefore, we have decided that this is an occasion that requires some form of formal festivity. Babaji has employed a team of carpenters and decorators to prepare for the event, but he has also asked for Bishnu to make some repairs to the central house since he trusts him."

He grinned. "This is why I told Babaji that Bishnu works under a contractor now and to invite him, you need to invite the contractor, too. That's where you come in."

"So, the way I see it," I responded, "this is not really a matter of choice, since, if Bishnu goes there alone, Babaji might ask where his contractor is."

"He may, or he may not," Babu Bhairab said. "Even if he asks, I can simply tell him that his contractor decided not to come because he trusts Bishnu's capacity to get the work done by himself. So, really, it's up to you."

"Well—" I sank back into my seat, thinking. "—if I don't go, there's still a chance that Babaji might want to know more about Bishnu's contractor. And if he finds out that I am not a contractor of any sort, that could get both Bishnu and me in trouble. By lying to your father, you have essentially put us both in a compromising position."

"You can see it that way if you want. That's your prerogative," Babu Bhairab said, leaning back in his chair with a look of satisfaction. "So, are you coming or not?"

"I don't think I have a choice," I commented.

"Well, that's settled, then!" Babu Bhairab took his bottle from Nondi's lap, got up and hastily walked out of the restaurant, down towards the boat shed. "Come now, Nondi. The sun is setting. Maaji gets worried when I stay out after dark," he cried out.

"You can choose not to go if you don't want to, you know?" Nondi said quietly. "Babuda has a way of putting people in uncomfortable situations, but if you choose not to go, I can manage the situation with Babaji."

"No, I'll go," I responded. "Firstly, because frankly, I am curious to see what happens." I glanced at Bishnu. "Secondly, I have a feeling that Bishnu might get in trouble if I'm not there with him. Even with your assurance, I don't want to take that chance."

"You wanted meet the Bhairabs." Bishnu finally spoke. "So, I thought this would be a good opportunity to arrange that." He looked towards the boat shed, where Babu Bhairab had already settled himself on a large boat and was waving at us. "Although I have to admit, I didn't know he would put you in a situation like this."

"Don't bother, Bishnu," I assured him. "I would have gone anyway."

We left the restaurant. The daylight was fading and the never-ending emptiness on both sides of the road felt eerily inviting.

13 AN INTERMISSION OF REFLECTION

When winters are harsh, rainy seasons are plentiful—a common saying among the villagers.

In harsh winters, people suffered. And sometimes, that suffering led to death. On more than a few mornings, I heard news of some old soul passing away because their weak, aging body couldn't withstand the long, cold nights.

"What a terrible way to die!" Dadima once said. "Let's thank the Almighty they didn't burn their house down."

"What do you mean?" I asked.

"Oh, that is a tragedy of far bigger proportions, my boy," Dadima replied. "You don't need to know about that."

"Please, tell me."

Dadima sighed. "These poor souls, desperate in the unbearable cold, sometimes light fires on earthy floors of their hay-covered huts. During the night, when they are fast asleep, the unattended fire would catch on something; a piece of cloth or dry hay hanging down from the roof. It doesn't have to be much. From there, it spreads—"

"That's enough," I interrupted Dadima. "I get what you mean."

As tragic as all these deaths were, in a twisted way, they were seen as signs of a plentiful rainy season. No one would openly admit it, but if you paid attention, you would sense it. The speeches delivered by Imaams[xxiv] in mosques whenever there was a death in the locality went along the lines of, "May Allah to grant this poor soul Jannah[xxv]. May he take notice of this loss and suffering and give us plentiful rains and harvest."

In one of those plentiful rainy seasons, I made a friend named Bishnu, who taught me how to fish, told me ghost stories and took me to a mysterious old man named Arup Sai.

"How is the filming going?" Bishnu asked me one late night when we were enjoying the quietness of the sleeping village on a bamboo mat in the yard of Dadima's house.

"It's going alright," I answered casually.

"How many more days will it take?"

"Not more than a week, if I go every day," I estimated. "The old man...he is surprisingly eloquent with his words and his work."

"Is he now?"

"He is," I admitted. "I wanted to ask you something."

"Ask away."

"These ghost stories you tell," I said. "Do you actually believe in them."

"You think I don't?"

"You don't think these stories are a bit...fantastical?"

"Hmm...on the contrary. I think are very real?"

"Really? Djinn possessions, laughing girls with mangled bodies in tattered clothes on top of trees, fish hags, drowned dead people staring back at you from underneath the water surface. If these are all real, where do you think they come from?"

"From suffering."

"What do you mean?"

Bishnu breathed in and closed his eyes for a few moments. "To answer your question, let me present you with a scenario. Let's say a specific area is used to maim, torture and kill hundreds of people."

"What? I didn't—"

"Do you think a place with so much pain and agony buried in shallow graves would be peaceful, like everywhere else?"

"I...why would there—"

"Don't you think it is a little self-centered to think people's sufferings leave no trace behind?"

I stared at Bishnu with awe. I didn't expect the conversation to take such a morbid turn. "I didn't mean to offend you, Bishnu," I said.

"Oh, I'm not offended." He smiled, to my relief. "But I want you to understand that accepting the presence of the paranormal isn't a work of your imagination, but simply that of empathy."

"How so?"

"A lot of people live and die in agony in this part of the world. They curse, they lament and they die in despair. Do you really think all that pain and desolation just live and die with the people who experience them?"

"They...don't?"

Bishnu's laughter caught me off-guard. "No, they don't. How can they?" He continued. "The residues of their suffering live on. That's why there are abandoned houses, woodlands, water bodies, fields that people forbid you to go to. And it is wise to pay heed to those advices."

He glanced at me meaningfully. "This land has gone through so much! People have died of famine, been tortured in camps, faced cruelty by overlords of far-away worlds. People instigated rebellions against oppressors, faced genocidal massacres and they still face misery and desolation to this day. Do you really think that a place with so much history of agony would be perfectly peaceful and quiet? It isn't." He shook his head, starting at me eye-to-eye. "You just have to open your senses and you'll find the anguish of souls from past and present all around you. You'll realize that these things are not to be feared, but only to be understood."

The citrus smell in the wind from the grapefruit trees was lovely. Floating clouds in the sky hid and revealed the moon in turns. The rainy season was over, but if I concentrated, I could feel tiny raindrops drenching us gradually.

14 AN UNFINISHED STORY

"Did they tell you about my wife and children?"

It felt like the hardest question in the world to answer. By that time, my frequent visits to the old man had been noticed by the villagers and out of curiosity, many had approached me with questions. Out of respect for Arup Sai, I avoided answering them. That didn't stop the villagers from being vocal with their own opinions. But I was convinced, that almost everything the villagers (except for Bishnu) had told me about the man sitting in front of me was not true. The man I was seeing now, with eyes full of perplexed pain, could never have murdered his own family.

"Nothing of substance," I replied. "Nothing that matters, anyway."

"You know, you should stay away from me," he said, looking away. "You finished whatever little filming you had to do days ago."

"Yet, here I am," I said.

"Yet, here you are," replied the old man.

An uncomfortable silence followed. I gave out a chuckle to make the situation lighter, but it didn't seem to work. I was sitting on top of the huge, dusty white log and the old man was sitting cross-legged on the ground. All around me was a swath of natural destruction. The sun poured all its light onto an empty, dead ecosystem with no framework. It felt like the universe was trying to present this tragedy on a brightly lit stage and I was the audience.

"Well, if you have grown tired of my presence, I have some good news for you," I said. "This is probably my last visit, at least for a while."

"You have finally decided to go home?" Arup Sai asked.

"No, I am going across the river to an island," I responded.

"You were invited by the Bhairabs?" The old man's reply was unexpected. I didn't expect him to know about the Bhairabs.

"Yes…yes, I was," I said.

"I see," Arup Sai commented. "Make sure you take that boy, Bishnu, with you. It is not wise to go to a foreign place like that alone."

"He's going with me," I assured him. "How well do you know Bishnu?"

"Hardly," the old man said with a chuckle. "He appeared in my periphery years ago, when I was collecting branches for my flutes. For days, he quietly observed me from a distance. Then one day he came to me and told me that he could sell the flutes I make to people in Choubazaar. I gave him some to humor him.

"I never expected people to buy my flutes. But, to my surprise, he came back a week later, with money. Since then, he comes to me every now and then to take my flutes and then comes back later with payment. I asked him if he kept a commission for the sales, to which he replied, 'Naturally.' Strange boy."

"He does seem like someone who has a lot going on underneath the surface."

The old man's face hardened and eyes became narrower, as he surveyed the horizon.

"I didn't kill them, you know? I could never have done that," he said.

"I know that," I said assuredly. "Do you really think I would have come here time and time again, for months, if I thought of you as a murderer?"

"I don't know," he replied. "I barely understand the people in this village, let alone a capital-folk like you."

The old man seemed have gotten lost in his own thoughts again.

"What I do now is the only thing I can do to restore whatever is left of my life." The old man finally broke the silence. "They were all I had…my family." There was a slight jolt in his voice. "I loved this place. It was where I found meaning and where I belonged?"

He went quiet again. It didn't seem like he would start unless I ask something. "What do you mean?" I asked finally. The old man turned towards me an and in his eyes, I saw a hollowed-out man—a soul in so much pain that it wanted to be spared.

"The forest was a whole life form by itself. Interconnected parts, making up an ecosystem like no other," he went on, "It was deep, mysterious, beautiful and fertile. It grew plants other areas couldn't. And they were amazing life forms, capable of unforeseen healing abilities. Studying and understanding them was my life."

His eyes were gleaming. "I've been doing this since I was a boy. If I had made different choices, I could have had a life of better means. But I always knew that choosing another life wouldn't make me happy. What's the point of having everything while you experience nothing in here?" He touched his chest.

I nodded in agreement.

"So, I made my choice to be here, living a life of isolation. But you see, the universe had a different plan for me. It didn't let me be by myself for too long." The old man's jaws clenched. "One day, this young man knocked on my door. With horror and despair in his eyes, he said that his sister was sick. He wanted me to go with him immediately.

"'What's she suffering from?' I asked.

"'Please, come with me!' The man begged. 'She is in great pain and she doesn't have much time.' I tried to learn more about his sister's condition because I didn't necessarily have the tools or resources to take care of all kinds of illnesses. But the man insisted I came with him. So, I did. When I reached his house, I heard the constant wailing of women from inside and I realized it was either someone dying or childbirth gone wrong. Further inspection confirmed it was the latter."

"You see, childbirth here is a complicated thing. Some men don't want their wives to see doctors when they are carrying a child or when they go into labor. Women who have the misfortune of being married to such men only get midwives, who claim to be specialized in overseeing childbirth, when they are pregnant.

"The condition of the household was horrid. The husband, a well-to-do farmer, was sitting in the corner on a chair, muttering unspeakable things under his breath. I heard the voice of a woman from inside the house, shouting out instructions to men, who were running around like rats in a maze to bring things, such as, buckets of water and cloth.

"'I can't do anything here,' I finally said, turning to the man who brought me there. 'This is not something that my skills cover.'

"'Please, Arup. I beg you!' The man threw himself to my feet. 'I don't know what to do. They are not letting me get a proper doctor. I…I don't think my sister has much time.'

"Seeing the desperation on his face, I realized there was no way I could explain to him that I had no idea what to do. So, I tried the best I could. I was not allowed inside the house, but I gave them pain medication that might help the woman who was in labor. I stayed until midnight. In the end, the woman didn't die, but the child was stillborn. After the woman who had been giving instructions emerged from within and gave everyone the news, the man in the corner finally stood up.

"'Arup Sai,' he said, in a firm voice. 'I thank you for the services you have provided. I will pay you generously. But for now, you have to go.' His hardened face told me that insisting on staying wouldn't be a wise decision. So, I left.

"The next day, I was coming back from the forest after my morning walk when I saw the same man, who knocked on my door the day before, sitting in my yard. His lips pressed against one another, trying to block a stream of tears from adding to his already tearful face.

"'What's the matter, Abir?' I inquired. 'Is your sister all right?'

"What he told me saddened me, but didn't surprise me. The child that the housemaid announced as stillborn was not stillborn at all. The rich farmer's wife had given birth to stillborns twice in the past, but not this time. This time, the child started crying a few minutes after I had left. But that still wasn't good enough. The child was a girl. The father expected a boy to carry his wealth.

"This didn't sit well with the father. He had already given his wife taalak[xxvi] and kicked her out of his house, along with the newborn. Her brother, Abir, who lived in the same household, working in the rich farmer's fields, was kicked out as well, for good measure.

"'Where is your sister? Why isn't she with you?' I asked.

"'She is sitting on a bench in Choubazaar,' he said, in a trembling voice. 'No one is taking her in. I didn't want to walk her here, since she is already very weak. I just came here to see if—'

"'Bring her here, right now,' I said instantly. I let the woman and her newborn child stay with me for the time being. I hoped that her brother would eventually return to take her back. But he didn't. I assumed that being shunned by a rich family didn't earn him a good enough reputation to find any work.

"So, not being able to show his face to me as a brother who couldn't find a way to take care of his sister, he disappeared. The villagers eventually got weary of a woman living alone with a stranger like me. And being in a profession that depended on maintaining a good face, I did what I had to do. I married her out of necessity. A marital life wasn't what I planned for myself, yet there I was—married and already with a newborn. I wasn't expecting to be happy with this predicament. Yet, I was…until all was taken from me."

The old man stopped. He brought his gaze back to me. I didn't know what to say.

"You should go," he said, getting up. Then, without giving me a chance to respond, he walked back to his hut.

I felt overwhelmed by the story I had heard. The day, however, had some more curious events stored for me. But I will come to that later.

15 AN ADVENTURE BEGINS

On a late-autumn afternoon, we started for the Bhairab Island.

"Look after him, Bishnu. He's from the capital and he's going to the most untrustworthy house in this village," Dadima muttered under her breath as she kissed our foreheads.

Right then, Babu Bhairab appeared out of Ustadji's restaurant with a couple of new bottles in his hands. His seemed tidier than usual, in an ironed-out beige dhuti and a yellow fotua. He climbed down the stairs leading to the boatshed, gave me a snarky look, ignored everyone else and jumped into the husk of the large boat he had brought in to take Bishnu and me to the island. We heard his harsh, loud voice.

"You people want to reach the island at midnight? Say your goodbyes and come in. We're already late. Biruda, start the engine."

A large, muscular man with a pronounced moustache came out of the husk and smiled amicably at us. He pulled the cord of the engine at the end of the boat closest to the shore and it started with a loud roar. He smiled at us again before taking his seat near the engine. We peeked in to see Babu Bhairab had already made himself comfortable inside and was opening one of the bottles.

"What an unpleasant lad!" Dadima commented. "Why do you keep his company, Bishnu?" She glanced at Bishnu and me worriedly. "He'd better not make trouble with my boys. Bhairabs aren't the lords of everything. I will show them—"

"I will ensure that nothing happens to any of them, Dadima." Nondi's soft voice came from behind us as she came down the stairs, smiling. "I won't let anything get out of hand."

Dadima sighed and kissed Nondi's forehead. "I know you won't, Nondi," she said. "I'm counting on it."

We climbed into the boat, got inside its husk and it left the shore. The river started narrowly with open waters in the distance. The water rippled and sparkled in the fading yet still bright sunlight. On both sides, localities were greener, with fewer houses than the mainland.

"I assume that's the Hindupara?" I asked. Bishnu nodded in agreement.

"Keep the boat in the middle, Biruda," Babu Bhairab cried out to the muscular man sitting near the engine, guiding the boat. "You are straying off to the sides too much. These people start smiling and bowing whenever they catch sight of me."

"They do so because you are a Bhairab, Babuda," Nondi said calmly, looking at the two bottles he had brought in. He had already finished one of them. "Your family name carries respect all across these lands."

"Hah, family name!" Babau Bhairab scoffed. "What did I do for them and what did they do for me? I am just as much a stranger to them as our guest from the capital is. Speaking of—" He brought his attention towards me, grinning with mischief. "How do you feel, my dear guest? Excited to be part of such a unique event?"

"Not sure at the moment." I smiled politely.

"Not sure?" He took a few swigs of the second bottles. "Well, you'll find out soon enough." He wiped off his mouth with his sleeve.

It was evident from the start that Babu Bhairab had not been making the least bit of effort to make a good impression on me. We remained silent in the awkwardness that he created. Bishnu looked at him with clear disdain, but Babu Bhairab ignored it and kept drinking, while mumbling indistinctly.

"Are you enjoying the view, at least?" Babu Bhairab asked, breaking the silence.

"That I am," I assured him, trying not to aggravate him any further.

"That's good," he said, gazing out of the window. "You see all this beauty?" His voice was quickly losing its constitution as he mumbled along. "This wide-open sky, rippling waters, woodlands and fields? None of it is yours or mine, or anybody else's, for the matter. You hear me? We have no business in…" His mumbles started to become incomprehensible as he fell sideways onto the bamboo mat.

Nondi quickly caught him and helped him lie down on his back. She snatched away the bottle, which was just about to spill the little remaining content it had, put the cap back on and set it aside.

"Steady yourself, Babuda," she said. "We are with new company. What will he think of you?"

Nondi went back to her seat with the bottle and Babu Bhairab lay there, muttering gibberish. Eventually, the gibberish subsided into silence and then, to my relief, he finally dosed off. I turned to see Nondi covering her face with her orna. Sensing that she was being observed, she quickly wiped her eyes and smiled at me.

"Babuda doesn't know how to behave appropriately. I apologize on his behalf." Her voice had that softness of a woman who just had a silent sob by herself.

"Please, don't apologize," I insisted. "I don't get bothered very easily. I am a little worried about him, though. It is not my place to say this, but it does seem like he has a drinking problem."

"He's just under a lot of stress with what's happening around him," Nondi said.

"I understand," I said, nodding.

"What stress?" Bishnu's dejected voice joined the conversation. "Everyone does everything for him, anyway. What does he have to worry about?"

"Bishnuda, this is not the time or place," Nondi said firmly. Then she smiled at me again. "Let's go outside. The sun is about to set. It should be nice and breezy out there."

We stepped out of the husk, leaving a snoring Babu Bhairab inside. The evening was dawning on the distant horizon. We had left behind the narrow waters of the Hindupara and ventured into the open river. The steamer engine was shredding through the watery pathway, but I had gotten used to the noise.

16 A TALE OF MADNESS

"Bishnuda has told you many ghost stories. But do you know the scariest things in this part of the world are not ghosts at all?"

I appreciated Nondi's poise. She was trying her best not to make this journey a sour experience for Bishnu and me. The two of us were sitting on the deck while she was sitting at the edge of the husk, occasionally checking on Babu Bhairab.

"What is it, then?" I asked.

"Madness," she said, trying to sound secretive.

"Are you trying to emulate me again?" Bishnu asked.

"I can never recite stories the same way you do, Bishnuda. But I try." She chuckled. A glow of childish carelessness had prevailed on her face. I felt relieved.

Darkness didn't fall on the waters the same way it fell on land. On land, night came abruptly. When the sun melted itself on the horizon, painting it bright red, everything close to you would already be engulfed in darkness. But on water, the environment absorbed that red glow and everything stayed relatively visible for a while. Shapes of small fishing boats scattered around us across the vast waters with ripples of colorful patterns.

"Madness?" I asked.

"Yes, madness," she said. "Madness susceptible to possession."

"Possession?" I asked. "You mean by evil spirits or Djinns?"

"Sometimes, yes. But people can also be possessed by grief. They can get raving mad purely through the sufferings they endure. And that is more frightening than any paranormal thing you can experience."

"How so?"

She took a breath to gather her thoughts. "Because when you see people, you have known for years, turning, through grief, into something you don't even recognize, it gives you a glimpse of how terrifying it can be to sink into the darkness of your own heart. The realization that, under certain circumstances, it could happen to you is petrifying."

"And you can tell when someone reaches that point?"

"Oh yes, I have seen many such instances."

"Is that common here?"

"Very common. Poverty and suffering can do that to you."

"How so?"

Nondi took a deep breath, eying the dark water. "For example, a child with multiple elder siblings in a poor family would always hear something like, 'I cannot feed you for too long, why don't you go and find some work?'" she explained. "Listening to this over and over, with the stimuli of poverty, hunger and deprivation, for years, can drive that child mad. You will often see young people who have lost their mental constitution, muttering something along the lines of, 'I cannot feed you for too long, why don't you go and find some work?' repeatedly."

I looked at her, stunned.

"But this is a very common and tame example," she said. "In many cases, the insanity is so twisted that you cannot really identify whether it is the mind itself or something else. In their eyes, you see something otherworldly. You realize that the person is merely a shell to something foreign within. That terrifies you to your core because suddenly, these unholy things are not different from you anymore. They have taken a familiar form."

I had to admit, that unnerved me a little in the dark, empty atmosphere, as the light of the setting sun faded. "Can you tell me one of those stories?" I asked.

Nondi smiled and nodded. "One time, I was returning home late at night. Everybody was asleep. I noticed, in the middle yard, a grown woman, standing still with her head down. She had no shari on and was only wearing her blouse and petticoat[xxvii]. The wind was howling that night and her long, clumpy hair was swinging.

"I'm used to seeing people lose their minds, especially women. So, I thought she was just another housewife in grief who walked away from her home because she couldn't take it anymore. However, as I approached her, I observed that her eyes were wide open and bulging as if they were about to pop out. Yet her face was expressionless and trance-like.

"That's when I knew that this was different than just a simple case of insanity. Instead of going across the yard to the main house, I went into the eastern house and locked the doors shut. I peeked through my window to see if she was still there before closing that one, too. I kept an eye on her through the crack. Biruda was doing his night-rounds and would eventually come to the yard and that's when I planned on coming out. But I fell asleep.

"Biruda's voice woke me. 'Just tell me where your house is and I will escort you there,' he said. I gathered up the courage and peeked through the cracks of the window and I almost fell off the bed when I saw a wide red eye staring back at me.

"'You have been found out. They are coming for you,' she whispered.

"'Biruda!' I shouted, not knowing what to do. Hearing my voice, she suddenly took a step away and turned her back to me, only to face Biruda on the other side of the yard. After a few seconds, she kneeled on the ground and started chanting.

"'I come and go and no one cares. I come and go and no one cares.'

"For some reason, this gave me some courage. I opened the door and confronted her. 'Who are you?' I asked.

"She stopped the chant and looked up at me. This time her eyes weren't bulging, but the same unnerving expression remained.

"'Where are you from and why have you come here?' I asked again.

"She raised her trembling hand, pointing directly towards the river. Her lips shook, tears formed in her eyes and her face distorted as she started to sob silently.

"'Hey,' I said as I approached her and gripped her shoulders.

"'Nondi, don't!' Biruda cried out, but it was too late. The woman pushed me with tremendous force that couldn't possibly have come from a human being. I was hurled backward and my head almost cracked open on the concrete wall of the eastern house. Her eyes were bulging again.

"'Do not touch me, you insect!' she said, in a guttural voice that was definitely not her own.

"I tried to tell her that I meant no harm. But she screamed in that same guttural tone, only amplified tenfold. Then, with inhuman speed, she darted towards the river and jumped in.

"Biruda later told me that he had also tried comforting her by touching her shoulders, but she pushed him away with ease. And you can see that Biruda is not a feeble person."

She pointed towards our bulky, muscular boatman. He was sitting quietly, lazily gazing at the dark waters. He hadn't spoken a word throughout our trip and probably couldn't hear our conversation over the sound of the engine.

"So, what happened next?" I asked.

"Nothing," replied Nondi. "She dove into the river and never came up."

"Never came up? You are telling me that a human being jumped into the river and never came back to the surface?"

"Biruda went to check in the morning, but all he found was her clothes," said Nondi, smiling at my stunned expression. "These kinds of things happen in this part of the world, my dear guest. You just have to accept it."

"So, you believe in these things too?"

"I do. Not as passionately as Bishnuda, but I do."

"You would believe in them like me, as well, if you went to the places I had been." Bishnu joined in our conversation.

"Yes, Bishnuda. We all know about your adventures with swamp monsters and ghost villages," said Nondi, giggling.

"Just admit it, Nondi," said Bishnu. "You had one experience with these things and it spooked you."

"That, I have to admit." Nondi nodded. "Especially when the lady told me that something was coming for me."

"That, I think, is probably something you heard in your head," Bishnu said. "In my experience, these things usually have their own business and don't attach themselves to other people."

"You sound so sure, don't you, Bishnuda," Nondi protested. "Tell me, then, why would I just make it up in my head?"

"Because you have heard it all your life," replied Bishnu. He pointed at the now-snoring Babu Bhairab. "Our friend over there has been telling you this since we were children. 'Bhairabs will turn on you, Bhairabs will turn on you.' He had set that thought in your head and in that fearful moment, you heard what you always feared."

"I have never feared that, Bishnuda," Nondi said, in a firm voice. "The Bhairabs have been taking care of me since I was a child. Babaji is like a father to me. I would never think that they could cause me any harm."

"Well, that's what you always say," Bishnu commented.

"Tell me more about the Bhairabs," I said, changing the subject.

"What would you like to know?" she asked.

"Tell me about Babaji. I guess he will probably be the first person I meet," I said. "From what Babu Bhairab has told me, he sounds like a man who exudes a lot of power."

Nondi chuckled. "Never fully believe what Babuda tells you," she said. "Babaji used to be quite powerful, yes. But now he is old and is about to pass his reign to his successor."

"Then I guess Babu Bhairab has big shoes to fill," I said.

At this, Nondi broke into full-blown laughter, which echoed across the waters—although, it didn't seem to have bothered our snoring companion in the husk. "Babuda taking over Babaji's role. Wouldn't that be a sight!" she said. "No, he is not expected to take up his position. He is Babaji's youngest son. You must have thought Babuda is Babaji's only son; that's perfectly understandable. Rich folk seem to be satisfied as long as they have a male heir to pass their wealth to. But no, Babaji doesn't have just one son. He has three."

"I'm assuming I will be meeting the other two, as well, when I get to the island?" I asked.

"Hmm…that's tricky," Nondi replied. "I would say, for now, Babuda is the only one you will have to interact with on a daily basis."

"Why so? Are they away? I assumed, on such a big family occasion, they wouldn't be far from home."

"Oh, they are on the island, that's for sure," Nondi said promptly. "It's just that they are in positions where you wouldn't really get to meet them right away."

"Why not?"

Nondi sank back against the wall of the husk. "His eldest son, Meghab Bhairab, is the heir to all his wealth. He is always busy, looking after his father's affairs. He lives in a separate section of the estate with his wife and children and comes out only when it's necessary. Babaji's middle child, Kuber Bhairab—" Nondi pursed her lips, trying to figured out how to word her explanation. "—he currently lives with Ponditji, the priest of the Bhairab Temple, on the other side of the island from the Bhairab estate."

"I see."

"He needs…to be taken care of," she said. "He's had health problems since he was born. Since Babaji and Maaji are quite busy organizing the event, he is being kept in the temple, under the care of Ponditji. He is to be there until the event is over."

I nodded politely, realizing that I had unintentionally trod into an uncomfortable matter.

"We need to wake him up now." Bishnu pointed at Babu Bhairab. "We're here."

About a few hundred meters away, an island started to take form in the darkness. We were approaching what seemed like a very large, bustling boatshed with boats of different sizes jammed together. Behind the boatshed, stood a large estate with festive lights of various colors. Behind the lights, the isle opened up into a wider curve, turning into a large piece of land that appeared dark and menacing.

Book 2: The Gathering

CHILDREN OF DECAY

17 A NIGHT OF MISCHIEF

As we sat quietly, desperate wailing echoed from somewhere in darkness ahead of us. It had been a fantastical day and it was barely the break of dawn. It all started when the night-guard, Biruda, burst into the concrete, single-storied accommodation at the eastern section of the Bhairab estate where Bishnu and I were fast asleep.

We sat up on our beds with eyes half open and faces asking: "What's going on?"

So, Biruda explained. "Sorry to wake up the honored guests," he said hastily, "but has Babuda been here?"

Babu Bhairab had the habit of barging into our room late at night after his lonesome evening trips to Choubazaar since we lived right next to the boatshed. He couldn't ask Bishnu to accompany him due to the ongoing feud in their friendship and he couldn't ask Nondi as she wouldn't let him do what he wanted to. So, he would venture alone, get back too drunk to show his face to his family and fall asleep on the floor of our rooms. However, that had not been the case last night.

"Babuda wasn't here last night, Biruda," Bishnu confirmed, rubbing his face. "What's going on?"

For a brief, uncomfortable few seconds, Biruda eyed Bishnu with a frown. The muscles on his juggernaut body flinched and tightened before he went on.

"A prisoner from the district jail has escaped. I got a phone call from the police constable. Some of his men had seen the convict make his way towards our island. I couldn't find Babuda in the main house. So, I ask you again, do you know where he is?"

"Babuda didn't spend the night with us," Bishnu said, calmly. "But he did say yesterday that he was taking the boat to the Choubazaar after sunset."

"That puts him directly in the route of the convict!" Biruda ran out the door towards the boatshed. We got up from our beds and followed him. Sleep had escaped our eyes.

When we approached the boatshed, we heard Babu Bhairab's sober voice from inside the husk of the steamer boat.

"I am here."

The three of us ran towards the boat and found him leisurely leaning on the inside wall of the husk.

"What in the seven seas are you doing here, Babuda?" Biruda muttered. "Why did you sneak off into the night again?"

Babu Bhairab remained silent. Carrying a nonchalant smirk on his lips, he avoided eye contact with all of us.

"You could have at least taken Bishnu with you," Biruda muttered.

"I would have made my way into the household, as I always do, Biruda," Babu said calmly. "But I didn't, because I saw someone I don't recognize wandering about. I couldn't call for you since it might have gotten his attention."

"Someone was wandering in here?" Biruda said. "And you're only just telling me?"

"I would have told you earlier if you hadn't showered me with hundred questions."

After giving Babuda a tired, dejected look, Biruda stood up, tightening his lungi, glancing at us. "You three sit tight. Don't make a sound," he said. "Come on, get in."

We followed his order.

"Don't make a sound," he repeated. Then his eyes narrowed towards Babuda. "Where did he go?"

Babuda, still surprisingly calm, raised his hand, pointing towards the way we came from.

"He's headed for the estate!" Biruda said and sprinted off in that direction. The wet clay on the river shore clapped with his heavy, hurried footsteps.

We sat inside the husk. The night was dreadfully quiet, like the world settling down before or after chaos. The air seemed heavy and motionless. Light ripples rapped on the boat and it swayed side to side. The river beyond seemed vast and secretive, enveloped in darkness. *Somewhere out there, policemen are searching for an escaped convict.* The thought felt surreal.

"You could just take me with you to these evening trips, you know?" Bishnu said in a whisper.

"I know," Babu Bhairab said as he sat upright, folding his legs. "But I don't like being taken care of like some child. I was feeling out of breath. I needed to get out of all this drama."

"Oh, but I thought you like all the drama?" Bishnu whispered, with a touch of sarcasm in his voice.

For the first time, I felt that the exchange between the two childhood friends had lightened up enough to be enjoyable.

"At first I did, yes," Babu Bhairab said, staring sideways towards the river pensively. He stayed like this for what felt like an eternity. "But things were getting out of hand."

"And by drama, you mean all that is happening in preparation for The Gathering?" I interjected.

Babu Bhairab glanced lazily at me. "Oh, there's always drama in my family," he proclaimed. "The Gathering just amplified it. All this is about money, anyway. Money, wealth and pride. Secret treasure trove full of valuables." He scoffed as he made the shape of a box with his hands. "It's just becoming too much to handle. I had to do something."

"What do you mean by a secret treasure trove?" Bishnu asked.

"In the secret room," Babu Bhairab said, narrowing his eyes at us. "That's all that's there. More wealth. More gold, jewelry, expensive silverware…you know, the typical things in a treasure chest."

"And you know this, how?" Bishnu inquired.

"What else would it be?" Babu Bhairab replied. "That's all that rich folk care about. That's what they mean when they say 'our family name is perishing,'" he said in a mocking voice. "Rich folk are both proud and insecure about their wealth. It's a hilarious juxtaposition. That's why they have been tucking away their fortunes in secret places forever. Why would this be any different for the Bhairabs? It's all—"

Babu Bhairab's speech was interrupted by a loud thud, followed by muffled sobbing and pleading. To my surprise, Babu Bhairab snapped out of his comfortable position and hurled himself out of the boat in the direction of the noise. Bishnu and I glanced at each other confusedly. In the distance, the muffled wail continued.

18 AN ESTATE ON THE CURVE

Old and new was what defined the Bhairab estate. Like a massive, ancient fig tree, the center of it was mythical and rustic, while the outskirts sprouted with colorful modern additions. The estate was situated on the eastern curve of the island. On that shore, the Bhairabs' private boatshed housed about thirty boats, which mostly belonged to the guests currently residing at the estate. A few meters inland, through some wild bushes, was the eastern side—the most utilitarian and the least illustrative part of the Bhairab estate. Beside a tin and bamboo shed full of essentials for boat-maintenance, there was a concrete, elongated, one-storied house with two rooms.

The smaller, northern room belonged to the guards and the bigger southern room was for the lower-class guests, where Bishnu and I resided. The Bhairabs often needed to accommodate people of lower socioeconomic classes in their household, for varying amounts of time and for various reasons. Contractors (like Bishnu and I), wholesalers and small-time businessmen, village spokespersons requesting an audience to talk about concerns of the community—they all got their place in that room.

The southern part of the estate, to an outsider, would seem like a separate household altogether. High walls and a thick, iron gate guarded a two-storied, concrete building and a generous amount of land surrounding it. It was resided in by Meghab Bhairab, the heir apparent of the Bhairabs, with his wife Mala Bhairab and their son Bipul Bhairab.

The northern part held two long, two-storied concrete buildings, perpendicular to each other. These buildings housed guests of religious influence from all over the district who had come to observe The Gathering. Hindu pondits[xxviii] resided with Muslim imams in different rooms. They had been chattering about their thoughts and theories on what would or would not happen at the event. The tension and underlying conflict among the representatives of both faiths was a complex narrative all by itself. But that's not my story.

In between the two buildings, there was a yard, with a decorated sitting area overlooking a large pond that spread from the north-west to the western part of the household. On the far western side of the pond, the surrounding land had patches of tall trees—mangos, jackfruits and guavas.

On the bank of the large pond's north-western side, stood two of the most ancient and significant parts of the Bhairab estate. The central house was where Babaji resided with his wife Modhura Bhairab and his two younger sons, Kuber and Babu Bhairab—although, as Nondi had explained, for the duration of the event, Kuber Bhairab had been moved to the Bhairab Temple across the island.

The central house was enormous and complex. On strong, earthy foundations, cleverly-done concrete modifications held up the massive, ancient home. The upper portion was built with giant tree trunks, lined together, holding up the vast tin-shed rooftop. Layers of intricate bamboo carvings in bright colors protected the tree trunks from weather damage. Bishnu's job was to remove the layers with cosmetic damage and replace them with fresh ones while also livening up the colors. He was instructed not to participate in any other heavy-duty tasks being done by other workers and focus only on the house, for which he only worked a few hours in the evenings.

Beside the central house, near the pond, stood the mythical, massive banyan tree—the pride of the Bhairab family. It looked rustic, powerful and sprawling when I first saw it from a distance. The three of us—Bishnu, Babu Bhairab and I—were taking a late-afternoon stroll. The sun was fading out over the pond, which we were circling and the tree came into our view. It had an extensive exterior of what looked like multiple trunks that had solidified themselves into the ground, like pillars protecting the center.

"This…is quite a tree!" was the only comment I managed to muster.

"Those are not trunks, if you were wondering," said Bishnu.

"They're not?" I asked in puzzlement. "Then, what are they?"

"They are vines," answered Babu Bhairab. "Vines that started as feeble additions, but grew in thickness and stature until they became significant parts of the tree, forcing he center into irrelevance."

"Must you be dramatic about everything, Babuda?" asked Bishnu.

"But this just isn't any other tree. This is…*the* tree," Babu Bhairab said with mischief in his eyes.

"Since when did you become serious about tradition?" asked Bishnu.

"I am not serious about tradition," proclaimed Babu Bhairab. "I am just entertaining our guest here. After all, his trip here is all about this tree, isn't it?"

"You know very well that Babaji told us not to allow his guests to see the decay," Bishnu said in a stern voice.

"But he is not Babaji's guest, is he?" Babu Bhairab said, nonchalantly. "He is *my* guest and, therefore, must be treated with full exposure. Please, come." Babu Bhairab motioned for me to step closer.

"I thank you for your hospitability," I interjected. "But I don't want to be treated any differently than the other guests."

"No, I insist. I promise you won't be disappointed," Babu Bhairab persisted. "You will know how—"

"I think it is best for all of us if we maintain the rules Babaji has set for the guests." Nondi's ringing voice interrupted what Babuda was about to say. The three of us turned to see her walking towards us. "And we should be considerate to guests who respect these rules." She looked at me and smiled.

"But this is harmless fun," Babu Bhairab said.

"Maybe to you, Babuda," Nondi responded. "I know Babaji will not be hard on you, no matter what you do. But he is not as kind to everyone else. There are many guests in this house, so we should not be setting bad examples."

The two of them stared at each other, Nondi with a firm face and Babu Bhairab like a wounded animal.

"There's no point arguing with you," he said, finally. "Why are you here?"

"Babaji has summoned you all," Nondi answered. "Please, come with me."

19 A DREAM OF A NESTLING

"Sorry to keep you waiting, Constable Jafar. As you might have heard, I am tending to the preparation of an important event." Those were the first words I heard from Babaji. He made himself comfortable on the bed, resting on his back in the room allocated to Bishnu and I.

In front of him, on the floor, was a thick, red cotton mat, which extended to the other end of the room for people to sit on. One of the people sitting there was a stout man of short stature in a police uniform: Constable Jafar. When Babaji saw us enter the room from the corner of his eye, he lazily pointed us to take a seat with the constable.

Nondi disappeared back into the central house and within a minute, came back with a large, covered bowl, a few glasses and a jug of water. She gracefully handled the delicate objects balancing on her hands and placed one glass in front of each of us, filling them up with water. The bowl, placed in front of us, was revealed to be full of various sliced fruits. She filled another glass and presented it to Babaji, who took it and looked back with warm affection in his beady eyes.

Babaji was a tall, bony man. Narrow eyes sat in caves of protruding cheekbones, with almost indistinguishable smidges of white eye-brows above and tightened cheeks below. His pronounced, yet broken jaws were covered with short, white beard. His lips were thin. Receding black and white hair covered his head. His complexion was that of a faded, golden metal that hadn't yet lost all its blaze.

He was wearing a minimalistic white shirt made of a thin layer of cotton, typical wear of the elderly in this part of the world. A sienna-tinted shawl hid his nearly skeletal body. A bright white dhuti covered his thin legs in a seamless grace. Old age was quite evident in his features.

"It was my pleasure to wait for you, Babaji." My train of thought was interrupted by Constable Jafar's reply.

"I see," replied Babaji. "Then I am afraid you will have to indulge in that pleasure a bit longer. My eldest son is going to be here any moment now." Then, with annoyance in his voice, he called out, "Prithu!"

A low voice from the shadows in the corner of the room said, "Yes, Babaji."

"Is Megha here yet?" he said, but immediately after, swayed his arm in a dismissive fashion. "Don't waste my time. Just go and get him and bring the brute with you. Go."

Prithuda walked soundlessly and swiftly towards the door. Before I could get a look at him, he was gone. All I could register was a lean and meek presence and long raven hair that waved as he walked out of the room.

"In the meantime—" Babaji brought his gaze towards Babu Bhairab. "Might I ask, what exactly were you doing last night, Babli?" He frowned, displaying a veneer of annoyance, hiding an amused smirk. "You made your mother very worried. You know that?"

"I couldn't sleep with all the ruckus going on," answered Babuda, with characteristic nonchalance. "I needed some fresh air."

"And to get some fresh air, you took one of our steamer boats and headed to Choubazaar without Bishnu?"

Babu Bhairab drew a deep, contemplative breath. "I like the river. It helps me gather my thoughts."

"What thoughts do you need to gather? I have given you everything you could..." Babaji looked around at our agitated faces and calmed himself. "You could have taken Bishnu with you."

"Bishnu was asleep."

"Then you should have woken him up."

"Is that why you brought him here, then? To take care of me?"

Babaji stared at Babu Bhairab in awe, which I understood. He had been doing his best to maintain his poise in dealing with his volatile young son. I could imagine the anxiety he must have felt, along with his wife, on hearing the news that their son was missing at a time when a convict had escaped from prison.

Taking another stock of all the people around the room, Babaji finally said, "Yes. That is the truth. You know it, Babli. I have a whole horde of people organizing this event for me. I didn't really need Bishnu." He exhaled. "The reason I brought Bishnu here is that he is the only decent boy in this district you get along with and perhaps, he can keep an eye on you while your mother and I put our attention into the event. That's the only way I could keep your mother from worrying herself into madness. Do you not understand that?"

Babaji stared at this reckless son with a frown of tired dejection, while Babu Bhairab stared back with sheer nonchalance. A few moments passed by. Then Babaji brought his attention to me and smiled. "I apologize for my honesty, my dear guest," he said. "I suppose, keeping my reckless, young son out of harm's way was not really what you had in mind when I invited you here, was it?"

"I don't mind," I answered. "The task is just as hard as what we came here to do…if not harder."

To this, the room broke into laughter, except Babu Bhairab, who, to my surprise, appeared unaffected by all the attention and seemed to be lost in his own thoughts.

"You and Maaji shouldn't worry about me," he said in a calm voice. "I've traveled across those waters at the dead of night since I was a child and I have survived 'til now without anyone's concern. I have dealt with things worse than escaped convicts. I am perfectly capable of looking after myself."

"I agree, Babu, but that's not the real reason you shouldn't be trusted with a boat in the depth of the night." A deep, raspy voice came from the door. "We need eyes on you because otherwise, you bring trouble."

My first impression of Meghab Bhairab was that he looked how Babaji would have when he was young. He had the best of his father's features: a tall stature and a pronounced bone structure with just the right amount of lean flesh on it. It was evident that he was physically quite active. He was wearing a white dhuti and a grey fotua[xxix] covered with a yellow shawl. His face was square and sharp—as if the sculptor who made it had ensured all the corners were cuttingly defined. His jawline was strong and crisp. Cheeks tight, with clear, protruding cheekbones. Above the cheekbones rested a narrow set of eyes that pierced everything they gazed at. In the middle of the two eyes descended a long and narrow nose that cast a shadow over his thin lips as he stood in the doorway.

In this part of the world, body complexion worked as a proxy for social status. While farmers toiling away in the harsh tropical sun had dark skin, the rich walked proudly among them with lighter complexions. However, when I saw Babu Bhairab for the first time, although he was evidently fair, it didn't have that air of superiority. Instead, his pale complexion made him seem a little otherwordly. When I first saw Meghab Bhairab, however, his fairness seemed much more conventional. The spotless, fresh metallic glow pronounced pride and opulence. Both brothers had an abundance of physical beauty, but each was beautiful in their own way.

Despite his pronounced physical presence, we really didn't see him coming. As he entered the room and took a seat at the foot of the bed, two men followed him in. The first was a short, rotund fellow, with rough black and grey beard all over his face and similar, long hair all over his head. He was barefoot, wearing a cotton shirt and a grey lungi, both dirty.

Behind him entered the meek day-guard of the Bhairab Estate. I struggle to picture the moment I had first laid eyes on Prithuda. He had never possessed any noticeable physical attribute. Most of the time, he wore a striped shirt and a worn-out grey dhuti. He had a thin, long nose—much like Meghab Bhairab. But unlike Meghab Bhairab, his other facial features were not young and crisp. The bottom half of his face was cramped together to make room for his large forehead. He had black eyebrows, which connected with each other over the bridge of his nose. Under his brows, two thin slits displayed narrow, drowsy eyes. He had swollen cheeks that were darker in the middle and murky, thin lips that bore obvious marks of cigarette-consumption. His face was quiet and expressionless and body skinny and docile.

The rotund man stood about a couple of meters from the door as Prithuda stood in front of it.

"Is this the man who escaped from your jail?" Babaji asked.

"He is," Constable Jafar replied. "Criminals escaping from prison isn't very common here. Perhaps that's why my guards have become complacent. He managed to knock out one of our guards delivering food to the inmates and take his key to free himself." He looked at Babaji. "Once these convicts get past the guards in the cellar, there's nothing much to stop them from escaping, as our prison isn't manned all that well."

"Oh, come now, Constable. You and I both know it's neither the prison walls, nor the laws, nor the guards that keep these convicts in jail in this part of the world," Babaji interrupted. "It's their circumstances. Most of them have crippling debt or have gotten themselves on the wrong side of local politicians." He took stock of the rotund man. "To the point where getting themselves locked up turns out to be a better life than dealing with their problems on the outside. Isn't that right, convict?"

The dirty, rotund man looked up, with profound tiredness in his eyes.

"Start by telling me your name," Babaji said calmly. "Then you can tell me why you were in jail and why you are here now."

The rotund man brought his head down and mumbled something inaudible.

"Speak up. We cannot hear you," Meghab Bhairab said in an authoritative voice.

"Suba. My name is Suba."

"Suba what?" spat out Meghab Bhairab. "Tell us your full name."

"Suba Kashem."

"All right, then," Babaji said, sitting up. He clenched his jaws and stared intently at the man named Suba Kashem. "Tell me, Suba Kashem. Why did you end up in jail?"

Suba Kashem looked at Babaji, then at Constable Jafar. He seemed like an animal being hunted "I… I…" He mumbled.

A frustrated scoff broke our concentration. It came from the northern end of the room near the window, from Babu Bhairab. "Can my guests and I be pardoned?" Babu Bhairab asked. "I don't see how this applies—"

"They are not your guests, Babli." Babaji didn't let Babu Bhairab finish his sentence. "And no, you cannot leave. We all need to see this through, together."

Babu Bhairab frowned at Babaji, as if he was measuring up his father for what he was about to say next. "Very well, then," he said. "If you are not going to let me off the hook from this…slobbering, fear-mongering charade, allow me to contribute, at least."

"What can you possibly contribute to this, Babli?" came the calm yet firm voice of Meghab Bhairab. "What you need to do is sit and listen to—"

"I think I can contribute a great many things, Meghabda," came Babu Bhairab's defiant, interruption. "For starters, I can ask the right questions."

Meghab Bhairab began to say something, but Babaji raised his hand to stop him.

"Go on," Babaji said. "Let us hear what you have to say, Babli."

"We might start by asking why he headed west instead of east," Babu Bhairab said. "From his name, it is quite clear he is a Muslim and being a convict on top of that makes it quite risky for him to head west, to this unwelcoming Hindu island. He could have headed for the district-town if going back to the Muslim side of the village was too dangerous for him." He drew a deep breath and looked around the room. "Which means that he is in trouble with someone bigger than just some village landlord. It has to be something political. But that doesn't explain why he escaped in the first place. If he was indeed in trouble with someone dangerous, it makes more sense to just stay in jail, as Babaji pointed out." He glanced at Babaji, who nodded back to his son. "Which means only one thing. He had a stronger motivation to break out of jail than the fear he felt that kept him in it all this time. So, the question is, why now and what has changed?"

"ENOUGH IS ENOUGH! I HAVE HAD ENOUGH!" The rotund convict, Suba Kashem fell to his knees, covered his ears and started sobbing vigorously and loudly.

This went on for about a minute until Constable Jafar stood up and said, "I have seen enough. "I need to take this brute away from this honorable house to-."

"You will do no such thing, Constable," came the calm, firm voice of Babaji. "Please sit down."

Constable Jafar silently followed his command.

"This is a very critical time for the Bhairab household," Babaji continued. "A lot of things are happening. News and rumors are spreading.

A lot of people related to us and our business are saying various things and possibly conspiring about how they can profit from it." He looked around the people in the room. "We should be cautious of the unexpected. We need to be aware of any and all events that are out of the ordinary. So no, Constable, you are not going to take him away from me until I reach a resolution to all this."

He smiled approvingly at Babuda. "My unruly, yet highly observant, youngest son, has asked some good questions. We need to understand why this convict broke out of prison and headed west, right to our doorstep. If he is feeling unwell, he will be cared for." He turned to Suba Kashem. The hysterical sobbing had simmered down to indistinct murmur, yet his posture remained unchanged. "But you will tell us where you came from, why you escaped and why you came here, won't you, convict?"

Suba Kashem looked up at Babaji. He mumbled something. "Make yourself heard if you want me to hear what you have to say. Mumbling will not get you anywhere," Came Babaji's commanded.

"I... I had a dream," answered the man, this time with more composure in his voice. He stood up.

"So, you are telling me," chuckled Babaji, "that you came here because you had a dream?"

"Yes."

Babaji's face hardened, jaws clenched and eyes narrowed.

"If you want me to believe your lies, convict, at least make them believable. If you make up stories like this, make no mistake, I—"

"A dying nestling," murmured Suba Kashem, at which Babaji stopped in his tracks.

The convict and Babaji stared at each other. Suba Kashem seemed much calmer than moments before, while Babaji stared back with bewilderment.

"What...did you say?" Babaji asked.

"A pigeon... a wild, spotted pigeon," came the response, at which I saw a shade of color drop from Babaji's face. "A nestling," Suba Kashem continued. "I...I somehow knew in the dream where its nest was. I made a move towards it, but my limbs had frozen. The bird was tethered between life and death—hungry, tired and cooped up under a bush for warmth, but I couldn't move a muscle. I could see it breathing irregularly, its chest trembling in a broken rhythm. This is a sign of a bird that is drawing its last breath." Suba Kashem paused to sob for a few moments silently. "Then, the breathing stopped. And I could see the dying strength with which the little bird was holding itself together fade away. It tumbled forward. But I couldn't do anything.

"I felt horrible guilt and remorse." Suba Kashem wasn't sobbing anymore as he went on. "The bird died near the east riverbank and I somehow knew in the dream that the its nest was to the west...which is here."

The whole room was silent for what seemed like forever.

"This is the most nonsensical story I have ever heard." Constable Jafar broke the silence. "I am going to take you back to jail right now."

"Constable Jafar, I am telling you one last time, do not interfere in my work," came the firm voice of Babaji.

"But I am to take him back to—"

"You are to do what I tell you to do. You are young. You don't know how things work in this part of the world. You don't know the consequences of not taking into account what I wish to happen and for that, I will forgive you, for now. But interfere with me one more time and you will find out." Babaji gave one last look at the convict Suba Kashem. "Prithu," he called out.

"Yes, Babaji." Prithuda quietly stepped out from behind the convict.

"Take him to the eastern section of the guesthouse. You understand what room I am talking about?" Babaji asked.

"Yes, Babaji, the farmers' room."

"Yes," said Babaji. "Clean up two of the neat beds and make them look presentable. You and the convict are to stay there. Make sure to never let him out of your sight."

"Yes, Babaji," said Prithuda obediently.

"I want this to be discrete. Do you understand the delicateness of the situation?"

"Yes, Babaji," replied Prithuda. "If the guests know an escaped convict is among them, they will become agitated."

"Yes," Babaji affirmed. "Give him a proper bath. Dress him up as a Muslim imam and introduce him to everyone as our new guest. We are all out of guest rooms, so it will make sense that we are accommodating him in the farmers' room. Tell them, also, that you are staying there temporarily to give all the guests better protection."

"Yes, Babaji," answered Prithuda. He gripped the convict's arm and walked him out of the room without noiselessly.

Babaji then brought his attention to me with a surprisingly sweet smile and said, "You are our honored guest. And even more so, because you are a friend of my Babli. I apologize for all the strange things that you have just witnessed. I did not anticipate things to turn out this way. However—" His face tightened. "I would really appreciate if you keep all that happened here to yourself. Can I have your word?"

"Of course," I said courteously.

Babaji's look of cold speculation filled me up with dread. "Good," he said finally. "I appreciate your support." He then turned to Constable Jafar. "Constable, I would like to make a request. Go back to your superior and tell him I've decided to keep the convict with me. He will understand. I will send the convict back when the time is right. That is a promise."

Constable Jafar nodded and made himself scarce.

Babaji took a deep breath and turned to us. "Now, if everybody could leave this room to my two sons and me, I would really appreciate it."

20 A CHEST FULL OF IDEAS

From the eastern curve of the island where the Bhairab estate was situated, there was a narrow, dense, woodland stretching to the north. It stopped abruptly at the Bhairab Estate. It was fenced off rather diligently—an unwanted bushland trying to creep into the well-kept estate. I would sometimes see Biruda pruning out the greyish green weeds trying to burst out of the fence. Babu Bhairab would be there—not necessarily helping Biruda, but chatting away in a leisurely manner.

On the other side of the island, near its southern border, was the public boat line, where boatmen offered their services to the general population needing a ride. Due to the Bhairabs occupying the narrow eastern curve—the shore closest to the mainland—the boatmen had to essentially row beside the southeast shoreline for a while before they could get to the deep waters on their way to the district. So, whenever I'd take a stroll along the Bhairabs' private boat-line, I would often see boats coming up from the side. If I happened to make eye-contact with the boatmen or their passengers, they would smile and bow. Although I am not one of the Bhairabs, having the privilege of staying at their estate carried its weight.

Life in the Bhairab estate surely wasn't short of extravagance. Late autumn is harvesting season. That, coinciding with The Gathering, ensured that the estate was buzzing with festivity. At least two guests were greeted in and taken to their allocated rooms every day. The closer we got to The Gathering, the more important guests we received.

Inside the estate, men and women all over the island had their hands full. While hordes of men were busy building and organizing the upcoming event, the women of the village were employed to take care of the harvesting. Crops were brought in on boats and then transferred in bunches to different sections of the Bhairab estate to be harvested by loud, humming machines.

Baby Bhairab, Bishnu and I would take part in all these festivities. Housemaids would present servings after servings of pithas[xxx], sweetmeats and fruits. Sometimes, during late evenings, when things had settled down, Nondi would come to our shed and chat with us, but other than that, she was always busy. Yet, I had never really seen her participate in any of the work the women were doing. So, I wasn't sure what kept her occupied at the time. She was hard to read as she carried her self-reservation everywhere.

The southern part of the estate, which belonged to Meghab Bhairab, was always locked shut and no one got in or out except Meghab Bhairab himself, who would occasionally come out. Avoiding eye-contacts with the guests, he would go inside the main house and then come out a few hours later to go back to where he came from in the same fashion. Prithuda sat quietly and inconspicuously in front of the gate of the southern section on a chair. He never provoked much attention from anybody.

"Babaji must be really busy taking care of all this harvesting. Makes sense that we don't see him too often," I said casually one day to Babu Bhairab, which made him break into a laughter.

It was that awkward time of the day when Bishnu was working on the house for a few hours and I was left alone with Babu Bhairab. My tolerance for Babu Bhairab was a slow work in progress. We hadn't started off on the right foot and he hadn't made a very good impression on me thereafter. His absentminded, entitled behavior bothered me, but on occasions, when he was sober, sparks of intelligence would come out, which intrigued me. In his behavior towards me, I sensed a playful disrespect. I felt, just like the day he invited me to come closer to the decay, he was always daring me to do something drastic. But I never entertained his taunts.

"Oh, no, Babaji is not concerned about harvesting at all." He picked up a fallen branch from the ground and started whipping the air with it. After doing this for a bit, keeping me in the dark (to my annoyance), he finally answered, "If he was concerned about it, he wouldn't have left it to me."

"You are in charge of harvesting?" I could barely hold the sarcasm in my voice. "I haven't once seen you tending to anything related to harvesting."

"Oh, I don't worry about that," Babu Bhairab said as he sat underneath a tall mango tree. The thick shadows of the tree's leaves made a strong contrast on his pale face. "Our workers are pretty self-sufficient. And Prithuda takes care of all the distribution."

"You mean to the wholesalers at Choubazaar?" I asked. "I have never seen him set foot on any of the boats going in that direction."

Babu Bhairab smiled at me, with the same arrogance with which adults smile at children asking questions beyond their comprehension.

"Prithuda does a different kind of distribution. A more important kind," he said, smugly.

"What kind?"

"He makes sure all the proceeds of the harvest go to the right people, so everyone is happy. You know…that sort of thing."

I gave up asking questions. I was pretty used to his antics by then. I assumed that it was Prithuda who took care of all the harvesting. Babu Bhairab was simply set up as an honorary supervisor to keep him busy. *Why would Babaji make him, of all people, responsible for his family's business? The wealthy cannot afford to have arrogant imbeciles in charge of what makes their wealth.*

"You should be wary of Prithuda, you know." Babu Bhairab broke my train of thought. "He is a quiet fellow, but he takes care of a lot of important family matters." He nodded at me as if I had actually understood what he was saying.

"What do you do then?" I asked to humor myself.

I hoping the question would take him by surprise. But instead, he looked at me seriously, breathed in, threw away the branch and leaned on the tree.

"I do the opposite of what Prithuda does," he said with calm speculation in his voice. "I make sure the proceeds of all the things we put out come back to us," he answered.

I hadn't really expected an answer any less vague, to be honest. So, I decided to end the conversation there and gazed across the pond. The massive banyan tree seemed surreal in the dying light. Looking at it, I felt a tingle of dread. I felt out of place and contemplated the hospitality of the Bhairabs, not just towards me, but towards all the guests. I felt that beneath the surface of their accepting nature, there was something dangerous and unknown lurking. *Was it really crazy to think that a family whose belief and sense of prestige depended so much over a myth about a tree would have a lot going on under the surface?*

I thought about how Babaji and his eldest son had almost never interacted with us and Babaji's strange decision to house an escaped convict for talking about a dream he had. All this indicated underlying tension beneath the seemingly settled and friendly attitude of the Bhairabs. I honestly couldn't imagine what to expect the closer we got to The Gathering.

"Don't worry about The Gathering." Babu Bhairab broke my train of thought. "It won't be anything more complicated than a stash of gold and jewels."

"How…what makes you think I was thinking of that?"

"You have been staring at that blasted tree for the last five minutes."

"I guess I was," I said, chuckling nervously. "What makes you think it's just going to be gold and jewels?"

"I don't romanticize things. I prefer to take things for what they are," Babu Bhairab said in a nonchalant tone. "Historically, it's not really an uncommon practice. Agriculture propels this economy, but agriculture is also unpredictable. You are at the mercy of nature, with possibilities of floods, droughts, infestations, weather damage and so on. This makes the poor miserable and the rich fearful.

"So, the rich do what they always do when they fear the unpredictable: they store away their riches for their future generations. They become so deluded by their own comfort, they worry about their bloodline far into the future—people they would never even meet."

"So, to you, caring about future generations is a bad thing?"

"It's not a bad thing. Just deluded."

"How so?"

"You only think this way when your own ego supersedes your pragmatic constitution. When you're so comfortable with your life that you no longer worry about your own survival. You no longer feel any pain from the actions you or the people in your life take. In some twisted, misconceived way, you have managed to make peace with the grotesque wrongness that happens around you, by you and with you. That's the state of mind you need to be in to be so unaware of the present, that you start thinking about the future. You want to extend your seed in some twisted idea of immortality. You try to make as many versions of yourself as possible. One more perfect than the other." Babu Bhairab chuckled maniacally as he squinted up at the sprawling tree above.

"So, you think the desire to bear children is all about ego?" I asked.

"At a fundamental level, it is. It's madness, really," he said. "You take that madness up a few more notches and you start becoming so consumed with the legacy you would leave behind, that you worry about the time when it will end, even though by that time, there will be no trace of you left behind. That's when, to you, stashing a chest full of gold for generations far into the future would seem rational. For the Bhairabs, it's just the same thing—only bigger and more mythical, because it's our family."

"So, you think you have all this figured out?"

"Yes."

"Then what about all this religious sentiment?"

"Such as?"

"Preachers of two religions gathering here and interpreting all this from a religious perspective. What's that about?"

Babu Bhairab breathed in contemplatively.

"Religion in this part of the world is…complicated," he went on. "We have two religions here: one built over thousands of years of beliefs, traditions and knowledge passed through generations and the other a foreign influence layered on top of it as a unifying, divine and otherworldly set of codes."

"That's…one way of looking t it."

"Two very contradicting concepts, don't you think? The second eventually overtook the first, but the traces of the first still remain. How can it just go away? It had been our way of life for thousands of years. You cannot expect a nation of people built and shaped by one underlying way of life to just cleanly accept another based on a different and in fact, opposite idea." He smirked. "Do you see what I'm getting at?"

"I'm trying."

"You see, no matter how our religious preferences have changed over the years, we still adhere to the principles of what we were used to for thousands of years."

"Hmm…interesting ideas, but I still don't see how it answers my question," I said. "Why are men of both religions gathering for this event?"

"Because this event is all about tradition—fulfillment of an old prophecy. That subtext fascinates the religious people of both sides because they want to believe in traditions and prophecies and attach significance to anything that adheres to these ideas."

"So, that's why they're observing this from a religious point of view?"

"You bet."

"It'll be a real disappointment when they find out that it's just a chest full of riches…given that you are right."

Babu Bhairab shrugged. "You don't understand this world, do you?" he said. "People will attach religious significance to it, regardless of what lies on the other side of that door. If they find the branch of a tree in there, they will call it the tree branch of the first prophet who came to these lands, which he used to split open the Great Green Lake to make his way."

We both chuckled out loud at the comment. It was moments like this when Babu Bhairab became unexpectedly pleasant to converse with—when he isn't trying to get a rise out of people and his sharp, introspective mind full of odd, yet evocative ideas come out. I could see glimpses of an intelligent, curious young man, which made me wonder. *What could have happened that made him the way he is.*

I gazed up ahead. Bishnu was coming back after his day's work. The daylight was starting to fade. Thick shadows of leaves covered the ground and roots of the trees. Nesting birds were calling out for their partners to come back.

"I am getting restless again," said Babu Bhairab to Bishnu, when he made it to us.

"Well, if you want to go out boozing at Choubazaar, at least take me with you this time. Babaji gave me an earful the last time you disappeared," Bishnu responded.

"Oh, come on," Babu Bhairab said instantly. "Babaji and Maaji only noticed because of the ruckus Biruda and that convict created."

Bishnu stared at Babu Bhairab with raised eyebrows.

"Fine," Babu Bhairab said, waving him off. "I don't have to justify my actions to any of you. Besides, I'm not keen on getting on the water again. I was simply thinking about taking a walk outside this estate, away from all these fanatical sycophants."

"They are the religious spokespeople, Babuda," said Bishnu. "Not sycophants."

"Everyone's a sycophant if you are a Bhairab—everyone with an ambition at least," said Babu Bhairab. A mischievous grin spread across his face. "I bet Kuberda would agree with you, eh, Bishnu? Why don't we pay him a visit?"

"That's a good idea, actually," acknowledged Bishnu. "That is, if you stop aggravating him like you always do."

"I don't aggravate Kuberda," said Babu Bhairab. "We only aggravate the people around us when we talk to each other because we speak the truth. People don't like hearing truths too often or for too long. But we are not people-pleasers. Kuberda tries to be a people-pleaser. Unsuccessfully, but he tries. I, on the other hand, don't bother."

"Well, thanks for your valuable insight." The sarcasm in Nondi's voice as it came from behind us was very clear. "However, I would prefer our dear guest to find out whether Kuberda is a people-pleaser or not by himself." She looked at me. "And you will get that chance today. Kuberda has invited all of you to spend the evening with him."

"The three of you can go. I will get some rest," Babu Bhairab interjected.

Only moments ago, he was the one talking about going to see his brother, what's gotten into him?

"Kuberda has invited you, too, Babuda," Nondi said.

"Tell him I will see him later," Babu Bhairab mumbled, avoiding eye contact. He departed abruptly, pacing towards the central house and disappearing behind it.

I looked at Bishnu and Nondi in confusion.

"It's alright," Bishnu said, putting a hand on my shoulder. "Leave him be. He usually needs some time to gather himself after causing a ruckus."

For the first time since I had arrived, I got out of the estate. Beyond the pond to the west was the Bhairab's well-maintained garden, from where we started our journey. We walked out of the open, barred iron gate, which was kept unlocked to make way for the farmers, who were carrying in the harvest in large bamboo containers balanced on their heads.

From the narrow, eastern shores where the Bhairab Estate was situated, the island opened out like a wide, misshapen egg. On the northeastern shores, dense bushland bordered the island. Parallel to that strip of bushland was a strip of crop fields, full of rice paddies that farmers were busy reaping with large kachis. The heavy waves of golden tops over light green stocks glistened in the sun as they swung gently in the wind.

To the south of the crop fields, the locality was quite different from what I was used to back on the mainland. It wasn't the organized, quaint little northern community; neither was it the stretched-out swampland to the south. Instead, the locality on the island spread out in an unorganized clutter that felt much more primitive. Green pastures, with tall, unattended grasses. Small but dense woodlands with waterbodies scattered here and there. Small pieces of independent lands where crops were grown, with farmhouses bordering them.

Within this diverse landscape were independent little houses. They were mostly bamboo-built, yet they didn't look any less affluent than the tin-shaded ones on the mainland. In fact, they were more elaborate, with spacious, smooth yards and I could see people in those yards, busy wiping them with wet mops. They smiled at us cordially as we passed by.

"Hmm. These yards are cleaner than the ones I saw on the mainland," I commented. "Dadima's yard was clean but dry. She didn't mind the general dust or fallen leaves, either. But these yards, including the estate, are kept pristine."

"Muslims are keen on keeping the insides of their houses clean, whereas Hindus focus on the outside," Bishnu replied.

"Why so?" I inquired.

"It's related to how and where we worship," Nondi joined the conversation. "Muslims pray inside, whereas we worship outside. The basil plants that grow in our yards are sacred; the cow is sacred. Your God is in your prayers, in your thoughts, in the scripts you keep on your shelves and in the prayer mat you tuck away. Whereas our Gods are spread out in different forms, in the very nature we live in."

Nondi beamed at me and her dark pupils glistened. I smiled back, then gazed towards the houses again. Their clean yards glowed like golden amber in the sunlight.

21 A GRACIOUS WEAKLING

My first sight of Kuber Bhairab, the one 'misfire' of the great Bhairab seed, didn't quite fit the picture other had drawn of him. He clearly was nothing like his handsome, healthy brothers, but he didn't seem all too weak and docile either. We had just entered the wide front yard of the Bhairab Temple to see him repeatedly running and crashing into a tall, sprawling tree. Every time he did it, green fruit of various sizes rained on top of him, making him cover his head with his bony arms in defense.

"Kuberda, what are you doing?" Nondi shouted out and ran to hold him steady.

Kuber Bhairab couldn't be more than five feet tall, as he stood about a forehead short of Nondi. He wore crisp, clean matt-white dhuti and a yellow fotua with a white shawl wrapped around him. The layers of his dress made him seem bigger than he was.

"Don't worry, Nondi. I am fine," Kuber Bhairab squeaked out, followed by a few coughs. "I was just getting some starfruit for our guests."

"Settle down, Kuberda," Nondi said. "This is why I don't leave you alone." She coaxed him onto the mat, which had been laid out under the tree along with pillows, soft cushions and thick blankets. "Look at the mess you've made!" she said as she started to clear out the tree-debris from the mat.

"I needed the exercise," Kuber Bhairab said, catching his breath. "Besides, I wanted our guests to enjoy the juicy starfruits we have here."

"You couldn't ask for that from Ponditji?" Nondi asked.

"I think he is asleep at the moment. He usually is at this time of the day. Besides, I'm getting tired of asking people to take care of me, Nondi. I can do it myself."

Nondi closed her eyes and shook her head. She then pointed at me and said, "This is our guest."

A friendly smile stretched his thin lips thinner. He had a small, ovular head with puffs of black, thinning hairline on top. He was quite fair, yet, like his siblings, he was fair in his own unique way. He was pale, with reddish smudges on his cheeks, possibly due to his exercise we had just witnessed. He had a sharp nose, tight cheeks and big, spread-out ears. His thick eyebrows squinted together as he smiled invitingly at us.

"And also, Bishnu!" exclaimed Kuber Bhairab, with excitement in his voice. "Haven't seen you for ages, my dear friend. How is Dadima?"

None of the Bhairabs until that point had asked about the people in Bishnu's life on the other side of the river, not even Babu Bhairab.

"She is doing okay," Bishnu replied.

"Can't imagine how she's coping after Dadaji's departure!" There was genuine concern in his voice. "How long has it been? Two years?"

"A little over a year," said Bishnuda.

"Hope you're taking good care of her," said Kuber Bhairab.

"Oh, well, you know Dadima. She doesn't like living in the past," Bishnu said, smiling. He put his hand on my shoulder. "Our guest has been giving her good company."

"Has he now?" Kuber Bhairab turned his attention to me. "It is a pleasure to finally meet you."

I smiled back and nodded.

A streak of child-like exuberance appeared on Kuber Bhairab's face. "Nondi, pick up the good starfruits that I have extracted, take them inside, prepare them with salt and chili powder and present them to our guests. I—" He stopped to gather his breath.

"I will, Kuberda. As soon as you lie down, please." Nondi said as she was trying to coax him to lie down from his upright position from which he had been maintaining the whole conversation. With Nondi's insistence, he finally laid down.

After settling Kuber Bhairab down, Nondi picked up some tree branches and leaves that had been scattered around us and threw them to the side. Then she began picking up the bottle green fruits Kuber Bhairab had harvested from the tree, putting them into a make-shift pouch—made with her orna. The fruits were oval, but with sharp angles that would make four- or five-pointed stars if you cut them out diagonally, justifying their name.

"Only pick out the nice and ripe ones. Keep the green ones for later," Kuber Bhairab interjected, as he lifted his head to see what Nondi was doing. "Leave the botched ones as they are. They are good bird-food."

"I will, Kuberda, I will. Please, lie down," came Nondi's response as she waved at him while concentrating on her work. After collecting the fruits, she looked at me and smiled. "Come with me. Let me take you to Ponditji. He is eager to meet you, as well."

CHILDREN OF DECAY

In the fading light of the day, the Bhairab temple looked like a mythical structure rooted deep into its landscape. It almost seemed too enormous to be man-made, with its thick stone walls decorated with various wild forest-mosses. Only closer inspection revealed the joints in the stones. It stood as the last sign of civilization at the south-western part of the island in front of a stretched-out swampy woodland. Beyond it, murky water gradually morphed into the river beyond.

Entering the temple with Nondi, I heard noises from all sorts of birds and critters around me. The whole ecosystem had come to life to settle itself for the night. I heard shuffling over my head. A few monkeys on all fours disappeared from sight.

A few paces from the entry-point was the main hall of worship. It was spacious, with rows of bamboo mats hanging from the walls and the altar at the far end. I could imagine those mats set out on the floor for people to sit on during worship.

Paralleling the main hall of worship were two corridors, one on either side, the shorter one on the left and the longer one on the right. Both had a door at the end. Nondi turned to the left one and I followed. Her jaws were clenched beneath her soft cheeks. When we reached the end of the corridor, she rapped on the door loudly.

"Ponditji!" She said, in a controlled, yet sharp tone.

"Ponditji!" She repeated as she rapped on the door louder and this time we heard shuffling and a small commotion coming from inside. I looked at Nondi again; her jaws were still clenched, added to that were narrowed eyes and flared nostrils.

I heard a cough from inside, followed by a muffled voice. "Please, come in. The door is unlocked."

I saw something much different from what I was expecting when I met Ponditji. Having grown up in a Muslim community, I had quite antiquated ideas about Hindu Pondits. I was expecting a full, bright white dhuti, seamless clothing and a shaved head. What I saw instead was the most normal-looking person I could possibly had met.

He was wearing a dirty, grey dhuti and a green checkered shirt. He had blunt nose, thick lips and a small round head with thin, receding hair. His deep-set eyes carried the blank expression of a person who had just woken up. As we stepped into the room, he stood up. He was of medium height, with a lean body and a dark complexion.

"This is our guest," said Nondi. Before Ponditji could say a word of greeting to me, she interrupted, "Ponditji, why didn't you keep an eye on Kuberda when I left?"

"I..." Ponditji's face lost a bit of color. "I didn't know you were gone."

"I knocked on your door quite loudly, Ponditji," Nondi said. A slight sliver of disdain flashed underneath her usual respectful expression. "And told you that I was going back to the estate to run some errands and bring in our guests."

"I was probably still asleep, Nondima," Ponditji said as he cracked an affectionate smile, breaking out of his drowsy state. "You know I have to prepare pujaris[xxxi] all night for The Gathering?"

Nondi closed her eyes and drew a deep breath. "All I ask of you is to keep an eye on Kuberda while I am gone," she said. When Ponditji tried to respond, Nondi ignored him and continued, "This is our guest."

"It is a delight to meet you." He smiled at me. "Babuda befriends all kinds of folks. But you are the first of a kind."

"What do you mean?" I asked, perplexed.

"I have never seen him befriend someone like you, that is all." He looked at me intently for a few moments before Nondi interrupted.

"Kuberda needs you to prepare these for our guest." While we were exchanging greetings, she had poured the starfruits into a steel bowl.

"Yes, of course," Ponditji said. "I will tend to these."

He walked over to the corner of the room opposite the bed and opened a small pantry full of little jars of spices, cutlery and cooking utensils, stacked from top to bottom. Right beside the tap was a single gas stove. He extended a hand towards Nondi, who handed him the steel bowl, which he took and began rinsing its contents under the tap. Sunlight from the window made the fruit seem like precious green rocks. Through the window, I could see Kuber Bhairab there, excitedly pointing up the starfruit tree and talking to Bishnu.

"Kuberda loves that tree." Nondi's ringing voice broke my contemplation. She carried a serene smile on her face. "He keeps an eye on its fruits and what level of ripeness they are at. He loves to show them to people."

"Why are you two standing? Please, take a seat on the bed," Ponditji said, turning towards us as he finished rinsing the fruits. He then pulled out a piri[xxxii] from the pantry and took out a dao[xxxiii] from its side. He put the dao on the ground and started slicing up the star fruits. He would first peel away the thin outlines of the fruit and then start cutting it out at the short end, creating little green stars that shone in the light. The fruits came out of the bowl whole and went back in pieces.

He looked up at me and grinned. "So, it must be quite strange for you, here...being in the middle of¬—" He took a short breath. "—all this."

"It is," I answered after a few seconds of contemplation. "But I'm interested to see how things turn out."

"Aren't we all?" came the instant response. "What do you think lies on the other side of that door?"

Nobody had asked me that question before, so I hadn't given it much thought.

"Honestly...I am barely still figuring out this predicament. Heh." I admitted. "It all feels different and new."

"Is it different because you are a Muslim, or is it different because you are not religious?" Ponditji asked. *Is it meant to rattle me?*

"Does it matter?" I said, deciding not to be rattled.

Ponditji had finished cutting the fruits. He got up and handed the bowl back to Nondi. He then gazed at me contemplatively.

"To me, it doesn't," he said. "My religion is not as black and white as yours. You may or may not believe in a divine being, but you will have your journey."

He gave me an approving nod and went back to sit on the piri. He opened the pantry again. From there, he brought out a small ceramic cup and two little boxes—one contained chili powder and the other contained salt.

He opened both and muttered softly, "It's never where I look for it, is it?" He opened the small pantry again, shaking the different containers in there until one of them made a faint rattling noise that made him go, "Ah!"

He took that container out and opened it. The strong fragrance of coriander filled the room. He dipped his index finger and thumb carefully into the container and brought out a small, white, semi-transparent plastic spoon. It was still laced with coriander, which looked like little specks of blemishes as the sunlight passed through them. He tapped it on the inside walls of the container, which cleared it off most of the blemishes.

He then took the spoon in one hand, closed the lid of the container, put it back in its place and went back to the two containers of salt and chili powder. He took out two spoonful of salt and one spoonful of chili powder and shook the small ceramic bowl to mix the two ingredients together. When they were mixed evenly, he gave the bowl to Nondi. He put the white plastic spoon in the salt container and put everything back into the pantry.

"What did you mean by saying that your religion is not as black and white as mine?" I asked. I had been contemplating whether or not to ask, fearing it would mean disrespect.

Ponditji smiled cordially as he sat beside me, wiping off his hand with a cotton towel. "In my religion, the choice between good and evil is not bound by rules. They are merely open choices of various degrees that have their appropriate consequences," he said, nodding. "If you make the right choices, your life on this earth might be difficult, but the journey of your soul in the grand universe will be short. If you make the wrong choices, then it will be longer. You will experience more rebirths, more chances to make amends until you do."

He looked at Nondi. "Now, let us get back to Kuberda," he said to both of us. "We shouldn't be keeping him waiting."

"What do you think is beyond that door?" I asked as we walked along the corridor.

"Whatever is on the other side of that door, I am sure it will make us more aware of the creator of this universe and bring some of his grace back into this household. We could really use some right now."

The crickets had started chirping; evening had just fallen.

22 OF GODS AND WORSHIPS

"Starfruit trees are like Gods as we perceive them, while mango trees are like Gods in their true nature," said Kuber Bhairab.

"What do you mean?" I asked as I bit into my first starfruit piece. It was watery, sweet and sour, with a comforting citrus undertone. After finishing that piece, I took another and followed what others did. I tapped it on the mixture of chili powder and salt and took a bite. This time, the taste was enhanced by an herbal kick. The flesh inside the fruit disintegrated inside my mouth into watery, pulpy goodness. The pieces had varying degrees of balance between tangy and sweet. Some of them were sweeter than others and the sweetest ones shone the brightest in the sunlight and left a lingering taste on my togue.

"Delicious, isn't it?" Kuber Bhairab asked, resting his back on the starfruit tree, supported by a pillow.

"It is. Quite a nice complex taste." I nodded. "You haven't answered my question,"

"Oh... right. It's how they give us their fruits," he said and then closed his eyes as if that answered the question.

"How so?"

Kuberda opened his eyes and stared at me, perplexed. "You really don't understand?"

"How would he understand, Kuberda, if this is the first time, he's having a starfruit?" Nondi said, giggling. She was clearly in a good mood, which wasn't all that common.

"Fair point," said Kuber Bhairab. He put the propped-up pillow flat on the bed and laid down, gazing up at the fading light of the fresh evening sky.

I gave him time to contemplate. The sun was setting and darkness was quickly engulfing the world. The temple was a few hundred meters away from the village where people lived, separated by a patch of woodland with a narrow road in the center. So, as we sat in the front yard of the temple, there was the woodland to our east and shadowy swampland in all other directions. If I concentrate, I could make out the texture of the trees. I could hear skittering noises of critters running around. Infrequent gusts of wind made the leaves sing in broken rhythm. The whole swampland felt like a living being around us; its features gradually faded into the looming nightfall. Sitting at the center of all this felt surreal.

"You see this tree, such beautiful fruits. Delicious." Kuber Bhairab's voice broke my trance. "All year, these fruits come out—for us humans, birds, bats, sheep and goats. They grow like a million stars in the night sky and fall on us like rainfall—an abundant, constant supply. This is how we expect Gods to be."

"In contrast, think about the mango trees. They give out their fruit only for a couple of months a year. And for that, we need to tend to them, protect them from insects, keep them healthy with fertilizers…throughout the year. Then and only then, when summer comes, we get their sweet yield. And even then, we don't get the best at the beginning. The lesser-quality mangoes need little heat to ripen and thus come in early. They have less fiber and thus store less juice. Their sweetness is less intense." He stopped to draw a deep breath.

"But the best of the mangoes—the most densely sweet ones—they take longer to ripen and come in only for a few days before the season ends and then we have to go through another whole year of preparation. That is how Gods really are. They answer our prayers in small increments, in long intervals and the best of their blessings can only be felt for a short, short time."

"Interesting perspective," I commented. "So, what is your point? Do you mean to say that we need to be patient with God's blessings?"

"There's no point to it. It is only an observation," replied Kuber Bhairab. Then he turned to Nondi and muttered, "I am thirsty, Nondi. Will you help me?"

"Of course, Kuberda." Nondi turned around promptly to fetch the glass and the steel jug from around the corner of the tree, poured some water into the glass and handed it to him. As he drank the water, Nondi maintained her grip on the glass.

"However," he said, in a reenergized voice after he was done, "it is a perspective on the Gods' motivations—why they act the way they do, isn't it?"

"What do you mean?" I inquired.

"Look at how we treat starfruits. We trample them; we get annoyed when they fall on our heads. We don't invite guests just to treat them with starfruits, unlike I did today. Yet they are just as delicious as mangoes, if not more, in their own right." He kept going, with eyes full of wonder, observing the starry night sky, "We treat these fruits poorly because they are plentiful and always there for us."

"Compare that to how we treat mangoes. We take care of the trees all year, keep an eye on their growth, whether they are growing enough leaves or the right kinds of branches, we give them fertilizers when the season is approaching, we protect their sprouts, we protect the green fruits from critters, we wait and we wait until we get their sweet, sweet yield." He paused and exhaled contemplatively. "And when the yield comes, we celebrate it. We invite guests to eat our mangoes. Social status is measured by how good of a mango-yield a house gets. This fruit is our cultural treasure and we worship it like a God."

He sighed and nodded contemplatively. His chest was thumping with irregular breaths and he seemed tired. He had probably been running into that tree all afternoon. But in his eyes, I saw satisfaction for being able to talk to someone.

I smiled at him. "But what does it say about Gods' motivation?"

"That Gods understand our nature," came the response from Kuber Bhairab. "When the supply of blessings is abundant and constant, we take them for granted. But when the blessings come as a result of long, dedicated devotion, that's when we treat them with Gods' love. We don't really worship the Gods. In reality, we worship our own devotion. Gods know that and that's why they treat us the way they do because that is the way to achieve devotion from us."

Kuber Bhairab closed his eyes. Night had fully fallen and the chirping of crickets filled the environment. But the sky was still relatively bright. In this region, when night had only just set in, the sky didn't lose all its color. A strange hour passed where everything above would still have the dim glow of late afternoons, while the world closer to the ground would be enveloped in darkness. The moon was a flat, faded orb, gradually gaining color. The stars came out one by one and, the world above turned gradually into a proper night sky.

"You know, Nondi, if you stayed with Babaji at least a few hours a day, it would have made both his and my work much less stressful." Meghab Bhairab's deep, commanding voice brought us out of our collective trance.

He made it right behind us, with Prithuda in tow, without any of us noticing.

"I was looking after Kuberda," Nondi's voice went back to its measured calmness.

"Yes, but Ponditji had been tasked with that responsibility."

"No disrespect, but you and I both know Ponditji doesn't take good care of Kuberda." Nondi reply came instantly. "Last harvesting season,

Kuberda was sent here, just like now and he had a very painful food poisoning. This time around, Ponditji has even more to do, as he is preparing the Pujaris for The Gathering. He is often sleep-deprived and dozes off during the day." She glanced at Ponditji, who stood up with nervousness painted on his face. "I don't think the task of taking care of Kuberda should be thrust upon someone who is that much occupied with other things. I come to Babaji's aid whenever he calls for me. But Kuberda has been left stranded here."

Meghab Bhairab seemed bit taken aback by Nondi's defiance. I admired the girl's courage to stand up to him, but I also wondered if she had gone too far. I heard a faint exhale of breath and turned to see Kuber Bhairab grabbing the trunk of the tree behind him, trying to use it as leverage to get up. He clearly didn't have the energy to do so. The reddish glow on his pale face had disappeared. His thick eyebrows came together to form a look of profound fear.

"What are you doing, Kuberda?" Nondi muttered, turning towards him.

By that time, Ponditji had already come to his aid and helped him up.

"You...you should listen to Meghabda, Nondi," Kuber Bhairab said, breathing laboriously. "I can look after myself here."

The stern expression on Meghab Bhairab's face softened as he gazed at Kuber Bhairab. He walked towards his younger brother and guided him away from Ponditji and into his embrace.

"I would like to apologize on behalf of Nondi," Kuber Bhairab murmured, resting his head on his older brother's shoulder. "She just cares for me and is always worried that something bad will happen to me."

"I know," Meghab Bhairab said, patting Kuber Bhairab's back, with is eyes on Nondi.

"She has been caring for me since we were children. I hope you don't mind?"

"I don't, Kuber, I don't mind it at all." Meghab Bhairab smirked, but Nondi maintained her frown of speculation.

"Anyway," Meghab Bhairab said, releasing his younger brother from his embrace and coaxing him back to Ponditji. He brought his attention to Bishnu and me. "Babaji has invited you two for dinner, along with the estate's most honorable guests. But, you, my dear guest—" He smirked at me. "You need to come with me to the estate a bit early."

"W-why?" I asked.

"You are a popular man! Maaji wants to see you personally, in her kitchen," Meghab Bhairab replied, as he glanced at Kuber Bhairab.

The two brothers grinned at each other. The tension of the conversation seemed to have subsided.

"Babu's never told him, has he?" Meghab Bhairab asked.

"I suppose he didn't," Kuber Bhairab replied. He then explained to me, "You see, Maaji adores Babu. He is the delight of her world. And so, she is very observant of the company he keeps. You came to this island as his new friend. You are a well-mannered companion and you seem to be spending a lot of time with Babu, as I've heard from Nondi—" He looked at Meghab Bhairab. "—which, I assume, makes Maaji very happy."

"It does." Meghab Bhairab took over from his brother, putting his hand on my shoulder. "And frankly, I am happy as well. You are Babu's new friend, so you might not know him as well as we do, but soon you will see that the company he keeps is nothing worth mentioning."

"Oh, I know. I had a glimpse of them," I said, to which both brothers broke into laughter. I joined them nervously, thinking about how it would make Bishnu feel, but when I glanced around, I realized Bishnu was nowhere to be seen. He had quietly slipped away and I saw him already making his way along the narrow road to the east.

"And you still tolerate him? That's impressive," Meghab Bhairab said. He didn't seem to have noticed Bishnu's departure. "Well, then. Let me be the first to tell you: seeing you as Babu's new companion is, for all of us, a refreshing change. Perhaps he is learning to be civil after all these years." Meghab Bhairab took a deep, thoughtful breath. "Problem is he has somehow convinced Babaji to hire one of his entourages as the estate's night guard. Can you imagine that? The whole estate asleep while that brute roams about everywhere. That boy has so much influence over his parents. Its unhealthy." Meghab Bhairab shook his head and glanced at Prithuda behind him, who stared back blankly.

"But we'll get to that when the time is right." He smiled at me. "For now, Maaji is interested in getting to know you better. She has invited you to her kitchen while she prepares dinner for the guests. So, I request you to, please, start for the estate at once with me. It will be a late-night dinner, as Babaji is still busy closing off his affairs for the day. So, Maaji should have you at least for a few hours. She loves to talk to people when she cooks. Ever since preparation for The Gathering had started, Babaji and I had become quite busy and Babu has, well—" He glanced towards Kuber Bhairab. "—he is just being Babu. So, Maaji has been working away all by herself. She would enjoy your company, trust me."

I glanced at Nondi. She hadn't taken part in any of the conversations we just had, looking sideways towards the ground with a dejected look.

Meghab Bhairab stared at Ponditji. His face hardened and smile faded. I saw a bit of color drain from Ponditji's face.

"Ponditji, you take Kuber and tuck him in for the night. The next time you take a nap with Kuber lying alone outside, it won't end well for you."

Ponditji's, with head down, nodded. Meghab Bhairab stepped forward and kissed Kuber Bhairab on the forehead. They exchanged a nod as Ponditji hastily guided Kuber Bhairab towards the temple.

"You look confused, dear guest," Meghab Bhairab said, as we watched Ponditji and Kuber Bhairab disappearing into the temple.

"Kuberda isn't invited to the dinner?" I asked.

"He is not strong enough to make it all the way across the island this late. We will send them both leftovers," he said. "And, besides, there will be a lot of important guests tonight."

23 A SUPERSTITION ABOUT INEVITABILITY

"Come here. Let me get a better look at you."
The first thing I experienced after entering the central house of the Bhairab estate was Modhura Bhairab, known by everyone as Maaji, walking out of her bed-chamber and wrapping her short arms around me in a tight embrace. It felt like dropping onto a soft pillow of unbridled affection, tainted with the tart smell of paan[xxxiv]. She kissed me on my forehead and stared at me with glinting eyes.

She was a handsome, plump woman, with a thick line of shidur[xxxv] across the middle of her temple, matched in brightness by the crimson red paan in her mouth. Her cheeks were soft, despite showing the wear and tear of old age. She was short in stature and wore a golden red shari with blue streaks for the occasion.

The interior of the central house was rustic, lit by electric bulbs as modern additions. It had two sections, of which the southern section was bigger than the northern. In front of the immense, decorated bed in the southeastern corner was a large table with eight heavy set chairs circling it. To the west of this arrangement was a few other smaller dining tables, with smaller chairs. It was clear that the room was not only Babaji's bed-chamber, but also where he conducted his affairs. Further west, two rooms next to each other belonged to Babu Bhairab and Kuber Bhairab. I wasn't sure which one belonged to whom at that time, as both were empty. Through the open door of one of the two rooms, a grilled window gave me a glimpse of the Banyan tree and the pond beyond.

"Come now, Modhubi," came a deep, crackling voice. "Let the poor boy breathe."

Babaji looked at us with a smile on his face. Just like his eldest son, his expression was much more amicable when he spoke to me, compared to the stern demeanor he had maintained while talking to the convict, Suba Kashem. He got up from his giant bed, put on the shawl that was folded neatly on the large table beside him and picked up a large steel torchlight from the table. He then put on his slippers and walked towards us.

"Your Maaji has been waiting eagerly for you," he commented, placing his hand on my shoulder. "Go ahead, take a seat in her bed-chamber." I obliged. He then turned his gaze to Maaji and smiled. "Are you happy now? Look at this boy. He came right to your doorstep when he heard you wished to see him. And where's Babu? Probably back at Choubazaar again. I keep telling that boy to stay on the island 'til The Gathering is over and he keeps running off."

"Why do you have to bring that up now? You have no sense of context, Raghabji."

It took a moment for me to realize that Maaji was calling Babaji by his real name. I hadn't heard it since Babu Bhairab said it in Ustadji's restaurant.

"Anyway, Nondi will greet the guests. You finish your work with Megha and come back as soon as you can," Maaji said. "I don't want the guests to wait any longer. The only reason they don't mind waiting so long is that it is you. But, don't push them any further."

"I can push them as far as I want to and you know it," Babaji said. "But yes, I will be back soon. I don't want you and Nondi serving guests into the depth of the night." He let out a quick sigh. "What choice did I have? I had so much to do today, yet Megha insisted I make the announcement no later than tonight. So, a late dinner for the guests would have to suffice. Anyway, chat with your new naat and cook dinner." He gazed lovingly at his wife. "I'll see you all when the guests arrive."

Before heading for the high-walled home of his eldest son, Babaji looked over his wife's shoulder towards Nondi and nodded with a smile. Nondi, who was preparing the kitchen, smiled back.

"Don't be scared, little one. There will be some big guests coming today. But they are people, just like you and me," Maaji said as she entered her bed-chamber.

I gave her a courteous nod of acknowledgment. Maaji's bed-chamber contained a single bed to the east and a kitchen to the west. A proper, modern stove is a rare luxury in this part of the world, but so far, among the Bhairabs, I had already seen two. A small, single-stove setup in Ponditji's room and an elaborate four-stove setup in Maaji's chamber. The stoves were set close to the ground, just like the earthen ones typical in this part of the world, but instead of jute-stock and firewood, they ran on gas.

Maaji and Nondi sat on piris and went to work. Nondi was cutting potatoes. She ran their outer surfaces lightly along the blade of her dao, peeling them in the process, before cutting them into four even pieces. A wrinkly old lady sat on the steps at the chamber's northern exit, peeling potatoes of a different variety in a steel bowl with a spoon. Each potato couldn't have been bigger than a sizable pebble. ┐┐

"Never seen gol alu[xxxvi] before, naat?" Maaji's voice broke my train of thought. She glanced at me, smiling, while hastily caramelizing onions on a korai[xxxvii] that sizzled with shots of hot oil spitting out. She very quickly brought the intensity down with a splash of water and carefully stirred the concoction until it simmered into a thickened, consistent mix.

"I have," I responded. "Dadima puts them in when she cooks shaak[xxxviii]." I immediately regretted my answer, as I remembered that I was supposed to maintain my identity as Bishnu's contractor and drawing attention to Dadima might jeopardize that.

"It's so great to have grandparents alive, isn't it?" Maaji didn't seem to have picked up on it. "Babli has never seen any of his. They were long gone before he was born. Meghab got all four of them. He even got a bit of his great grandfather on his father's side. His boro-abba[xxxix]," she said. "Nondi, that's enough potatoes. Go and help the maids with the shaak and fish. I'm getting the meat in."

Following her instruction, Nondi walked out through the northern exit into a small bamboo shack outside, which I had initially thought to be a storeroom. But as my gaze followed Nondi into the hut, I saw a glint of burning amber. While the hut was indeed a storeroom, it also had a couple of earthen stoves, where a few women, including the one who had been peeling the potatoes just before, were busy cooking.

As Nondi disappeared into the shack, I sensed quiet resentment in her movements. *The confrontation she had with Meghab Bhairab must have left its mark on her.* I decided to leave her be and brought my attention back to Maaji, who was carefully releasing some pieces of meat from a large steel bowl into the korai as it sizzled. The potatoes Nondi prepared went in as well.

She picked up a small metal tray that had been sitting beside a pata-puta[xl]. On the tray were little mounds of colorful spices, emanating zesty scents; yellow-ochre ginger, white garlic, bottle-green nutmeg and fresh yellow turmeric. Maaji slid all the little clumps of paste into the korai. In went some garam masala, a healthy dose of chili powder, a couple of sticks of cinnamon and a few whole cardamoms. Maaji then opened a small plastic box, from which she picked out a few dried red chilies, crushed them in her hands into little flakes and added them to the mix.

She then added water and stirred everything up into a simmering mixture of thick, uncooked curry with a wooden spatula. The room filled with a strong aroma. She put a lid on top of the pot and sat down on her piri in front of me, wiping away sweat with her shari.

"This vita[xli] had so much life, once!" she said, with a sigh. "When I got married to Raghabji, this house was bustling with life. It wasn't as big as you see it now. It didn't have the guest house, only the farmer's quarter. Raghabji was always there, working with the farmers." She looked out the gate into the night. Loud chirping of crickets filled our silence.

"You are from the capital, aren't you? Don't lie." She surprised me with a difficult question, smirking.

"I...I..."

Maaji broke into full-blown laughter. "You have that clueless glare. It's pretty obvious. Raghabji hasn't picked up on it yet, but I have. Don't worry, I won't pry. Babli doesn't like me asking too many questions about his friends."

I didn't know what to say except to nod and smile nervously.

Maaji gazed at me with squinted eyebrows, still smiling. "I knew something was afoot when Raghabji said Bishnu was bringing a contractor with him. That boy is too independent to work for any contractor, but when I saw you, I knew what was going on. Babli wanted to bring a friend of his to the island and this was his way of doing it." She giggled. "Nobody understands my Babli, but I do. He has been told not to get off the island. But he is not the kind who can just stay put. So, he brought the most civil of his friends so that he had someone to talk to." She nodded. "I understand."

"But even after bringing me in, he made trips to Choubazaar anyway." I chuckled.

"Yeah, that he did. He doesn't like following orders. Especially Raghabji's orders," she said. Then she glanced up at the wall-clock behind me and muttered, "Oh, look at the time." She turned her attention towards the northern gate and shouted, "O, Nondi, did you put the polao[xlii] on?"

"I am about to, Maaji," came Nondi's voice.

"Put that on. The guests are about to arrive," she said. She gave me a calculative stare. "Do you have brothers or sisters?"

"No. Just me."

"That's good. It's not pleasant growing up with siblings. So much animosity. Opinions. Pride. Jealousy." She said shaking her head. "I should have been happy with Megha."

I smiled nervously. I was enjoying her insightful commentary. But I wasn't prepared for her blunt honesty about having children.

"Don't get me wrong. It was absolute bliss to have my Babli. Such a beautiful child he was!" she continued. "But it's hard to have beautiful children. You get bad gaze from people."

"What do you mean?" I asked.

"Well, you'd think it's superstition. You are a boy from the capital, after all." She went on, "But I've seen it happen. If you have beautiful children, people tend to be jealous of you. They observe the child with impure thoughts. These bad intentions ultimately rub off on your child. If not on the child you have now, then on your future children. But ultimately, their curse catches on."

Maaji got up from her piri and sat beside me on the bed. Concern and despair were prevalent on her face. I felt that she had been agitated about something ever since she started the conversation. But me giving some credence to her superstition seemed to had opened her up to be more honest with me.

"You are a good friend to my Babli," she said. "You might not be close enough to him yet, but I encourage you to be. He needs a friend like you."

"I will do my best."

"You know where my Babli is right now?" Her voice vibrated a little.

"Where?"

She glanced through the window, which afforded a glimpse of the main yard. It was still empty; the guests hadn't begun to arrive. She went on in a low, trembling voice. "Passed out in the Eastern room. He came to the estate a few hours ago and wanted to enter the main house and make a scene. Biru had to subdue him and take him away. Raghabji doesn't know yet, but Nondi and I know that he is in no state to join the guests for dinner. Can you believe that? The embarrassment." She looked away and wiped her eyes with her shari.

"He is getting worse as The Gathering comes closer. Whatever is beyond that door, I hope it brings some peace to my Babli. Perhaps you are a sign of that." She gazed at me with teary eyes that held a glimmer of hope. "This is what happens when people's bad intentions go into your children. They go mad," she said. Twinkles of more tears appeared in her eyes. She hastily rubbed them away with her shari again. "And sometimes, you give birth to a monster."

"And why did you say I was lucky that I was the only child?" I asked. This strange conversation almost had me in a trance.

"Because the curse never falls on the first child."

I heard footsteps coming from the yard. The guests had started to arrive.

24 A DRUNKEN MALFEASANCE

"Three nights from today will be the night we have all been waiting for," Babaji announced, sitting near the window at the edge of the large, oval dining table. "Therefore, it is paramount that, from this point on, until The Gathering, none of us leave the island and no one gets in."

He surveyed the room with a tight smile that carried heavy authority. There was a nervous shuffle among the guests, but they nodded in unison.

"For this event, I have invited many honored guests," he continued, "and I have invited the very few I consider the most honorable to dine with me today." He nodded. "And out of this respect, I have explained to you all very clearly the implication of joining this event...that when we are a few nights away from The Gathering, a full lockdown of the island would take effect."

"That starts now. I have placed guards all over the island's shores." His let his demeanor soften and his smile felt more genuine. "However, I have strong faith that the guards' jobs will only be blocking intruders coming in, as I know very well that you are all men of principles and thus, you won't disrespect me. Many guests did not accept my invitation due to this very condition. I have nothing against them for making that decision, as they gave respectable consideration to my rules. I am sure you will give these rules the same respect."

An uneasy silence followed. Neither Nondi, nor Babu Bhairab had told me about this stipulation. I glanced anxiously at Bishnu sitting to my right near the doorway and he stared back with the same perplexed gaze, which meant that he didn't know of this either.

"Hold on a moment. Where is Babu?" Babaji turned to his wife and Nondi. Standing at the door between the two bedchambers, they stared back in silence. "Has he..." He paused and surveyed the room. The guests avoided his gaze. "Has he gone off again?" He muttered.

"He did, Babaji, but he has come back." Nondi said calmly.

"So, why isn't he here?" asked Babaji.

"He... he isn't feeling well," Maaji responded.

The uneasy silence was broken mercilessly by the loud, gurgling voice of Babu Bhairab as he stumbled into the room from outside.

"I don't understand why you think I am unwell, Nondi. I am as good as I have ever been and my mind is clear of all resentments."

"Babuda!" Nondi cried out. "I told you to join us later when you are feeling better. Biruda, you were supposed to keep an eye on him."

"He slipped past me," came Biruda's low, guilt-ridden voice from the yard.

"Look, you all need to stop worrying about me," said Babu Bhairab, in a surprisingly composed voice for his inebriated state. "There are people in this world that need far more help than I do."

He stood upright in the middle of the room and drew his breath. "My dear guests, I know that you might be thinking, 'Will I be stuck on this island forever?' To that, I say...no. No, you won't. You will receive a hasty goodbye, so you have nothing to worry about." He took another deep breath. The entire room lingered in stunned silence. "Moreover, due to your loyalty to our family, you are going to get rich."

"That's enough, Babuda!" Nondi said as she tugged on his arm, trying to pull him towards the door.

But Babu Bhairab didn't budge. "For beyond that door lies riches beyond imagination. I know it!" Babu Bhairab said. His voice started to finally break down. "And by bestowing these riches on all of you, we Bhairabs will clear our name of all our misdeeds and we will be sacred once again."

Suddenly, Babu Bhairab lost his footing and Nondi caught him from tumbling onto the floor. "Biruda, please help!" Nondi pleaded.

In came Biruda, who applied the natural strength of his body to carry Babu Bhairab out of the central house. Nondi followed. It didn't seem like Biruda was applying any real force, which was a mistake. As soon as Biruda got Babu Bhairab into the middle yard, Babu Bhairab's body suddenly jolted back into motion as he slipped out of Biruda's grasp.

"Babuda, no. Just—" Biruda stopped talking, as he realized that Babu Bhairab had no intention of having an exchange with him and had already started to stumble his way to the north of the estate. His steps were uneven yet agile. It seemed like he had faced this scenario before. As he disappeared into the night, Biruda chased after him.

The heavy silence in the room was made unbearable by the chirping of crickets. I saw Babaji's right hand curl into a fist on the table. My heart skipped a bit as he turned sideways to give a piercing gaze at me, which then moved to Bishnu. I realized then that in that congregation of important guests, Bishnu and I were invited only under the grace of us being his youngest son's entourage. But since that very son had caused this embarrassment, part of the blame had fallen on us.

I heard hurried footsteps as Nondi came back into the room. She glanced at Babaji, who looked back with a stern face. He gave Nondi a light nod. She had a quick, whispered conversation with Maaji and came directly to Bishnu and me.

"Come with me," Nondi said in a hushed voice. "We'll be spending the night at the temple. I'll pack up food for all of us."

As Bishnu, Nondi and I stepped out into the yard, we saw Biruda, with guilt written all over his face. It was clear that he hadn't been able to get hold of Babu Bhairab.

"When he comes back, please take care of him, Biruda," murmured Nondi.

"I will do my best," he muttered.

Helped by a kerosene lamp, Nondi guided us across the island to the temple. From a distance I saw people sitting out in their yards, whispering to each other, but they went silent as we passed them by. Curiosity and fear were written all over their faces.

"So, Babu made another little mess, did he?" Kuber Bhairab said as we entered through the front gate of the temple.

"Have you eaten?" Nondi inquired.

"Yes, yes, I did. Don't worry, Nondi," Kuber Bhairab said. "Ponditji was quite insistent that I have my meal on time. Fear is good motivation. Especially when it comes from Meghabda." He took a small breath to collect himself. "However, seeing the big pots of food in Nondi's hand, I am guessing none of you have had your supper yet. Babu made his mess early. So please, I insist you all finish your meal here. I'll get Ponditji to arrange your beds."

As we ate in silence, sitting around the desk beside Kuber Bhairab's bed, Ponditji came in, took out a folded mattress from the bottom of the bed, rolled it out on the floor and covered it with cozy blankets and pillows.

"This is where our guest and Bishnu will sleep," said Nondi. "I will go and—"

"Sleep beside the altar," Kuber Bhairab completed her sentence, smiling. "I know that very well. But, before you go, perhaps you can accompany us for a while. What do you say?"

"I am fine, Kuberda," replied Nondi, quietly.

"No, you are not. Don't lie to yourself," Kuber Bhairab responded. "You are never fine when either Babu or I are in trouble. You consider us your brothers. You took care of us and despite us growing older, you are not convinced that we could ever take care of ourselves. I don't blame you. One of us is an impulsive boor and the other a cripple."

"Kuberda, that's enough!" Nondi snapped at him.

Kuber Bhairab ignored her and continued, "But you need to internalize that both of us can take care of ourselves despite our flaws and you don't always have to be there to save us." He breathed in again to regain himself. "I know that Babu messed up again. He went to Choubazaar and got himself drunk. He made a scene and then ran away. I know what will be the consequence; I've seen this happen too many times. There will be no consequence.

"Babu usually gets away with whatever chaos he causes. He'll sneak back into the western guest-house at some point in the night. Babaji would brood. Maaji would sob and pray for his salvation. But come morning, they will both forget what happened. Meghabda will make an attempt at giving him a few stern words, but by the time he makes it to his room, Babu will be long gone, on to his next adventure." Kuber Bhairab chuckled.

"But this is not like the other times, Kuberda and you know it,"

"No matter the significance of the time, place, or the actions he takes, nothing will happen to Babu. And you know why? Because both Babaji and Maaji think that his actions are not a result of his choices and he is simply a victim of his circumstances. So, trust me, he is safe." He nodded at Nondi. "Now, please...instead of worrying yourself to sleep in that giant altar room that constantly carries in the cold wind through the cracks of that rusty front gate, come sit with us. Bishnu will tell us one of his fishing stories."

Kuber Bhairab smiled at Nondi with the warmth of a friend and motioned for her to take a seat. Through the window, the misty swamp looked surreally inviting as Bishnu started to tell one of his stories. This one was about a pale white ghost-girl that kept appearing and reappearing in different corners of the woodland surrounding his house.

25 ANOTHER FISHING STORY

"Bishnu, go fetch Babu after you finish," said Kuber Bhairab, as we were sipping the milk tea Ponditji had served us after finishing off our morning breakfast of paratha served with loti poti[xliii]. The milky sweetness of the tea balanced out the smokey spiciness of our main course.

Compared to Ponditji's modest, small room, Kuber Bhairab's room on was more spacious. However, despite the large, square size of the room, the contents were quite minimal. Near the entrance, was a small fridge—another modern luxury in this part of the world. To the western side was a single bed, where Kuber Bhairab sat. The window overlooked the swamp and let in the thick smell of wet grass at night and bright beams of light in the morning as the sun floated over the river. Beside the bed stood an elongated table with a few chairs surrounding the other side, where we sat having our breakfast. In the spacious eastern side of the room was the mattress where we had slept the night before.

"Did you enjoy the shaluk I sent you?" Bishnu asked Kuber Bhairab.

"Ah, yes. Yes, I did," Kuber Bhairab said, with a rising smile. "Haven't had those in ages! These sludgy swamplands don't grow shaplas." He looked up contemplatively. "Last time I had shaluks was over a year ago. Babu brought some." He sighed. "He was so much better in those days. He was still unruly but his mischievousness was amicable and enjoyable, compared to the hothead he has become these days."

"I agree," Bishnu said, nodding. "He has really deteriorated over the last year."

"Ever wondered why?" Kuber Bhairab narrowed his eyes with a smirk.

To this Bishnu, gave a dry chuckle. "What do you mean 'why'?" he said. "Babuda's mood has never been consistent. And besides, I've had enough problems of my own. I had to get everything sorted after Dadaji departed."

"I see," Kuber Bhairab said.

Bishnu glanced at Nondi, who gave him a disenchanted look. "Oh, don't you two start with me," Bishnu muttered. "I have had more pressing concerns than deciphering Babuda's drunken whims."

We sipped our tea in silence for a minute, until Bishnu broke it. "Anyway, what makes you think he will just come to us when we ask him to? Specially after the mess he made last night."

"Oh, he will. Trust me," Kuber Bhairab replied. "Tell him that Nondi told me about the macha[xliv] that were planted at night and we are about to capture the little fish it caught."

We finished our breakfast, after which Bishnu left for the estate.

"Come now, dear guest. We are going fishing," Kuber Bhairab announced. "I will tell you some stories on the way."

"You're really going to catch fish with that thing?" I asked Kuber Bhairab, pointing at the simple, bamboo-woven mat he was carrying.

It seemed less like a fishing implement and more like a long serving mat. The only difference between that and a tabletop was that it had two bamboo-woven handles at its two long ends. Kuber Bhairab had slipped his thin arm through one of them and he let it dangle at his elbow. He held a long bamboo staff with both hands to help him walk.

Kuber Bhairab gave me a playful smirk without answering. We were going through the swampy woodland towards the shallow waters near the river. Kuber Bhairab, with remarkable agility, traversed through the landscape, using the bamboo staff as leverage. I, on the other hand, was getting ice-cold, swamp-water all over my trousers.

The swampland, simmering in thick early-morning fog, felt unnerving. Contrasting with the busy noises of critters last night, it was dead silent in the morning—as if the whole ecosystem had quieted down to listen to us. Our footsteps felt uncomfortably loud. At odd moments, I'd be startled by the flutter of wings as wild pigeons burst out of bushes.

"It always feels awkward traveling through this place for the first time, but you'll get used to it," assured Kuber Bhairab. "I have ventured across this swampland ever since I was a child. Babaji would place me here whenever important guests visited us. And since important guests were frequent for Babaji, so were my days at the temple. This is practically my second home."

There was something charming about the way Kuber Bhairab always ended his sentences with a smile—even when talking about something profoundly heartbreaking. I felt, at the time, that the innocence in his heart kept him from understanding the darkness of the world. I was proven wrong.

"Bishnu has told you about many of his paranormal fishing stories, I presume?" he asked.

"Yes, he has," I replied. "If you're going to tell me horror stories about this place as well, save your breath. I am already creeped out to my wits' end."

"My stories are not like the ones Bishnu tells you because the things he talks about are from the other realms." Kuber Bhairab sighed, looking around. "But the horrors of this place are all too real."

"Oh, wow. Thanks for that," I responded, with thick sarcasm in my voice. "I wasn't terrified already at all."

Kuber Bhairab laughed at my remark. We went on quietly for a minute.

"Ok, now I'm curious," I said with a nervous chuckle. "What's so horrific about this place?"

Kuber Bhairab drew a deep breath.

"During the Liberation War[xlv], the Hindu population was the most miserable," Kuber Bhairab said. "This island has seen many horrific things. Localities burned down, people executed by the hundreds, torture camps, you name it. And the bodies of all the people who drew their last breaths in these brutal acts were just casually thrown here into this swamp, in shallow graves. Guards used to patrol these swamps so that people wouldn't be able to retrieve the bodies of their friends and families. Muslims bury their dead while we Hindus cremate them. Not giving our loved ones the opportunity for a proper send-off was their way of breaking our spirits."

"You are telling these tales to our guest now?" came Nondi's soft voice. "You can see how frightened he is getting, right?"

I had almost forgotten that Nondi was with us. She was carrying a large empty metal pot with a lid.

"But it is the perfect place for these stories, Nondi," Kuber Bhairab commented. "Scary stories are at their most enjoyable when the fear factor is more palpable."

Kuber Bhairab was right. In some twisted way, I was indeed enjoying the morbid history he was telling me about.

"There is, however, a pragmatic reason why I am telling you all this, my dear guest," Kuber Bhairab went on. "As you are clumsily walking across this area, don't be afraid if you step onto something that might feel like a tree-branch, but is in reality, something vastly different."

"What do you mean?"

"Well…in here, things that feel like branches might be something else—" he cracked a dry smirk. "—like skeletal remains of a human body."

"Wow, really?" I exclaimed. "You can find such things here?"

"I have found many of these things here all throughout my life and I still do to this day," Kuber Bhairab responded. "Well, if you happen to step on something like that, just hand it over to me."

"And what would you do with it?" I asked, dreading the answer.

Kuber Bhairab smiled without responding.

"Kuberda keeps them under his bed in a bag," Nondi answered for him.

"Why…why would you do that?" I asked as, glancing at the bemused expression on Nondi's face.

"I don't know," Kuber Bhairab replied calmly. "I feel these souls are better off with their bones in a safe, warm place, rather than the cold ditch they died in."

"That…sounds strange, yet quite thoughtful," I admitted. "What do you eventually plan to do with all that…uhm…collection?"

"Not sure. Haven't figured it out yet," Kuber Bhairab admitted.

We walked on in silence for a minute or two.

"Well, now that I've told you about the real horrors of this place, let's lighten the mood with some stories," Kuber Bhairab said. "Has anyone on the island told you about the story of the child-thief rajakar[xlvi]?"

"Is this how you 'lighten the mood,' Kuberda?" Nondi said. "Why are most things you and Babuda talk about so morbid?" She shook her head.

"Well, what is it? I want to know," I said.

Nondi sighed as she went on, "Well, during the Liberation War, when the occupying army came to this island, they brought in a rajakaar with them to keep an eye on the locals. After the war ended and the invaders left, the rajakaar was stuck on the island. He couldn't get a safe passage home and he knew people would try to kill him on sight. So, he hid in these swamps, eating raw fish for sustenance. But sometimes he would want to have a proper meal.

"So, at night, he would slither his hand through the open window of houses and snatch children from the embraces of sleeping women. He would then demand a ransom of a hot meal in exchange for the abducted child." Nondi smiled at my awe. "That's a tale parents tell their children to scare them into being obedient. 'If you are naughty, the child-thief rajakar will get you,' they say."

"Oh, well," I chuckled. "That's definitely a tale for children."

"It doesn't have to be," Kuber Bhairab commented.

"Well, you are perhaps the only mature person on the island who believes in this story, Kuberda," Nondi responded.

"You do?" I asked.

"Well, not the exact details of the story. But we *were* quite cruel to rajakaars after the war. We slaughtered them…maimed and tortured them wherever we found them. People in general won't tell you these little details about the war. But that doesn't make them not true." Kuber Bhairab sighed contemplatively. "So, given that historical context, can we really discard the possibility of a rajakaar being stuck on this island with no way of going home, shivering and dying in cold in this swamp?"

We all remained silent for a while.

"Well, if he did die here, his remains could be in the pile of bones you collect," I said.

"It is possible, yes," Kuber Bhairab replied.

"Doesn't it taint the purpose for which you're collecting them?"

"How so?"

"Well, you collect the bones to give warmth to the people who died in the massacre. Doesn't having a rajakaar's remains in that pile defeat that purpose?"

"Does it?" Kuber Bhairab asked, gazing at me intently. "Bones are just bones. Suffering is just suffering."

"We are here," Nondi announced.

"Ah, great," Kuber Bhairab said. "I always feel excited when I get to harvest a macha."

Ahead of me was the end of the swamp where the murky water smoothed out into the river beyond. The fog had cleared up quite a bit and the sunlight finally hit us uninterrupted. At the edge of the swamp and the river, a few muddy holes held some water. From one of these holes, Kuber Bhairab pulled out a cube-shaped cage made of thin bamboo strips. As water spilled out of the cage, the bottom half was revealed to be bustling with little fish of different kinds, madly flickering to get out. A couple fell back into the river, but the rest were caught as Nondi put the large metal bowl she was carrying underneath. The bowl had a few small holes at the bottom that let the residual water out. Kuber Bhairab then carefully unlocked a small latch on the side of the cage to split it open, which let all the fish fall into the bowl.

"Not as much as it would have been a couple of months ago, but that's still plenty," commented Kuber Bhairab. "Now put that away and let's start scorching these holes."

Nondi put the bowl, topped off with a metal lid, under a tree on a piece of dry land nearby. By that time, Kuber Bhairab had started dipping the bamboo-mat-like fishing implement into one of the other water-holes.

He smiled at me and said, "Come closer, but fold up your trousers first. These pre-winter waters are cold and will give you a fever if you're not careful."

I followed his instructions.

He held up the mat in front of me. "See here? It actually has two layers of bamboo textures. The weave is wide and intentionally out of sync, so that little fish get stuck inside it when we run it through the water, with very little possibility of getting out."

I concentrated on the design of the bamboo mat. Kuber Bhairab was right. Indeed, the gaps in the two layers of bamboo were not consistent. In the places where one layer had a gap, it was solid on the other side.

"Ready when you are, Kuberda." Nondi had tied her orna around her torso and folded up her trousers to her knees.

Kuber Bhairab held the handle at the one side of the bamboo mat, while Nondi held the other. Standing at the opposite ends of the hole, they gave each other one last confident look before violently swinging the mat side to side, in and out of the muddy water. The bamboo mat thickened as it gathered black mud.

After about a minute, Kuberd Bhairab cried out, "Alright, I think that's enough!"

They moved towards the tree with the metal container, carefully holding the mat on its two ends to ensure minimal movement. From a distance, I saw that the mat was thick with mud stuck between the two sheets. But as I got closer, I caught sight of little fish, clinging to the mat, sparkling in the sunlight, like jewels in a coal mine.

Kuber Bhairab knelt down and pulled out a small knife from a hidden chamber in his dhuti, near his waist. Its sharp edge shone in the sunlight, just like the fish. Using the knife, he started to extract the fish at different corners of the mat and they fell into the metal container with chunks of mud.

They repeated this process on a few other little holes near the river and the large metal container filled up to brim with fish and mud.

"Let's head back," Kuber Bhairab said finally, panting. He tiredly tucked his little knife back into his dhuti and extended his hand towards Nondi.

"Do you want to sit for a bit to catch your breath?" Nondi asked as she helped him get up.

"No. I'm good to go. I will shower and rest when I get back to the temple," responded Kuber Bhairab.

Nondi took the bamboo mat from his hand and started cleaning it up in the water. Kuber Bhairab reached for his walking stick, which was leaning on the other side of the tree and started to make his way back to the temple.

"Kuberda, slow down!" cried Nondi, struggling to keep up with him while carrying the heavy metal container full of small muddy fish. "What's gotten into him?" she murmured.

"Maybe I can carry the container and you can catch up to him?" I said.

"No, just leave him be," she said quietly. "When he's in the mood for something, there's no stopping him. He can be quite stubborn sometimes. He'd have to rest up the rest of the day; he wasted all his energy so early in the morning. I told him to rest while Ponditji and I did the fishing, but no, he had to go by himself."

"He was just eager to show me around," I commented.

"Yeah, probably," Nondi said, absently. "Where is Ponditji, anyway? Haven't seen him since this morning. Probably sleeping like a log in his room again." She sighed.

We looked up ahead. Kuber Bhairab had made it to the temple already. I saw a figure come towards him. It as Babu Bhairab. I was not looking forward to dealing with him after what he'd done last night.

26 AN EXILE FOR TEMPORARY PEACE

"Here we are again, with our whole gaggle of misfits and more."

Babu Bhairab's comment made Kuber Bhairab chuckle. Nondi and Ponditji were serving us our meal. Beside a steel bowl of soft, thick brown rice was a ceramic bowl containing a curry of small fish of various colors and sizes, cooked with fresh, viney vegetables. The curry smelled earthy and appetizing.

"Has Babaji asked you to be at The Gathering yet?" Babu Bhairab asked.

"Not yet," Kuber Bhairab replied.

"He won't. So, don't put your hopes up," Babu Bhairab said. "Who wants to watch one of the Bhairabs jittering about with a staff?" He then looked at the cold stare that Nondi was giving him. "Come now, we are all thinking it!"

Kuber Bhairab chuckled out. "I guess me needing a staff to stand on wins over your drunken antics for best reason to get uninvited to The Gathering," he said.

"Says a lot about our family, doesn't it?" Babu Bhairab commented.

"Babuda, why do you have to aggravate people around you?" Nondi interjected. "Do you find it amusing?"

"Why would I find it amusing?" Babu Bhairab said. "I consider it a service to society, ripping off the mask of pretension and showing them its true nature."

"Hah," Bishnu joined the conversation. "A lot of good you are doing, making a fool out of yourself."

"I don't need your approval to be good," Babu Bhairab answered instantly. "I can be good in my own way."

"But I feel that you are contradicting yourself," I interjected, feeling that I had enough of him already. "You are saying that you're being a good person, yet none of the things you're doing are good. You are embarrassing your parents, making fun of your older brother's disabilities. These are not things recognized as good behavior."

"Look at our guest, with his sweeping wisdom!" Babu Bhairab pointed at me. "I knew he would be a good addition to the circus."

"Why don't you make a counterpoint to his argument instead of brushing it off with sarcasm?" Bishnu asked firmly.

Babu Bhairab broke into laughter. "What was his point? That if people find me unpleasant, I'm not a good person. Is that it?" His face turned serious. "You know what's pleasant? Lies. You know what else is pleasant? Mediocrity. Doing the bare minimum, to make sure no one gets under the ire of anyone, instead of doing something about the glaring wrongness staring in your face. Doing the right thing doesn't always mean being what we consider as pleasant."

"So, tell me then, Babuda," Bishnu said. "All the things you did last night…was that your attempt at doing the right thing?"

At this, Babu Bhairab chuckled loudly. "It wasn't an attempt. It was a success," he said.

"A success?" Bishnu asked to which Babu Bhairab nodded. "How so? What did you accomplish by embarrassing Babaji in front of—"

"Let me clarify something, Bishnu," Babu Bhairab interrupted. "The Bhairabs aren't embarrassed by anybody. Not in this part of the world. They own this district. If a Bhairab murders someone in front of a group of people, they'd just stare, terrified and then walk away when they are told to, like obedient children. And this feat can be accomplished even by the weakest of Bhairabs." He casually pointed at Kuber Bhairab, much to my disgust.

"You seem to be quite proud of that privilege, aren't you, Babuda?" Bishnu muttered.

"I am neither proud nor ashamed of it. I am just stating facts," came the instant reply. "You underestimate the Bhairabs' power, Bishnu; you always have. But that's not what puts you in danger. What puts you in danger is that you also underestimate their lack of humanity, their lack of empathy and their capacity to commit atrocities. And this cluelessness of yours is dangerous." Babu Bhairab went on as Bishnu stared at back, jaw clenched. "Bhairabs don't listen to reason or to any call for compassion. So, the only way to get our attention is madness."

"Madness?" Bishnu asked dejectedly.

"Yes, madness," Babu Bhairab went on. "If you want progress from the Bhairabs, you have to be a little mad."

Silence followed as we went on with our food. Bishnu stared at Babu Bhairab with discontent for a few seconds before joining us.

"So, is that what you were doing last night, Babu?" Kuber Bhairab broke the silence. "Being…mad?"

"Yes," Babu Bhairab said in a surprisingly meek voice, that contrasted his arrogance just before.

"And is that your excuse for being drunk and rude all the time?" Kuber Bhairab asked.

"Interpret it how you like," Babu Bhairab replied. "I have my reasons for what I do. As long as I am doing what's right, I don't have to be likeable."

Kuber Bhairab nodded calmly and for about a minute, silence returned to the group.

"But have you ever thought, Babu, that people who want to do good need to be amiable, not necessarily to make themselves acceptable to society, but rather for their good intention to accomplish something?" Kuber Bhairab's words were calm and collected.

"Why would I need to please people to accomplish anything?" Babu Bhairab asked.

"Because we live in a society and you cannot really accomplish anything if you can't get people to agree with you."

"Oh, really?" The irritable egotism was back in Babu Bhairab's voice. "What have you accomplished by being pushed around by your own family? Has anyone respected you for being such a mild-mannered child? All I've seen them do is put you away in this ghost-land for being a cripple."

"That's far enough, Babuda!" Nondi snapped after quietly absorbing the heated conversation.

"Let him finish, Nondi," Kuber Bhairab said, raising his hand.

"The only thing you managed to accomplish was to make people sorry for you," Babu Bhairab continued. "You stick around in this temple so people can come here and feel pity for the weak boy living down the corridor. You live with the sole purpose of feeding on other people's pity."

Kuber Bhairab took a quiet, deep breath, he put his head down and continued his meal. Sitting beside Kuber Bhairab, I stared across in wonder at Babu Bhairab. He seemed to feel no remorse for the things he had just said.

After we finished the meal, Kuber Bhairab got up and said, "Babu, why don't you follow me?"

"Why? What's going on?" Babu Bhairab asked as if nothing had happened.

Kuber Bhairab gave him a grim look and walked down the corridor to outside. Moments later, to my surprise, Babu Bhairab followed.

The two brothers stood under the starfruit tree. Bishnu and I observed them from the window. Ponditji stood at the gate of the temple.

"What are they talking about?" Bishnu murmured.

"Don't know," commented Nondi, as she sighed and started to tidy up the table.

I watched the conversation intently. Kuber Bhairab was mostly talking and Babu Bhairab was listening. At one point, Babu Bhairab took a step back and hastily looked around and towards the temple. But Kuber Bhairab advanced forward to close the gap and kept talking, this time with more assertion. Babu Bhairab tried to interject a few times, but Kuber Bhairab cut him off.

"Good to see Kuberda finally standing up to him," Bishnu muttered. "Every time these two get together, Babuda says things like this."

"Doesn't it bother Kuberda?" I asked.

"Surprisingly, it doesn't. Despite these incidents, the two of them get along fine."

I glanced around. Nondi had already left the room after cleaning the table. I returned my gaze to the window. Kuber Bhairab waved towards Ponditji, who started to approach the two brothers. Then, to my surprise, the two brothers hugged each other tightly. Kuber Bhairab placed his hands on the Babu Bhairab's cheeks and gave him a kiss on the forehead. Babu Bhairab walked away with Ponditji, with his head down.

With one last, lingering look at his departing younger brother, Kuber Bhairab made his way back to the temple. "He's gone, now," He said after getting back to us.

"Good riddance!" muttered Bishnu.

I nodded in agreement.

27 A TREASURE OF MISFORTUNE

Two days before The Gathering, Babu Bhairab was nowhere to be found. The island was guarded, but somehow, no one knew where Babu Bhairab was. After failing to locate him on the island, men were sent all over the district. Yet there remained not a trace of Babu Bhairab.

"I brought you here to look after him," Babaji snapped at Bishnu, on the night before The Gathering.

"Both Nondi and I had been doing that until we were sent to the Temple," replied Bishnu.

"I knew that unruly boy would cause trouble right before The Gathering," Babaji said.

"Is that all you care about?" Maaji said. "The Gathering. Our youngest son is missing. My Babli is missing."

"Oh, don't create drama, Modhubi!" Babaji waved at her. "He's not missing. He is probably wandering drunkenly somewhere in the mainland with a bottle. How many times have we found him in that state?"

"I told you many times that he is different from his brothers," Maaji went on ignoring Babaji's comment. "He doesn't like people buzzing around in the house. Yet you brought in this horde of religious fanatics-."

"Measure your words, Modhubi," Babaji said, in a firm voice. "There are guests everywhere."

"Then let them hear!" Maaji protested. "My Babli is missing. I don't care. You could have invited them on the day and our lives would have been much easier. I could have spent time with my children. Yet you had to invite hundreds of Imaams and Pondits from everywhere to stay in our house for weeks."

Babaji looked at Maaji for a few seconds with dreadful calm. He finally got up from his comfortable position in the bed and sat at its edge, resting his hand on the table.

"You know very well why I had to invite the guests, Modhubi," he said. "How they interpret this event will make or break the Bhairab name for generations. If we don't treat those the general population considers to be spiritual leaders with good hospitality, then people will spread rumors. Our family name will gather blemish."

Maaji scoffed. "But according to our legends, what's in the room will restore our name, won't it? So why do you care?"

"Don't disrespect the Bhairab tradition, Maaji." Meghab Bhairab joined the conversation. He was sitting on a chair across from Babaji, with Prithuda standing behind him. "Tradition is everything. A lot of the beliefs we held previously do not apply in today's world. The world has changed and we had to change with it. But that doesn't mean we should give up tradition.

"What's in that room could be anything; a book of discipline, a statue of a deity, a set of clay-made tableware with symbolic decorations. Anything! I'm fairly certain there isn't any magical entity or power inside that will suddenly rejuvenate the Bhairab name. It might have done hundreds of years ago, when people interpreted simple objects with deeper meanings, but not today.

"But we are not doing this because of what's inside the room. We're doing this for the idea it holds. This event carried significance to people of both religions and they are curious. Now, if we don't entertain that curiosity to some extent, then, as Babaji pointed out, we will fall on the wrong side of people's perception. We cannot afford that since we do business with everybody."

"What should we do, then?" asked Maaji. "Give up looking for Babli?"

"We are not giving up, Maaji," came the response from Meghab Bhairab. "Right at this moment, people are scouring the district searching for him. He will eventually be found, just like he is always found when he goes missing. He's spent his entire life roaming around the district. He's mixed with all sorts of people. He can take care of himself until he is found, or until he decides to come back. In the meantime, we should not waste time being worried about him when we have The Gathering is in less than a day."

I admired the composure Meghab Bhairab displayed to calm Maaji down. What I found curious, however, was that nobody actually talked to Kuber Bhairab about any of this. I felt that the conversation he had with Babu Bhairab that day in front of the temple and the way Kuber Bhairab came back to us and mysteriously announced, "He's gone," definitely had something to do with Babu Bhairab's disappearance.

But since I observed that neither Bishnu nor Nondi was saying anything about it, I chose not to interfere. Kuber Bhairab had been told strictly to stay in the temple until The Gathering was over, as Babu Bhairab predicted. This meant that on the day of The Gathering, he would be all by himself in the temple, which made me feel bad for him. I realized that I had already developed an affinity towards him and it was perhaps due to this affinity that I decided to keep my mouth shut.

In the late afternoon of the day of The Gathering, I stood in front of the elaborate stage the workers had built. About one hundred feet from the great Banyan tree, the stage had levels for the audience to sit on. The seats were relatively empty, as the main event would happen when the full moon was visible. At the bottom-most level sat a group of Hindu pujaris, led by Ponditji in proper, appropriate attire. The bright white and silver dhuti, kurta[xlvii] and the orange scarf made him look out of place. The whole congregation sang Mantras[xlviii], with light music in the background.

"Nervous?" Bishnu startled me.

"Define nervousness." I said, as we both chuckled. "Not nervous. Perhaps a little daunted."

"You feel afraid?"

"Yes. A little."

"Why?"

I squinted my eyes. "I feel something is about to happen that will make things volatile. Meghabda said there's probably nothing magical in there that we should be worried about and his logic makes sense. But I've had this feeling in my gut ever since I landed on this isle. Something just doesn't feel right."

"What made you feel this way?"

"Well, have you been observing how strangely people are behaving? Like Babu disappearing, Nondi acting increasingly quiet and distant…"

"Neither of those two things is outside the reasonable boundaries of what is considered normal behavior for them. Babuda is volatile and can disappear anytime. And Nondi's mood goes through ups and downs based on how she gets treated by people around her in the estate, specifically Babuda."

"Okay, then," I said. "But don't tell me you aren't feeling this too! They're about to open a room that has been locked shut for hundreds of years. A gate with so much significance and mystery. Can it really be something as simple as some gold and riches, as Babu claims, or some object, as Meghabda claims?"

"You just told me that you agree with Meghabda's rational estimation of what's inside the room."

"I did. But…I don't know…"

Bishnu looked at me with a playful smile that I hadn't seen since we had landed on the island.

"So, you think there's something in there that cannot be explained in real terms? Something paranormal?" he asked.

"Would it be too far-fetched to think there might be?" I muttered.

"I wouldn't expect anything unreal in there."

"Wow, that's surprising!"

"How so?"

"You, of all people, thinking that there's nothing strange inside that room."

Bishnu chuckled in response. "Yes, I do believe in the paranormal. But I don't believe in dark fairy tales about ancient magic. My learning from dealing with these things is this—they exist, but there's no grand purpose behind their existence. They exist just the way animals or birds exist. They mind their own business and don't meddle with the affairs of men. They are either strange creations of nature or traces of past sufferings that haunts the present.

"And the Bhairab Estate is neither one of those places. Believe me. Even during the Liberation War, families like the Bhairabs managed to buy their protection. So, you don't have to worry about the unexplainable here. Whatever happens here has and will have its reason well within the realms of reality." He put his hand on my shoulder. "And besides, I will ensure that you are safe, no matter what happens. That was my promise to Dadima."

"Thanks for the assurance."

The crowd started to grow. The sun had melted on the horizon and darkness was quickly covering the area. I saw Biruda switching on the lights set up around bamboo frameworks. The lights were of bright, hot colors—red, orange and golden yellow. They surrounded the Banyan tree, creating mesmerizing works of colors that illuminated the leaves, vines and branches of its elaborate structure. The large pond to the west was quiet—not a single ripple. The full moon was slowly becoming visible. The mantras and the music were increasing in tempo.

It all felt, to me, a little sad. I felt for the Bhairab family for not having the opportunity to handle a sensitive family event with privacy. *What if they find something that casts them in an embarrassing light in front of others? To do all this with the risk of such embarrassment!*

But then I remembered Babu Bhairab's words: "'The Bhairabs aren't embarrassed by anybody. Not in this part of the world. They own this district. If a Bhairab murders someone in front of a group of people, they'd just stare, terrified and then walk away when they are told to, like obedient children.'

Are they really that powerful? Or was that just another unhinged rambling of Babu Bhairab?

"Babu Bhairab's disappearance in all this makes it all the more unstable," I reflected.

Bishnu shook his head in irritation. "He is better off being out of this, trust me."

"You know, I don't understand what you feel about Babu Bhairab, exactly," I said. "Him, Nondi, Kuberda and you seem to be childhood friends. But compared to Kuberda and even Nondi, you seem to have very little patience for his idiosyncrasies."

"Babuda is a good person at heart and despite his antics, he is a relatively good company to be with," Bishnu responded. "But lately, his buffoonery has been out of control."

"And have you ever asked him why he is acting this way?"

Bishnu gave out an exasperated sigh. "I just never had the time to have that conversation with him. A little over a year ago, Dadaji passed away and I have been dealing with the loss ever since." He glanced at me with a frown. "And instead of being supportive of me, he has been acting like a fool. And both Nondi and Kuberda have been acting as if I am supposed to condone his nonsensical behavior…this entitled brat, who had everything handed to him…who walks around in questionable company, mostly drunk…" He looked down, shaking his head. "That's why I decided to take a break from all this." He looked at me and smiled. "Thankfully, you showed up around that time and taking the responsibility of giving you company provided me with the necessary distraction to create distance from—" he spread his hands out wide. "—all this."

"Well, I'm glad that my friendship helped you cope with the loss you experienced," I said putting my hand on Bishnu's shoulder. "But abandoning your friends is not a healthy way to deal with difficult times."

Bishnu glanced at me and nodded. "Well, if you can get that drunken fool back to this island, maybe I will finally have that talk," he commented.

The sound of the northern door of the central house opening ended our conversation. Babaji, accompanied by Meghab Bhairab and Maaji, came out and started towards the Banyan tree. Darkness had fully set in and the full moon was visible. The mantras were at full intensity.

"Come, The Gathering is starting." Nondi's ringing voice came from behind us. She ushered us to one of the front seats, sat beside us and looked on intently.

In front of the sitting area, near the pond, Biruda stood, facing the audience. The colorful light glistened the curves of his muscles. As soon as Babaji, Meghab Bhairab and Maaji reached in front of the banyan tree, the mantras stopped.

"Greetings, my dear guests!" Babaji's crackling voice brought silence to the crowd. "The time has come for a very important event for my family. As you all have shown interest in observing this event, I have given you that opportunity. I have treated you with heartfelt hospitality. I want you all to observe and enjoy this event."

He stopped to draw a deep breath and his face tightened. "However, as I have told all of you, this is, at the end of the day, a family event. It's a day of tremendous importance to our family's fabled name. Therefore, I request all of you to take a strictly viewers' role in this event and not to interfere, verbally or in any other way. Please, respect the significance of the event in silence as I, my eldest son Megha and my wife Modhubi, descend into the room.

"Once we retrieve whatever is waiting for us in there, we will take it into our house. Then, you may all start to socialize again in your merry way. After we have examined what we find in the room, we will come back out and tell you all what decision we have made. If we feel that it is something that we can share with you all, we will. However, if we feel that it is something that should be kept to ourselves, then I would kindly request you all to respect our prerogative. Either way, you will all be treated to a hearty feast. So, please sit back, relax and enjoy." He breathed in again and looked up. The full moon was visible in the clear late autumn sky. "Alright, it is time."

Meghab Bhairab produced two shovels from behind the banyan tree. Then he and Babaji proceeded towards the western wall of the central house nearby, leaving Maaji in front of the tree. Meghab Bhairab started digging into the soil, along with Babaji. They kept going for a few minutes in pin-drop silence. The sound of the shovels hitting the soil echoed. My heart skipped a beat as we heard a sharp, metallic clunk. Meghab Bhairab looked at Babaji, who handed him a long dark key, which glimmered in the moonlight.

Meghab Bhairab knelt down and cleared away some dirt to insert the key into what I presumed was a keyhole. There was resistance in turning the key and Meghab Bhairab's face tightened. But a few seconds later, we heard a metallic snap.

I heard shuffling noises. The crowd remained silent, but their nervousness was palpable. Meghab Bhairab scraped some more soil away with his hands to reveal two rusty, metal handles. Babaji took a couple of steps back. Meghab Bhairab stood up and yanked at the two handles and they opened with a loud thud as a plume of dirt went up and blurred the scene for the spectators.

I heard a couple of coughs. Meghab Bhairab and Babaji took off their shawls and started to clear out the dust. As it cleared, I saw that an opening had been revealed, with steps descending into the ground. Meghab Bhairab and Babaji waved at Maaji to come. The three of them glanced at each other one final time before descending.

For what seemed like forever, nothing happened. It felt like everything had gone silent and the wind had ceased. Then I heard a faint shuffle from the cellar. Suddenly, there was a thumping sound of something heavy falling on the ground, followed by Maaji's high-pitched voice.

"Hold him, Megha! Hold him, he's collapsed!"

Some more shuffling followed. Then I heard her voice again, "Megha, hold your father! Leave her! Leave her now and hold your father."

A few more unnerving seconds went by before I head Maaji's voice again. This time it was a full-on scream.

"MEGHA, TURN AROUND! MEGHA, HE CAN'T BREATHE! B-BISHNU…NONDI, COME HERE, RIGHT THIS MOMENT!"

Bishnu and Nondi both jolted towards the opening. I stood up and took a few steps forward as they both disappeared into the cellar. After some noise of struggle, I heard Bishnu's faint voice. "Here, here. Hold him here."

Then, after a few seconds of shuffling, Bishnu and Nondi appeared, holding an unconscious Babaji between them. He was frothing at the mouth. Followed by a sobbing Maaji, they carried Babaji to the stage and sat him down. His eyes were closed.

"Nondi, bring a bucket of cold water and a towel, right now!" Maaji instructed in a broken, teary voice. Nondi obliged immediately.

We all heard a single set of heavy footsteps coming from the cellar and looked up to see a dirt-covered Meghab Bhairab ascending. All the madness going on around me escaped my senses and the world became silent. Electric lights pierced through the swirling dust and I could clearly see Meghab Bhairab approaching us. In his careful hands, he was carrying a dirty blanket made of old rags.

Coming out the side of the blanket hanging from his right arm were two thin, fair legs, covered until the knee with a white cloth that glistened in the moon. In his left arm rested a girl's head, turned towards his chest. Long, raven black hair came down from her head. Some of it even touched the dusty ground.

Book 3: The Capture

CHILDREN OF DECAY

28 A PREMONITION

With each labored breath, it was getting increasingly obvious that she was not going to last too long. Something heavy was pressing against her ribcage and digging into her lungs. She pushed against the weight, trying her best to keep herself alive. She needed to be alive.

As my senses adjusted to my surroundings, I realized that I was in the mass graveyard of trees, near the old man's hut. But Arup Sai was nowhere nearby and, as I looked down the slope into the distance, neither was his hut.

That haunting, labored breathing again. A movement. I gazed towards the numerous giant tree trunks laid out in front of me in an endless landscape. I ran towards the direction of the sound and tried to move the first log I saw. *Why is this so heavy?* As far as I remembered, these were supposed to be hollow. But instead, the one I was trying to move felt as if it were filled with concrete. *Am I just not strong enough?*

I managed to finally roll it to the side, only to reveal a bare sandy surface. The shuffling noises came again—this time more frequent. This time it came from everywhere. I kept going, from one fallen tree to another—a frantic surveyor searching desperately to save a life in a sea of death. But no matter how many logs I rolled over, I found nothing underneath any of them.

The shuffling got louder, overlapping. They were no longer coming from any of the fallen trees, but from under the ground itself. Someone, or something, was trying to reach for freedom from the very ground I stood on.

I know now where I need to go.

I ran towards the waterbody in the distance. My feet thumping on the damp ground couldn't deafen the noise of death and despair. I climbed up the mound to reach the shore of the waterbody. The factory in the distance wasn't there. I looked down. The water was clear with beautiful, green leaves swaying under light ripples. I felt relieved for a moment until I saw something rising from the depths of the water.

A plume of blood.

I woke up sweating. I was sleeping on the floor of a room in the Temple near the swamp. My heart skipped a beat as I started hearing the shuffling noise again. This time, it was coming from the main hall of worship.

A faint voice uttered, "Shani!"

29 A NIGHT OF CHAOS

It was chaos at the Bhairab estate. Outside, hundreds of guests were left alone. They murmured frantically without anyone to tend to them but Biruda, who had been told to not let anyone near the Banyan tree.

Bishnu and Nondi carried Babaji to his bed-chamber. Maaji followed them, weeping. Meghab Bhairab came up from the cellar. I didn't realize that I was walking behind him in confusion until he glanced back at me with a cold stare that stopped me in my tracks, but I didn't turn back.

Meghab Bhairab ascended the steps up the northern entry of the central house, into Maaji's chamber. I stood outside the gate, stunted, in a trance. He laid the malnourished girl he was carrying down on the bed where I had sat three nights ago while Maaji was cooking. I caught a glimpse of her pale face before Meghab Bhairab turned around, gave me a tight look and closed the door.

I only caught a transient glimpse of the girl, yet her appearance had been etched in my memory. A single piece of white cloth covered her nearly-skeletal body. Her eyes were disproportionately large, with strikingly dark pupils that evoked in me a sense of dread-filled wonder that I couldn't explain. Those eyes were settled in dark, bony sockets, with cheekbones prominent and sharp; cheeks tight and sickly pale; lips thick and dark; long, raven black hair sprawled all over the bed, smooth and seemed almost painted on. Everything about her felt unreal. Everything about her felt rather ethereal.

I stood outside, not knowing what to do. Biruda stood in front of the guests and the group of pujaris led by Ponditji. I was expecting him to instruct me to join the guests. Instead, he stared at me like a large, muscular child—stunned and confused, like the rest of the congregation. Ponditji sat among the pujaris with his head down. I brought my attention back to the central house and listened intently.

Maaji's sobbing had quieted down. I heard Meghab Bhairab's voice.

"Bring her some food. She looks like she hasn't touched anything edible for years."

Some shuffling followed and it all went quiet again. Then the door burst open and I almost cried out in fear. Imposter syndrome finally kicked in, but out of sheer dread, I couldn't move a muscle. Before I knew it, Meghab Bhairab stood in front of me, smiling. He was wearing a different set of cleaner clothes.

"Hello, my dear guest!" he said. "Can you go tell Ponditji that I want to see him?"

His words brought mobility back into my body. I nodded and started walking briskly towards the stage. I heard the door close instantly behind me.

In front of the stage, Ponditji was already standing, ready. "Meghabda called for me?" he asked.

I nodded. He paced towards the door and I took a seat. There was some soft murmuring among the guests. Up ahead, the dust had settled down around the tree and the open cellar.

The lighting around me blazed the entire environment in an unearthly, bright light and I felt, for some reason, that the place shouldn't be so visible to the rest of the world. The wide-open, metal cellar doors were rusty and thickly layered with dust. I was expecting the door to have some kind of extravagant designs or carvings on it, but it seemed like a simple, rusty iron gate with thick, long handles. The stairs leading down seemed to be simple concrete rather than stonework. Nothing about the cellar seemed ancient.

Considering the cellar doors—the loud thud they made when it was opened—it did seem like it had been shut for a long time. If not for hundreds of years, then at least quite a few. I couldn't think of any way that door could have been opened recently. Neither could I rationalize in any way how a human being could survive in there for that long. The girl that came out, despite being malnourished, would have required at least a minimum level of sustenance to survive.

Desperate mumbling, followed by noises of a struggle was coming from inside the house. I heard Maaji's uneven, indistinguishable voice. I listened intently and heard the fading murmur of Ponditji reciting mantras. There was another scuffle, followed by a screeching, high-pitched voice, full of panic, which I had never heard before.

"Shani! Shani!"

I heard the desperate words being uttered repeatedly, interrupted by mumbling from other voices. That prompted the guests to start making their way to their quarters. Unlike me, they understood the fine line between curiosity and danger. I glanced at Biruda, who lowered his gaze after we made eye contact. Never had I seen a person with that much physical presence be so frightened. *What is so he scared of?*

Soon, the entire sitting area was empty. There was only Biruda and me. When I finally decided that I, too, should head to my allocated room, I realized the problem I had at hand. The other guests had the luxury of leaving quietly back to their accommodations in the northern part of the estate, which was right behind the sitting area. My accommodation, however, was the eastern house. To reach it, I had to walk past the central house into the middle yard. I had no intention of getting close to the central house again. In retrospect, I could have taken the round trip through the northern guest house to reach my room. But at that moment of confused nervousness, my brain didn't register that as an option.

So, I nervously started making my way. I heard the word 'Shani' repeated in that same voice, but as I was tip-toeing past the central house, the voice stopped and everything went silent. The sounds of struggle and crying had made me nervous, but the silence terrified me. I hurried my steps and when I was just about to step into the middle yard, the northern door of the central house swung open again.

I gasped and turned around to see Meghab Bhairab calling out, "Biruda!"

Biruda instantly ran towards him. I stood there, frozen, not knowing what to do.

"Gather all the guests to the sitting area again," Meghab Bhairab said, without acknowledging my presence. "I will sort everything out, now."

Then, with the same suddenness with which he had swung the door open, he closed it.

30 A DISPLACEMENT OF AMBIGUITY

All the Imaams and Pondits were treated to a quick dinner and given a short farewell. There was no protest, no commotion. People understood the sensitivity of the situation and made themselves scarce. Before midnight, the once-crowded Bhairab boatshed was almost empty, except for the two large-engine boats and four smaller ones Bhairabs owned themselves.

I saw Biruda prepare one of the larger ones and assumed it was for Bishnu and me. So, I went back to the eastern house and started packing. I heard footsteps behind me and turned around to find Bishnu, looking tired, dejected. The daydreaming, curious boy I was used to seemed to be carrying the weight of the world on his shoulders.

"What's the matter, Bishnu?" I asked.

But before he could answer, Meghab Bhairab and Prithuda came in and silently closed the door. Meghab Bhairab then turned around and gave me a tight smile.

"Quite an eventful day, wasn't it?" he said.

"It was," I said, with a polite smile.

"You must be exhausted. However, I need to ask you for one last favor. As you can see, there have been some delicate situations developing in our estate and it is time our family gives itself some privacy as we find a way to deal with this...predicament."

"Fair enough," I commented.

"Nondi told me how you enjoyed spending the night at the Temple," Meghab Bhairab said. "So, I think it would be best for you to stay there. Bishnu and Nondi will look after you. Prithuda is going to accompany all of you to the Temple."

"I have no problem with that," I said calmly. "But what I find curious is why you are asking me to stay while all the other guests have received an abrupt goodbye."

Before Meghab Bhairab could answer, the door opened wide as Maaji burst into the room. Tears were running down her cheeks as she was panting.

"You send that wretched girl to the Temple, too!" she said. "The mere sight of her has put my Raghabji to bed. I don't want her here."

"We've talked about this, Maaji," Meghab Bhairab said as he coaxed her to sit on the bed.

"Talk is talk!" she snapped at her son. "Talking won't fix anything. This girl is bringing ill wind to this house and I want her gone."

Meghab Bhairab put his hand on Maaji's shoulder.

Without a warning, she started sobbing uncontrollably. "Oh, my Babli-re[xlix], where have you gone?" she repeated, as she rocked back and forth. "Your father is now bedridden. Come home!" After a minute of bawling, she calmed down.

"Look, Maaji," Meghab Bhairab finally said. "She came from the cellar, which means she is important. We need to figure out–"

"I WANT HER GONE!" Maaji's high-pitched voice startled me. She took a moment to catch her breath. "Besides, she didn't eat anything from anybody until Bishnu stepped in. I tried to reason with her and so did Nondi. We even brought Ponditji in. None of it seemed to work. She took food from no one, except Bishnu."

"I know that, Maaji. And we have talked about it, too, just now," Meghab Bhairab said. "Whoever or whatever she is, we are supposed to figure out what to do with her. Those *were* the instructions. We are supposed to understand why she behaves the way she does. If we don't–"

"You actually believe this nonsense, don't you?" Maaji interrupted him. "You actually believe in this wretched old prophecy?"

Meghab Bhairab glanced at me and then smiled at Maaji. "We shouldn't be discussing delicate family matters in front of guests," he said.

"I...I can just get out of this room. I don't mind," I said, but when I was about to get up, Meghab Bhairab put his hand on my shoulder.

"It's all right, my dear guest. You are already part of this and you are a good friend of Babu. You can stay," he said as we exchanged a hesitant glance with each other. "Please stay."

I sat down.

Meghab Bhairab drew a deep breath and went on. "I'm a pragmatic man. I don't believe Gods reveal themselves to us through magical miracles. The times of Godly incarnations living among us is long gone. I never believed that I would find anything extraordinary behind that door. I expected something symbolic—a scripture, an idol or any other artifact that is supposed to carry some kind of a grand meaning, which we would then have to interpret and let others make their own interpretations. My expectation was that, ultimately, this would result in our family name becoming more widespread, which in turn could help our business.

"My unruly and arrogant little brother had his own ideas. He thought the only logical thing that could be behind that door was more gold and riches. And to his credit, there was wisdom behind this idea. Historically, families had indeed stored away their riches for a rainy day, to be dug up generations later." After what seemed like a well-rehearsed oration, he paused and gazed out of the window, towards the central house. "But regardless of all our rationalism, we went into a cellar that had been locked shut for centuries to find a living, breathing person. How would you interpret that, Maaji?"

Maaji remained silent.

"Whoever or whatever she is, we need to understand her nature and her purpose. *That* is the prophecy."

"Then deal with her in the Temple," Maaji finally said, as she got up.

"But Maaji, we cannot understand her if we put her far away, on the other side—"

"Let Kuber figure her out. Keep her with him in the Temple. If she stays in the house, she will only bring more misfortune." She had calmed down quite a lot during the course of the conversation and had now started to sound authoritative.

"And you don't mind if that misfortune falls onto your middle child?" Meghab Bhairab echoed what I was wondering.

"Don't put words in my mouth, Megha," Maaji snapped at him. "We cannot have her here. Not until my Raghabji recovers and my Babli comes back. Besides—" she took a few moments to calm herself, "—if she is some kind of Godly incarnation, the most appropriate place for her is the Temple, not a home."

While I finished packing my bag and Bishnu gathered his belongings, Meghab Bhairab took Maaji back into the central house. After a few minutes, he came out into the yard, wearing a frown on his face.

"Biruda!" he shouted out, at which the guard appeared from behind the eastern house. "Is the boat ready?"

Biruda nodded.

"Good," Meghab Bhairab said. The frown and the irritated expression on his face deepened. "Run back to the temple and get the cart."

"Um…but Kuberda is alre—"

"Just do as I say," snapped Meghab Bhairab as he walked back to the central house. "And wake up Prithuda," he muttered as he closed the door.

Bishnu and I waited for Biruda to come back at the eastern house. Bishnu didn't sit down—he just stood near the door, gazing out. The light from outside illuminated the outline of his dark face, which was as still as stone. His eyes carried a mixture of anxiety and desolation that I had never seen in him before. I left him be.

Biruda eventually got back to the estate, rolling a wooden cart inside. Prithuda was already up. He quietly took over the handle of the cart from

Biruda and stood there, as docile as always. Biruda gave him one last glance before making his way to the southern house.

Shortly after, Meghab Bhairab came out of the central house in the same fashion in which he came out of the cellar a few hours ago, carrying the skeletal girl in his arms. He carefully placed her on the cart.

As soon as she was out of his grasp, she slid to the furthest corner of the cart, away from Meghab Bhairab and tightly covered herself with the large white cloth she was wrapped in. She glanced around the yard with eyes full of terror. Her body trembled. Nondi came out of the central house, too, with Ponditji, who was now in his normal attire. Both of them carried a small bag of clothes on their shoulders. Bishnu and I joined them.

"Prithuda will escort you all to the temple," Meghab Bhairab said calmly.

I heard the gate of the southern house open and for the first and last time, I saw Meghab Bhairab's wife and his only son. Mala Bhairab was a petite woman wearing a white shari, who, without letting me get a better look at her, walked across the middle yard towards the boatshed with her head down and face half-covered. Biruda followed behind, with their belongings in one hand and holding Bipul Bhairab's little hands in the other. The boy couldn't have been more than five years old. He struggled to keep pace with Biruda as he glanced in confusion at his father, who stared at the girl on the cart with a hardened face, without paying attention to anyone else. Soon, Biruda and the child disappeared behind the eastern house as well.

"Stay safe, dear guests," Meghab Bhairab's said, turning to me. "Make haste on your path. Deep nights are not kind to outsiders." He gave me one last still stare and went quietly into his walled southern house.

The estate, which bustled with people, songs and intrigue only a few hours ago, had descended into silence. I glanced at the malnourished girl on the cart. Her dark lips were trembling and wide eyes stared into nothingness with palpable terror. Prithuda pushed the cart forward. We followed.

Behind them, I walked alongside Nondi and Bishnu walked noiselessly a few paces behind. I left him alone while Nondi glanced back every now and again, covering most of her face with her orna. Everyone was quiet and no words were exchanged. The whole island felt stunted. All the houses were closed and the windows were shut. The kerosene lantern Ponditji held was the only source of light we carried.

"Shani," were the repeated, weak whispers from the cart as the only disruption to the stillness.

31 A CHILD OF REDEMPTION

"Boinji¹, what is your name?" Kuber Bhairab asked, crouching down in the main hall of the Bharaib Temple.

The malnourished girl's large eyes full of anguish stared at Kuber Bhairab. "Shani!" she said and buried her face in her knees. Her skinny body stiffened.

"Is that what you would like us to call you?" Kuber Bhairab asked.

"Shani," she repeated, in a fading voice. This had been her only verbal response to every question.

Kuber Bhairab glanced at Nondi, who shook her head subtly he brought his gaze back to the girl. "Ponditji is cooking some food for us," He said, calmly. "Would you like to join us for supper?"

The girl kept her face tucked within her knees but, to my surprise, nodded in approval.

Kuber Bhairab gave a sigh of satisfaction. "That is great, Boinji. We shall call you Shani from now on, but to me, you will be my Boinji. What do you say?" he asked, putting a hand on her shivering back.

The girl lifted her head and looked at Kuber Bhairab without taking evasive action. Her eyes started to water.

Kuber Bhairab smiled warmly at her. "Good, then." He got up, using his staff as leverage. "Ponditji," he called out.

I heard footsteps. Ponditji came out of his room across the corridor. The herbal smell of a fish-curry hit us.

"When you're done with cooking, set up a bed in here for both Nondi and Boinji," Kuber Bhairab said. "Sorry to keep you up so late. I know you've had a long day, but, as you can see, unexpected situations call for unexpected work."

"It's fine, Kuberda," Ponditji said.

"I can prepare the bed while Ponditji cooks." Prithuda's voice startled me and I realized he had been in the room the entire time.

Kuber Bhairab closed his eyes for a few seconds before turning around to face Prithuda. "Prithuda," he said, with non-characteristic firmness, "I thank you for escorting my guests across the island. I do! But I think it's time you leave us to take care of ourselves."

"Meghabda told me to put everything in order," Prithuda said.

"And you did," said Kuber Bhairab. "Like I said, you brought our guests here safely. You've done your job. You're already working Biruda's shift and he won't be back before late evening since he's taking Boudi[li] and Bipul all the way to the next district. You have a long day ahead, so I suggest you go back to the estate and get some much-deserved rest."

Prithuda looked at Kuberda meekly for a few moments before nodding and disappearing out of the front door.

Kuber Bhairab leaned against the wall. Standing close by, I saw his knees buckling slightly. Nondi stepped forward and helped him stand back up.

"Ponditji," Kuber Bhairab called out again, as he was escorted to his room. "Fix that awful front door tomorrow, as soon as you wake up. Winter is almost here and the wind keeps rushing in through the cracks. We have two guests living in the main hall now. So, replace those worthless wooden planks, if you can." He stopped to breathe in. "And install a good lock."

Ponditji nodded approvingly and went back to his room.

Nondi quickly helped Kuber Bhairab back to his own room and then came back and sat down with Shani, whispering, "It will be okay, Boinji. It will be okay."

When I entered Kuber Bhairab's room with my belongings, Through the window, I saw the familiar silhouette of Bishnu leaning on one of the trees, with his back towards us. Regardless of how familiar his outline was to me, somehow, I felt I wasn't seeing the same fisherman boy I used to know. I was looking at a man.

"Leave him be," Kuber Bhairab said, as he settled on his bed with his back resting on the wall. "He will come back to us in time."

"Is he okay?" I asked.

"He will be, eventually. We all are dealing with this…situation in our own ways."

"How come you're so calm?"

"You think I'm calm?"

"Well, compared to everyone else, yes," I chuckled. "You don't agree?"

Kuber Bhairab took a deep, exasperated breath. "I don't know how I feel," he said.

"What do you think of the girl?"

"I think she's terrified. I think she feels alienated here and making her comfortable will be a daunting task."

"That's all of your thoughts on her?"

"More or less. For now, anyway."

"You don't wonder where she came from, or how she could have survived in that place for so long?"

"That's not for me to ponder on. It was the Gods' will for her to be there. So, she was."

"So, you believe that she is some kind of Godly incarnation, just like your mother does?"

Kuber Bhairab looked at me blankly for a while. "That's what Maaji thinks?"

"That's what I gathered from what she said, yes."

"I see," Kuber Bhairab said, pensively. "It makes sense, I guess."

"What do you think?" I asked again.

"I think she is a Godly incarnation, yes."

"You do?"

"Yes. We are all Godly incarnations. Our humanity is a reflection of the Gods—our rage, our pride, our despair—they all tie into a complex consciousness that is the image of God."

"So, you think the Gods put the girl in that room?"

Kuber Bhairab chuckled. "Does it matter?" he said. "Gods could have put her there. Some human could have put her there with magic. The important thing is that she was there when we went in. *That* was Gods' will."

I sighed and nodded. "Hope I'm not bothering you with all these questions."

"You're not bothering me. But I am bothered."

We both sat quietly for a while. I started to recount the day's extraordinary events. I couldn't wipe away, from my memory, the image of Meghab Bhairab ascending from the cellar with Shani in his arms. All the other things that had happened were just details in my head, but that particular sight flashed vibrantly in my mind.

I pondered what Kuber Bhairab must be going through. One of his brothers had disappeared, he had just gotten the news that his father was bedridden and a strange, malnourished girl had arrived for him to take care of.

"Babu Bhairab disappearing in the middle of all this has made the situation more difficult," I said, in an attempt to empathize.

"Oh, I'm not worried about Babu," Kuber Bhairab assured me. "He knows his way around. He can take care of himself. He's clever when he needs to be."

"I've been thinking about him lately. I admit that I didn't quite like him at the start, but now that I see the environment he grew up in, it explains his mannerisms."

Kuber Bhairab gave out a dry chuckle. "Oh, there are so many things you don't know about what makes Babu do the things he does!"

"Enlighten me then."

Kuber Bhairab played with his fingers for a bit before giving me a stoic smile. "When Babu was born, I was a child of five," he said. "As soon as I had the sense to understand the world, I realized that my family was embarrassed by me. I was mostly looked after by the housemaids; my parents barely touched me or even talked to me.

"When they had Babu, I knew it was their attempt at redeeming themselves. They wanted to prove to themselves that their seed was still strong. They wanted to feel proud again, as they had felt when they brought Meghabda into the world—their perfect son and heir to their throne. Beautiful, strong, intelligent and, most importantly, obedient to family values and interests. They wanted to bring another son like him into the world, to be absolved of the shame they felt for birthing me."

Kuber Bhairab went on exposing sensitive family history to a man he had met only days before without any flinch in his voice.

"When Babu came into this world, they were beyond happy. I remember being woken up by Ponditji early one morning. 'Wake up, Kuberda! You have a new brother,' he said. I walked across the island and entered my mother's bed-chamber. My heart melted when I laid my eyes on Babu. He was a beautiful…beautiful child! His light brown hair rose up in swirls and his plump little hands rested on his belly. His large, dark pupils stared back at me with wonder."

"Seems like that day had really stuck with you," I commented.

"It did." Kuber Bhairab nodded with a childish glow on his face. "Ever since I heard I'd have a brother soon, I was afraid that when my newborn brother would saw me, I would scare him. Growing up being shunned for my ugliness made me feel that way. Yet, when I looked into Babu's eyes that day…all that wonder…I felt, perhaps for the first time, accepted. Unconditionally." Kuber Bhairab's face radiated a joyous glow of nostalgia.

"My family was overjoyed to give birth to such a beautiful child. And as Babu grew, he became even more beautiful. People started calling him *Deboshishu*[iii]. With all the attention he got, people sometimes felt bad for me, thinking that I was being left out—"

"As if you weren't left out before," I commented sarcastically.

"Yeah." Kuber Bhairab chuckled. "The truth is, they couldn't have been more wrong. I didn't feel left out for all the attention Babu was getting. In fact, for the first time in my life, I felt I had a purpose. Seeing the love my little brother was receiving finally gave me closure from the rejection I'd felt until that point in my life. I was happy that he was happy. I cried when he cried and laughed when he laughed. We were tied by an invisible string."

"That's wonderful," I said.

"Not really,"

"What do you mean?"

"My happiness was tied to Babu's acceptance and belonging to the family," Kuber Bhairab went on. "But that faltered as he started to grow up. They realized that Babu wasn't like Meghabda. He didn't gloat in the family pride or strive to uphold its virtues. He was a curious boy who liked to question things. My family thought he would be a close friend to Meghabda and learn the family values. But Babu developed a cold, distant relationship with Meghabda and started to spend more time with Nondi and me.

"While Meghabda was an obedient child who stuck by his father to learn about the family business, Babu would barge into the house with mud all over his dhuti. He mixed with people my parents didn't approve of and did things they didn't want him to do. Their unbridled joy of having such a beautiful child slowly turned into covert disappointment."

"Looks like being beautiful wasn't enough," I said.

"It was, but it also wasn't," Kuber Bhairab said with a dry smile. "They still loved him because the youngest child is expected to be loved unconditionally, but they pushed him away from serious conversations. They admired his intelligence, but preferred not to let him apply it to anything that mattered. He was still the pride of the family: the beautiful son with subversive wisdom. But they gave no credence to his subversion. And that..." Kuber Bhairab stopped and sighed. "And that, over time, made Babu depressed. He got attention, but not acceptance. He was admired but not listened to. Everybody loved him, but nobody liked him. And so, with time, he became disobedient, pessimistic and bitter."

"That explains a lot," I admitted.

"Explains what? His current behavior?" Kuber Bhairab asked as I nodded back. "I guess. At least, some of it."

32 A GUARDED SWAMPLAND

Winter had come and gone and spring brought color into the world again. The gloomy swampland came alive with verdant patches of grass adorned with yellow flowers around the muddy swampland. The trees were greener and the daylight started to last longer. The silent swampland turned into a noisy ecosystem of chirping birds and the mating cries of monkeys.

Shani had been living with us in the temple since just before winter, when we found her. On days of worship, she would sit on the bed she shared with Nondi at the corner of the main hall. Her hair would be parted in the middle and tied into long braids. She would wear a thick, white shari with red working on the edges. People would look at her with wonder, but nobody would dare interact with her. They would smile and bow whenever she gazed back at them. Her eyes carried the fidgety fear of a caged bird, as Nondi would whisper comforting words in her ear. After the event, when the people had left, Shani would fall into Nondi's arms, sobbing. From a distance, I would hear the repeated murmur: 'Shani, Shani.'

On those days, people paid their respects to Meghab Bhairab, who attended with Prithuda by his side. I never saw Babaji and when people talked to Meghab Bhairab, I heard words along the lines of, 'hope he comes to his senses,' and 'quite unfortunate.' From these interactions, I assumed Babaji was still bedridden. I didn't realize at that moment how wrong I was.

On days other than those of worship, we saw a gradual rise in Shani's comfort level. She still sat quietly on her bed in the corner of the main hall with her head sunk onto her knees, but the desperation in her gaze abated over time. Kuber Bhairab and Nondi ensured that she received regular meals. During meals, we had casual conversations and Shani sat in between Nondi and Kuber Bhairab and quietly ate her food.

With time, as Shani became healthier, she started to look much less foreign compared to the way she looked the day we found her. Her cheeks became less tight and developed a rosy glow. The dark patches under her eyes lightened and so did her dark, thick lips. I started to realized that she was actually quite beautiful. Her face had an innocent glow that made the look of constant fear she carried hauntingly heartbreaking. Despite her acclimatizing with us more and more, every once in a while, I would hear her, mutter, 'Shani,'. It continued to be the only word she spoke.

Bishnu had essentially become an outdoor-dweller. He wouldn't join me on the walks I had with Kuber Bhairab. We sometimes saw him sneaking out of Ponditji's room through the main gate before disappearing into the swamp again. Nondi, with Shani in her arms on their bed, would look at him with discontent. I sometimes saw him in the distance while I was taking a stroll around the swamp, but Kuber Bhairab advised me to "Let him be."

On some late nights, I would see him sneaking into our room and slide into his side of the bed beside me, but he'd be gone when I woke up in the morning. I had no idea what he was up to. Since he'd told me countless stories about camping out on his fishing trips, I had no doubt that he was able to live outdoors. What perplexed me was why he chose to be this way.

On my strolls through the swamp with Kuber Bhairab, every so often, I would spot gangs of men, wandering, carrying spears in their hands.

"Sometimes, when an unexpected piece of land cleared up in the middle of the river, with fertile sediments, men like them fought for their landlords' ownership," Kuber Bhairab said.

"Seriously?" I asked. "Like…actual battles, with sharp weapons?"

"Yes," Kuber Bhairab said. "It's not that common these days."

"Why?" I asked again. "Land like this doesn't come up anymore?"

"It does," Kuber Bhairab said, calmly. "But you know how warfare goes…one of the sides eventually wins more battles than the others. Eventually, they become more powerful than everyone else and people realize that it is foolish to test the power of the most powerful."

"And that side, I am guessing, is the Bhairabs?"

"For most of our history, yes,"

"Okay. Fair enough," I commented. "Tell me, then…if those men are meant to fight for sediment lands in the river, what are they doing here?"

"Meghabda has possibly employed them,"

"Why?"

"To keep an eye on Shani, I'm guessing," Kuber Bhairab said. "Our family obviously has a vested interest in the girl. This side of the isle is open and could be infiltrated by intruders."

We fell silent as we traversed the grassy swampland.

"I'm going to ask a question and I want you to be honest with me in answering it." I broke the silence.

"I'll do my best," said Kuber Bhairab. "Go on."

"Are we guests here, or prisoners?"

We stared at each other a few moments before Kuber Bhairab shifted his gaze towards the ground.

"Don't know," he finally admitted.

33 A PLAUSIBLE INVITATION

"So, she does eat without Bishnu's help."

Meghab Bhairab's voice startled us. He was standing at the door of Kuber Bhairab's room. The early spring sunlight, glancing in from the window, drew a long shadow over his thin lips, cast by his sharp, protruding nose.

"Shani! Shani!" the girl muttered beside me, clutching Nondi's orna tightly.

Nondi quickly rinsed her hands in the washing bowl, wiped them with her orna and took Shani in her arms. "It's okay! It will be all right. Shh, shh..." Nondi whispered.

Shani's fearful chant faded but didn't stop.

"Nondi, take her to the main hall," Kuber Bhairab said.

Nondi guided Shani out of the room. Meghab Bhairab observed them with a smirk on his face as they disappeared down the hall. Prithuda stood behind him, head down.

"Join us for lunch, Dada[liii]," Kuber Bhairab said with a warm smile. "It's been ages since you had a meal with me."

Meghab Bhairab smiled back at his younger brother. It felt like, for the first time, I saw a glimpse of genuineness in his expression. "Of course, Kuber. I've always wanted to have a meal with you and your friend."

Kuber Bhairab glanced at Ponditji, who was already rinsing his hands in the washing bowl. He got up from his seat and indicated for me to replace him. I obeyed and I got up from my place beside Kuber Bhairab at the edge of the bed and sat on the chair Ponditji had been in, on the opposite side of the table. The side of the bed where four people had been sitting on just minutes before now accommodated only two brothers.

"Our guest is a friend of Babu," Kuber Bhairab commented. "He brought him here."

"All friends, good and bad, are brought here by Babu," scoffed Meghab Bhairab. "The bad ones stay with him and the good ones stay with you."

Kuber Bhairab smiled and shook his head.

"You don't believe me?" Meghab Bhairab pointed at me. "Look at this gentleman. Knows how to speak with tact, knows culture and good behavior. And he's here, eating with you." He nodded at me with arrogant respect on his face, which, for some reason, gave me an unwanted sense of validation. "On the other hand, where is that wretched fisherman boy? Wandering about the island, spending his days in God knows where."

"Dada, you know that Babaji trusts Bishnu and depends on him to keep an eye on Babu," Kuber Bhairab said, calmly. "He keeps him in check and I can vouch for that."

"Great," said Meghab Bhairab, dismissively. "Then explain to me this: if Bishnu is so good at keeping Babu in check, why has he disappeared?"

"That's on Babu," Kuber Bhairab said. "We all try to keep him in check. You, I, Maaji, Babaji, Nondi…who doesn't? If a house full of people cannot reign him in, why do you expect a poor fisherman boy to?" Kuber Bhairab stopped to catch his breath. "He's trying his best, just like everyone else. Yet, just like everyone else, Babu finds a way to get under his skin. He's only human."

Ponditji had placed a set of fresh silverware down for Meghab Bhairab and had already served him some rice. Meghab Bhairab pointed at the curry cooked with garden vegetables and small fish. Ponditji took the cue and served some of that along with the rice. He then bowed at all of us and quietly left the room, passing Prithuda, who was sitting on the floor near the door, cross-legged and head bent.

"So, what's he doing now?" Meghab Bhairab broke the silence. "Disappearing and reappearing everywhere, as my men tell me…is it his attempt at finding Babu?"

Kuber Bhairab took a breath. "Don't know," he said finally. "I'm sure he has his reasons."

"Does he now?" Meghab Bhairab muttered as he started to dig in. "I never trusted the rootless hoarders Babu brings into this house."

I saw a flash of dissonance on Kuber Bhairab's face, which he wiped off with a quick gulp and a smile.

"Bishnu is not a hoarder; neither is he rootless," he said. "He is responsible, industrious and knows full well his place in the world. He doesn't try to be what he isn't. He doesn't go looking for trouble. The troubles he finds himself in are usually brought about by our younger brother."

I admired the tact with which Kuber Bhairab had shared his disagreement. But I wasn't sure how open Meghab Bhairab was to Kuber

Bhairab's views.

"You're not happy with Babu at the moment, are you? That's a first," Meghab Bhairab exclaimed. "What horrible thing has he done to get you, of all people, irritated?"

Kuber Bhairab fiddled with his food for a while before answering. "What do you think? Disappearing like that, with all of us in this mess."

"We finally agree on something," Meghab Bhairab chuckled. "I did tell Babaji to keep him on a tight leash 'til The Gathering was over, but he thought keeping Bishnu with him would do the job." He sighed. "Now look at us. We're in a mess and our pretty little beloved brother is gone, leaving everything in chaos."

"I can only imagine what Maaji is going through," Kuber Bhairab said.

"Well, she is in distress and that's unfortunate. But she's also partially to blame."

"What do you mean?"

"She keeps letting Babu get away with whatever he wants and that is exactly why he had the nerve to leave us all in the middle of this. She keeps putting herself in between Babu and the rest of the family, every time he does something wrong." Meghab Bhairab drew a deep breath and looked at his younger brother. "And she is also not fair. While she keeps indulging and favoring Babu, she keeps you isolated from everything."

Kuber Bhairab glanced at me and for the first time ever, I saw a smidge of embarrassment on his face. "Is this really something to bring up in front of our guest?" he said finally.

"Oh, I don't think it makes a lot of difference, Kuber. Your friend here has already witnessed quite a bit of the chaotic side of this family and so far—" Meghab Bhairab gazed at me with a friendly smile. "—he hasn't caused much disturbance. He knows his place, keeps to himself and doesn't meddle where he isn't supposed to. He is a bit curious, as I can see in his eyes, but he knows how to keep it under control. I don't really mind that."

"I...I didn't mean to follow you to the front door of the house on that day," I mumbled. "I was just—"

"Curious," Meghab Bhairab finished my sentence. "Your curiosity led you to follow me when I came out of the cellar. And why wouldn't you be curious? The events of that day were quite extraordinary. But what's important is that you didn't force yourself further into the matter and kept your distance. I appreciate that." He nodded approvingly. "And now you are here, helping my brother with this situation, which I highly appreciate."

He turned to Kuber Bhairab and grabbed him by the shoulder with his left hand. "My brother, here, is a very sensible, intelligent boy. People underestimate him, including my own parents. They adore Babu but push him to the side. Yet when our family is in crisis, he has stepped up and taken care of this girl and generally handled the situation well." He glanced at Kuber Bhairab with clear admiration in his eyes. "And where is our beloved little brother? He ran away to some isolated corner of the world to get away from a bad situation like he always does."

"It's a little bit more complex than that, Meghabda," Kuber Bhairab said calmly. "Why Babu behaves the way he does. Why Bishnu behaves the way he does. Why Maaji and Babaji behave the way they do. You cannot just—"

"I'm just telling it like it is, Kuber. Sometimes, that's the right way to go."

"And is this one of those times?" Kuber Bhairab asked. "…when Babaji has become bedridden and Babu has mysteriously disappeared without a trace, leaving Maaji in disarray…is it really the time to take people's behavior at face value?"

Meghab Bhairab looked away for a few moments before turning to me and beaming in a broad smile. "My little brother is a philosopher!" he said. He wrapped his arm around Kuber Bhairab and ruffled his puffy hair. "He sees people as bigger than they are." He got up and rinsed his hands in the washing bowl. "Well, you are wrong about one thing, Kuber, Babaji is not bedridden."

"He isn't?" Kuber Bhairab asked in disbelief. "Then why do I hear people say that it's unfortunate what is happening to him?"

"Something *is* happening to him, all right and it *is* unfortunate," Meghab Bhairab said, wiping his hands with a towel. He walked towards the door. Prithuda stood up as well. Meghab Bhairab turned to us and announced, "You two are invited to lunch at the house tomorrow." The affectionate softness he'd carried in his face while he was having a meal with his younger brother had disappeared, replaced with a look of cold speculation. He glanced towards the window with a frown. "See if you can get that wretched fisherman boy. In that case, he is invited, too. Nondi and Ponditji will stay back and look after the girl."

Him, along with Prithuda, departed the same way they came—silent and sudden.

34 A RIGHTFUL MADNESS

The Bhairab household was nothing like how we'd left it. The middle yard was riddled with the dark, pebbly dust that yards gathered when they are not tended to for too long. The room Bishnu and I used to live in was empty. The whole estate seemed gloomy and ghostly.

"Where are all the decorations?" Kuber Bhairab asked. "I was looking forward to finally seeing them."

"Maaji had Biruda take them down early in the morning, after The Gathering," said Meghab Bhairab. "She didn't want any trace of the event in the house."

"That's fair," Kuberd Bhairab commented. "Knowing Maaji...this is something she would do. She blames the event for Babu's disappearance and Babaji's illness, I presume?"

"Yes," Meghab Bhairab replied.

"Always the fault of the circumstances, never the fault of Babu," muttered Kuber Bhairab. The two brothers shared a glance, smirking.

"To be fair, you are also among the ones who have tied Babu's actions to his circumstances," Meghab Bhairab said, raising his eyebrows.

"I tie them in, yes...quite sensibly. But I don't use them to absolve him of his deeds."

The two brothers pensively observed the central house for a while.

"Speaking of shifting blames," Kuber Bhairab finally broke the silence. "What I'm still struggling to figure out is why I've been invited here, with all that's happening."

"Ha," chuckled Meghab Bhairab. "Now, you're asking the right questions."

"I'm listening."

"You're the best person right now to go fetch Babaji."

"Fetch?"

"Come with me," Meghab Bhairab said. Then he glanced at me. "You can come, too."

"He...can?" Kuber Bhairab said in a confused voice.

"Yes. Who knows what might work." Meghab Bhairab had already started walking and we followed.

The guest-quarters at the northern part of the Bhairab estate were elaborate additions to what it originally was: the farmers' house, situated at the ground floor. It was a long room full of racks of farming implements, lines of hay-stacks. On lined-up beds at its south-western corner, men in the typical farming attire of tight, white tops and lungi rested. One of these men, I recognized, Suba Kashem, the escaped convict. He seemed quite civil, as his thick, unorganized beard had been shaved off. Seeing us coming in, he sat up on his bed.

"How are you, Subaji?" Meghab Bhairab said, smiling.

"I am all right," Suba Kashem replied. "Has...has the inspector come to take me away?"

Meghab Bhairab sighed deeply and sat in front of him. "Look, Subaji. We've given you a good life here. You work in the fields, get three square meals a day. Why do you want to go back to jail?"

"I just feel that the longer I'm here, the more I am in danger," Suba Kashem muttered.

"What are you afraid of, Subaji?" Meghab Bhairab crouched down and put his hand on his shoulder.

At this, all of a sudden, Suba Kashem's eyes started to tear up. "I'm such a coward!" He started to sob.

"That's all you keep saying," Meghab Bhairab said with a dejected sigh as he stood up. "Either 'I am a coward,' or 'I want to go back to jail.' What are you a coward for? What are you afraid of? Tell me."

Suba Kashem calmed himself and looked up at Meghab Bhairab, tightening his jaw.

"If you are afraid of doing something, but you also feel you are a coward, then I would advise you to embrace your fear and do what you have to do," Mehghab Bhairab said.

Suba Kashem kept silent, carrying the same expression.

"Tell me, Subaji," Meghab Bhairab asked. "What do you fear?"

"He fears what we all fear. He fears the inevitable." A familiar, gruff voice came from behind us, as one of the farmers who had been lying down with his back to us got up and turned around. At first, I didn't recognize him due to the thick layer of white beard covering his wide yet broken jaw. He wore the same attire as the other farmers, but as he glanced at them, they got up and left, including Suba Kashem.

"How are you feeling, Babaji?" Meghab Bhairab asked.

"Wonderful," came the immediate response. "Never felt better."

"That's great," Meghab Bhairab said. "I brought you a visitor."

Babaji's face lit up after seeing Kuber Bhairab. "Kuber! My Kuber. Come here." He got up from the bed and fumbled towards Kuber Bhairab and hugged him. Now that his frame wasn't covered in a decorated shawl, as I was used to seeing, his body seemed more withered than I thought it was.

"I...I was meaning to come to the Temple," he said, letting Kuber Bhairab out of his grip. "But I never had the time. The winter crop was amazing this year! I...I was meaning—"

"We don't grow winter crops anymore, Babaji," Meghab Bhairab interrupted him. "You are just keeping these poor farmers here from going back to their families, making them grow crops that we don't want."

"But you haven't seen the harvest, Megha," Babaji responded. "You wouldn't believe the yield of cabbages and cauliflowers—"

"Meager farmers grow cabbages and cauliflowers in their yards to sell at Choubazaar, Babaji," Meghab Bhairab said. "We grow rice in our fields, in the right seasons every year. When we are not growing rice, we give our fields rest to rejuvenate them for the next season. Growing winter vegetables by employing farmers is just not profitable enough to—"

"Who said I'm doing this for profit?" Babaji said. "I'll give them away."

Meghab Bhairab closed his eyes and drew a deep breath. "Babaji, we talked about this before. We don't grow acres of crops, employing farmers, just to give them away."

"Why not?" Babaji asked. "All we do is take and take. Why can't we give some back? Ever thought about it that way, Megha?"

Meghab Bhairab sighed again and glanced at his brother on the side.

"That's all right, Babaji. We'll talk about this later," Kuber Bhairab said as he guided Babaji back to his bed. He glanced at his brother, who nodded dejectedly.

"I'm so glad to see you, Kuber!" Babaji said. "I wanted to go to the Temple and bring you home. You are my child and you belong in my home. I have three sons...three beautiful sons. One of them lives across the island and another has abandoned me." Babaji broke into a loud sob as Kuber Bhairab placed his head on his chest. "Come back to your home, Kuber. Your Maaji has tended to your room every day since you left. She..." His voice broke and he took a moment to regain himself. "She doesn't show it, but she loves you."

"I would love to come home, Babaji," Kuber Bhairab said. "But, I am currently taking care of somebody."

Babaji stared at Kuber Bhairab for a while before looking down. "I understand," he murmured. When he looked up again, tears slid down his cheeks. "I know why you are here," Babaji said. "You're here to take me back."

"That's right," Kuber Bhairab said. "I'm here to take you to your bed-chamber."

"I don't belong there. It is not mine," came the prompt response. He then wrapped his arms around himself and started whimpering. His body contorted into a shrunken, skeletal form. "I don't deserve to be there," he whispered.

I observed him in amazement. This powerful man, who had previously maintained a tact and command that suited his position, had been reduced to a soft-spoken farmer. *What happened to him?*

"I cannot go back there," Babaji went on. "I don't deserve the warmth of my bed and the grains and the fish I eat. I don't deserve the privilege. The things I have done…" He finally looked up. He wasn't sobbing anymore. Perplexed tiredness had set in his eyes. "And besides, I am not yet ready for what will happen when I go back."

"And what do you think will happen?" Kuber Bhairab asked.

Babaji gazed out the window with a stoic expression. "The inevitable," he said finally.

"Fine, then. We will eat here." A voice I hadn't heard for months startled me. Bishnu had quietly made his way into the room, carrying a rolled-up bamboo mat.

"You…you will…eat with me?" Babaji said in a confused voice. "Why? You have no reason to—"

"Come now, Babaji. Let's get our hands washed," Bishnu said, as he rolled out the bamboo mat on the ground. "I've asked Biruda to bring the food here. We'll have a nice meal." He smiled at him warmly. "And I will tell you a story."

35 A TEST OF HUMANITY

"A long time ago, on a bright autumn day, you took your two youngest sons, Kuberda and Babuda, across the river to see your crops. 'Well, I guess it's time for you two to get to know about our lands, too,' you told them.

"When you crossed the Great Green Lake and landed on the shores of Choubazaar, little children gathered around you and your two sons with curiosity in their eyes. Your two sons were children themselves and stared back at them the same way. As your party walked, the band of children walked with you. But the more you walked, the more the crowd thinned until there was a crowd of only one—a lanky boy with shiny, dark skin. His eyes weren't full of wonder, like the other children's. They were too observant and serious for a little boy.

"You didn't pay much attention to him, but he paid attention to you. He kept his distance, but made no attempt to hide himself. He followed you all the way to your hut in the middle of your lands. While you were talking to your supervisors, your children saw the lanky boy sitting in an alley between two crop fields. He observed them intently, with deep sorrow in his eyes.

"After you were done supervising, to the lanky boy's great surprise, you cried out, 'You can sit with my two boys and play with them.' The boy looked at you, stumped.

"'Come here, boy. Don't sit over there like a stranger,' you said, again. The boy fearfully stepped forward. 'You want work, yes?' you asked and he nodded. 'I cannot give you work in the fields yet. You are too small and skinny. My men cutting the tall jute stems might not see you and slice you in half!' You broke into laughter as the white beard across your powerful jaws glistened in the sunlight. 'You entertain my two boys and I will give you some money to buy a clean set of clothes from Choubazaar. What do you say?'

"The boy nodded. 'What is your name?' you asked.

"'Bishnu,' the boy spoke for the first time. I was the boy.

'A Hindu boy in a Muslim village?' you said. 'Did you swim across the river to come here, boy?' You chuckled and I shook my head, side to side. 'How did you make it here, then?' you asked. I remained quiet.

"'Well, Bishnu,' you said. You kneeled down at my level and squeezed my shoulders. 'If you ever need any work or any help with anything, come to me. You can also play with my boys when they are here. Okay?'

"And that's how I met you and your two wonderful sons, who would grow up to be my life-long friends."

"Babaji," Kuber Bhairab said. "Would you like to start?"

Babaji was looking down at the food, which Biruda had placed on the mat in the middle of the circle we had formed. He hadn't said a word throughout Bishnu's story.

"You shouldn't care for me," he finally spoke, glancing at Bishnu. "You don't know—"

"I know you enough to know that you are capable of doing good," Bishnu said. "And that's what matters. What matters is what you do now, not what you have done in the past."

There was a long, stunted pause. Sunlight was creeping into the room through the window, illuminating on the smokey white rice in the big bowl. After what felt like forever, Babaji started serving himself some of it.

36 A SECRET CARRIER

"Maaji would like to see you," Biruda announced as I was leaving the farmers' house with Bishnu and Kuber Bhairab. I saw nervousness in his eyes, which intensified when Meghab Bhairab came out of the farmers' quarters.

"Let me guess, Maaji wants to see our guest?" Meghab Bhairab said, approaching us.

"She wanted to give the people in the Temple some new blankets, Meghabji," Biruda said, with a wide smile. "The winter blankets are too heavy and should be pretty worn out by now. So Maaji wants to take this opportunity to send some lighter, cleaner blankets."

"And she also wants to talk to our guest because she thinks he knows something that might help find Babu," said Meghab Bhairab. "I understand."

Meghab Bhairab brought his gaze towards me. "It is unfortunate that we couldn't yet find your friend," he said, "but my men are looking all over the district. However, managing Maaji, in these trying times, has been quite a challenge," His face hardened. "So please, do your best."

Meghab Bhairab walked away, with Prithuda in tow. He paid no attention to Bishnu or Kuber Bhairab.

"You can take yourself back to the Temple, right?" Kuber Bhairab asked.

I nodded.

"Good," he commented. "We'll make our way back. I'll see you with the new blankets."

I looked ahead to see that Bishnu had already progressed some way ahead of us. Kuber Bhairab followed him, supported by his long staff.

"Biru, guard the door," whispered Maaji as she entered Babaji's bed-chamber moments after Biruda had brought me into the central house. He obliged by closing the eastern door quietly and standing in front of it.

I took a seat on one of the chairs. Maaji went and closed the door to her bed-chamber, glancing stealthily through the window. She then turned around and smiled cordially.

"How are you keeping, my naat?" she asked.

"I am doing all right, Maaji," I replied.

"Are Nondi and Ponditji keeping you well?"

"Yes, they are."

"That's good. This vita had a lot more people, once. I could have sent out more people to look after you back then." She sat on the bed next to me. "Now look at us. Barely anybody to tend to the house, let alone the guests."

Maaji wore a light blue shari and the shidur on her temple had a fresh touch of crimson. But she wasn't chewing paan and her face had lost a lot of its luster. Her cheeks showed signs of wrinkles and her eyes had dark circles under them.

"I hope my Babli keeps himself well-hidden, wherever he is hiding. I don't want him to find himself back in this mess. He's suffered through enough mess already," she said. "If you're the one who gave him the idea to run away, you have my thanks!"

"I...it wasn't me," I said in confusion.

"Who was it, then?"

"I mean...I don't know if anyone put the idea in his head, but—"

"You don't need to tell me," she said. "The important thing is that my Babli is safe." She leaned back and glanced out the window into the front yard. No one was around. "How are things in the Temple?"

"We are managing," I said. I chuckled dryly and she joined me.

"Can I rely on you with something?"

"Of course, Maaji."

"If anything goes awry, you run back here, okay? You bring everyone right back here and go to Biru's room, over there and tell him what's going on." She pointed towards the Eastern house, across the yard. "He'll help you."

"I will," I assured her.

She nodded, got up and walked over to the narrow space behind the chairs near the bed. She reached up to the wooden shelf high up on the wall and brought down a tied-up mound of cotton sheets. She carefully counted the layers before reaching high up again. This time, she brought down a wooden box. She opened the box and counted its contents. A sliver of frown formed on her face as she made her way towards the chest of drawers behind the second set of chairs. From the top drawer, she took out a few spools of cotton and put them carefully into the box. She made one last count of the objects inside the box, closed it and carried both the mound of sheets and the wooden box to me and put them noiselessly on the table, all the while eying the yard through the window.

"You know the way back, I presume?" she asked.

"I do."

"Good. I want you to carry these two things as quickly as possible across the isle to the Temple and hand them over to Nondi."

I nodded.

"I would send Biru with you, but I cannot afford to do that, right now," she said, with palpable fear on her face. "Can you make it?"

"I can, Maaji," I assured her.

She drew a deep breath, leaned down and kissed me on the forehead. "You are a good child. Any mother would be proud to have you."

I chuckled to myself as I stepped past the gate of the Bhairab Estate and made my way to the temple, thinking about the first time I made this trip—I, along with Nondi and Bishnu, merrily making our way there. The second time was the three of us again, making our way there as a result of Babu Bhairab's drunken actions. On the third occasion, I walked among a group of people carrying a malnourished girl we found in an ancient secret cellar.

Since then, I had been helping Kuber Bhairab, Nondi and Ponditji nurse the girl back to health. As I was making my way there for the fourth time, each of the last three trips felt like three different timelines of my life, with three completely different versions of me that I no longer related to. Something inside of me had fundamentally changed.

I examined the package I was carrying—a few clean blankets, tied together and a sewing kit. Maaji desperately wanted me to take them to Nondi. It was a secretive operation. No longer was my visit to this island just curious exploration. The stakes were higher. I had gotten myself tangled in the web of sensitive secrets of this powerful family. I couldn't imagine the consequences this would bring. Yet the uncertainty didn't unnerve me. I wasn't quite sure then why I felt that way.

I realized, even in broad daylight, all the houses had been locked shut, along with the windows. Not a single living human soul was visible. Birds were chirping away and the light spring breeze was whistling past the tall grasses near the water bodies. Nature was at its regular rhythm, yet everything felt breathless, like the calm before the storm.

I suddenly felt a piercing gaze on me. I glanced back to see Suba Kashem standing behind the gate of the Bhairab Estate, clutching the iron bars, resting his face on them. For reasons I couldn't explain, I knew then and there that he, too, wanted me to take what Maaji had given me to the temple, desperately.

I turned my gaze ahead and hastened my steps.

37 THOUGHTS AND DEEDS OF UNWANTED CHILDREN

The Bhairab's boatshed was over-crowded during The Gathering. But that was nothing compared to the lines of numerous boats gathered in the common boatshed at the southern border of the island. People of all kinds, from all social classes, had come from all over the district. They wore the freshest set of clothes they had and carried large folded jute bags with wonder in their eyes and smiles on their faces.

About fifty paces in front of the boatshed stood a large, tented establishment, where farmers sat in front of wide-open, round bamboo baskets, full of vegetables. The western side of the tent had two enormous baskets, full of beans and okras. The fading late-afternoon sunlight illuminated their fresh green textures. Besides that, a basket three times larger carried brinjals of various sizes and shapes, clustered together in shades of violets and greens. Next to that, three more baskets of the same size held mounds of cauliflowers and cabbages.

Well within the shade of the tent, on a large bamboo mat, was a mountain of bottle gourds, resting on each other like round, green stones. Deeper inside the tent were four rows of more vegetables, just like those displayed at the front, piled up haphazardly on long strips of jute-mats. They were the inventory, which the farmers used to replenish the baskets at the front. These stocks were quickly depleting, as lines of people took what they wanted, served by the farmers.

Babaji was busy running around with Suba Kashem. He chatted, laughed and hugged his way around the crowd, as people watched in wonder.

"Never seen him this happy," said Kuber Bhairab, smiling joyfully.

We were sitting further onto the shore, under a tented area a few hundred meters away from the large tent. A few similar, tented arrangements had been made around us, with propped-up wooden chairs where guests sat, many of whom I saw at The Gathering.

"Forgive my intrusion, but you seem to be invested in seeing your father happy," I commented.

"And that is odd to you?"

I took a moment to gather my words. I had gotten used to Kuber Bhairab's openness, but I didn't want to push my boundaries.

"Well...I just thought...the way you and Meghabda described your relationship with your parents...the way they–"

"Treated me?" Kuber Bhairab finished my sentence. "I see your point." He nodded. "It's understandable that you think that I might not be as invested in my parents' happiness as my brothers. Yet I feel elated to see my father like this and it confuses you."

"Should it not?" I asked.

"No, it definitely should. In all honesty, I'm confused, as well. I'm trying to understand why I feel so happy, seeing him the way he is now. A part of me believes that the reason is selfish, while the other part thinks it's quite altruistic."

"How can it be selfish?"

Kuber Bhairab sat more upright, cross-legged. "It's selfish because, like you said, I wasn't at the receiving end of the best treatment from my father, most of the time. But the few times he treated me like a son was when he was happy...truly happy. When he didn't have ambition or didn't need to feel powerful. When he was accepting everybody, in all shapes and forms—" I heard a little vibration in his voice. "—those were the times when he was at his most accepting of me. Those were rare, but I remember them."

He paused to gather himself. "You see, in our lives, we see people as representations of ideas. Each of us represents an idea—wisdom, strength, perseverance, opulence—just like the Gods. But unlike Gods, we don't represent each of our defining ideas through and through. Someone who represents arrogance and ambition can, on odd occasions, be kind and accepting. I see these ideas that we enforce on people as burdens. We are built in a way that when the rest of the world assigns an idea to us, we subconsciously work towards being as much of a representation of that idea as possible.

"That's how we try to gain acceptance. We mold ourselves in the form society puts us in...so that we become easily definable. But this burden is too heavy and at times, we take it off our shoulders, put it down and rest. We are not Gods and so we cannot carry the burden like Gods do. Yet when we put down the burden, that's when we are at our most beautiful. That's when we are truly free. To think openly. To do great things. And that's when we become more than just an idea."

I followed Kuber Bhairab's gaze. Babaji, indeed, seemed quite happy. His silver shawl glistened in the light of early spring. His abundant smile, peeking out of his thick, white beard, made him almost look like a different person altogether.

"Oh, Dadima is here." Kuber Bhairab pointed towards the boatshed.

I was elated to see Dadima. She got off a hired boat, rowed by a hired boatman, which surprised us both.

"Where's Bishnu?" Kuber Bhairab muttered—echoing my thought.

Bishnu had been sent by Babaji to the mainland. We assumed it was to go and get Dadima. But Dadima had arrived by herself. I went and greeted her and brought her into our sitting area. Kuber Bhairab wasn't there anymore.

"Are you absolutely sure you don't want to go back?" Dadima's concerned voice made me smile. I'd missed her abundant affection and care.

"Of course, I will go back, Dadima," I assured her. "Just...later."

"If you say so." Dadima nodded. "The Bhairabs are treating you well?"

"They are. Umm...where's Bishnu? I thought he went to fetch you."

"He did," Dadima said. "But right after he boarded me on the boat, he said, 'I will catch up with you. I need to take care of something,' and left. That boy and his errands!"

"I'm sure he's just going to get some things from Choubazaar for the day."

"Don't lie to me, Naat! I know what I have seen in his face. He seemed like he has aged a decade." She sighed. "Has he been like this for long?"

"For the past few months, yes." I decided not to lie. I thought it would distress Dadima, but she simply pursed her lips and nodded.

"Well, I sent him here to look after you, but now I guess you are the one who needs to look after him," She glanced around and then moved close to me. "The news is all over the district. Did—" She lowered her voice. "Did they really find a girl in there?"

I nodded.

"Oh, Dadima, I haven't seen you in ages!" Kuber Bhairab's voice from behind us cut our conversation short. He approached us with Nondi by his side, who was holding Shani gently in her arms.

Shani was looking peaceful, despite carrying that characteristic alarm on her face. She was wearing a white shari with blue-lined edges and her long, raven hair was tied in a thick braid. Nondi was whispering comforting words in her ears, as usual. Nondi was wearing her typical attire—faded old, red salwar kameez with a white orna. Ponditji, in a clean yellow fotua and bright white dhuti, followed them.

"Boinji, this is my Dadima," Kuber Bhairab said when they got to us. "Go sit beside her." He smiled at Shani's distressed face. "Don't worry,

Boinji. Dadima won't hurt you. She's one of the most caring people I know. Go on now. Nondi will stay with you."

Shani glanced at Nondi, who nodded back at her. The two girls sat beside Dadima and Ponditji followed, standing beside Nondi.

"Come with me," Kuber Bhairab said suddenly, turning his gaze towards me. His voice was calm and collected, but I sensed a touch of hurried anxiety in it too. I smiled at the girls and then followed him. 'Shani,' I heard the faint whisper.

Using his staff to leverage himself, Kuber Bhairab was moving quickly towards the shoreline, in the direction of the stalls. I followed him quietly.

"We are going to Babaji, in case you are curious," Kuber Bhairab said.

"I gathered that," I said. "Any particular reason?"

At this, Kuber Bhairab took a short breath and chuckled. "If I had a notebook with a thousand pages, I wouldn't be able to fit all the reasons in it. Let's just say, Bishnu will be here soon and when he is, I want to be there."

"Expecting trouble?" I chuckled nervously, but Kuber Bhairab remained silent.

We reached the tent where Babaji and Suba Kashem were working. They were opening the last few slabs of tied-up vegetables to replenish the empty bamboo baskets.

Suba Kashem looked tidy and comfortable. He moved with urgency and grace. But in his eyes, I sensed an anxious fear. Desperation and fear was a common theme in the eyes of many people around me at that time—Kuber Bhairab, Nondi, Ponditji and now, Suba Kashem. It felt as if they were all waiting for something horrifying to happen.

The only person who seemed calm in this situation was Meghab Bhairab. Despite giving off an aura of superiority, until that point, he had made a good impression on me. He wasn't the most down-to-earth person I had ever met and he didn't go out of his way to be friendly with people, but I could see his effort to deal with the situation we were in.

He sent us away to stay in the Bhairab Temple so he could take care of his emotionally-volatile father and his grieving, dismissive mother. He had been working towards getting his father to come back home while also sending people out to find his younger brother, who had disappeared without a trace.

He'd also planted men everywhere to keep an eye on us. This had made me skeptical at the beginning, but with time, I realized it was the sensible thing to do. He needed to establish some sort of control over what was going on. He had also put his trust in the caring nature of his other brother, Kuber Bhairab, to nurse Shani back to health after she appeared in our lives out of nowhere. In these times of ambiguity and distrust, Meghab

Bhairab remained calm and collected.

My gaze fell on to Babaji. Even while cordially meeting and greeting different people, Babaji kept eagerly looking towards the boatshed. The daylight had started to fade away as the horizon of the river began to darken. On that horizon, a shape started to form on a boat—the singular shape of a boy, standing and rowing vigorously to make it to the shore. Kuber Bhairab stood up from his chair.

In the sitting area we had left, Shani, Nondi, Ponditji and Dadima had gained more company. Meghab Bhairab had finally joined the party, with Prithuda behind him. Meghab Bhairab was carrying his characteristic tactful, polite smile as he shifted his gaze towards us. He started pacing towards us. Kuber Bhairab exhaled a worried sigh.

"You really managed to give it all away, Babaji!" Meghab Bhairab commented, indicating towards the depleting mounds of produce, which were mostly scraps of cauliflower-leaves and cabbages by then. "Never realized there was that much demand in the village for brinjals and cauliflowers." He squinted his eyes and looked towards the shoreline. "Is that Bishnu?"

"That's..." Kuber Bhairab stepped forwards eagerly, to see more clearly in the dying light. "That's Bishnu, all right."

After reaching the shore, Bishnu parked the boat, got off and knelt down to pick up his fishing spear, a net which he slung over his shoulders and some bamboo containers tied together with rope. He took the containers in his left hand and the spear in his right and walked towards us.

"Gone fishing?" Meghab Bhairab asked.

"No, but hopefully soon," Bishnu said with a smile. "I was bringing Dadima here, but then I thought, I should just get my fishing implements and join Kuberda on his fishing trips. Didn't want to miss out anymore, you know?"

Maintaining a smile on his face, Bishnu stared piercingly at Meghab Bhairab and tightened his grip on the spear. The broad smile of Meghab Bhairab's face faded away as he stared back at Bishnu. To my surprise, Prithuda, who usually always stood just behind Meghab Bhairab with his head down, looked up at Bishnu as well. His eyes seemed reptilian and calculative.

"Good idea," Meghab Bhairab said. "Keep yourself busy with fishing as much as you want." He gave one last gaze at all of us and brought his attention towards Babaji. "Time to go, Babaji. You need a good night's sleep."

"I'm not tired," Babaji said, which Meghab Bhairab ignored as he coaxed Babaji away.

"Subaji, stay with them in the Temple tonight," Meghab Bhairab said.

"But–" Suba Kashem tried to protest.

"Stay in the Temple, Subaji," Meghab Bhairab commanded, which rendered Suba Kashem silent.

Meghab Bhairab walked away with Babaji and Prithuda followed them. Babaji looked back at us. The man that I had seen to be full of life all day seemed rather defeated. With one last glance at Bishnu, he turned away.

"God, I wish Babu was here. Could have used one of his bottles right about now." Kuber Bhairab's snarky comment made us snigger.

"I will be taking Shani to the Temple," came Nondi's dry voice. She had quietly made her way among us.

"That's good," Bishnu said. "I'll be taking Dadima back to the mainland."

"I've already tasked Ponditji with that responsibility, Bishnuda. Don't go out into the waters again at night," Nondi said promptly. "Say your goodbyes to Dadima and let us go back to the Temple."

"You can all go. I'll catch up to you later," Bishnu responded.

"You know, sooner or later, you need to start being around us in the Temple," Nondi said, eying Bishnu judgingly.

"I know," Bishnu said, bringing his head down. "I've been busy."

"Busy?"

"Yes."

"What I see here is that you went back brought your fishing implements so that you can fish whenever you want."

"These things?" he said with a boyish smile, pointing at his spear. "They can be handy, sometimes. You know, fishing isn't always a hobby. You don't really know when it might become a necessity. It's better to be prepared for it when the need arises."

Nondi eyed Bishnu for a while, keeping her calm demeanor. "Well," she said finally, "if you stayed with us, you could have been of much more help than...whatever kind of *fishing* you are preparing yourself for." She sighed. "Anyway, come back to the Temple as soon as you can, then."

Nondi went back to the sitting area where Shani was curled up on the matted floor with Dadima sitting next to her. We followed Nondi and said our goodbyes to Dadima.

"You two look after each other. Okay?" Dadima said, kissing Bishnu and me on our foreheads. "Help each other with whatever you are going through. I'll leave you be."

We went to see Dadima off at the Bhairabs' private boatshed, but only I came back to our group. Nondi woke up Shani. Then our company—Nondi, Kuber Bhairab, Shani, Suba Kashem and I—started heading back to the Temple. We stayed silent throughout the trip. A bit further down our way, I heard footsteps. Bishnu was following us at a comfortable distance, holding onto his fishing implements.

We finally reached the Temple. Suba Kashem hadn't talked much throughout the trip, keeping his head down and muttering indistinguishable things. In the same manner, he disappeared into Ponditji's room. Nondi tucked Shani in and we had our supper, which was leftovers from the day's event. Then we went to sleep.

At around midnight, I heard the familiar noise of Bishnu climbing on to the bed on my side. Only this time, I also heard the clinking metal of a sharp spear being put down on the concrete floor.

38 ASHRAF UL MAKHLUQAT[liv]

"Tell me one of your fishing stories, Bishnu. It's been a while since I heard one."

Bishnu gave a dry chuckle at Kuber Bhairab's suggestion. "Why? So you can make fun of my ghosts again?"

"I don't laugh at your ghosts, Bishnu," Kuber Bhairab said with a smirk on his face. "I just like to question the logic behind their choices. When you talk about scary Banshees laughing at the top of coconut trees in plain white, loose clothing, for example. It makes me question—how on earth did they get up there? Climbing a coconut tree takes a lot of effort, strength and agility. How did an undead, old witch manage to do that?

Also, while they were getting up the tree, hasn't anyone ever caught sight of them and thought, 'How is that really decrepit-looking old lady getting up a coconut tree so easily?' Why don't strangers ever find them while the Banshees are preparing to scare them? Why do they always find them already up there?"

Laughter broke around the circle. It was midday. Shani was feeling feverish and deep in slumber inside the temple, giving Nondi a chance to relax and spend time with us. Bishnu had appeared from wherever he kept himself and joined us on a large bamboo mat under the starfruit tree. We were in late spring and the world was full of noise. Bird calls were a constant hymn, interrupted by the flutter of wings and rustling of leaves as forest critters shuffled from branch to branch.

"You don't believe in the paranormal and I do. That's perfectly fine," Bishnu said, "but there are things out there and it's smart to acknowledge that. Denial is not a smart response to fear—preparation is."

"So, you think I don't prepare for scary possibilities?" asked Kuber Bhairab.

"That's…not what I implied and you know that," Bishnu said.

"I'm not challenging you, Bishnu," Kuber Bhairab said. "I genuinely want to know. Do you think…when unexpected things happen, I am prepared enough to deal with them?"

"You are more prepared than the person you're talking to will ever be, Kuberda," Nondi said before Bishnu could answer, putting her hand on Kuber Bhairab's shoulder. "Look how well you dealt with Shani."

Kuber Bhairab breathed in. "I'm doing the best I can. Don't know if that's enough."

"Your best is more than enough, Kuberda," Nondi said.

Kuber Bhairab glanced at Bishnu, who had his head down, resting on his knees, nibbling at the stitches of the bamboo mat. "You shouldn't be harsh on Bishnu, you know?" Kuber Bhairab said. "Like I said before, we're all dealing with this predicament in our own way."

"What Bishnu is doing is not unique," Nondi responded immediately. "I have seen him do that many times."

"And what is it you think I am doing, Nondi?" Bishnu said, looking up.

"Running away," replied Nondi calmly. "That's what you've always done. When life presents you with ambiguity, you run away."

"I'm here right now, am I not?" Bishnu said. "I'm not necessarily living every hour of every day in the Temple, but I'm here, keeping an eye on all of you."

"We don't need anybody to keep an eye on us," Nondi said.

"You think so?" Bishnu chuckled. "You think all these men walking around the edge of the swamp with spears are always going to keep their distance? You really think it's safe to let them know that the people they're measuring up are all in one place so that they can do to us whatever they intend to do, whenever they want to do it?" Bishnu took a pause to lower his voice. "…not to mention whoever orders them to do it!"

"These people are employed by Meghabda to look after us," Nondi said.

"And you think that's all Meghabda's intentions are?" Bishnu asked. "You put a lot of trust in the Bhairabs. And speaking of the Bhairabs, where's Babuda? Where is he in the middle of all this? If you're so concerned with us sticking together, why haven't you ever blamed him for disappearing from this island?"

Nondi's lips pursed and her chin started shaking. She quickly rubbed her eyes with her orna. "I admit," she said in a broken voice, "Babuda is an irresponsible hothead."

"Wow, look who's—" Bishnu snapped.

"Bishnu, stop talking. You have talked enough," Kuber Bhairab said, commandingly.

"But when I said that you're running away," she continued, trying to keep as calm as possible, "I didn't mean running away from all of us and you know it."

Bishnu breathed heavily and looked at the ground. His jaws were clenched together.

"Bishnu, listen to me," Kuber Bhairab said, breaking the silence. "You don't have to—"

Bishnu stood up and took a last glance at everyone before walking away towards the swamp and quickly disappearing into the tree line. We sat in silence.

"Well, here goes my attempt at bringing any kind of stability to this group." Kuber Bhairab chuckled. "Anybody have any ghost stories like Bishnu's to share? Any story will do, really."

Nobody had any response to that. It was the way it had been all throughout the spring so far; while the universe was celebrating life, we were stuck in a world of anxiety about something none of us could either fathom or convey.

"I don't believe in ghosts; I don't have to. There is a much simpler explanation to things of paranormal nature." Suba Kashem's comment broke the awkward silence.

I'd almost forgotten he was there. He had been quiet as a mouse. His voice, at that time, was surprisingly calm and his eyes carried innocent wonder and eagerness.

"Finally!" Kuber Bhairab said, breathing a sigh of relief. "Someone who can talk. Tell me, Subaji, what do you believe in?"

"Djinns," said Suba Kashem.

"Ah, Djinns," Kuber Bhairab responded. "The fabled astral beings of Islamic mythology. Please, do tell. Where do they live?"

"With us," Suba Kashem responded. "Their dunya[lv] exists in the same place as ours, but most of us don't see them."

"Is it because they are rare and hard to find?"

"Not really. They have their own homes, cities and workers."

"Really? Then, why are they so hard to find?"

"Because you see them and their dunya only when they choose to make themselves visible to you...or if they are forced to."

"So, you're telling me there's a whole world of these astral creatures living in the same space of reality as we do, but we don't see them?"

Suba Kashem nodded.

"Fascinating," Kuber Bhairab commented with curious wonderment in his eyes. "So, how can you force them to reveal themselves to you?"

"Through being a favorite of Allah," Suba Kashem said, eagerly.

"Okay," Kuber Bhairab said. "So, forcing an astral being to show themselves is not some dark magic. It's rather a reward?"

Suba Kashem nodded again.

"What a strange concept!"

"Well, it's not like they come to you unwillingly. Most of the time, they come to you happily. Well...at least, the good Djinns do."

Kuber Bhairab stared at Suba Kashem with puzzled awe.

"Let me explain," Suba Kashem said, smiling. "You see, in our religion, Allah made us humans his most superior work of creation and as such, his next two superior creations—the Firishtas[lvi] and the Djinns—are expected to respect the humans. If a human reaches a certain point of closeness with Allah through dedication, then Allah commands a Djinn to answer to that human's call and provide him whatever he wishes. In the world of Djinns, this is considered a great honor—to be chosen to be of service of an elevated human being."

"That's a really interesting concept to motivated people to do good."

"I guess," Suba Kashem said, with a proud smile that clearly showed his gleefulness of having bestowed this knowledge among us.

The daylight had started to fade and so had the noises of the forest critters. The shadows of the trees were getting longer. In this swampy woodland, the darkness fell quite abruptly compared to the rest of the island.

"What makes us better than them?" Kuber Bhairab asked.

"What do you mean?" Suba Kashem asked.

"You said humans are superior to the Firishtas and the Djinns. What makes us superior?"

At this, Suba Kashem drew a long breath. "It's a complicated concept," he said. "To put it simply, we humans are better than them because of our limitations."

"So, we are superior, not because of our powers or greatness, but our limitations?"

"Yes. Two of them, in fact."

"And they are?"

"The limitation of matter and the limitation of conscience."

"Care to explain?"

"Well..." Suba Kashem said, measuring his words. "The limitation of matter means that we live in a dunya of limited things. Money, water, food, space—they are all limited. We have to make do with the limit of what we live with." He paused again to clear his throat. "The limitation of conscience means that we have the capacity to do evil despite the drive to do good."

"So, we humans are superior to Firishtas and Djinns *because* we have these limitations?" Kuber Bhairab asked.

"Yes," Suba Kashem said, smiling.

"Sounds a little contradictory to me."

"Well..." Suba Kashem said, "...the fact that we have these two limitations means that we, the humans, survive, despite the greater odds.

Does that make sense?"

Perplexed, Kuber Bhairab stared at Suba Kashem for a few moments and then broke into a smile. "Oh, now I's starting to understand."

"You see, Firishtas have none of these limitations. They live in a world where everything is boundless and they are incapable of doing evil," continued Suba Kashem. "While Djinns have only one of these limitations. Their dunya has boundless things, but like us, they too have the capacity to do evil." Suba Kashem grinned. "And trust me, you don't want to be part of the evil things they do."

"Why?" Kuber Bhairab asked.

"Well, you know they live in a world of boundless things, right?"

Kuber Bhairab nodded.

"Well, think of it in human terms…if you had everything you needed but still chose to do evil, what kind of person are you and what kind of evil things would you choose to do?"

Kuber Bhairab nodded with wonderment in his eyes. "Wow, Subaji, let me tell you: this is the first time in a long time we've had a moment to unwind and that's thanks to you."

"Don't mention it," Suba Kashem replied, smiling.

"Well, Subaji…I guess you've seen this question coming," Kuber Bhairb said. "Why don't you tell us a bit about yourself? Who are you? Where did you come from?"

"I am a convict," Suba Kashem said, calmly. "What else do you need to know?"

"Well, you're not *just* a convict, Subaji. You were someone's brother, or someone's husband, or someone's son. You were at least one of those things. Am I right?"

Suba Kashem looked down. His face no longer carried the childish wonderment. "I've been in jail for years and the people I cared about are long gone into obscurity. At least, that's what I thought when I was in jail." He went on. "I thought the people whom I loved had perished at the hands of those who didn't want them found. I thought the children I spent nights telling stories to were nothing but insect food in tight little graves."

"Subaji?" Kuber Bhairab said. "Did you have your own children? Do you know where they are?"

Suba Kashem suddenly broke into a haunting laughter. "No, I didn't. I never even had a wife," he said. "I'm an escaped convict with my time running out. That's who I am."

"I get the feeling that what you really want is for us to see you as a convict and nothing else."

"Why don't you ask the people who already know who I am?" Suba Kashem said. "A few months ago, I was in a cell and nobody knew or cared about who I was, but now, I find that there are people who know plenty about me...more than I know about myself. And the knowledge they bestowed upon me put me in the situation I'm in right now."

"And you don't want to be in the situation you're in now?" asked Kuber Bhairab. "You would rather be in jail?"

Suba Kashem stayed silent. "What I am is a coward," he muttered finally.

For about a minute, Kuber Bhairab observed Suba Kashem intently, who kept his head down.

"All right, then. I won't prod into things you're not comfortable talking about," Kuber Bhairab said. "If you don't want to tell us where you came from, then at least tell me why you came here. Nondi told me you came here because of a dream?"

My heart skipped a beat as Suba Kashem broke into laughter again. "I didn't see any dream," he said.

"You didn't? Then what was the dream you mentioned to Babaji?"

Suba Kashem stood up. "I didn't see that dream. I was told to recite it, word for word," he said, fixing up his lungi.

"Who told you to recite it?" Kuber Bhairab asked.

"Babu Bhairab," he said. "He's the one who broke me out of jail. He paid off the guards and told me when the gates would be left unlocked at night."

A dreadful calm took over Suba Kashem's face. His eyes carried no fear.

"This has been a relaxing chat and I thank all of you," he said, finally. "But I have to go now."

"Where?" Kuber Bhairab asked.

"To Babaji. He needs me," Suba Kashem muttered, as he hastily made his way south.

The daylight was at its last, dying glow; darkness would soon take over the world. We rolled up the large bamboo mat we were sitting on and made our way to the temple. Little did we know, we had a long night ahead of us.

39 A SHIMMER OF LIGHT FROM THE OUTSIDE

"Well, I guess we're back to the five of us again," Kuber Bhairab scoffed. "Whenever we acquire a new friend, we somehow drive that friend away."

"Maybe it's not a good time to make friends, Kuberda," Nondi said.

"I disagree," Kuber Bhairab said. "I believe this is exactly the time when we should be sticking together and looking out for each other."

We were all back at the Temple. Ponditji sat with his back to the altar-base, while Kuber Bhairab and I sat on the floor. Nondi, now awake, sat in her usual place on the bed with Shani.

I remember her face at that moment very clearly, because perhaps for the first time, she didn't seem agitated. Her eyes weren't fidgety. She didn't sit close to Nondi, hiding her face in her orna; instead, she sat comfortably at the corner of the bed, legs folded. She realized that I was observing her and brought her gaze towards me.

I thought I might have scared her, but to all of our surprise, she smiled at me. Suddenly, the whole room seemed to have brightened. I remember discovering at that moment that one of her teeth, under the left side of her lip, sat higher than it should and as a result of that, her lip in that area was slightly elevated. That little imperfection made her more beautiful. I realized that she was not some Godly being; she was probably someone's daughter, or someone's sister, or someone's niece, or any or all of those things.

I remembered a similar comment that Kuber Bhairab made to Suba Kashem, but he seemed to be set on making us believe that he was nothing but a convict. *What does Shani want us to believe about her? A captured Godly being, or a girl just like any other?*

She looked at Nondi and her smile became more gleeful.

"Are you ready?" Nondi asked.

Shani nodded enthusiastically.

"What is my Boinji ready for?" Kuber Bhairab said as he stood up.

To everyone's surprise, Shani sprang off the bed, walked towards Kuber Bhairab and hugged him. Nondi covered her face with her orna.

"I know you appreciate me, Boinji," Kuber Bhairab said. "You don't have to—" Kuber Bhairab stopped as Shani tightened her grip.

He then gently placed his hands on her long braid. After a minute of silence, she finally let go of him, revealing her tearful face. She went back to her bed and started clearing out the jumbled blankets to the side, which revealed two neatly-folded katha[lvii]. She picked one of them up and let the folds fall as she held one end. Needlework of red, blue and green vibrantly contrasted with the bright white cloth, which was reinforced along the edges with velvet-red layers.

"This is beautiful, Boinji," Kuber Bhairab said. "Is...is it for me?"

Shani nodded enthusiastically, beaming. She carefully re-folded the katha, presented it to Kuber Bhairab. Kuber Bhairab took the katha from her. She looked down, folding her hands and mumbled something that made my heart skip a beat.

"Boinji." Kuber Bhairab sounded just as astonished as I was. He quickly handed the katha to Ponditji and came back to her. "What did you just say?"

"Birji!" the girl said, in a slightly raised voice.

"Birji?" Kuber Bhairab asked.

"Birji," came the response.

"Kuberji?" Nondi's joyful voice came from behind as she walked over. She put her hand on Kuber Bhairab's shoulder and looked at Shani. "Kuberji?" Nondi said again.

The girl finally looked up at them with teary eyes. "Kub—" she mumbled. "Kub-birji!"

"That's good enough for me," Kuber Bhairab said, in a trembling voice. He wrapped his arms around Shani as she placed her head on his chest.

"Birji," she said, this time more commandingly as if to claim something.

"Yes, Birji," said Kuber Bhairab. "I will always be your Birji." He then looked towards the bed again. "And I am guessing the other one is for Nondi?"

At this, she went quiet and all of a sudden went back to looking down at the ground.

"I already got mine," Nondi said, as she pointed at the red katha she was covering her legs with.

"Well. I see you get preference over everybody," Kuber Bhairab chuckled.

"I didn't get any preference," Nondi said. "She was just too shy to build up the courage to give it to you."

"I see," Kuber Bhairab said.

Shani looked up at Kuber Bhairab with nervousness on her face. She then walked over to her bed again, picked up the second folded katha and walked back to Kuber Bhairab. This one was bottle-green, with red and black needlework.

"You want me to have another one?" Kuber Bhairab asked.

"Shani," she said.

Kuber Bhairab's smile went away from his face.

"Shani," she said again, this time with more eagerness.

Kuber Bhairab nodded silently and took the katha from her.

A loud knock on the front door startled all of us. Ponditji stood up and went to open the gate.

"Kuber, I am afraid I have some bad news," came a commanding voice. In the darkness of the night, Meghab Bhairab looked frighteningly calm as he entered the hall. Prithuda was standing behind him inconspicuously. Nondi guided Shani back to their bed.

I heard a whimper and looked at Kuberda. His lips were trembling, holding back tears. He held the folded katha Shani had given him tightly in his hands and looked at his older brother in deep despair, jerking his head side to side.

"No!" he whispered.

"Babaji hanged himself in the cellar last night," said Meghab Bhairab calmly.

An awful silence filled the room.

"I should have been by his side," Nondi's sobbing voice echoed through the hall. Shani observed her in stunned silence. "I could have gone and—"

"Babaji had people by his side, Nondi," Meghab Bhairab interrupted her. "He had Maaji and me. And yet, he chose to run off with farmers and convicts. He lost his mental constitution in the face of obscurity and gave up in the end."

Nondi looked at Meghab Bhairab. She was clearly about to say something, but chose not to. Shani stared at her in confusion.

Kuber Bhairab, in the middle of all this, had already settled himself. He looked at Meghab Bhairab and said, "So, you want us to come back to the estate for—"

"—for the funeral, yes." Meghab Bhairab finished his sentence.

40 A GARDEN OF INNOCENCE

"You, my dear guest, have an important responsibility when we reach the estate," Meghab Bhairab told me while we were traveling across the isle in the late hours of the morning. "You have to give my mother company."

I stared at Meghab Bhairab in confusion, but he walked away, glancing meaningfully at Kuber Bhairab.

"You are the only person, at this point, who can talk to my mother." Kuber Bhairab explained his brother's words.

"How so?" I asked.

Kuber Bhairab gave me a painful smile. "Babu is my mother's favorite son," he said finally. "She cannot stand anyone in her family at the moment and you are the friend that Babu brought home."

I nodded. Silence followed as I walked side by side with Kuber Bhairab with Meghab Bhairab a few meters ahead, with his hands clasped behind him. And a few meters behind me came Nondi with Shani in her arm. The doors and windows of all houses were closed, as I expected. Up ahead, the high walls of the Bhairab Estate stood with its authoritative presence.

"Nondi, I want you to do exactly as I say," said Meghab Bhairab, when we were about to walk into the estate. "Take Shani with you straight to the Eastern house. I want you to ensure she gets anything she needs."

Shani stared back at Meghab Bhairab with a nervous frown as Nondi took her away along with Kuber Bhairab, who went dejectedly alongside the girls.

Up ahead, I saw Maaji sitting on a bamboo mat in front of the high walls of Meghab Bhairab's living quarters. Her legs were spread wide as she gazed at the ground. She didn't look up at us, even once. Meghab Bhairab placed his hand lightly on my shoulder, gave me an approving nod and went inside the southern house. Prithuda followed.

So, I stood there for a minute, assessing the situation. So far, I had received clear hints that she didn't see Kuber Bhairab in a very favorable light, but why she was dismissive of her eldest as well wasn't clear to me. *Was she unappreciative of Meghab Bhairab's failure to control his father?*

"Come here, naat, sit with me." Maaji broke my train of thought with a voice numbed by insurmountable grief. She was wearing a plain white shari and her reddish-brown hair was loose, down to her waist. The shidur on her head was gone and her mouth was no longer red with paan.

I smiled and sat in front of her on the bamboo mat. She gazed blankly at me for a few seconds and then yanked me towards her and embraced me, breaking into a catatonic sob.

"O, my Babli-re...my Babli!" she cried, in a rhythmic howl. "Come back to your father! He is on his way. O, Babli-re, come back!"

She let go of me and pounded on her chest repeatedly, sobbing and howling, rocking back and forth. Her tearful eyes showed deep despair and sorrow. As her wailing went on, she lost her balance and almost fell to the side before I intervened to hold her steady.

It was at that point that the weight of loss in the air struck me. I realized that I had never really felt the hopelessness that this family had been going through. So far, I had been curious and inquisitive for my own sake. I feared for my own safety and wondered about the strangeness of the whole situation. I did recognize the predicament the Bhairabs were facing. I acknowledged that Meghab Bhairab had been doing his best to bring some sanity to this chaotic predicament. I appreciated the emotional intelligence of Kuber Bhairab and the perseverance of Nondi. But I never had, until that point, truly empathized with the strain this family was feeling, with their youngest missing and their patriarch losing his sanity before passing away.

No longer did I fear for my safety, for Meghab Bhairab keeping me hostage on the island. Why wouldn't he keep me hostage? I had been introduced along with Bishnu as the friend of his little brother, who had disappeared. Why would he just let me go, knowing that I might have valuable information that can potentially lead to Babu Bhairab?

No longer did I wonder who Shani was or where she had come from. I realized the wisdom behind what Kuber Bhairab said. The fact of the matter was that she was here and we were all simply managing the predicament, except for Babu Bhairab. I felt profound anger towards Babu Bhairab. I had found him unpredictable and irritating until that point, but now, for the first time, I felt genuine resentment towards him for leaving his family in the middle of all this.

"Baba[viii], do you know where my Babli has gone?" Maaji asked me in a tired voice.

I felt a lump in my throat. I really wanted to help this poor old woman. But I couldn't figure out what to say.

She sighed and went on, "Perhaps it's better if he doesn't come back for a while. He doesn't react well to people passing away. He was never the same after his aunt, Shormi, passed away."

I kept holding on to her hands, not knowing what else to do.

"He loved visiting her. He ran around the garden and woodlands around that place. We couldn't keep him here. We would ask him, what does his Aunt Shormi's place have that the estate doesn't?

"'Everything here is pretty and tidied-up. The birds don't tweet too loud, so not to annoy the guests,' he explained. 'But at aunt Shormi's place, the birds chirp in unison, the foxes hide in bushes as I chase them and I can catch snails near the wetlands!'" For the first time, I saw a dry smile form on her face. Her breathing had calmed down.

I stared at her in wonder. The memories of the same boy who, to some extent, was responsible for this woman's grief had finally brought a smile to her face. It astonished me how deeply she loved her youngest.

"So, I used to slip away from the house when Raghabji and Megha were busy with family business and take him across the river to his aunt. When Raghabji found out about it, he forbade me to take him there. We didn't always fare well with that family. But in the end, he too saw how happy it made Babli." She exhaled heavily. "It was his favorite playground. Talking to the trees. Talking to the animals. He gave the animals names of his own making. He used to call Shormi's domestic hens *baan*. And the roosters *raata*. Some people call roosters raatas, but baan was his creation."

She chuckled like a little girl. "'Maaji, I will stay the night here and when the raata calls in the morning, we will head back home before Babaji even notices. You will see!'" After reciting this in a child-like voice, Maaji broke into a quiet sob. "And now his Babaji is gone and no one is here to notice that my Babli is gone, too!"

"He will be back, Maaji," I assured her. "Don't worry, he will be back eventually."

She looked at me with a glint of hope in her eyes and nodded. "He was never the same since his Aunt Shormi died. I don't know what will happen to him when he learns about his father."

I was startled by the loud, metallic sound of the gate to the southern house being opened. Meghab Bhairab stepped out, carrying a frown on his face. It was obvious that he wasn't very pleased with her. *Was he listening in on the conversation this whole time?*

"Time to prepare you for the funeral, Maaji," he said. "Let's get you inside."

To my surprise, Maaji didn't seem to be affected by Meghab Bhairab's aggravation. Instead, she stared back with her, jaws tightened. Before Meghab Bhairab could get a hold of her, she raised a hand to stop him and then stood up by herself, using the wall as leverage. She staggered over to the gate and got in. Her unorganized, clumpy hair and shari full of creases made her almost seem like a prisoner.

"Kuber! Nondi!" Meghab Bhairab cried out. The two of them came out from the eastern house into the yard. "Nondi, come and prepare Maaji. Kuber, you know what to do."

Kuber Bhairab nodded and went back to the eastern house where Shani was.

Meghab Bhairab then smiled at me. "Come with me, my dear guest. It doesn't look good for a family who has just lost one of their own to wander outside."

41 A GAME AMONG CHILDREN

Right after Nondi and I stepped into the high-walled southern house, a single, loud bark sent me into a fight-or-flight mode. I jolted to my right to see a hairy, grey dog, at least the size of a fully-grown wolf, staring at me, showing its long, sharp fangs and salivating. Its body was full of thick muscle and its eyes stared into the core of my fear. Yet something about the dog told me that it wasn't seeking the crazed violence that other dogs seek when they are about to attack. Instead, it seemed silent—vicious, yet calculating. It seemed like a different animal.

"Prithuda, keep Bagha under control. Why does he react to strangers this way? Didn't we train him to stay quiet?" Meghab Bhairab said as he followed his mother into the two-storied building.

"Settle, Bagha. Settle," Prithuda muttered. There was no affection. It was a silent order and the dog stopped showing its teeth and went silent, still eying me. Prithuda pulled on its leash and they walked noiselessly into a small concrete room, near the wall.

I stayed on this estate for weeks and I never heard a single bark from this dog who lives just on the other side of the wall.

"Come." Nondi's broke my trance. Her eyes were full of fright. "Let's get inside."

The concrete, two-storied house was built quite sparsely, but it didn't have a terrace in front. Everything was closed in. Behind the house, to the south, Ponditji was working with his Pujaris, preparing for the funeral. I didn't get a chance to observe that scene in detail as I was ushered inside by Nondi.

"I really appreciate you calming Maaji down," Meghab Bhairab said as soon as I entered.

The interior of the house started with a stretched-out hallway, which quite evidently, had once been an open terrace. The walls separating it from outside were thick and new with a fresh coat of white paint covering it and two windows bringing in rays of sunlight. Concrete pillars stood in long intervals with red bricks showing in different areas where the cement had wilted away. I saw a couple of closed doors across the hallway. Beyond them, at the far southern end, was a set of stairs that led to the second floor. While Nondi was guiding Maaji up the stairs, Prithuda appeared in the doorway, closed it and went up with them.

"Nondi will prepare Maaji for the funeral. Don't worry about her." Meghab Bhairab's voice interrupted my observations. "Come, sit with me."

Meghab Bhairab was sitting on one of the lavish sofas in the living room near the door, concentrating on preparing his hookah. He carefully slid a lit match inside the coconut-shell bottom. As he put his mouth to the opening, I heard a gurgling noise and soon, swirling smoke came from his mouth.

He sat back on the sofa comfortably, gazing out the window in the hallway behind me. Sunlight coming from the window dropped a sharp shadow of his protruding nose over his thin lips. He was quite good-looking. I estimated that he was at least a decade older than his siblings, but even though his body showed signs of maturity, his face had a boyish charm that made him appear friendly even when he was serious.

When I took a seat on the sofa beside the one, he sat on, he smiled at me with genuine appreciation. From his smile, one could easily tell when he was genuinely happy and when he was just being courteous. More often than not, it was the second case and therefore, when he did smile genuinely, it was noticeable.

"You develop care for the people around you easily. I like that quality," Meghab Bhairab commented. "That's the reason why you get along so well with Kuber. Anybody who gets along with Kuber gets along with me."

"You think very highly of one of your brothers but don't think much of the other."

"They deserve what they get from me. Babu is intelligent but defiant, unpredictable and low-cunning. Intelligence is good when it is used in the right way. Kuber's intelligence can compete with Babu's any day, yet he has no ego. He is tactful and he listens to reason."

"You mean your reason?"

"I am a reasonable man," he said, after releasing a swirl of smoke. "Babaji raised me to maintain good poise and reasonable thinking in times of calamity. If you listen to me and let me counsel you, you are a reasonable person by nature, as well."

He sighed and went on. "It is alright to question things. It is welcome, even. But, at the end of the day, when one is faced with good reason, one must accept it. Reasonability is not a natural quality—it is learned. And the eldest son of the family must be raised with good reasonability. The younger ones have the freedom to place themselves anywhere on the spectrum of reason and chaos, but the eldest must follow the path of complete reason because the future of his family balances on his shoulders.

"Babu had placed himself far towards the side of chaos. He regularly brings embarrassment to his family. Kuber is much more reasonable, but he isn't seen by the family as someone of importance, which is a shame. Yet, it has to be this way. You need to seem dignified if you are a Bhairab. That's just the way it is." Meghab Bhairab leaned forward. "My two younger brothers had the opportunity to choose their paths. But I hadn't. My path was chosen for me. Following my whims is not a luxury I share with my siblings."

He leaned back, took a deep breath and looked at me. "Are you the eldest in your family?"

"I am the only."

"Oh, that's trouble! Single sons ruin their fathers' legacies. It is not wise to raise a male heir as a single child. You must give your eldest siblings to compare himself with and it is preferable that those siblings are notably younger. That's how you build character."

He went back to his hookah. After letting out another plume of smoke, he leaned back on the sofa as his eyes narrowed. "Single children turn out to be irrational and impulsive," he finally said. "They get plenty of time to get through their phase of irrational choices, but most never evolve." He then smiled at me. "But I have high hopes for you. You have good composure and observation. I believe you can come out of your phase soon enough."

"You think I make irrational choices?"

"Don't you? Leaving your family in the capital to come all the way to this distant village to film some old man's flute-making?"

"I—"

Meghab Bhairab broke into gleeful laughter. "I know, I know," he said. "You came to this island, introducing yourself as Bishnu's contractor. You thought it would be your little secret and that's all right. But I like to know the truth behind everybody my family comes in contact with. I have eyes everywhere in the district. You have to be very crafty to keep secrets from me."

He smiled at my terrified face, leaned forward and squeezed my elbow. "Hey, don't worry! There's no reason to be afraid. You are a city-dweller, an adventure-seeker. You wanted to observe the interesting event the whole village is talking about, so you made up a harmless lie to get yourself what you wanted. It's all right to lie for innocent reasons. As long as your lie doesn't have an ulterior motive that could potentially be a threat to me, I don't really mind lies. I'm glad that you satisfied your curiosity."

I smiled at him nervously.

"People's innocent little lies are the least of my worries, trust me," Meghab Bhairab said as he released his grip on my elbow and sat back comfortably. His face hardened. "Anyway, the reason why I brought it up now is that I want to counsel you. You are your father's only child and you have traveled far to satisfy your curiosity. You have seen and experienced many interesting events. I think now it's time for you to head back home.

"After the funeral is over, I advise you to cross the river, say your goodbyes to your Dadima and take the earliest bus to the capital. I don't know about your family, but I'm absolutely sure that they need you. So, whatever drove you to leave your family to go on an adventure, you must resolve that in your mind and go back. Every family needs its eldest child to carry its legacy." He nodded with a sigh. "Even if he is the only child."

42 A FUNERAL, AN INEVITABILITY

Suba Kashem, looking docile and defeated, sat on a bench about a hundred feet from the pyre made of large, chopped-up logs upon which Babaji's body was resting. We were at the southernmost part of the Bhairab Estate in a private orchard within Meghab Bhairab's high-walled living quarters. All around us were tall trees and pruned, green grass with a sharp, freshly-cut smell. Ponditji had washed and prepared Babaji's body for the cremation all night. His team of pujaris had placed the body gently on the pile of logs. Biruda had cut down the logs of the pyre from trees of the orchard.

"Should I cut a piece from the Banyan tree?" Biruda inquired.

"No, leave it be," Ponditji replied. "It has shown its decay, so its purity is broken."

Subaji and I, as the two sole Muslims, kept our distance from everything. Behind us the eastern sky was showing the first sign of dawn. The still body of Babaji was loosely wrapped in white, red and yellow ochre sheets of cloth. It seemed that the three layers were intentionally wrapped out of sync so that all three colors were visible.

"White represents purity." Ponditji's soft voice broke my trance.

I was dreading that he would ask me to keep my distance, but instead, he gave me a broad smile.

"Red represents happiness, celebration and Godly presence in everyday life. Yellow ochre represents holiness. That's how we send off our departed. We acknowledge the purity of their soul, celebrate the happiness they felt in life and wish them redemption in their holy journey."

"And where does that journey lead to?"

"To Bramhan, to Nirvana."

"Is that like heaven?"

"Things are not as binary in our religion as it is in yours. Good, bad, reward, repentance…These are not things set in stone."

"So, is it more like…a spectrum?"

"A little bit, yes. But it also depends on your point of view. What your Nirvana is might not be the same as others'. Therefore, your journey is unique from everyone else's because everyone experiences life differently."

I nodded at Ponditji.

"You seem distressed," commented Ponditji.

"To be honest, I'm thinking of Babu Bhairab. I feel worried about him."

Ponditji shook his head. "Don't be. He's on his own journey just like everyone else. And besides, you cannot really prevent the inevitable."

"You say that everybody has their own journey, but Babu Bhairab once said that the idea of good isn't variable, just misunderstood. He thinks that being good doesn't need to be popular or accepted. He thinks that only his idea of good is right and the others are wrong. Might that be his problem? That he thinks everything is absolute?"

"He thinks he is right. But if you disagree and want to advocate the idea of taking other people's views into perspective, that means you need to put his view into perspective as well and not just dismiss it."

"That's paradoxical, don't you think?"

Ponditji chuckled and shrugged. "Being good isn't easy. It's a complex concept that we're still trying to figure out. But that doesn't mean we don't need to strive towards it. Whatever idea of good we have, we need to apply it, regardless of the consequences. That's the only way to know whether that idea was right, to begin with."

"What happens when those consequences make you a bad person in the eyes of the others?"

"Then, that's a sacrifice we should be willing to make. Perhaps our journey towards Nirvana isn't a specific path of righteousness, but rather an intent on making sacrifices in trying to find that path."

He drew another deep breath. "The journey of the righteous is a difficult one. In many ways, being good is like being the sole living tree in a polluted wasteland. You know the pollution is affecting you, yet you need to survive because you are the only thing in your environment that represents life."

Ponditji's eyes had formed a frown and his face gave me the feeling that he was carrying the weight of the world on his consciousness. "I was appointed as the head Pondit of the Bhairab Temple when Babu was a child of five, Nondi was about the same age and Kuber was ten. The two boys' parents treated them quite differently and Nondi was always worried about Kuber. Even as a child, she worried that the world's cruelty would one day crush Kuber's spirit. 'Ponditji, can you please keep an eye on Kuberda? Nobody cares for him.' She used to say.

"But I was never worried about Kuber. I knew that the same thing that Nondi thought made Kuber vulnerable made him stronger than others.

He had experienced the darkness and hatred in people's hearts since the day he was born. I was rather always worried about Babu. I was worried about him because he had something in him that made him very vulnerable: innocence. Innocence, in its purest form, is volatile. A child who has never seen the uglier side of the world, with a heart pure and without blemish can evolve terribly when introduced to the ugliness of the world all at once, in a large dose. Kuber and Nondi didn't have that weakness, but Babu did."

"I guess his aunt's death really didn't sit well with him," I commented.

At this, Ponditji stared at me with stupefied bewilderment. "Who told you about his aunt?"

"Oh, sorry, I...I heard it from Maaji."

Ponditji stared at me in awe for a few seconds before taking in a deep breath. He smiled courteously at me and then, without saying another word, made his way towards Babaji's still corpse.

He was holding a piece of wooden cylinder, smoothly carved into about a couple of inches in diameter. He planted the bottom half of it into Babaji's mouth, looked at his pujaris and nodded.

He and the pujaris began reciting mantras. The Pujaris took hay from the stacks behind them in large bunches and covered Babaji's body with it while circling the pyre. A couple stayed with Ponditji as they started sprinkling chunks of a white substance on the body.

"Those are lumps of butter." Kuber Bhairab's voice startled me.

"Butter?" I asked.

"Yes, butter. It comes from the cow, which is considered sacred in our religion. This will also help with the cremation. You see the pujaris putting hay all over the body? That's food for cows. Another symbolism."

"How are you holding up?" I put a hand on his shoulder.

"I'm doing what I can, I guess. Nondi has put Shani to sleep in the Eastern house." He sighed with a frown. "Bishnu is nowhere to be seen."

"You feel worried?"

"Yes."

"But he's been inconsistent in showing up to things for a while."

"This is different. This is not normal. Bishnu wouldn't miss this."

The place was now surrounded by people. I could see faces I recognized from The Gathering. A murmur in the crowd drew my eyes to an opening, through which Meghab Bhairab walked in with his mother. They were both dressed in all white. Meghab Bhairab coaxed his mother to a bench set close to Babaji's body. She looked nothing like the disheveled woman I saw a few hours ago.

Ponditji was preparing fire-torches and lining them up around a small fire he'd made with a few dry branches. Seeing Meghab Bhairab come in, he took one and lit it up. He walked over to Meghab Bhairab and handed the torch to him.

My memory of Meghab Bhairab at that moment is strange. He seemed more defined than others, as if drawn with a darker lining. He started making his way towards Babaji's body, which was covered thickly with hay. After circling the pyre a few times, he silently lit the protruding piece of wood Ponditji had placed in Babaji's mouth. He held the torch to the wood for a good minute to ensure that the fire was well lit. Then he handed the torch back to Ponditji and rejoined his mother on the bench.

Kuber Bhairab had made his way to the congregation. He was given a torch as well, like a few other people from the crowd, who I assumed were esteemed members of the society or extended family. They all lit the mound in different places. I walked over to sit near Subaji.

The fire spread across the mound and when my eyes fell on the Babaji's head, I was met with the unnerving sight of the skin of his face being burnt away as his teeth and tongue became visible. I felt like I was seeing a face of eternal pain.

I felt exhausted. We were up all night preparing for the funeral. I looked at Suba Kashem. He was looking on intently. The muscles of his body were tight and trembling. He hadn't spoken a word throughout the evening. *What's gotten into him?* I laid down on the concrete bench beside him and fell asleep.

"YOU MURDERED HIM! YOU MURDERED YOUR FATHER WITH YOUR OWN TWO HANDS!"

Suba Kashem's deranged voice jolted me awake. I took stock of my surroundings. The guests were gone and Ponditji and his pujaris were carefully collecting pieces of burnt amber and clumped ashes. Suba Kashem gotten up and was looking straight ahead.

Meghab Bhairab was directing Ponditji others in the clean-up, but he turned around towards Suba Kashem. He seemed menacingly calm.

"What did you say?" Meghab Bhairab asked as he approached us. He stopped about ten feet away as Suba Kashem spoke again, this time in a low, trembling voice.

"You murdered your father, Meghab. Don't pretend you didn't. He wanted to be free. He wanted to make amends and that didn't sit well with you. So, you killed him and then told everyone that he took his own life. But I know Babaji would never do that to himself. He was the happiest he had ever been."

I felt unnerved as I stood up and took a few steps back.

"Suba Kashem," Meghab Bhairab said calmly. "I have invited Constable Jafar to come here and take you back to jail. He will be here any minute now. Babaji tried to give you a good life here. Out of respect for him, I allowed you to stay. I thought you could be a caretaker for the farmers.

"But you don't follow my command. You mutter incomprehensible things. You disappear and reappear everywhere. And now you have just accused me of murdering my father. I don't think you are fit for civil society. Solitary life had made you paranoid. So, I think it's time—" Meghab Bhairab stopped as he shifted his gaze from Suba Kashem's eyes to his hands.

I followed his gaze and saw something glinting. It was a small knife.

"Subaji, what are you doing?" I murmured.

"I am not going to go to jail. I am ready to meet my fate," Suba Kashem muttered as he charged at Meghab Bhairab, raising the knife.

In a matter of a split second, he was interrupted. Prithuda appeared from behind his master and caught him about a couple of feet from Meghab Bhairab. He tightened his arm around Suba's neck.

"Let me go!" Suba Kashem said as he wrestled around to face Prithuda and drove his knife towards him.

With a terrifying jolt, Prithuda caught Suba Kashem's elbow mid-motion with his right hand and planted his left elbow on Suba Kashem's arm, twisting it at an uncomfortable angle. Suba Kashem winced and dropped the knife, which Prithuda caught with his left hand, still holding Suba Kashem's right hand at that painful angle.

For a moment, I was relieved and I admired Prithuda's hand-to-hand combat skills, which had saved us from a violent outcome. However, what happened next stunned me. Prithuda, still subduing Suba Kashem's arm with his right hand, looked at Meghab Bhairab, who, completely unnerved, gave Prithuda a subtle nod.

In a blindingly fast motion, Prithuda let go of Suba Kashem, transferred the knife from his left hand to his right and caught Suba Kashem's throat with his left hand in a vice grip that made Suba gasp for air. Suba Kashem looked at Prithuda with terror in his eyes and shook his head in a plea for a reprieve. Prithuda gazed at him without a hint of emotion and then planted the knife into his abdomen.

A thick gush of blood flowed out. Prithuda took the knife out and stabbed Suba Kashem again. And again. And again. Suba Kashem opened his mouth, but being strangled, he couldn't make a single sound. When his body started to buckle, Prithuda let him go.

Suba Kashem fell to the ground with a thud. He didn't struggle; almost all his strength had been wrung out of his body. He twisted his head upwards to look at me with a pale expression. That's when I saw life leave his body.

43 A FATEFUL IMPRISONMENT

Prithuda was standing with his shoulders slouched, staring coldly at Suba Kashem's corpse. The bottom of his right forearm and his right fist, with which he held the knife, were bloodied.

As I was petrified by the events that had just unfolded, I heard heavy breathing behind me that made me stumble in a rush of fear. But I managed to keep my footing and turn back to see Constable Jafar and Biruda.

"Jafarda, I apologize for you having to see such an unfortunate event transpire," Meghab Bhairab said, coming forward.

I hastily took a few steps back to give him way.

"I…I…" Constable Jafar mumbled.

"I told the convict that you were coming to take him back to prison, but in response to the news, he attacked me. The two guards of the estate have a sworn duty to protect the Bhairabs, so Prithuda here had no choice."

"I…I understand." Constable Jafar said, finally recovering.

"Let me reinforce that the Bhairabs have a very good relationship with the police," Meghab Bhairab said. "Babaji has told me all my life how much he appreciates the work of men like you do to keep order in the district. As his successor, my sentiments are no different. You and your men have always been very cooperative with us and right now, I would like one more display of cooperation from you."

"Of course," Constable Jafar said with a nervous laugh.

"I would like you to go back to your station. I will have the convict's body sent to you soon. For the next couple of weeks, please order your men to keep themselves at the station and not to come to Choubazaar or the surrounding village as my men will be carrying out some important operations in that area."

Constable Jafar glanced at me and back to Meghab Bhairab. He clearly didn't know what to say.

"Just say yes, Jafarda. Like Babaji once said, you are new and inexperienced. Please know that saying yes to Bhairabs can only be good for you."

"Yes, sure. I will tell my men to not do patrols."

"Wonderful," commented Meghab Bhairab. He then turned his attention towards Biruda. "Biruda, I am afraid you have to get on the boat again. Please take Constable Jafar back to his station."

Biruda and Constable Jafar quickly made themselves scarce.

"I am deeply sorry that you had to see this, my dear guest," Meghab Bhairab said. "I would have sent you off on the same boat Biruda is about to take Constable Jafar in, along with…" Meghab Bhairab motioned towards Suba Kashem's body. "…This convict. I would have had Prithuda see you off on a bus to the capital, but unfortunately…" He drew a quick breath. "…I am afraid I need Prithuda now, for plans I was initially looking to execute much later on."

I took a nervous gulp. The Pujaris were gone, along with Ponditji. In their place, I saw men with spears. I had seen them before, walking around the edge of the swamp.

"Shani, Shani!" came the piercing, familiar voice.

Prithuda had brought Shani in. He wasn't forcing her to come here. He simply held her left arm and she walked. She was terrified. Prithuda took her near a tree about a hundred feet away from Meghab Bhairab. He had already changed his blooded attire and washed his hands. His face carried no remorse.

"Prithuda, let her go!" Nondi's defiant voice startled me. I looked at her and saw Kuber Bhairab put a hand on her shoulder.

"Nondi, I…" Kuber Bhairab said in a broken voice. "I am sorry."

"What do you mean?" Nondi asked.

A couple of guards came from behind her and gripped her arms tightly.

"Let me go!" Nondi screamed, struggling.

The men dragged her in front of Meghab Bhairab with ease.

"Now bring the last of our unwanted guests," Meghab Bhairab said, looking towards a few of the men circling us.

I heard a struggle and saw a couple of men holding Bishnu tightly and pushing him forward. A third man walked behind with Bishnu's spear in his hand, which he handed to Prithuda.

"Shani!" I heard the murmur of the familiar, fearful voice.

"I am afraid I have to ask you to take a break from your fishing trips, Bishnu," said Meghab Bhairab. "My men had been looking for you all over the island. It wasn't easy; you know your way around here. You're a slippery one, Bishnu. But I finally got you."

"If you are as smart as you claim to be, Meghabda, then you should know very well who is responsible for all this," Bishnu answered with a surprising calm in your voice. "So, if you want to understand what is exactly going on, then find and ask the person responsible. And let us all go."

"Shani!"

I heard struggling and saw Prithuda tightly gripping Shani's arms from the back as she fought to get free. There was no sign of effort on his face, just a vapid expression.

"I can let all of you go, for sure," Meghab Bhairab said. "But that wouldn't teach people the right lessons." He started walking towards Prithuda and Shani.

My heart stopped for a few moments, but he interacted neither with the captor nor the captured, walked right past them and picked up Bishnu's spear, which Prithuda had leaned against the tree. Then he walked towards Nondi and me.

I took a nervous step back, but he went past us all, towards Bishnu, flipped the spear to hold it with its blunt end up and in one swift motion, whacked the end on Bishnu's head. The sickening thud made my stomach squirm. Bishnu collapsed on the ground and curled into a ball before going motionless.

"Shani!"

Meghab Bhairab gave the spear to one of the guards. He then turned and started walking back to us. To my surprise, Nondi threw herself at Meghab Bhairab's feet.

"Meghabda, I am sorry!" she said. "But if you please let me explain, I will—"

Without letting her finish, Meghab Bhairab did something that made my blood run cold. With his left hand, he grabbed Nondi by her hair and dragged her up to her feet. She was weeping and biting her lips.

I couldn't hold myself anymore and flung myself at Meghab Bhairab, but out of nowhere, the back of his right hand swung round in terrifying explosiveness and the left side of my jaw went numb, as I dropped to the ground. Things went dark for a few moments. A line of blood slithered down from my left nostril.

"Don't overstep your boundaries, you miserable drifter!" Meghab Bhairab said in a gritty voice. "I was about to send you back where you came from, but now, you should consider yourself lucky if you can get out of this place alive."

"Shani!"

Meghab Bhairab, still holding Nondi by the hair, brought his face inches from hers. "You think you're smart, don't you? You whore!" Meghab Bhairab said.

"Meghabda, please let me explain," Nondi said in an uneven voice.

The terror in her eyes was unnerving. "I didn't—"

Meghab Bhairab whipped his right hand round again. This time, it landed palm first on Nondi's right temple. My body shivered in rage and pain, but I didn't have the courage to do anything.

He finally let her go and she fell softly to the ground, sobbing.

"Shani!"

"You think I don't know what you did?" Meghab Bhairab said.

"P-Please," whispered Nondi.

"I know exactly what you did. In the cellar, there was a secret passage. It was covered quite cleverly with dirty blankets. One has to look for such a thing to find it. But I knew what I was searching for. I knew that a living human being couldn't just survive there. It took me a while to figure it out and I found it. It led right to Babu's room. Right underneath his bed, carefully hidden away behind the large cooking pots that you put in. You thought no one would ever suspect anything. But I figured it out. I always do. Hiding things from me is not smart and you should know that, Nondi.

"You dug that hole, right into the cellar. The foundation of the central house is made of mud, so it wasn't very difficult. At first, I thought it was all Babu's doing. He is the kind of person who would do such a thing. But then I thought, Babu doesn't have the kind of determination to pull this off, at least not by himself. So, I kept looking."

He walked back to the tree, from where he had picked up Bishnu's spear. This time, he went behind the tree and leaned downwards to fetch something tucked under the root. He picked up a steel water bucket with a ceramic plate on top.

"This," he proclaimed. He put the bucket in front of Nondi.

Nondi had become deadly calm, now. She was no longer weeping and she sat in the dirt with her left hand supporting her weight.

"Shani!"

"Look at it, Nondi," said Meghab Bhairab, with a victorious smile. "I found it in the cellar, hidden away, near the opening of the passage."

Nondi stayed silent. Meghab Bhairab knelt down and pulled on her hair again to make her face him. With his other hand, he removed the ceramic plate from the top of the bucket and pulled out a water-soaked cloth. And held it in front of Nondi's face.

"LOOK AT IT, WHORE!" he bellowed, in an inhuman voice. "What is it?"

"My orna," came the cold response.

"WHAT IS IT DOING HERE?"

"I used it to soothe the girl's fever when your drunken brother brought her in there."

Meghab Bhairab slapped her again. But his time, Nondi took it and turned back to stare back at Meghab Bhairab.

"Shani!"

"Now, why would Babu do that?" Meghab Bhairab said.

"You ask him," Nondi said, as she stood up. "You drag him out of whatever hole in whatever jute-field he has gotten himself into this time, passed out in his own piss. Then you ask him. Ask him why he brought her here."

A stunned silence followed. I stared at Nondi, dumbfounded. The right side of her upper lip was swollen and had clearly sustained a nasty cut, but she stood up to Meghab Bhairab when everyone else shivered and did nothing. But I saw Kuber Bhairab approach his older brother, balancing himself on his staff.

"Meghabda," Kuber Bhairab said softly as he put a hand on his older brother's back. "Please, Meghabda, that's enough. You discovered the truth. Babu brought the girl here and Nondi looked after her. She was only helping the girl stay alive."

Meghab Bhairab shoulders relaxed as he gave his younger brother a glance before bringing his attention towards Nondi again. "I don't think so, Kuber," Meghab Bhairab said. "I know that Nondi is your childhood friend and you want to give her the benefit of the doubt. But I don't trust her. Babu doesn't have the determination to do such a thing. All his life, all he did was avoid responsibility. She helped him."

Nondi took no part in the conversation as she gazed down to her side with a stoic nonchalance.

"Shani!"

"In fact, I think she made him do it," Meghab Bhairab said, at last. "I think this boba[lix] girl is somehow tied to her. Perhaps one of her relatives, from whatever slum she came—"

"Babaji adopted me as an infant. I have no memory or knowledge of my family or lineage," Nondi's finally joined in. "I am a nobody and I have always been happy that way."

"That's what you are saying now. But I will get the truth out of you," Meghab Bhairab said.

He looked at the men surrounding us. They took the cue and escorted Nondi into the southern house. I saw Maaji standing in front of one of the windows, looking on with a blank expression.

I heard movement from behind me and saw, to my great relief, that Bishnu had started moving again. Kuber Bhairab and I ran to help him get up. Meghab Bhairab observed us without impeding our actions. The men surrounding Bishnu had already joined the rest in the southern house.

"Kuber, you take these two worthless fools to the guard's room," Meghab Bhairab ordered. "After Prithuda takes the girl into the house, he will come join you."

"Shani!"

Without letting his brother respond, Meghab Bhairab strode into the southern house as Prithuda watched, holding Shani by her two arms. Taking advantage of Prithuda's lapse of concentration, Shani freed herself from Prithuda's grip and ran towards us. She crashed into Bishnu's arms and Bishnu started sobbing quietly.

Holding Shani's head tightly in his chest, he kissed the top of her head. Shani was also weeping as she breathed unevenly into Bishnu's chest. Prithuda was slowly making his way towards us in his characteristic docile manner. *Fight him!* Said a voice inside my head. But I couldn't process my thoughts due to what I heard next.

"Shani, Shani-re." The girl's first full sentence came out in a broken murmur. "Take me back to Tadiji. I don't want to be here anymore!"

"I will, my Boin[lx], I will," whispered Bishnu, running his shivering hand over her head and down her long hair. "I will come back for you. I promise."

By then, Prithuda had reached us. He pulled the helpless girl out of Bishnu's embrace and guided her into the Southern house. A few guards approached us from behind. There was no chance of an escape. Meghab Bhairab had finally captured us all.

CHILDREN OF DECAY

Book 4: The Release

CHILDREN OF DECAY

44 KOMLA BIBI

"My dear capital-dwelling friend, tell me," Babu Bhairab's voice pierced through the buzzing music and the bustling crowd. "Has Bishnu ever told you the story of Komola Bibi?"

On my last visit to Arup Sai before I sailed to the Bhairab island, he shared with me stories from his past that were a lot to absorb. But I didn't get a chance to contemplate on them right after leaving his hut. I saw a plume of smoke in the distance. Never before had I seen any villager other than Bishnu and Arup Sai venture into that barren moor. As I got closer, I discovered a gathering of people from where I heard Babu Bhairab's voice.

The crowd stood aside to give me way to the center of the congregation, where Babu Bhairab and Bishnu were sitting near a fire pit. Babu Bhairab's dark eyes glistened in the glow of the pit as his face carried an aura of contentment. Bishnu sat beside him with a frown, looking to the distance dejectedly. The heat of burning coal came from a hole in the ground, over which, over a few metal grills, laid the carcass of a skinned, headless goat on its side, marinating in a thick coat of spices and yoghurt. Babu Bhairab was intermittently throwing water into the pit to make it hiss and redden, while poking at it with a stick to distribute the coal.

As I got closer, Babu Bhairab chuckled. "Come sit beside Bishnu and me," he said. "It will be a while before I come back to the mainland for longer than an evening, so my friends insisted on me giving them a feast. So here we are."

I sat with Bishnu near Babu Bhairab. Among the crowd, I recognized people I met at Ustadji's restaurant a few days earlier when Babu Bhairab told me about The Gathering. There were a lot more of their sort. Giggling and merry-making was going on all around. The two short, moustachioed men I'd seen the other day were playing a tobla[lxi] and an ektara[lxii]. To their melodic beat, the masculine-looking women were dancing alluringly. Men circled them, clapping loudly.

"Never seen Hizras[lxiii] before?" Babu Bhairab broke my trance.

"I have," I replied. "Just never in this setting."

"Nasrin and her girls are wonderful." Babu Bhairab's face carried mischief. "If you pay them well, they will–"

"Babuda, that's enough," Bishnu interrupted our exchange. "Not everyone is like you. He is an honored guest from the city and Dadima has trusted me with–"

"What do you know about me, Bishnu?" muttered Babu Bhairab, stoking the fire carefully. "…or people like me. You know nothing."

Bishnu ignored Babu Bhairab's comment. "It's bad enough that you make such a big mess with the people from Hizrapara every time you come here and now you're dragging–"

"He's not dragging me into anything, Bishnu, calm down," I said, putting a hand on Bishnu's shoulder. "I can take care of myself and I know where to draw the line. We're just having a conversation."

"You come from a much less affluent background than I do, Bishnu, yet I can accept people's differences better than you," Babu Bhairab commented. "Look at our capital-friend here. He is more comfortable here than you are and he has never seen this crowd his entire life."

"Mixing with the wrong crowd is no noble pursuit, Babuda," Bishnu said, frowning. "They are just taking advantage of you and you don't even realize it."

Babu Bhairab chuckled loudly. "I am a Bhairab, Bishnu. Don't you forget that," he said. "Nobody knows sycophants better than Bhairabs and let me tell you, as a Bhairab, these people aren't taking advantage of me. You just don't understand them."

"Well then, tell us about them," I said, to diffuse the exchange. "Who are these people? From what I have gathered so far, these people live in a place called Hizrapara. What is it like?"

Babu Bhairab got up and reached for the goat carcass in front of him. He carefully held on to the dry hoofs of its two back legs and flipped it. The fire pit hissed and a meaty smell filled the air. The visible side of the goat-carcass looked succulent and mouth-watering. Babu Bhairab returned to his seat and breathed in.

"Hizrapara is a small locality in the forest on the northern shores of the Great Green Lake. It is for the ultimate outcasts; snake charmers, black magic practitioners, hizra dancing girls, the bobas, the lolas[lxiv]—they all live there. The two religions in this part of the world are instruments of social divide, but they are also necessities of social acceptance. You need to boldly cling to one of them if you want to be a part of the civil society.

"But some people choose or are burdened with lives outside the boundaries of the two religions. They live there. Very few know where they live. Very few bother to care. They come to the mainland to earn a living by entertaining people, which young men delight themselves in. The murubbis of the village discourage these young men from doing so. Yet, they don't go out of their way to abolish the practice because they understand the very necessary economic exchange that ensures that these people stay out of their world."

Babu Bhairab glanced at Bishnu. "And that's why you look down on them, don't you Bishnu?" he said. "You were raised by a murubbi and you like to believe in his ideals. Tell me then, Bishnu, why do you venture there?"

Bishnu gave Babu Bhairab a cold stare.

"Tread carefully, Babuda," he said. "We have a guest present."

"I asked you an innocent question," Babu Bhairab said.

Bishnu switched his gaze to me and smirked. "I am a fisherman. In my trade, I need to explore all places with water bodies," he said, eying Babu Bhairab. "Nobody questions a fisherman for venturing wherever he wants."

"All right, then," Babu Bhairab said. "Let's go with that."

"So, you were talking about the tale of Komola Bibi?" I asked, changing the subject.

"Yes," Babu Bhairab said.

"Tell me about it."

"To understand the story, you must first understand the rituals of marriage in this part of the world. Do you know what a palki is?"

"Of course. It's a little carriage transported on the shoulders of men. The carriage houses a bride on her way to her husband's home. It was a practice of generations past."

"Correct. But do you know the cultural significance of the palki? Why are these brides carried by a congregation of men, rather than on boats or carts, both of which are faster and cheaper options?"

"Hmm...I never thought of it that way," I admitted. "Why do they do that?"

"Aha! Now you are asking the right questions." Babu Bhairab smiled victoriously. "The idea is to make the journey as slow as possible. When a bride is married off, it is expected that she takes her new family as her primary family. The family she was raised in will, thereafter, be her secondary family. They might come visit her from time to time, but until she establishes herself as a trusted part of her husband's household through years of service as a housewife, she is not allowed to visit her parental home."

"Quite tragic, when you put it that way."

"It is. When a girl gets married, she needs to abandon her parental home for years. She needs to mentally give herself closure from everything she grew up with—the fields she played in as a child, the friends she made, the people she cared for. She has to leave it all behind."

"That's why she is carried off on a palki with no more than four men, two front and two back. They would transport her carriage on their shoulders, led by a ghotok[lxv] on a horse. These men won't hurry their steps. They won't waste their energy on long, uninterrupted passages. They will stop to rest frequently. If there is a river on the way, they won't take the ferry. They will go around the shore. They will bear through calamities and they will camp during nights. But they will eventually get the bride to her new home. On their path, in this slow journey, the bride will bid her teary farewells to her home, her friends and family and everything she grew up with. That's what a palki is. It's the bride's last voyage. Her one last opportunity to have closure from everything she knew."

"That's insane," I commented.

"It is." Babu Bhairab nodded.

An exhaled chuckle made us look at Bishnu.

"You have anything to add?" Babu Bhairab asked.

"You are blowing this way out of proportion." Bishnu scoffed. "The symbolism behind a palki is that it is like a gift, a treasure. Brides are considered to be treasures to a grooms' family. So, they bring her in a fancy, treasure-chest-like carriage. That's what the palki represents. You made that whole thing up."

"Perhaps," Babu Bhairab admitted. "I didn't make it up; I was just trying to rationalize it."

"Rationalize it? How?" Bishnu asked.

"Well, think about it," Babu Bhairab went on. "They don't do this anymore, do they? They don't carry brides in palkis anymore. Why? Because times have changed. Today, we have railroads, buses. Quick, cheap and easy transport that let married women visit their parents whenever they want. There's no stigma attached to it anymore. This idea that a bride comes under the ownership of her new family after marriage has virtually died and so has the necessity of palkis."

For the first time, a relaxed grin formed on Bishnu's face. Babu Bhairb drew a deep breath and gazed pensively at the firepit.

"Why does it matter, anyway?" he finally said to Bishnu. "Your explanation is symbolic; mine's functional. Doesn't change anything, one way or the other."

"So, how is it relevant to your story?" I asked.

"The story of Komola Bibi?"

"Yes."

"Well, the story is about one of the long voyages of a group carrying a bride home on a palki. This was one of the rare occasions when the husband rode a horse with the ghotok to bring his bride home. The story is about the husband."

"I'm listening," I said.

"Well, it's not very long. As the congregation went on their way, they made camp near a large water body for the night. All the men and the bride fell asleep. The husband was awake, resting. As he was about to doze off, he heard water splashes.

"It was one of those wild, bushy waterbodies with no houses nearby. So, he thought to himself, *who could be taking a dip in this isolated place at the dead of night?* As he approached the shoreline, he saw a dark woman's shape, bathing. He got closer. The woman was beautiful in every possible way, but the one feature that got to him was her skin, which had an unusual orange glow[lxvi]. Mesmerized, he walked towards her.

"When the woman realized his presence, she looked back at him with alluring eyes and walked deeper and deeper into the water. The man quickened his steps, but by the time he got there, she was gone. A piece of string from her shari was stuck on one of the low branches. It trailed into the water, where the maiden had gone. The husband took the string in his hand and looked back to his group, where his newly-wed wife slept peacefully. But he had no desire to go back. He had made his choice. He pulled on the string as he walked into the water, following the lady's path." Babu Bhairab stopped with a content smile as if he had finished the story.

"Well, what happened then?" I asked.

"Well, there are two versions of the story's ending. In one version, the one told to children, it is said that the man goes into the water and finds an underground palace with beautiful jewels and architecture. There, he finally finds his Komla Bibi and stays with her for the rest of his life."

"What's the other version?"

"In the other version, the men find the husband's corpse floating in the river the next morning, with all the blood drained off his body."

45 RIGHTEOUS OLD LOVERS

Setara Begum dreaded that she, too, would one day be alone, holding onto her last piece of land that nobody wanted to look after and pass away into insignificance. To her relief, though, she never had to share the fate women like her often did. And for that, she was always thankful to two people—her recently-departed husband and her boy.

Her husband, unlike other men in the village, didn't become emotionally distant and dull with old age. He was full of life. He had his lands and a steady income and if he wanted to, he could have spent all his time leisurely chatting with other old men about village politics. Instead, he walked all over the village all day and came back to her with stories.

To the villagers, he was a respectable old man. They came to him for advice. He would spend the day advising farmers on investing in good seeds or giving blessings to the newly wedded bride of some young man. But they never realized that, deep down, he was a child, with eyes full of wonder. After being the village's lead murubbi all day, he would come home to his wife, talking about the curious things he had seen. How the enormity of the katla fish he saw at Choubazaar blew his mind, or how he found a rare, blue waterlily peeking out of the mud, or how good the broad-bean harvest of his neighbor was. And when he told stories, that's when she loved him most.

He was a religious man, but unlike other religious men, he didn't use his beliefs to express narrow-minded ideas. However, he had his own beliefs about how God's earth was meant to be.

"We are not supposed to alter Allah's dunya for our own extra comfort," he always said. "Allah has already made it comfortable enough for us to live in. When we try to alter it more to further our well-being, that's when we stop receiving His rahmat[lxvii]."

For many years, youths in the village had been demanding a cinema hall like the adjacent villages. And when the free market finally paid attention to them and built the cinema, Setara Begum's husband protested vehemently.

"This will make young men forget Allah," he said. "They will forget their prayers and responsibilities."

But the businessmen didn't hear his protests. They brought in the cinema, market complex with cafeterias for highway drivers and so on. He protested against them all, gathered troops of murubbis and stood against the progress. Setara Begum lost track of how many things he protested against. She didn't mind. She loved how her husband could stand for his ideals.

Her husband had always had problems with progress, or at least what people perceived as progress. But there was a time when he went uncharacteristically quiet. A large tannery plant was being built at the eastern fringe of the village. In the beginning, he protested in his characteristic way, rallying support around the village. But one day, he came home with a grimace on his face. He didn't tell his stories and he didn't interact. He simply sat in his bed quietly and counted the beads of his tasbeeh[lxviii]. Setara Begum approached her husband to ask what was going on, but the moment he saw her, he spoke out.

"I don't understand this dunya anymore, Khuki[lxix]. It has changed beyond recognition for me."

"What happened?" Setara Begum asked.

"Maybe the things I stand for aren't relevant anymore. Perhaps my time has come. I should accept who I am—an old man with antiquated ideas."

"What happened?" she asked again. "Did the factory people do something to you?"

He stared at her with eyes full of agony and sighed. She had known him long enough to understand what this meant. He had lost his spirit. She took his hand in her lap.

"Who are these people anyway? They never show themselves. This Godforsaken plant came out of nowhere," she said, trying to empathize with him, hoping for him to open up. But he remained silent. "Your ideas aren't antiquated and you're not an old man whose time has come. Get that idea off your head. You can still do the right thing. You don't have to wage wars with people you cannot survive against, but you can change little things."

A year passed, but Setara Begum's husband was never the same. Nobody else noticed, but she did. He didn't have the spring in his step or daydreams in his eyes. He was uncharacteristically pragmatic and it broke her heart. Then one day, he came home with a dark, little boy in his hands.

"I am getting too old to watch over my lands, Khuki," he said. "I have decided to take a caretaker."

Why the caretaker had to be a boy that couldn't be more than half a decade old, she didn't quite understand. But she saw something more in her husband's eyes than just the need for a caretaker. She saw hope. He introduced the boy to her as Bishnu. He was a stray child who'd come from Hindupara in search of work. Setara Begum knew that there was more to the story, but she didn't pry.

Most women would have been annoyed at the prospect of raising a child at such a mature age, but she didn't mind. She appreciated the fact that life had given her responsibility.

Over time, Bishnu became more than just a caretaker for her and especially her husband. He became their boy. As Bishnu grew up, Setara Begum saw the youthful exuberance return to her husband. He went back to his crop fields and taught the boy farming with his own hands. He taught the boy how to take care of himself.

And the boy was a fierce learner. He absorbed everything her husband taught him and then went to places and learned more. He learned carpentry and made a place for himself. He learned fishing to earn some extra money. She admired Bishnu's prudence in saving up for his future.

One day, Setara Begum's husband made one of his long trips to Choubazaar to say his evening prayers as usual. But after returning home, he laid down quietly on his bed and asked his wife to bring in some of his closest friends and his boy.

"I am about to pass away now," he announced in a calm voice. "If any of you had any qualms with me, I would like to seek forgiveness. I will meet you all in the field of Hashr[lxx]."

Then he asked everyone to leave, except for his wife and Bishnu. First, he wanted to be alone with Bishnu. Setara Begum looked on from behind the curtain with teary eyes as her beautiful husband said his last few words to the boy they raised together. Then he asked her to come in.

"I will be waiting for you, Khuki. But 'til we meet again, I don't want you to feel alone. I'm leaving Bishnu with you. He'll look after you," he said. "But a day will come pretty soon when he won't be a boy anymore. He will have to be a man and that will involve some painful experiences. But you need to let him endure it and embrace the change that will come with it."

"You don't have to explain that to me," she said, holding his hand tightly. "I know you more than you think I do."

They exchanged one last loving stare. Then Setara Begum's husband closed his eyes and passed away peacefully. Gracefully.

People, including Setara Begum herself, mourned for a few days. However, the sense of loss dissipated soon enough, not because people never cared for him, but rather because they were happy with him and the way he had lived his life. His children came from the capital and organized the funeral and everyone eventually moved on. Setara Begum's beloved husband passed away, but he had left a part of himself with her.

46 A TUG OF THE LEASH

Before I knew any better, I had taken Prithuda for a docile little man. Possibly a drug-addict, due to those narrow, dejected eyes that seemed to never blink. But by the time I was sitting in his shabby little room just inside the high walls of the southern house, I had seen him brutally murder an adult person twice his size only hours before. Somehow, being a prisoner to a ruthless, powerful man didn't faze me. My mind fixated, instead, on this submissive, yet dangerous man and for the first time, I started to really observe him.

The strong, yellow light from the bulb above made his dark, sunburnt skin highly visible. On his expressionless, pitch-dark face, I traced the mark of a scar, which spread across his right temple down his right cheek. Due to his dark complexion, the scar was almost indistinguishable.

He seemed out of place being so visible, sitting on a tool near the open door. He didn't make eye contact with any of us. His gigantic, vicious pet, Bagha, rested its long snout on the ground beside him, sleepily gazing into nothingness, just like his master.

How can he just be like this? He just stabbed a man to death.

"Prithuda, if you don't mind me asking," I said. He gave me a cold, lifeless stare. "What does Meghab Bhairab intend on doing with the girls?"

I immediately regretted asking the question, but nothing in Prithuda's face changed as moments passed.

"Questioning," he muttered, before looking away.

"What kind of questioning? Perhaps I—"

I felt a grip on my shoulder. Kuber Bhairab subtly shook his head. I got the message. I needed to stop asking questions.

We were all sitting on a minimalistic bed with a single blanket laid over the wooden framework. Bishnu was sitting with his back to the dirty wall, in the corner, with his face tucked into his knees. I pondered on the weight of the critical knowledge that I received about an hour ago: the girl they found in the cellar was no incarnation of Gods, no symbol or lesson—she was Bishnu's sister, who, unbeknownst to all of us, had been calling out to her brother all this time, in her own unique way.

Bishnu had known this all along and he'd chosen to keep his distance. Perhaps he didn't want the Bhairabs to know, or he didn't want to confront the reality that his childhood friend had dragged his psychologically-stunted sister into an underground cellar and kept her there for days. I wasn't sure at that time.

His eyes were shut. He had simply stopped communicating, which I desperately wanted him to. I wanted to tell him that it was not his fault that he was fighting against forces far greater than him. That his fishing spear wasn't enough to save his sister from the clutches a powerful, ruthless family.

I turned my gaze back towards the door and Prithuda was no longer there—just Bagha, sitting in its usual spot. I looked out the window to see him walking around.

Prithuda glanced at me and stopped, which made my heart skip a beat. In his hand was Bishnu's spear. He caressed the metal finish and the pointy top, which glistened in the moonlight. A furtive smirk formed on his face. He was toying with me. He was toying with all of us. He then turned around and went into the little bamboo-shaded latrine to the other side of the yard inside the southern house.

"At least he has the bodily functions of a normal human."

Kuber Bhairab's comment made me chuckle nervously. I looked at Bagha; the dog had closed its eyes in what seemed like a peaceful nap. But then I saw something that I wasn't expecting. A hand came from behind the door that opened outward, reached in and slowly picked up Bagha's leash, which was laying on the ground.

The owner of the hand stepped out a little, but I couldn't get a good look at him as the light, obstructed by the door, revealed only part of his face, covered with thick, greasy beard. The man carefully, but tightly, tied the leash to the door handle without waking Bagha with practiced precision. I heard a gasp from my side. Kuber Bhairab was looking on, too.

The figure finally emerged and walked very silently towards the latrine. In the dim light, he became fully visible. He wore dirty white clothes and had a head of long, curly hair and a face full of a thick, unorganized beard. He crouched and noiselessly tiptoed towards the latrine. He seemed familiar, but I couldn't quite recognize him. But Kuber Bhairab's anxious whisper gave my memory the assistance it needed.

"What are you doing, Babli?"

I glanced at the door. Bagha was still sleeping. Babu Bhairab reached the latrine and silently picked up Bishnu's spear, which was leaning on the bamboo wall. Right at that instant, the flap of the latrine snapped open and both Kuber Bhairab and I gasped. As Prithuda emerged, looking docile as usual, Babu Bhairab deftly pivoted behind the flap. That caused a slight rustle on the ground, which made Prithuda aware of another person's presence. By that time, Babu Bhairab had already positioned himself for what he was about to do.

The moment Prithuda turned and swung the flap back, he ran into Babu Bhairab's swinging spear. In the same fashion Meghab Bhairab had knocked Bishnu down, Babu Bhairab knocked Prithuda to the floor. Loud crack filled the silent void. Babu Bhairab stood on top of a motionless Prithuda, staring at us.

A lot of things happened within a very short space of time. First, I felt my heart jump into my throat as I heard a couple of loud barks; Bagha was finally up. The dog leaped fiercely at Babu Bhairab. But, in a fashion that would, on other occasions, be quite hilarious, the leash tightened on the door-handle and, the dog flipped backward, falling body first on the ground.

Babu Bhairab didn't stick around to entertain himself with the spectacle. He chucked the spear to the ground and ran out the main door of the southern house, yelling, "Biruda! Biruda! Biruda, I'm here. Biruda, I need you!"

As soon as Babu Bhairab disappeared from sight, I felt a jolt of movement behind me. I turned to see that Bishnu had flung himself out the door of our room. In a matter of seconds, he was outside, picking up his spear. I heard sounds from the southern house and at least a dozen men stormed out, spears in hand. Within a minute, the yard of the southern house had turned into a warzone.

Bagha finally got up and pulled hard on the leash but couldn't set itself free. Its viciously-defined muscles clenched. The men charged at Bishnu. I was about to run and join him, as I desperately wanted for him not to lose his life. But right then, in came Biruda with a large chunk of log—one of the leftovers from the wood he chopped for the funeral. He swung wildly, narrowly missing one man's jaw, but landing hard on the ribcage of the man beside him. The man fell to the ground, twisting in pain.

The message was clear: the two men were not about to let go without a fight and they were not easy targets. The men circled Bishnu and Biruda but kept their distance. Bishnu was holding his spear with sharp end forward and Biruda gripped his log tightly.

One of the men thrust the pointy end of his spear towards Biruda, but he side-stepped. Bishnu caught the spear and pulled it towards him. The man lost his balance, tumbled forward and ran into Biruda's upward-swinging log. His head popped upwards and ran into the butt of Bishnu's spear. Another man was down, this one motionless. The men increased the radius of their circle. Bagha kept barking away.

"Stop this nonsense!" Meghab Bhairab stepped out of the southern house. "Whatever ruckus you two are creating will achieve nothing. Just let me—"

Before he could say anything more, one of the windows on the ground floor of the southern house swung open and I heard a familiar voice.

"Shani!"

Whatever stability the situation had was gone as Bishnu charged towards Meghab Bhairab. The men weren't ready for it and couldn't catch him with their spear. However, they did manage to hold him back. In the process of keeping Bishnu contained, however, they turned their backs on Biruda, who came in swinging.

Within seconds, four more men were sent quivering to the ground before the remaining men finally managed to wrestle the log from Biruda's hands. But their long-range spears were of no use against Biruda up close. A couple of them still attempted to make it work by positioning themselves so that they could stick Biruda with the pointy ends. But Biruda used that split second to catch them and smashed their skulls against each other as they collapsed like a ton of bricks.

The remaining men then focused on holding Biruda in one place rather than fighting him. But Kuber Bhairab and I watched in horrified wonder as the muscular juggernaut used his trained strength and agility to pivot away from their holds and fought back. He took one man's hand and twisted it with a snap. The man cried out in pain and fell to the floor. He drove his elbow into the face of another, staggering him before finishing him off with his fist.

They were down to three men now, but one of them managed to run his spear in Biruda's left shin and it pierced right through to the other side. The man looked at his peers with a victorious smile and that was his mistake. As Biruda fell to his knee, he caught the man by his throat and brought him down with him. Screaming in agony and anger, he smashed his own head on the man's temple. The sickening thud made me shiver.

Only two men left, but they were the two holding Bishnu back from rushing Meghab Bhairab. They no longer had any leverage from their peers, which gave Bishnu the chance to kick one in the shin and set himself free. They tried to catch him, but Biruda, with the spear still tucked in his leg, flung his entire body weight on the two men, falling with them.

Meghab Bhairab watched in disbelief as his army of men thinned and the boy, whose sister he was keeping hostage, crashed onto him. He still had enough wit to catch Bishnu by the throat. When he reached for something in his pocket, I had finally seen enough.

A jolt of adrenaline surged into me and I flung myself out of the door past the barking Bagha, who was still tied to the door handle. My senses were sharp. I ran, anticipating that Meghab Bhairab might try to catch me by the throat as well. So, when he weakly extended his other arm to catch me, still trying to keep Bishnu at bay, I ducked low and spear-tackled him to the ground.

Bishnu, with nobody to stop him now, charged into the southern house and reemerged with Shani. I looked up to see Maaji at the doorway. Bishnu gripped Shani's hand tightly and they ran past the pile of stunned men, out of the door. Meghab Bhairab tried to take advantage of my lapse in concentration to grab at my throat, but I had decided that I had seen enough of this man today. I caught hold of his arm with my hands and bit his extended palm with every bit of strength I had in my body.

Meghab Bhairab winced in pain. I felt a bone joint dislodge under my teeth and tasted blood. I let go of his arm, stood up and kicked him in the side of his ribs without giving him a chance to recover. In the corner of my eye, I saw Biruda putting one man into a chokehold while the other was motionless on the ground.

Voices were coming from behind the southern house. More reinforcements were coming. I had no intention of dealing with them. So, I ran for the door. Before I got out, however, something metal struck my foot. It was Bishnu's fishing spear. I picked it up and went out of the door, running north where I could see that Babu Bhairab, Bishu and Shani had already covered some distance.

"All of you, follow me," Babu Bhairab said when I made it to the group.

I turned back momentarily to see Prithuda stepping out of the door of the southern house. He looked at us with a cold, piercing stare as we disappeared into the dense bushland.

47 A WHISPER IN THE WIND

"Still not talking to me, are you?" Babu Bhairab called out to Bishnu as he untied the little steamer boat from a protruding slab of rock on the ground.

Bishnu cast a tired glance at Babu Bhairab. We were in what seemed like the strangest little boatshed I had ever been in, outside of a muddy little cave, tucked into the wild bushland on the north-eastern fringe of the island. A small gas lamp was hanging above me, on the root of a tree curving down from the woodland above. At the furthest end of the cave, Bishnu was sitting with Shani in his arms on a dirty blanket that was already there, along with the lamp.

We'd reached the cave through some of the thickest bushes I had ever seen. Babu Bhairab led us as Bishnu deftly guided Shani through. It was obvious that they had traversed this terrain before. I followed them as branches swung at my face, thorny bushes tore into my clothes and skin and wet soil stifled my progress. The only thing that kept me going was the thought that there was no way I'd let Meghab Bhairab's find us.

A sudden burst of fury made me jump into a life-threatening combat, but now that I was out of that situation, I wanted nothing to do with our pursuers. Yet, I felt no fear, but rather cathartically liberated from it.

I looked eagerly at Babu Bhairab, untying the rope to set his little boat free. The boat shook in a jittery motion in the waves of the river.

"Your rotten-wood boat is going to sink us all in the middle of the river." Bishnu's annoyed voice echoed my concern.

"Finally, he speaks!" Babu Bhairab muttered. "Well, my boat is good enough for all of us. I made it myself."

"Yeah, that's exactly why I'm worried," Bishnu snapped back.

Babu Bhairab responded to the banter with a chuckle. "It will take us where we need to go, fast, without making too much noise. If I took

Ustadji's larger boat, it would have been too loud and we wouldn't have been able to accomplish what we have so far. Now stop whining and come on board. My engine is primed and ready."

"That is, if it doesn't blow off the side of the boat first," Bishnu commented.

"Look, do you really have a choice?" Babu Bhairab said as he splashed water around the side of the boat to clean off the muck. He took the rope in one hand and came forward a couple of steps. "Now stop being difficult and get in."

Bishnu gave Babu Bhairab another cold stare before getting up with Shani.

"We still need to do something about Nondi." I said.

Babu Bhairab smiled at me while helping Bishnu and Shani into the boat. "We will," he said confidently. "We'll come back and take care of her. I have it planned out. Meghabda has his army and I have mine. Now, if you don't mind, my dear guest, take that kerosene lamp and come join us."

"Out of the question," came Bishnu's sharp voice. "If we take a light source with us, that will attract Meghabda's men and we'll be bringing death on ourselves."

"Stop being so dramatic, Bishnu," Babu Bhairab said. "I need the light to guide this boat. If you don't want it to sink, don't let me propel it in pitch darkness. Besides, you know very well that Meghabda and his men have no idea where we are. By the time they see our light, we'll be too far gone. I told you, I've planned for everything." He looked at me. "Come now. Our little excursion is over. We need to get going."

I carefully dislodged the kerosene lamp from the protruding tree root and joined them on the boat. The boat was quite minimalistic. The deck was without a husk, lined with wooden slates. A dirty bamboo mat barely covered it.

After sliding his spear in along the side of the boat, Bishnu settled himself at the opposite end to the engine, where there was some room for him to rest his back with Shani in his arms. I sat in the middle and Babu Bhairab sat near the engine, taking the kerosene lamp from me and placing it carefully on a bamboo hanger attached to the boat. When he started the engine, the boat lurched forward with a terrifying jolt. Bishnu shrugged faintly.

The engine cut through the water aggressively, quickly creating distance from the shoreline. The water wasn't as clear and sparkly as it was on the other side of the river. It was murky.

"That cave fills up every rainy season," Babu Bhairab said, observing me looking at my surroundings. "The soil gets eaten away by the water as the shoreline is eroded. One day, that cave we've just left will collapse. Only the large tree's strong roots are holding the ground up. Don't worry, though. The soil will eventually come back to replenish the shore.

"We could build a dam here to stop the erosion, but nobody cares about this side of the isle. It's murky and ugly. We all love nature, as long as nature looks pretty. We don't really care if it's not easy on the eyes. That's a good thing, you know? The ugly parts are where things thrive most beautifully because no one cares to bend them to their will."

"Our Babuda, with his pearls of wisdom." Bishnu's sarcastic voice joined the conversation. "Answering life's great questions—not bothering to answer the simple ones."

Babu Bhairab looked away towards the dark horizon. His face hardened. "I brought her there so that Bhairabs learn their lessons," he said, to which Bishnu shrugged. Babu Bhairab stared at him with annoyance. "Stop being a coward, Bishnu!"

"You're calling me a coward?"

"I am."

"After all you've done. Running away from the island. Not bothering to show up at your own father's funeral. Leaving us in a dangerous situation that manifested as a direct result of your actions, which you took due to some kind of twisted logic of your own making. After all that, *you* are calling *me* a coward?"

"I am a coward, too. I've never denied it. That doesn't mean you're not one as well."

Bishnu stared at Babu Bhairab—nostrils flared and eyes narrow and sharp. He looked like he might just jump on Babu Bhairab.

"Yes, you finally got around to confronting the people who wronged you," Babu Bhairab went on. "But that came after I ensured that you had no other option. You lived in fear for years, hoping that someday these people would accept you for who you really are. You chose the peaceful option instead of taking action. These are all actions of a coward."

Bishnu contorted his face in disgust and turned it away. "I like to believe in the good in people," he said. "I looked up to Babaji. He saw me as a stray child and gave me a purpose. He let me be friends with you, Kuberda and Nondi. I had nobody." He paused, pursing his lips together. "Babaji gave me a childhood when I didn't have one."

"And he would have just as easily murdered you, if at any point he knew who you really were," Babu Bhairab commented.

"No! You don't know—"

"And if he didn't murder you, his monster of a son definitely would have. You never understood the danger you were always in, Bishnu. Nondi and I did, but you didn't. You and Kuberda wanted to bring Piplidi in, explain everything to Babaji. You expected him to show you grace. You, along with Kuberda, wanted to put yourself in the same danger you've been running away from for all your life. For what? For some misplaced idea that you can make people who slaughtered families have the heart to hear your plea? And you blame me for having twisted logic."

The silence that followed was frightful. It felt as if the whole river had gone mute—no splashing noises, just the thudding sound of the engine.

"Well," Babu Bhairab finally said. "I did what you wished for. I brought her in and look what happened. Meghabda went berserk, as expected. He murdered his own father, murdered an innocent man and took Nondi hostage. How else did you expect it to go down?"

Bishnu stared at Babu Bhairab, dumbfounded. "So, your reasoning for bringing my sister to that cellar was to prove a point to me? That's why you put all our lives in danger?"

"No, that's not why," Babu Bhairab replied instantly. "I did it to teach my family a lesson. They talk about how some hidden treasure is going to revive their name. Well, I think if they really want to redeem themselves, they should start by confronting their own wrongdoings."

"I don't understand," Bishnu said. "It was you and Nondi who advised Kuberda and me not to make Babaji aware of my sister, not to appeal to his good nature and tell him the truth. You didn't want me to do that, but you think it was right to bring her in unnoticed and put her into an underground cellar…so you can teach people lessons?"

Babu Bhairab smiled at Bishnu, who was breathing heavily in rage. "You do-gooders think in such simple terms, don't you?" he muttered. "Doing good isn't simple. It's not even the popular choice most of the time, because the world conspires to make it as hard as it possibly can for you to make that choice. When you decide to take action against a corrupt design, you often need to take the harder path. You have to do the unthinkable."

Bishnu stared at Babu Bhairab in confounded silence, but he went on. "People who turn into monsters aren't easy to defeat. You should neither run away from them nor should you try to appeal to their humanity, for they don't have any. The only way to make them do the right thing is to manipulate their conscience. Make them self-aware. Conscience is the only bit of humanity left in them, so that's what you need to work with.

"That's what I did with Babaji. I knew about his insecurity, how he talked about his dreams to Maaji. How he repented. So, I changed the environment around him to give him the idea that his crimes had come back to haunt him. I brought in ghosts from his past and had them recite to him his own dream. I made sure that, when he went down to that cellar looking for redemption, the only thing he would face was his own treacherous past.

"And it changed him. He spent his last few days as an honest man, as a man of toil. You wanted to change him by appealing to his humanity. I did it by manipulating his conscience. And who made real progress? Me!"

Bishnu remained speechless.

"It takes tremendous ego for a family to think that their name deserves to be redeemed, when all they've done is take what isn't theirs," Babu Bhairab said. "So, they must pay. If they want redemption, they must make up for what they did."

Bishnu's face no longer held the fuming rage it had minutes ago. Instead, he looked at Babu Bhairab in stunned wonder. "You talk about the Bhairabs as if you're not one of them,"

"Am I?" Babu Bhairab said. "You've seen me since I was a child. Have they ever acted like I was part of their family? They treated me like I was some kind of prop—the crown jewel of the Bhairab family. Distant relatives came to the estate asking, 'where is that deboshishu of yours?'" Babu Bhairab's voice started to shake. He took a moment to settle himself.

"They brought me in to parade me around, so that these sycophants could praise my milky white skin in the hope of getting some drippings from the generous Bhairab ego. Well, look at me now!" He spread his arms wide. "I am in dirty rags, face full of beard, hair all greasy and long. Am I ugly enough now for them to finally listen to me?"

Bishnu stared at Babu Bhairab in astonishment. "Who are you?" He spoke finally. "I...I don't know you anymore."

With the sleeve of his dirty white fotua, Babu Bhairab wiped his eyes. His heavy breathing made me realize that he had been trying to stop himself from breaking down. He muttered something under his breath.

"What?" Bishnu snapped out.

"I'm sorry," he whispered a bit louder.

Bishnu took a deep breath and closed his eyes for what felt like forever. "It's okay," he said finally. He looked at his sister, who was in deep slumber in his embrace.

Everything went silent for a while. The mechanical sound of the engine filled the void.

"Did you get to see Babaji's funeral?" Babu Bhairab inquired.

Bishnu nodded. "Yes," he lied. "He looked peaceful."

"Did he look happy when he was giving away the winter crops?".

"He did," Bishnu replied.

"That's progress," Babu Bhairab commented with a nod.

"I don't know if I'll ever understand you, Babuda!" Bishnu said. "You and your...thinking."

They smiled at each other silently.

"Well, we've given our honored guest quite a show, haven't we? How have you been coping, silent observer?" Babu Bhairab looked at me, smiling. "I took you for a town-dwelling, indulgent weakling, but you showed a lot of courage today. Very few people have the courage to physically combat my vicious older brother."

"I decided I'd had enough of him for the night," I replied. "...and the island, for the matter."

"Don't we all?" Babu Bhairab said, as we all broke into a nervous laughter.

I looked at Babu Bhairab. Despite the thick, mossy beard and long, dirty hair, he looked quite beautiful, which was tragic, given that he'd just proclaimed that his beauty had worked to his detriment all his life. In the light from the kerosene lamp, his pale face glowed. His ruffled, long, curly hair hadn't lost its raven-dark consistency, despite the lack of care. It drew intricate shadows on his face. Seeing Babu Bhairab at that moment in the light of the kerosene lamp, would become etched in my memory, for what happened next changed me forever.

The air whispered dreadfully with the sound of something piercing the darkness. Before I realized what was happening, Babu Bhairab's dirty white fotua split open and a gush of blood flickered onto my face.

Something dark protruded from a narrow gash just above his stomach. His laughter halted and his body gave out almost instantaneously. He clung on to the bamboo stand that held the kerosene lamp to keep himself from falling into the water. I got up to help him down and he fell face-first onto my lap. A spear was sticking out of his back.

A glimmer of light hit my face and I heard the sound of a second steamer boat, louder than ours. I saw Prithuda standing there without a hint of emotion on his face. He was covered in a grey shawl, but his right hand, which he had just used to throw the spear, was partially visible.

I looked at the kerosene lamp, still hanging on the bamboo stand. Bishnu had been right; the light had brought death upon us. Babu Bhairab lay face down on the deck. The other boat was approaching at a greater speed than ours. After exchanging a cold stare with me, Prithuda knelt down to the deck of his boat to pick up what I presumed was another weapon.

The burst of rage that had fueled me to run into Meghab Bhairab returned. I felt my nerves boil. I jolted myself up, making our small boat rock precariously.

"What are you—" Bishnu said in confusion, as he held onto the boat. Shani had woken up and looked on with the same expression.

I took the kerosene lamp from the bamboo stand, held it by its handle and slung it hard at Prithuda. He'd just straightened up with a knife in his hand and managed to partially get out of the way. The lamp hit his right elbow and the glass that held the flame inside crashed onto the deck of his boat. Kerosene spilled out of the broken container and set the deck near Prithuda on fire, along with a corner of his shawl, which grazed the deck. The fire wasn't big enough to cause any major damage, but it was enough to make Prithuda lose his footing. As he tumbled away from the fire while removing himself from his burning shawl. Right then, I felt a strong shove from behind me.

I tumbled forward onto Babu Bhairab's wounded body and had to catch hold of the protruding spear to keep my balance. I put most of the weight on my left knee, which pressed against Babu Bhairab's right shoulder. I was relieved to feel weak, irregular breathing under my knee.

The other boat was running parallel to ours now and Prithuda had managed to regain his footing. But, as soon as he turned around, he ran right into Bishnu's spear, which plunged in just beneath his chest. The momentum of Prithuda's boat worked against him. Helped along with Bishnu's forward motion with ill-intent, the spear was thrust further in.

Prithuda took a step backward, staring at his slayer with a vapid expression. Holding on to the spear that pierced him with one hand, he raised his other knife-hand and swung weakly. His target, however, was way out of reach. Bishnu's face contorted, full of hate.

"Die, whoreson! Die already!" Bishnu muttered.

Prithuda had to take further steps back to accommodate for the boat, which was moving away from underneath him. His boat floated past us. He ran out of ground to stand on and splashed into the dark water, but Bishnu still didn't let go.

Prithuda's twisting, flinging body sank as Bishnu forced the spear down, muttering, "Die," and "go to hell," under this breath. I heard some gurgling noises and struggle from beneath the water. Bishu's spear twisted violently, but he maintained his grip.

A cluster of small bubbles surfaced, followed by a few large ones. Then it all stopped. No more struggle. No more bubbles. Bishnu finally let go. Only then, I realized that this was all happening in motion when I saw Bishnu's dark fishing spear protruding from the water, fading further away from us into pitch darkness.

I looked up ahead. Prithuda's boat was now about a hundred feet ahead of us, lighting up the darkness with a dying flicker of flame.

48 A SLAYING OF DEMONS

"Keep it, don't throw it," said Bishnu, when I finally managed to get the spear out of Babu Bhairab's back.

I nodded and placed it in the same place where Bishnu had kept his fishing spear before. I felt a couple of rough coughs under the palm of my hand.

"Buji!" Shani cried out.

I flipped Babu Bhairab over, carefully sliding his head and shoulders onto my thighs as I slipped underneath him, resting my back on the side of the boat. Bishnu had placed himself near the engine and his sister sat beside me. I looked at Babu Bhairab. He was pressing on the wound on his abdomen tightly with his left hand, while coughing up blood.

"Bujiiiiii–" Shani started whimpering.

Babu Bhairab weakly extended a hand, which she came forward and held.

"We will get you back to Tadiji, okay?" Babu Bhairab said, breathing with a lot of effort. His face contorted as tears ran down it. "I am sorry, Piplidi! I'm sorry." He gazed at Shani with trembling lips. He then looked at Bishnu and me with deep sorrow in his eyes. "I apologize to all of you." He coughed with all the strength he had and a thick gush of blood ran out of his mouth. "For whatever I have put you–"

"Stop talking and keep pressure on that wound," Bishnu cried out. "We'll reach Ustadji's island soon and wrap you up."

"There's no point," Babu Bhairab said.

"Stop talking!" Bishnu snapped.

"My time has come."

"SHUT YOUR MOUTH, YOU MISERABLE BASTARD!"

"Bishnu–"

"Shut up!"

"Bishnu, just listen for once, instead of lecturing me. Come closer."

Bishnu looked at Babu Bhairab intensely. Then he slowly approached his dying childhood friend and sat beside me. Babu Bhairab coughed a few more times, wringing out all the strength in his body. He kept talking, though, this time merely in a whisper.

"All my life, I drank so much…I drank because I felt this pain in me. This monster that ate away my humanity, my peace. I wanted to kill it, so I drank all that poison." He coughed again before breathing in with a lot of effort. "But tonight, I feel that I am finally hit with something strong enough to slay that monster." He looked at Bishnu and grinned with bloody lips. "Now, I'm free!"

"Stop talking," Bishnu whispered.

"Bishnu, Bishnu-re!" Babu Bhairab said, at which tears finally broke out from Bishnu's eyes. "Take Piplidi to Ustadji, okay? Will you do that for me?"

Bishnu looked at Babu Bhairab and nodded, wiping his face with his elbow.

"And then, you need to get Nondi off that island," Babu Bhairab said, in the faintest of whimpers.

The two childhood friends nodded at each other. They understood.

"Summer's coming soon. I will miss all those mangoes this year," Babu Bhairab said as a subtle smile formed on his face. He looked sideways, towards the distant, rising sun. His gaze didn't shift to anything else from that point on.

49 PIPALI

"Her name is Pipali. Babu called her Piplidi."

Bishnu was guiding the boat, while Shani, now introduced to me as Pipali, whimpered on my shoulders, saying, "Buji," intermittently. She was almost weightless, as if a strong gust might whisk her away any moment. I put my arm around her shoulders lightly, driven by that irrational fear. I had seen three deaths that night and I wasn't ready to experience any more loss.

"Must have been awful to know that your little sister was stuck in that cellar," I said.

"She is not my little sister. She's a couple of years older than me. She came to this world around the same time he did." He motioned towards Babu Bhairab's body on my lap. It almost felt like he wasn't looking at me, but into the distance, with a saddened, stoic gaze. He wasn't a fisherman-boy anymore. He was a man, burdened with the weight of the world.

"I guess one upside is that Kuberda didn't get to see this," Bishnu said. "He loved his little brother with all his heart. Kuberda never had any influence over his parents, but Meghabda had an affinity towards him. All his life, Kuberda had used that affinity to keep Meghabda from harming Babuda. All that effort went to waste. Meghabda's monster finally got to him." Bishnu shook his head and closed his eyes.

I brought my eyes towards Babu Bhairab's lifeless body, resting on my thighs. For reasons I didn't understand back then, I straightened Babu Bhairab up. I turned his head back to a neutral position. He was still covering the gaping wound in his stomach with his left hand, but I adjusted it so that it wasn't visible. The blood under his palm was still warm. I wiped his bloody cheeks clean with my cloth.

After I was done, Babu Bhairab looked like he was just taking a nap on my lap. *What an absurd concept! Babu Bhairab wasn't the kind of person who would ever take a nap on anybody's lap, let alone mine.* I looked at him intently. *Or maybe he is that kind of a person, now that his monster is slain.*

"Kuberda is older than all of us. A good five years older than Pipali and Babuda. He doesn't look like it, but he is," Bishnu said, looking at me with a dry smile on his face as he observed me straightening up the body of his departed childhood friend. "When Babuda was a couple of years old, around the time when I was born, the Bhairabs adopted Nondi as a little girl." Bishnu gave a weak chuckle. "Nondi, Pipali, Babu and I. The four of us played together in the woods all day. We were inseparable."

"What about Kuberda?"

Bishnu smiled at my question. "No, Kuberda very rarely crossed the river. Maaji used to take Babuda and Nondi to the mainland, but Kuberda mostly stayed at the estate with Biruda, or in the temple with Ponditji. He never met Pipali, all these years, until–"

"–a few months ago," I finished the sentence.

Bishnu nodded. "For all the enthusiasm Kuberda has in his heart, he had never really gotten to see much of the world beyond the island. A tragic irony."

The whimpering on my shoulders had subsided. Pipali had cried herself to sleep.

"Pipali is…not like everybody else. She doesn't talk to everybody. The only people she opens up to are the three of us—Nondi, Babu and I. Her Didi, Buji and Shani."

I smiled at Bishnu and looked at Pipali. She seemed quite peaceful.

"She doesn't communicate with the world the way everybody else does. But she, in her own way, can reciprocate the way others behave towards her very well. If you show her that you care for her, she will trust you and care for you too. She's very sensitive to her environment. She knows when the world around her is friendly, dangerous, accepting or isolating and she behaves accordingly."

I understood that it was Bishnu's way of saying thank you, but he clarified it anyway.

"I am very thankful that you're here with us at this moment," he said. "If you weren't here right now, I don't know how I would be able to help Pipali. She doesn't react very well to violence." He looked up. "We're here."

we were approaching the shore of a small, bare island that rose up from the waters and at the tip of the island, behind a few trees, I saw the outline of a small hut.

"Tadiji."

I heard a whisper. Pipali had woken up. She took a nervous gulp and squeezed my hand. Bishnu parked the boat on the shore, on which two bamboos were firmly planted on the smooth, sandy shoreline. One had a larger steamer-engine boat tied to it. Bishnu tied our own vessel to the other. He then helped Pipali down from the boat.

"Wait here," he said and quickly guided Pipali up the island and into the hut.

The island poked out of the water, quite close to the mainland. It was clear that the hut ahead of me was the only habitation on it. On the other side, the mainland's shoreline loomed with thick woodland. But on the island, tall trees stood few and far between, looking like the lonesome silhouettes of broken statues in the early-morning light.

"I TOLD HIM! I TOLD HIM AND HE DIDN'T LISTEN."

A broken, familiar voice echoed across the water. The door of the shack at the top of the island burst open and a bearded man stormed out, with Bishnu behind him. I recognized him instantly. It was the man who ran the restaurant at the fringe of Choubazaar, where Babu Bhairab had told me about The Gathering.

He ran towards the boat with terror in his eyes. Ignoring my presence, he got down in the shallow waters and stood in front of the boat I was in with Babu Bhairab's body resting on my lap. His face was full of dread. He leaned forward and held Babu Bhairab's motionless, cold hand.

"How in God's grace am I going to explain this to Aru?" he muttered.

He looked up, but I knew that he wasn't really looking at me. His eyes were pondering.

"We cannot be here," he muttered finally and turned to Bishnu. "Bishnu, help me transfer Babli to the big boat." He looked at me, this time with intent. "You…go to the hut and get Pipali to the opposite side of the isle. Bring the blanket on the bed and close the door behind you. Bishnu and I will have to drag the boat around the isle."

I nodded and made my way to do as he'd bid.

50 A CRUELTY IN MOTHERHOOD

Bishnu lied to me about coming to the northern shores of the Great Green Lake. He didn't come here as a fisherman; he came here as a brother, as a protector. He lied to me, but I well understood why. I looked at him. The world of this day-dreaming, story-telling fisherman-boy had become much more real. He only barely managed to break his sister out of the clutches of the Bhairabs and had just lost his childhood friend at the hands of the remorseless henchman of a power-hungry psychopath. He looked dejected and broken as he sat with his head sunk on his knees.

A few feet away from us, under the husk, laid the lifeless body of Babu Bhairab, covered with a blanket. Ustadji was sitting beside it with Pipali in his arms. I heard her faintly whisper, "Buji," every now and then, with light sobbing.

"Close your eyes, Bhatiji[lxxi]. We will get you home," said Ustadji, repeatedly.

The isle that we had just left was less than a couple of hundred meters from the heavily-wooded northern shores of the Great Green Lake. Our steamer boat was barely about fifteen paces from the shoreline.

"Can't we go faster?" I asked.

Our much larger boat was going at about the same pace as Babu Bhairab's small boat had a few hours ago. I wasn't feeling comfortable with that slow speed. Getting into the open waters in the prevailing light of day ran the risk of bumping into men with evil intentions.

"The engine doesn't have enough depth in the water underneath to leverage itself forward, as it could if we were in deeper waters," Bishnu explained. "So, this is the fastest we can go, unfortunately. But don't worry—we won't be long."

I nodded. The dawn was breaking and the environment was

becoming clearer, which only made me more anxious. Piercing calls of owls startled me every now and then, but I knew that those, too, would subside as daylight prevailed.

"We were separated because our lives depended on it." Bishnu's voice snapped me back from my trance.

I looked at him.

"I never told you about her. I tell very few people about my sister." He said.

"That's quite understandable."

"Being a fisherman gave me a good excuse to frequent this part of the village. But with all that was going on with Babuda and Nondi surrounding The Gathering and my responsibility of looking after you, I became engrossed in other things and didn't have the time to visit. I had no idea Babuda was taking advantage of my absence to…do all this."

He sank his face in his knees again. I got close to him and put my hand on his back. His body was trembling. He was weeping silently. After about a minute, he looked up, quickly rubbing his eyes.

"I cannot break down now," Bishnu said. "If I break down, Pipali will break down with me."

"I think Pipali is stronger than you give her credit for," I said. "She survived being alone in an underground cellar for days; I think she can handle you shedding a few tears over your best friend."

Bishnu looked at me and gulped.

"And besides, you're not alone, Bishnu," I continued. "I'm here. Ustadji is here. You don't have to carry your burden alone."

Bishnu kept quiet. Tears started to form in his eyes, which he immediately wiped away. "I don't even know if I did the right thing…" he said, finally. "Keeping her away from the world. I feared for her life and mine, but keeping her away in an isolated place like this meant that she had no exposure to society.

"She was born with fear and desolation imprinted in her mind. She has the capacity to trust and care for the people who show acceptance, but almost all her life, all she's learned is that if she comes out into the world, she would put both herself and the people she cares for in danger."

I sighed and kept my hand on his back.

"The only way I realized that I could bring Pipali out into the world was to find acceptance among the very people we were running away from. So, as a child, with a mind full of mortal fear, I gathered up the courage to bring myself to face Babaji. I figured if he does anything to me, it will only be me. But, if he decides to accept me despite who I am, I could perhaps bring my sister to the mainland. I did it for Pipali."

"That was very brave, Bishnu."

"But neither of the scenarios I'd thought of played out. He didn't even seem to recognize me and I couldn't muster up the courage to tell him my real name. He let me be friends with his children. He gave me jobs and cared for my wellbeing. He looked for me every time he came to the mainland, to make sure I was all right.

"That's when I met Kuberda for the first time and I was reunited with Babuda since I escaped. But by that time, he had changed. I saw the seed to his path of destruction already planted in him." He glanced towards Babu Bhairab's corpse. "The path that led him here." He looked away, towards the water. "If I was only more present in his life—"

"You couldn't have been," I interrupted. "You had too many things to take care of all at once. You cannot be in all places at the same time."

Bishnu looked at me. I nodded in assurance. He went on.

"Over time, just like Dadaji, Babaji became someone I looked up to. The two of them never saw eye to eye. He knew that I was being cared for by Dadaji, but he never made the connection. He saw me as one of his children.

"As I grew up, I told Babuda and Kuberda about my intention to introduce Pipali to Babaji. Kuberda agreed and told me that he would handle things on the inside, but Babuda forbade me. He told me never to trust the Bhairabs. So, I grew up, torn between decisions. I just never had the courage."

"Don't tell me you don't have courage, Bishnu. If you didn't have it, you wouldn't have made it this far," I said, almost instinctively. "You're showing great courage right now. In fact, your courage is teaching me how to be brave. So, don't demean yourself."

Bishnu breathed in and looked at me. "You think so?"

"Of course."

Bishnu clenched his jaw, nodding to reassure himself. I breathed a sigh of relief. He steadied himself and spoke in a tranquil voice.

"The earliest memory I have as a child is the face of my mother and that of Pipali. I used to lay awake in the corner of my home, looking at mother making us supper. The thick forest mist would come in from the open door and coagulate with the smoke coming out of the boiling rice pot. The aroma of bubbling rice and freshly cut vegetables filled the room. Pipali and I would look on eagerly.

"'Will baapjan[lxxii] come home to eat with us?' I would ask.

"'Not tonight,' would be the answer, most nights. 'Your baapjan is busy with the protest.' I didn't fully understand what that meant; I had never seen my father too often and even when I saw him, he carried this unsettling anxiety and paid little attention to us. On most nights, he would come home late, after my mother had settled both of us in bed. Pipali used to sleep like an angel, but I would only pretend to be asleep, listening to my parents arguing in whispers. I would hear words and broken phrases like, 'gone too far,' 'must run away,' and 'my livelihood.'

"The next morning, Pipali and I would wake up to see that our father had long gone and mother curled up in bed, with dried tear marks on her cheeks. I used to wonder, all the time, who my father really was. Why he worried so much and what was keeping him from being with us.

"'Your baapjan is occupied with important matters,' my mother used to assure me. 'When you grow up, you will understand.' But I wanted to understand right then. I used to slip out of bed at night when everyone was asleep to look at my father. He looked...almost like a different person. When his face was relaxed of all the anxiety he usually carried, he seemed content. I once peeked into the bag he carried. It held so many things I didn't understand. Lightweight, sharp things. Blunt, heavy things. Things wrapped in cloth. Fragrant leaves tied in strings. I wanted to understand who my father was because, to me, he was nothing but the ghost of an unknown man.

"'Just you wait, Shanu. Once this protest is over, he will be back to normal,' Mother would say. 'He will play with you. Tell you beautiful stories. Teach you things. Wonderous things! He's just in a slump at the moment, but he will come out of it, believe me.' But that day never came." Bishnu stopped there and drew a deep breath. He looked back at the husk to see Pipali resting peacefully in Ustadji's arm. His eyes were breaking tears again. I knew then that his real name was Shanu and that's the name his sister was calling him in all those times in the Bhairab estate.

"You don't have to tell me any of this, Bishnu," I said.

"But I want to. I want you to know."

"Okay."

Bishnu looked at the waters as he went on. "On a familiar, winter night, mother was cooking dinner for us. I was dozing off, feeling tired from playing in the forest all day. I was content and peaceful, not knowing that everything in my life was about to change forever. I was jolted awake by a loud thud and a cry of pain in a male voice.

"'Shani?' Pipali said, sleepily. I looked in disbelief towards the other end of the room, to the kitchen, where the noise had come from. My mother had flung her hot cooking pot at someone. The man was small in stature and was holding the handle of the door with his left hand to keep his balance. His right arm was covering his face, which had just been splashed with boiling rice-water. In his right hand, he wielded a large butcher-knife. Its sharp edges glimmered in the light from the kerosene lamp.

"'Get out, you whoreson!' my mother screamed as she pushed at him with all her strength. He fell backward and out the door, which she quickly closed. I heard footsteps coming from the distance. Within seconds, loud slams were threatening to break open the door, which was held shut by a mere wooden slate.

"Mother ran to us, jumped on the bed and opened the window wide.

'Listen to me, Shanu,' she told me. 'Take Pipali and climb out of the window.'

"'Maajan[lxxiii]...' I said in confusion. With my child's instinct, I tried to grab hold of her, but she tore herself out of my embrace and pushed me out of the window in one swift motion. I had never felt that much strength in a human body before. After I landed clumsily on the tall grass, out came Pipali as well. Thankfully, she was much lighter than I anticipated and I managed to catch hold of her.

"'Run! Now!' she whispered to us. 'Run to the forest. Maajan will come for you.' That was a lie. After ten paces into the forest, we heard the loud crack of the door breaking and Maajan's scream.

"'Maajan!' Pipali tried to cry out, but I put my hand over her mouth. I was only a child of four, but the way my own mother had denied me her embrace snapped me out of the dream of being a child and into the dangers of reality. I knew, from there on, that it was up to me to look after Pipali."

51 A CARRIAGE OF MOURNING

"Wait here," Ustadji said. He jumped down from the boat and disappeared in the shabby-looking shed on the shore of the Great Green Lake.

"That's Ustadji's storehouse," commented Bishnu.

I heard something heavy being moved. Ustadji came out with a large cart that carried a folded yellow ochre blanket.

"Bishnu," he shouted. "We need to move quickly."

Bishnu pulled the boat parked on the shore in towards the land. I joined him. We got almost half of it on the shore and it became stable, compared to the way it had been jolting lightly with the waves.

Ustadji brought the cart close to it, opened the yellow ochre blanket and spread it open on the cart. Then, with the aid of Bishnu, he carefully carried Babu Bhairab's body onto the cart and wrapped the entirety of it tightly within the blanket. During the whole process, Ustadji kept frantically looking ahead into the river and sideways along the shoreline, like an animal being hunted. Daylight was about to conquer the last bit of darkness.

"Come," Ustadji said, as he settled himself at the front handle of the cart. "We need to disappear into Hizrapara as soon as possible. Pipali maa[lxxiv], walk beside me."

The two of us pushed the cart from behind, while Ustadji pulled it forward. We rolled the cart over the uneven patches of grass. Ahead of me, clumps of wild banana trees and bushes were scattered across the landscape. To my right, about a hundred paces away, I saw that the riverbank had cut sharply inwards, ending in a bend that had a long, plain slab of stone. To the side of the slab, a clothing line was tied between bamboo stands, carrying a couple of blouses and a dhuti that flapped quietly in the wind.

"Push harder!" Ustadji's crackling voice startled me back into what I was doing. "We need to get deeper in, as soon as possible."

After a hundred more meters, the landscape abruptly changed to dense woodland. The ground felt solid, held together by the roots of trees. Up ahead, I saw trees in lines and tiers as far as the eye could see.

It didn't seem, at first, like there were any sign of civilization anywhere. But as we went further in, lights of distant cottages flickered. We reached a clearing that had a clump of huts, strewn about in an unorganized fashion. Among them, muddy pathways were made easier to tread on with, with slabs of stones and tree barks. We stopped in front of the first of those pathways.

Even though the daylight had already broken near the shore, the sleepy locality simmered in foggy darkness with beams of sunlight penetrating through the dense tree-lines

"O, Nasrin! Nasrin re!" Ustadji cried out, in a broken, shaky voice. "Nasrin, come out here. God's wrath has befallen us!"

The first thing I heard in Hizrapara was an infant's piercing cry after Ustadji announced our presence. A skinny child came out of the closest hut, where the crying was coming from and stared at us. From one of the shacks in the middle, a muscular-looking woman came running out in a blouse and petticoat. I recognized her instantly.

"What happened, Ustadji?" she said. But her momentum stopped short when she saw the cart. Her eyes widened. "No!" she muttered. "Babu?"

Ustadji nodded with his face distorted in pain. The man who had been keeping us from mortal danger broke down into a sob.

"They killed him, Nasrin," he said, in a shattered voice. "They killed our boy! I warned him. I warned him for years not to defy them so much. They finally killed him."

For a few seconds, he kept whimpering as Nasrin looked on, silent and stunned. Then I saw her face distort, as well, as tears came down.

"Nituda!" she cried out. "Nituda re! They have killed Babu. Our Babu is dead!"

She came forwards and clutched Ustadji's fotua with her left hand while holding the rails of the cart with her right. She then hastily loosened the yellow ochre blanket, revealing Babu Bhairab's motionless face.

"Allah re, they killed him!" She broke down crying. "Oh Allah, they killed him!"

"What are you saying, Nasrin?" I heard a gruff voice and quick footsteps.

The short moustachioed man I saw before with Babu Bhairab had come running and stood at the opposite side of the cart. He was bare from the waist up, wearing a dirty, white dhuti. He was silent for about a minute, looking down into the cart before I saw his jaws clench.

"Who did this?" He asked.

"Prithu, that wretched guard," answered Ustadji.

Nasrin was still leaning on the side of the cart, running her hand over the cheeks of Babu Bhairab's motionless face.

"Oh, Babu re! What happened to you? Oh, Allah, why?" She looked at the moustachioed man. "What do we do now, Nituda?"

"I will hunt him down," said Nituda, in a calm voice. "I will carve that whoreson's face. I don't care how many Bhairabs I have to go through—"

"I killed him," Bishnu said, holding Pipali in his arms. "Sank him to the bottom of the river."

"Pipali!" Nituda muttered. He glanced at Ustadji. "You brought her here?"

"She isn't safe on my island anymore," said Ustadji. "We need to hide here until sunset and then take Babu's body to Aru."

"That makes sense," Nituda said, nodding at Ustadji. He walked over to Bishnu and put his hand on Pipali's back. "Pipali maa?"

Pipali, with tearful eyes and trembling lips, extended her hand to Nituda, who clutched. "Buji," she murmured.

"I know, Pipali maa, I know," he said quietly. "Your Buji has left this Dunya. We need to send him off properly, so he can be on his way." He sighed and gazed at Bishnu. "So, you avenged him?"

Bishnu nodded.

"Good," Nituda said. He came over and put a hand on Nasrin, who was still sobbing. "Nasrin, get a hold of yourself," he said. "We need to take Babu's body inside. Come on." He glanced at Ustadji. "Taking him to Aru is the right thing to do. Babu needs a sendoff in his favorite garden."

Subtle sobs and wails made me aware of my surroundings. The entire locality had circled us. They were the same people who had circled Babu Bhairab the day I met him on the moor near Choubazaar; only now, they were in a drastically different mood. Nasrin calmly unfolded the yellow ochre blanket. When I glanced at Babu Bhairab's exposed body, its paleness struck me. It looked as if he was emitting a strange ambiance into the shadowy depth of the forest. He seemed out of place.

As we pushed the cart forward, people gathered around us. A muscular woman like Nasrin came forward, muttered a Muslim prayer into her hands and then ran them lightly around Babu Bhairab's cheeks. The crowd made way for a sickly old woman, who came forward, tore a piece of her blood-red shari and tied it around Babu Bhairab's wrist before leaving quietly. A dark, skinny boy around Bishnu's age came forward in uneven steps and tightly clutched Babu Bhairab's hands, saying, "Stay well in your journey, my brother," in an unsteady voice, before walking off, wiping his eyes with his elbows. People of all shapes and mannerisms came forward to bid their farewell.

It took us about half an hour just to cover about ten paces of distance with the cart to arrive in front of Nasrin's hut. I looked at Babu Bhairab again. His hair was ruffled. His hands were no longer settled at his sides, as many had grabbed his wrists. His dirty, white fotua was slightly torn at the neck. The ambiance he had been emitting had subsided quite a bit as his fair face had gained many smidges, as had the yellow ochre blanket beneath him.

He didn't seem out of place anymore. He seemed rather happy.

52 AN ABANDONED TREASURE

"Would you like to take the bed?" Nasrin calmly inquired.

"Absolutely not," I replied immediately. "Put him where he usually stays."

I didn't need any context. The moment I entered Nasrin's hut, I saw the typical interior of a common-folk home, with the bed tucked at the back and mud-built stoves close to the door. Only in the case of Nasrin's home, right beside the stoves was some simple bedding, made of bamboo mats and soft blankets.

While Bhairab's men scoured the district for Babu Bhairab, this was where he had been spending his days. No one needed to explain this to me. We carefully guided Babu Bhairab's body onto the floor-bed and covered him to his neck with the yellow ochre blanket.

"I'll finish off the batch. You look after the guests." Nituda's voice came from outside. Nasrin nodded. Nituda went to the stretched front yard of the house.

Daylight had finally illuminated the yard outside Nasrin's hut, which stood at the center of the whole locality, with a large yard, shared by the houses circling it. A large bamboo mat covered most of the yard and on top of it were white, lumpy molds that looked like chunks of overcooked rice. At the other end of the mat was a large, fire-wood powered stove that carried three thick, terracotta cauldrons, one on top of another.

Nituda carefully removed the top one and put it on the ground. He sank his hands into the middle one while holding a thick piece of wet cloth and cautiously pulled out a smaller, metal cauldron. He emptied its contents onto a piece of cloth, which was tied over the top of another terracotta container. Chunks of white mold spilled out onto the cloth, while smoky white liquid passed through. He then carefully untied the sieve, lifted it with the rice molds and emptied it in a wide wooden crate waiting nearby. He covered the terracotta container with a thick wooden slab and went into the tree line.

"I should have taken him back to the shoreline when he came to me all those years ago." Nasrin's voice was numb as she put a hand on Pipali's forehead.

Pipali was lying on the bed, eyes closed and Nasrin was sitting beside her, close to the edge of the bed, with her back against the wall. Bishnu sat at the foot of the bed with his head tucked in his arms. Ustadji was beside him, sitting in front of crates of bottles of different colors full of liquid.

"Perhaps that would have prevented this," Nasrin continued.

"Nothing would have prevented what was coming to him," Bishnu replied instantly. "This happened because of his actions, his alone."

"Perhaps if you weren't this rude to him and listened to what he really had to say...I mean *really* listened to him, you could have understood his pain."

Bishnu frowned at Nasrin. She looked back tiredly. "He gave his life for you..."

Bishnu remained silent for a while gazing towards the window. "Tell me, then..." he said, finally. "How did he give his life for me? He brought my sister to a hole in the ground and kept her there for days. He started a string of events that ended in three deaths and put all of us in grave danger." He stopped to catch his breath. "So, please, tell me, on what line of logic did he die for *me*, or for anyone else for that matter?"

"He did this for you, Bishnu," came the tired interruption from Ustadji. "He did all this in his own unique way, which may not have been all that prudent, but he ultimately did all this for you. He wasn't trying to humor himself. On some level, he was also doing it due to his deep-seated hatred for his own family, but this hatred and his care for you are intertwined in a messy little knot that is hard to separate. You know this better than anyone.

"He wasn't enjoying what he was doing, either. He was drinking more than usual. He would come to me and babble drunkenly in my front yard as Pipali and I would look on." Ustadji drew a deep breath. "And then, one day, he did the unthinkable. I came home at dawn, after closing off the store, to an empty house and a heavy iron chest dumped carelessly in the muddy puddle behind my tube-well, sunk partially into the mire.

"He bought Pipali from me in exchange for a chest full of gold jewelry, ruby-fitted silverware and precious stones—a treasure chest straight out of a fairytale. I knew instantly who was responsible. Believe me when I say this, Bishnu, no one was more enraged about this than I. I was going to chase after him, but I heard on the radio that a convict had escaped prison and I decided not to venture into the water. I couldn't risk getting in trouble. I have a bad reputation in the village for selling contraband drinks and I knew if the police caught me prowling about in the water, it would compromise everything I had been protecting. Babu knew this. He planned this all out deftly.

"He showed up about a week later, not with Pipali, but with the Pondit of that temple the Bhairabs own. He seemed defeated and guilty. The Pondit assured me that Pipali was being taken care of and that there were people on the isle who were ensuring that she wasn't harmed. But if I interfered, it might no longer be possible. He left Babu Bhairab with me, but I knew he wasn't going to stay and as soon as the priest left, he took his little boat and went off to Hizrapara, like I predicted.

"I'd predicted it because I knew that regardless of the nerve, he'd gathered to commit such an awful act, he didn't have the courage to justify those actions to me. I didn't care; I just wanted Pipali to be safe, so I kept out of his way. Nitu and Nasrin kept me informed on his behavior."

"I wasn't aware of what was going on, but I knew something was different. Something was awry, yet familiar." Nasrin took over from Ustadji. "He was trying to feign a stable mental state, but in his eyes, I saw the same isolation and desperation I'd seen all those years ago." She shook her head. "It feels like yesterday. He came to me when I was collecting firewood. His bright white fotua and dhuti were tainted with forest muck and tears ran down from his eyes. I knew instantly that he wasn't one of us, that he came from privilege. I looked around and saw no one."

"'Are you lost, little boy?' I asked. He shook his head. 'You are not lost?'

"'I am not lost, but I don't want to go back,' he replied.

"'Why not?'

"He remained silent. His large, watery eyes reflected a pain that shouldn't have been in the eyes of a child his age.

"'Go back, boy!' I said. 'People will come looking for you.'

"'They won't,' he said, shaking his little head again.

"'Why?'

"'They are busy.'

"'What are they busy with?'

"The boy gave no answer, but brought his head down, silently sobbing.

"'What happened?' I asked, kneeling in front of him.

"'They are seeing my aunt off to her next life. Ponditji told me,' he murmured, as his little chest trembled in a broken rhythm. 'No one will come for me. Not my aunt, not my friends. They are all gone.'"

Everyone in the room gazed down towards the ground in a deafening silence.

"I couldn't be there and judging by how well you people knew Babuda, I think you all know why," Bishnu said, finally. "I was in hiding to save my life and the life of my sister. I didn't have the luxury—"

"Regardless of that, the truth is that when you were gone, Babu had nobody," Nasrin replied. "You found a new family and managed to get a shelter for Pipali. Babu was a stranger in his own family and he had nowhere to go to."

Bishnu stared at Nasrin with pain. He had no reply.

"I saw the same little boy in him when he came to me that morning a few months ago," Nasrin said. "The same look of desperate abandonment. He was trying to hide it, but it was written in his eyes. He spent his days either in bed with a bottle or sheepishly working in the yard with Nitu and me.

"Then, one day, he got up from his bed and said, 'I have to go back. I need to make things right, even if it kills me.'

"I made no attempt at stopping him. I knew that he needed to do whatever he was going to do. I also knew that, somehow, it was connected to the pain he'd felt all his life. It was his redemption."

53 A JOURNEY THROUGH DECAY

The cart was made of bamboo, with thick wooden borders. It was designed to carry products to Ustadji's restaurant. We pushed it across thick but thinning woodland, on muddy tracks that I assumed had been made by the very same cart. The cart carried sacks of grain, wooden crates full of bottles and hidden underneath all that, Babu Bhairab's body.

On the front of the cart, in an empty space, sat Pipali, nervously glancing at us. She was instructed to stay quiet under the hood of the grey blanket that covered her. Nituda and Nasrin pulled the cart from the front, while Bishnu and I pushed it from the back. Ustadji walked calmly beside us, supported by a large walking stick.

"Remember, this is just like any other shipment. That's how you need to act if you run into anybody," Ustadji had told us. "But, hopefully, we won't run into anyone significant and certainly not any of Bhairab's men." He breathed in to give himself some confidence. "We will continue to head north, past the bend of the Great Green Lake, 'til we run into a cluster of houses. A few poor, Hindu farmers live there and they won't pay us much attention. That's where we're going to curve towards the east. That's the only safe way."

Darkness had already enveloped us, but the moonlight gave enough ambiance to go by. Less than a year ago, if I had been told to venture into this area, I would have outright refused. About six months ago, if I were given that offer, I would have gone willingly and joyously with Bishnu for a night of stories and intrigue. But on that night, as I pushed the cart with Bishnu on my side, I didn't feel any fear or excitement.

Instead, I felt an urgency to take these people to where they needed to go, with Babu Bhairab's body. I glanced at Bishnu and realized that he was feeling the same way. No longer were we audacious youths looking for adventure. In the space of a few months, through experiencing the strange and the impossible, we had had gone beyond youth, into the bleating anxiety of manhood.

Cold wind hit me and I looked sideways to see twinkling lights on the shore near Choubazaar and the dark outline of Ustadji's store. But we were not going there. We continued our journey deeper into the north. A rush of memory hit me; sounds that I hadn't acknowledged when I experienced them. The clinking of nupurs[lxxv] from the feet of Nasrin and the other girls. The laughter and jest Babu Bhairab's voice. The eccentricity in his behavior, which I had viewed with so much judgment back then, felt beautiful in my memory. He was a person—a living, breathing person, with joys and sorrows of any other living being—a luxury he no longer had.

"You are crying." It wasn't a question from Bishnu, but simply an acknowledgment, perhaps with a hint of admiration.

Darkness had fully set in. I heard the strange cries of owls, with crickets chirping at their loudest. The moonlight peeking in through the leaves of tall trees provided a weak ambiance that wasn't enough for us to see what was ahead.

A light, metallic sound made me glance to my left and I saw Ustadji setting ablaze a small kerosene lamp without a glass covering. He held the small container in his right hand and raised it. It illuminated our path just enough for us to see a few feet ahead of us. He hurried his steps forward to the front of the carriage because the people pulling it needed the light the most. He ran his hand softly over Pipali's back.

"Just a bit more, maa, just a bit more," he said in a soft, assuring voice.

We pushed forward. As the lights of the shore faded behind us, we saw a few much weaker lights in the distance ahead of us. As we got closer, they revealed themselves to be kerosene lamps in the windows of four, very minimalistic, huts. Three were lined up facing south, with one facing east. All of them shared one middle yard. A little child was drawing shapes with a stick on the ground. His upper body was bare and he was wearing oversized legwear, tied at the waist with a string. Our party went past the four huts and turned east. Ustadji whipped his lamp sideways to make it go out in a wisp. The lights from the huts were enough for us to move forward now.

"Keep your heads down," he muttered as he surveyed the scenery ahead. "The forest will thin down enough to make us visible from a distance."

Following Ustadji's orders, Bishnu and I continued to pushed the cart forward. For some reason, I didn't feel any fatigue at all. I didn't feel much for my body. I was beyond its needs.

As Ustadji had warned us, the tree line started to significantly thin out and moonlight poured gracefully into the landscape. The ground I was walking on started to change; the soil started to feel loose. After a few hundred yards, I started to feel the all-too-familiar sandy soil with a hit of moisture under my feet. That didn't surprise me. I knew where we were going.

"By God's wrath, this place still had trees a few months ago!" Nasrin muttered, shaking her head. "If it goes on like this, it will spread to Hizrapara, one day."

Pipali's blanked flapped in the howling gust of wind. In the furthest distance, to the west, were the fading twinkles of Choubazaar. The market was closing for the night. I peered forward towards the emptiness ahead of me, trying to find the light of a contorted little hut until it finally appeared in the distance. Our journey was almost over. We were about to bring Babu Bhairab back to his favorite playground. The fallen garden, where his fallen body would be laid to rest.

"Aru!" Ustadji's cried out, in the same broken voice he'd cried out in when he brought us to Hizrapara. "Aru re! Open the door. See who we have brought to you."

The door of the hut opened and out came its inhabitant, in careful steps.

"Wh-what's going on?" Arup Sai asked.

"We brought our Babli's body," said Ustadji, as he settled himself. "Babli is dead."

"Bab—" Arup Sai muttered. "My bhatija[lxxvi]?"

He walked purposefully towards us. Ustadji proceeded towards the cart, but Arup Sai raised a hand to stop him. He somehow knew which bag hid Babu Bhairab's body. He pried it open, revealing Babu Bhairab's face.

He stared at it for a while before closing his eyes. A gulp moved down his throat beneath his glistening white beard. He leaned lightly on the wooden border of the cart.

"Look how beautiful you have become!" he said, caressing a hand through Babu Bhairab's curly, dark hair. "Shormi used to say that your beauty would one day win the world. What would she say if she was here today, Babu?" A single drop of a tear slid down his calm face, as it glistened in the moonlight. "So much youth. Wasted...all because of me,"

He looked up at Nasrin and Nituda. "Bring him inside. I need to give him a proper send-off. That's the least I can do." He turned towards Pipali, who was observing him from behind the blanket. He smiled at her, attempting desperately to hide his pain. "And who are you, maa?" he asked. "Are you Babli's friend?"

"She is," Bishnu said calmly as he walked over to the front of the cart and helped her down. He then looked disconcertingly at the old man. "And so am I. We are also your children, Arup Sai. Children you have fathered and adopted. You might have thought hiding away from civilization would let you rot away in peace without resolving your past, but this dunya has a different plan for you."

"You…you are my Shanu?" Arup Sai's voice tremored as he uttered those words. "You are—"

"Your two children lived their whole life hiding." Bishnu went on ignoring the old man's response. "But your bhatija that you see dead in front of you didn't want us to run anymore. So, he did something about it. Something catastrophic. But, in the end, the unintended consequences of his actions have brought us here. Pipali and I can no longer run away and fend for ourselves. There are men with bad intentions looking for us all over the village and a very important companion of mine is trapped as a prisoner on the Bhairab island." Bishnu sighed. "We need your help."

A second gust of wind swirled around us, bringing with it the fresh smell of rain.

54 A STORM OF CHANGE

Right at the end of spring comes a legendary storm called the Kalboishakhi Jhor[lxxvii]. It's a vicious disturbance of nature that rips into the landscape. Tin-shed roofs, torn from houses, are flung into the tops of tall trees. Haystacks are decimated and the small shacks of poor farmers get torn apart. From a distance, crop fields look like a sea struck by a mad tempest. The cattle wail and hide into their sheds.

The palm and coconut trees in the distance flail about like mourning giants. Sometimes it rains. Sometimes it hails. Sometimes, tides of wind come crashing in, full of soil and grass ripped up from the ground. It comes with tremendous force. With ill intent. In a violently beautiful display, it makes the world pay the price for the fortunes of a new year and a new summer.

As the terrible storm raged outside, we sat inside Arup Sai's little shack. The storm crashed itself against the door and the closed leads of the windows. The cart in which we had transported Babu Bhairab's body stood outside, under the shed of the slightly extended roof. Babu Bhairab's body laid inside, on the floor near the door. We all sat around the low table in front of Arup Sai's bed, where he sat. The kerosene lamp on the table lit up his face in otherworldly ambiance.

"Don't worry, I made sure the hut has good foundations," Arup Sai said, pointing at the corners of the roof, where pillars of cut-up tree trunks stood. His face hardened into a grimace. "So, Prithu killed him?"

"Yes," answered Bishnu calmly.

"And you killed Prithu?"

"Yes."

"Good." With a long, deep breath, he stared at Babu Bhairab's body. "You never told me who you really are," he said finally.

"Dadaji changed my name when he adopted me. He wanted to

protect me."

"I thought you and Pipali were dead. Everyone told me I was responsible for murdering my family and murubbis told me that whoever killed them probably took my children away and killed them elsewhere."

"And you were satisfied with that explanation?" asked Bishnu coldly, holding Pipali in his arms.

"Finding murdered children, along with their mother, could have a catastrophic impact in the villagers' minds, thus making it harder for the Bhairabs to put the blame on me," the old man replied. "It was easier to establish that a husband had put his hand on his wife and it had resulted in a fatal outcome, than to prove that he had murdered his own child, too. So, to avoid any foreseeable risks, the Bhairabs probably took my children away to be rid of them elsewhere—that's what the murubbis told me."

Arup Sai looked away towards the closed window and squinted his eyes.

"I was told by the whole world that my children were dead. I was told that I was responsible for it. I did everything to isolate myself from the world, not because I was shunned as a murderer, but because of the pain I felt from the loss of my family.

"If I hadn't been so stubborn, if I hadn't gone up against forces I couldn't survive against, if I'd just let go of my pride and focused on my family, then perhaps I wouldn't have experienced this loss. So, I thought to myself, even if my children had somehow survived, I should refrain from being involved in their lives."

The old man looked at Bishnu with desperation in his eyes. He wanted his son to understand. Bishnu broke the gaze to look at Pipali, who was shivering in his arms. He ran his hand through her long hair.

"You were right," he said finally, in a calm voice.

Arup Sai's face relaxed a little as he exhaled a sigh of relief.

"Dadaji told you that to protect us," Bishnu went on. "He was the one who found us running in the woods."

"It was a cold winter night when Dadaji brought them to me." Ustadji took over the conversation. "He was the last person I expected to see come to my establishment, yet there he was, with a little boy and a little girl in his hands, in the depths of a cold winter night. He told me that the children were in deep trouble and they needed to be taken far away, or else even he wouldn't be able to protect them.

"Dadaji was the lead murubbi of the village and I was a young Hindu restaurant owner who sold contraband to the villagers. I was in no position to say no to him. So, my course of action was clear. I took the two children to my island and took care of them the best I could. Then, about a year later, on a similar dark, winter's night, he came to my island on a boat again.

"He told me that he was there to take the boy away, as he would be able to look after him now that the dust had settled with the case of Aru's family being murdered. No one would bat an eye if he took a boy as his caretaker. But the girl needed to stay with me because it would be impossible for him to take her in without facing judgment and suspicion. So, that's how it's been…until now."

"And you never told me about any of this?" Arup Sai asked.

"Why would he?" Bishnu replied instantly. "It was the only way to keep us safe."

"Oh and one more thing…" Ustadji said, turning to Bishnu. "It was Dadaji who told Babu to find a way to bring Pipali to the Bhairabs. He asked me to bring Babu to the island so that he could talk to him. There, he explained to him that Pipali was growing up and needed to come back to society. He told Babu that his family owed her that, at the very least, after all they had done to her. Babu was the only Bhairab he could reach out to and he knew he was running out of time as his own health was deteriorating. So, he did the only thing he could do.

"I warned him. I told him that he didn't understand Babu Bhairab and the twisted way he thinks. But he was too noble to see the darkness in people and he was desperate. Babu promised him that he would do whatever it took to find a way for Pipali to be accepted by the Bhairabs."

I looked at Babu Bhairab's body. The flickering light of the kerosene lamp was making fluttering works of light and shadow over his face. The storm had subsided and gentler gusts of wind could be heard outside. We had weathered the tempest and now we had to wait until the morning—a fresh new start.

55 A SECRET INTERMISSION

"The earliest bus to the capital leaves in a couple of hours—enough time for me to take you to your Dadima's house. There, you can say your goodbyes, pack your bags and be on your way home. This is the safest time to go. So, come with me."

Arup Sai had noticed me waking up at the sound of him getting ready. It didn't wake anyone else; I was never a heavy sleeper.

"I am not going," I muttered. "I want to see this through."

The old man turned around from the small mirror he was combing his beard in and looked at me confusedly. I felt a strange sense of happiness seeing him at that moment. Arup Sai, to me, was no longer an old man shrouded in mystery. He seemed much more real. Perhaps even familiar.

"You don't want to go back to your family?" he whispered

"Not yet."

"You do understand that you escaped a very dangerous predicament, right? You escaped from a group of cold-blooded murderers who had no intention to leave any witness to their deeds, to which you are one."

"I am aware of that."

"So, why do you want to give these people the opportunity to get to you again?"

"Because there are people, I have grown to care about who aren't safe and I'm not going to leave them this way."

We stared at each other in silence. Gusts of wind could still be heard outside. Kalboishakhi had done its damage and left, but its residual effect lingered in the atmosphere.

"I know much about you, Arup Sai, but you don't know much about me," I whispered. "But if you did, then you'd know that being a part of all this...to care for these people, is perhaps the only thing that matters to me now."

I looked around. Bishnu had his back against the wall, with Pipali in his arms. Nituda and Nasrin had their back on one of the pillars, asleep. They all seemed deceivingly at peace, while their lives hung in the balance.

While all these people had to take their place on the muddy floors of Arup Sai's hut, I was given the honor of taking a spot beside Arup Sai on the bed, close to the window—the same bed where Bishnu spent the first four years of his life.

"So, do you have any plans to save Nondi?" I asked.

"I do," answered the old man.

"And how do you plan to do it?"

"By going to the Bhairab estate with Bishnu and confronting Megha."

"Good. Then I will join you. Now put down that comb and get some sleep."

Arup Sai put the comb down, but stared blankly at the mirror.

"Can't go to sleep, can you?" I chuckled silently.

The old man shook his head.

"Then let's go for a walk, shall we?"

We tiptoed past our sleeping companions and the dead one near the door and walked out into the dead forest for one last exchange of stories. However, I will come to that later.

56 WHAT MAKES A MONSTER

The two men were afraid of us. Instead of holding their spears confidently in their hands, they clutched them close to their chests and stared at us nervously. We walked up to them this morning, when they were sitting on the bench of a confectionery store.

"Take me to Megha," were Arup Sai's only words, at which they nodded obediently.

We got on their steamer boat and were on our way. We sat in the husk while they sat as close to the engine as possible, whispering amongst themselves and avoiding eye contact. Bishnu kept the spear he'd seen his childhood friend murdered with right beside him. He eyed the men and they nervously looked away. The riot we'd caused last night had left its mark. *If these men were cautious with us, then the Bhairabs couldn't have caused much harm to Nondi.* I knew Bishnu was thinking the same thing.

We had left Ustadji, Nituda and Nasrin at the hut to keep watch on Babu Bhairab's body and to look after Pipali.

"If you want, I can go back to Hizrapara and bring an army with me," Ustadji said.

"No," Arup Sai replied in a stern voice. "There will be no more bloodshed. I will handle this with Megha myself. I need to confront what I've been running away from my whole life."

"I can tell you now that the Hizrapara is not happy," Nasrin interjected. "They would like very much to see Babu's death properly avenged."

"Yes, but that will nullify the sacrifice he made for all of us," Bishnu said. He then looked at Ustadji. "And it is paramount that you, in particular, stay out of trouble. You and your restaurant are vital for this community."

I had never been prouder of Bishnu than I was at that moment. He finally understood.

"If you don't want to take us with you as reinforcements, then how exactly are you planning to survive on the island?" Asked Nasrin. "And how do you plan to get Nondi out?"

"You all seem to have forgotten that I am Nondi's childhood friend," Bishnu responded calmly. "I am not going to an unfamiliar place. I am going back to my friends." He paused to glance around the room as we looked on. "And nobody here understands my friends better than I do."

That was the last bit of conversation we had with people from Hizrapara before the three of us set sail for the island. Bishnu sat in front of me in the husk. His eyes carried burning determination. He was no longer afraid.

"How much did Babu tell you about his aunt Shormi?" Arup Sai's voice broke my train of thought.

"Nothing much, actually," I admitted.

"Those times feels like a dream now. Like a beautiful dream," Arup Sai said. "I used to come home from work, look through the window of my bed and see the children playing. All four of them." He glanced at Bishnu, who chose not to glance back. "I wish I had paid more attention. I wish I was more aware of the things that mattered. My beautiful children and my beautiful bhatija."

He took a deep breath. "When I saw Babu for the first time, it was a bright, late-autumn morning. The Bhairabs were busy celebrating the harvest and I didn't expect them to come to me for any reason whatsoever." He sighed. "But there she was. Modhudi! The last of the Bhairabs I expected to see in my yard. I was astonished. But when I saw the newborn, she was carrying in her arms, I understood her reason.

"This Deboshishu! Beautiful, wide eyes. Curly, raven-black hair. Rosy, pale cheeks. Thick, blood-red lips." He shook his head, measuring what to say next. "The woman who had looked at me scornfully all those years had come back with a friendly smile and the great news. I saw the pride behind her eyes. She had broken the curse that she blamed me for putting on her."

"You...cursed her?" I asked.

"It wasn't a curse and even if it was, I didn't mean it," he said. "You see, I was a Bhairab once, too. I was Arup Bhairab—Raghab's older brother and the first contender to all of my father's wealth. But I didn't want any of it for I wasn't like them in any shape or form.

"I had seen houses raided, lands taken over by force and families broken, all so that my family could extend their wealth and name. So, I decided I wanted none of it. I told my father that Raghab could take over the family business and decided to focus on what I found most pleasure in—understanding nature.

"That didn't sit well with my father. He told me that if I choose not to fulfil my role in the family, I should denounce my family-name and leave. So, I did. But before I left, I told them that if they continued to live by their pride and care for nothing else, one day, they would give birth to a monster."

"So, you did curse them?"

"In a way, yes. But it wasn't a curse. It was just cause and effect—an inevitability. Soon after I had left, I heard from people that Meghab had been born. But I was never invited to see him. I realized that my family had fully denounced me and I accepted it. I only saw Meghab from a distance, when he grew up and Raghab brought him to the mainland to administer his crops. However, I did see the other children right after they were born."

"Even Kuberda?"

The old man nodded with a sigh. "Twelve years after I had left the Bhairabs, on a late autumn night, when I got back from work, I was surprised to see Raghab standing in front of the door of my home with a grim face.

"'I hope you are happy, Arup,' Raghab said, ushering me to come inside. There, in my hut, on the bed was Modhudi, sobbing quietly.

"'What's the matter, Modhudi?' I asked. She stared at me with piercing eyes and lowered the small blanket she was holding close to her chest. I hadn't realized that the blanket wasn't empty. In there laid a new-born child, with bones as thin as jute stocks and a disproportionately large, oval-shaped head. The infant looked back at me with tired, narrow eyes that were almost closed. From his dull, pink lips, a gush of saliva descended, dripping onto his pale chest.

"'Look what your curse did,' she said. 'Your monster has finally come to this world.'

"'That's not what I-'

"'You want to keep it? Here.' She extended her arms, carrying the child with jerky motions that lacked any affection whatsoever. 'Take your monster away from me.' She started sobbing uncontrollably. 'Take it!'

"'Modhubi, that's enough,' Raghabda said, putting his hand on her arm. 'Let's go.' He left with his wife, giving me one last hateful glance. 'You cursed my family and hurt my pride. I will hurt yours,' he said.

"Since that day, I dreaded retaliation. I was a lonely man, so at least I had the comfort of knowing that if I ever was in danger, it would only be me. But a few years later, Shormi came into my life, with Pipali. I didn't want that life because it meant that I had to always look over my shoulder. But I had no choice."

Arup Sai looked pensively towards the water for a few moments. "When Shormi came into my life, I had a short period of happiness. I was at peace in my own little world. I sold medicine all day and came back to a pot of hot rice and freshly-cooked curry, made with love. I wasn't Pipali's father, but she cared for me in her own way."

The old man looked at me with a dry smile. Bishnu sat a few meters away, staring at the ground.

"I was starting to believe that, perhaps, there wouldn't be any retaliation and the Bhairabs had forgotten about me. After Shanu…" Arup Sai paused to glance at Bishnu who avoided his father's gaze. "…was born, I stopped looking over my shoulder. Around the same time, Babu was born, too and Modhudi started visiting us with her new-born baby. I understood her motivation for forgiving me; she wanted to prove to me that my curse was broken. I was content with that. I was happy to see her happy.

"With time, she became a family friend. I would come home from work to see her sitting on my bed, smiling merrily. Pipali sat beside her with needle and string, listening intently as her aunt, who held her tiny hands, guided her as she made patterns on a katha."

A streak of a smile formed in the old man's eyes as he went on. "Babu and my children grew up together in front of my eyes and I truly thought all of us had finally moved on. Seeing the innocent children playing in the forest made me hopeful that when they grew up, they would be able to look beyond our feud and rebuild the family." Arup Sai paused. The silence that followed felt natural. I gave the old man time to process his thoughts.

The new summer sun had fully taken over the sky and the water sparkled in its glow. There weren't any more boats around; the fishermen had all gone to the relative safety of their homes to weather the storm. The island I'd fled from last night was a visible blimp in the distance. It wouldn't be long until we reached it. I wasn't afraid. I was ready for anything.

"I didn't realize what Raghab really meant when he said he would 'hurt my pride.'" Arup Sai started again. "Across the river, in the glade beyond, I saw workers building something. When they brought in the machines, I knew what it meant. Even though the villagers were not clear on who was building all this, I knew who was responsible. The village murubbis organized a protest and I joined.

"Modhudi continued to visit us, despite the fact that the feud had rejuvenated. I avoided her. I worked on the protest all day and only came back at night. Amidst all the madness, I forgot what made me happy in the first place. I forgot about my wife and children…until they were taken from me." The old man stared at me in pain.

I put my hand on his shoulder. "Well, Arup Sai. All is not lost," I went on. "Your children have come back to you. You have a second chance."

"We're here." Bishnu's announcement startled us. He had quietly left the husk and stood on the deck.

We followed him out of the husk. The island seemed much less menacing than it had the last time I had been on a boat approaching the Bhairab boatshed. A few of Meghab Bhairab's men were standing on the wooden dock. My eyes searched for Biruda, but he wasn't among them.

57 'O-BROMHON, NOHO TUMI TATO'

"Meghabda, please hear them out." Kuber Bhairab's voice echoes the halls, the moment we were taken to the second floor of Meghab Bhairab's house.

In the concrete hallway was a bamboo mat, layered with a white cotton sheet. On top of that arrangement laid Biruda, eyes closed and left thigh heavily bandaged with bloody white cloths. A nearby door opened and Meghab Bhairab stepped out. He seemed calm and collected.

"All right, my brother. I will take your suggestion on this one, as well. I will hear them out before I decide what to do with them," he said, eying us. "You people should consider yourselves lucky." He then focused his gaze on me. "You have returned."

"I have," I said, glancing at the bandage on his left hand.

"If you had left for the capital early enough, my men wouldn't have been able to come after you. I was worried about that. But now you've come right back to my lair, like an idiot."

"I don't care for what you think of me," I said, calmy.

"All right, then, tell me, why have you come back?"

"I am here for the same reason all of us are: we are here for Nondi. Let her go and we can all leave peacefully."

Instead of answering me, Meghab Bhairab looked sideways, towards Kuber Bhairab. "Will he survive?" he asked, indicating towards Biruda.

"Yes," Kuber Bhairab said. "He has bled a lot and is very weak, but he will get through."

"Hopefully, when he comes to his senses, he will learn to appreciate the fact that I spared him, despite his disobedience."

"Well, showing obedience doesn't end well for your men, does it?" Bishnu's confident voice startled me. "Take Prithuda, for example."

Meghab Bhairab's jaw tightened as the lean muscle on his body rippled. For the first time since coming back to the island, I felt a pang of fear in my chest. I didn't understand where all this tenacity of Bishnu's was coming from. The guards had taken away his spear and we were surrounded by at least a dozen men.

"Bishnu, you need to stop aggravating Meghabda," Kuber Bhairab interjected, as he got up with the help of his staff. "Why don't we all go into the room and sort this out?"

He looked at Bishnu dejectedly as he ushered us to enter the room. Meghab Bhairab went in without making any eye contact. As soon as we entered, the guards closed the door behind us. Half of them remained outside, while the other half stood right behind us.

Meghab Bhairab's bedchamber was enormous. The northern side, where we'd entered, had an elaborate sitting arrangement. Meghab Bhairab took a seat on one of the sofas there with Kuber Bhairab and took the smoking hookah in his hand. A large bed rested in the south-eastern corner. Nondi and Maaji sat there, with their backs on the wall. They didn't seem to be physically distressed in any way, but their eyes told me they were exhausted.

"Well, Arupji," Meghab Bhairab broke the tense silence. "Your two friends have had their say. Why have you been quiet 'til now? Go on. See if you can aggravate me, too."

"I'm not here to aggravate anyone," Arup Sai spoke. "I have a simple proposition for you. The object that Babu took out of the cellar is a chest full of jewels and riches. It is now sitting in a hidden location, which only we know about. Let Nondi go and I can guide your men to that chest. And we will go on our merry way."

Meghab Bhairab broke into laughter. "You really think I care about some treasure chest? You, of all people, should have an idea about how wealthy we really are. A chest full of gold means nothing to me." His face suddenly hardened as he looked at us with a cold stare. "What matters to me is teaching lessons. Making people aware of what happens when you defy the Bhairabs. And the best lessons are ones that have consequences. You people are not leaving this island without consequence."

"Believe me, Megha, no one understands consequences better than I do," Arup Sai said. "The Bhairabs have taken everything from me. My forest, my family and my livelihood." He took a quick glance at Maaji, who looked back expressionlessly. "Whatever curse you people think I put on you, I can assure you that I paid for it tenfold. So, I am not here to defy you any further.

"I'm here because the people that you have put in danger are children, Megha. Children, who are dealing with the consequences of the whims of another child. They are not defying you; they are simply reacting to the situations they were put in and all they want to do is survive. I beg you to spare them. You know that there's nothing we can do to you. You have won and we can never retaliate for anything you've done to us. You own this world. Its people, its law. Everything."

"Yes, but you are not all from my world, are you?" Meghab Bhairab said. "You have a friend here from the capital, who can go back and get the law enforcement from the capital involved." He took a deep breath as he leaned back on his sofa. "That will result in me paying too many people off to get them off my back and even after that, rumors will spread. It will reach my buyers in the capital. I cannot afford that. My business hinges on reputation."

He gave me a calculative gaze as he leaned forward. "The kindest thing I can do is kill this capital rat and that fisherman boy, along with that old lady on the mainland."

My heart skipped a beat, but I looked on without flinching.

"The old lady has some influence in the village, so there might be some uprising. But I can manage that. I can get this done discreetly. Prithuda can take care of it. I'll consult with him when he comes back from his search." He got up and looked sideways towards Nondi, who gazed back. "Until I do all that, I can keep you and Arupji hostage here and then let you go when the dust settles. I do see Kuber's point, now. You were just taking care of the girl."

He then frowned contemplatively and took a couple of steps forward, looking up at Arup Sai. "But why should I be so kind? It will be far less problematic for me if I do all that and then kill you as well. So, unless you give me a reason not to—"

"Meghabda, you are overthinking," Kuber Bhairab said, as he got up and came closer to his brother. "These people have no leverage on us—even our guest from the city." He chuckled at his elder brother.

"Our connections in the capital are way too powerful than whoever he can summon on his side. We have it all; the transport, the policemen on the road. They are all bought and paid for. Babaji made all that investment solely for the purpose that we don't have to get our hands dirty unless we absolutely need to." Kuber Bhairab paused to catch his breath.

"If you let them go, they'll go away and live their lives, thanking their good fortune for leaving this island alive, let alone having the courage to retaliate." He nodded at his elder brother, who looked back contemplatively. "And besides, if you kill these people, the news will reach Babuda, wherever he is hiding and knowing him, the news of Bishnu's death will make him disappear forever and we will never have our brother back."

"You are a kind soul, my brother," Meghab Bhairab said. "But being a Bhairab sometimes involves making difficult decisions."

"You still seem to think Prithuda is alive, don't you?" Bishnu's cold voice came from my side, breaking the conversation. "I have slain your monster. Stuck my fishing spear right through his heart and drowned him in the depth of The Great Green Lake."

"Bishnu, stop being disrespectful!" Kuber Bhairab cried out, in the loudest voice he could muster.

Meghab Bhairab took a few steps forward and stood about a meter in front of us, leaving his brother behind. "What did you just say?"

"I killed your monster."

"You killed my monster?" Meghab Bhairab sneered.

"Yes, I did. He killed my childhood friend and I avenged him."

"Bishnu, what are you saying?" said Kuber Bhairab, dejectedly. "Stop making it worse for yourself with these made-up tales."

"It is not a made-up tale." Arup Sai joined the exchange. "Babu's body is lying on the floor of my house right at this moment, wrapped in a blanket." He looked back at Kuber Bhairab's shocked face. "He is dead. Prithu killed him while attacking your friends when they were fleeing from the island. He was about to kill them, too, but Bishnu stopped him."

The old man stared into the eyes of Kuber Bhairab as I saw the color drain from the weakling child's already pale face.

"Bab—" Kuber Bhairab muttered, taking half a step backward. "Babu is dead?"

Arup Sai nodded quietly.

"YOU KILLED HIM!" Maaji's cry shattered the stunned silence as she flung herself towards Arup Sai, crashing onto him, wailing in rage. The top portion of her white shari had unfolded and fallen off to the ground. With only the white blouse covering her upper body and her hands free, she reached for the old man's throat. Arup Sai took a step back, struggling to keep her at bay.

"You murdered my Babli! I always knew—"

"Maaji!." Meghab Bhairab came forward to break the commotion. He grabbed Maaji's shoulder and pulled back with great effort to separate her from Arup Sai.

"Leave me be, Megha!" Maaji cried out. "I am going to end him."

"Maaji...just...calm...down," Meghab Bhairab said, struggling to control his mother, who had lost her footing, letting all her weight go on her elder son's arms. "We need to assess what—"

It was that exact moment that was frozen in time in my memory— similar to Babu Bhairab's beautiful laughter before he was struck by the spear that took his life. As he wrestled to keep his mother from hurting herself, for a fleeting moment, the man who had been responsible for the deaths of three people seemed quite humane to me. *Has he ever had a chance to redeem himself?*

But just the way Meghab Bhairab couldn't finish his sentence, I couldn't finish that thought. I heard the metallic sound of a knife being unsheathed. It was Kuber Bhairab's—the small knife I'd seen him use while fishing. Clutching it in his skinny hands, he came charging in, diving right on Meghab Bhairab's back.

A meaty thud was followed by a spurt of blood that flickered back onto Kuber Bhairab's face. But that didn't faze him as his eyes carried unrelenting determination. He used all the weight of his body to wedge the knife further in as Meghab Bhairab's knees started to buckle.

The guards seemed to be in shock as they looked confusedly at each other. As Meghab Bhairab's knees finally gave out, with the last bit of grit left in his body, he knelt down, trying not to hurt his mother, who he was still holding onto. The death-scene of the villain of my story was anticlimactically humane. His eyes were full of shock and despair. Maaji, who had landed on the floor, turned around, but by that time, her eldest son's body was falling forward on top of her. No longer was she struggling as she looked back in disbelief.

Meanwhile, Kuber Bhairab kept on pressing. The gushing blood had painted all of his pale face, neck and hands in crimson. Meghab Bhairab tried to disengage by flinging his hands back, but to no avail. Soon, the flinging and flailing got weaker until it stopped altogether. Meghab Bhairab's lifeless hands dropped to the floor.

The two brothers went two ways. The elder fell face-first into Maaji's lap, while the younger went backward, lying flat on the bloody floor. Blood, flooding the floor, had completely soaked the portion of Maaji's shari that had previously fallen.

Despite the blood everywhere, I felt nothing. I felt empty and tired. I saw Nondi running over to Kuber Bhairab's side. She knelt down and took his crimson head on her lap. I saw bubbles frothing out of Kuber Bhairab's nose. Nondi took off her orna and wiped his face clean, which was revealed to be contorted in pain. His thin, trembling lips were pursed together as tears came gushing out of his eyes.

Looking at him, I realized, I had never seen Kuber Bhairab cry until that point. Perhaps for the first time, to me, he seemed weak. In my eyes, with his exuberance, curiosity and wisdom, he had defied all the images of a weakling that people had put on him. But for the first time ever, right after murdering his dangerous older sibling, he seemed incomplete. He seemed crippled.

"Babli!" he whimpered. "My Babli is no more. I tried. I—" He breathed unevenly. "I tried, all my life, to keep these monsters off him. But they killed him anyway. They killed him, Nondi! All for their greed and pride."

"I know, Kuberda. I know," Nondi whispered calmly, even though she, too, was weeping.

I brought my attention to Nondi. No longer did she hide her pain behind her orna. As tears ran down her cheeks and naked throat, with her hair tied into a bun and her upper lip swollen, she seemed Godly and blissfully so. She seemed like a person who could endure much and still remain vigilant. Kneeling on the floor, soaked in blood as she comforted a wailing murderer, she looked hauntingly beautiful.

58 A BUCKET FULL OF BLOOD

"I always knew, one day, all my happiness would fade away and you would be left standing," Maaji said in a numb voice when Kuber Bhairab stepped back into the room after getting himself cleaned. "I knew it in my gut and it happened. My Raghabji, my Babli...my Megha. All gone. And here you are."

The men took away Meghab Bhairab's body and wiped the blood from the floor. Arup Sai, Bishnu and I sat on the sofas as Nondi and Ponditji helped the men. Kuber Bhairab stared at his mother in wonderment for a while, as did I.

"And here I am," Kuber Bhairab said, smiling back at his mother. The calmness in his voice was frightening. Only a few hours ago, he was carried away from the room as he was bowling and howling after murdering his older brother. Although it seemed that a few hours of cleansing had calmed him down, there was something eloquently unnatural in his poise. It felt almost ritualistic.

"Well, like it or hate it, I am the last Bhairab heir standing and so the responsibility of looking after the family now rests on my shoulders," he finally said. "Unless you want to consider our extended family and in that case, Bishnu can be a contender, too."

For the first time ever, I saw Maaji look at her weakling, middle child. It was a look of tired rejection.

"While you're deciding, I would like to invite you all on a quick trip to The Banyan Tree for a sight of the decay," Kuber Bhairab said, looking around the room. He glanced back at Maaji. "There, I'd show you something that might change your perspective."

I remembered the last time Babu Bhairab invited me to see the decay, which I had rejected. *What was it that he wanted me to see?*

On his long staff, he led us all to the tree. It looked as mythical as the first time I saw it. Its thick, barky vines penetrated the ground like waves frozen in time. As I walked around those surrounding vines, the center stock became visible. Hidden inside the vines, the central body was smooth from the top and then seemed to break into a hollow near its roots. White, moldy borders surrounded the damage.

"Meghabda isn't as clever as you all think," Kuber Bhairab said, looking back at all of us—Maaji, Arup Sai, Nondi, Bishnu, along with Biruda standing on a staff just like Kuber Bhairab. "He investigated the cellar, sensing some foul play, but he never investigated the decay, which would have given him the simple answer to his question." He paused for a few seconds, eying all of us. "Who is behind all this?"

He then walked over to the sitting area beside the pond, supported by his staff. He crouched over, with effort and pulled out a bucket, covered with a lid, which he opened, revealing its contents. At first, I thought I was seeing a bucket full of blood. But within seconds, I was hit by a familiar scent. It was the same smell that I got when Arup Sai took me to the lake with blood-red waters—the smell of wet, rotting tannery.

"It was Babu's doing," Kuber Bhairab said, collecting his breath, pointing at the decay with his staff. "He had been collecting the water from the lake near Arupji's hut and dumping it here. He caused the decay himself to initiate The Gathering. Everyone thought it was possibly some form of infestation that trees as old as this one are prone to, but it wasn't."

Kuber Bhairab gazed back at us meaningfully.

"We all loved our Babu in our own way. Even Meghabda." He looked around, nodding. "But he never figured Babu out like he always claimed. Very few of us did. Very few of us took the opportunity to understand Babu. To *really* understand him. If we'd paid him even a minimal bit of attention, we'd have realized that the reasons why he did all the things he did weren't twisted at all.

"It was quite simple, really. Quite painfully consistent. He just couldn't bear the hypocrisy that a family that prides itself on the life-force of a tree could cause so much harm to nature. So, he made things…equal. He wanted to hurt our family pride, the same way we ruined his favorite garden. He wanted our family to pay damages for the sufferings we caused to other people." He paused to catch his breath.

"And we did pay our dues. Quite expensively. We punished people for their defiance, but we couldn't reason with the defiance of our own seed. We could neither love, hate, accept or reject Babu in any true form and in that willful conjecture, we lost him…and Meghabda too, for good measure." With a sigh, he carried himself away from the Banyan Tree and stood near the entrance of the northern gate of the central house.

We followed him.

"So, after so much bloodshed, so much loss, I, as the leader of the

Bhairab house, am going to make some decisions," Kuber Bhairab continued. "But first, I need to organize a few funerals. Starting with Babu's. Ponditji, get your pujaris ready and take a large steamer boat from the shed to go across the river to Arupji's hut. There, you should start preparing for Babu's funeral. People from Hizrapara will help you. Nondi, take Maaji and Pipali to the southern house and prepare them for the funeral."

He then turned to Arup Sai and me. His eyes carried a ghostly, hollowed sorrow. "Come with Biruda and me to the temple, my guests. I believe I have things there that both of you would like to see."

As we left Nondi and Maaji behind and started for the temple, the whole island seemed peaceful and sated. The people in their houses and yards went on with their business and the quiet chirping of the birds in the afternoon bore no signs of the violence we had experienced hours before.

59 A WARM PLACE

"Tha-that's Abir!" Arup Sai cried out.

We were standing just outside the front door, in the yard. Ponditji and his pujaris had already left. From behind the temple, Biruda came limping in, with his leg heavily bandaged, rolling in the cart we'd used to bring Pipali to the temple on the night of The Gathering. It carried the blanketed, lifeless body of Suba Kashem.

Looking at his body, I felt there was nothing left anymore. All the mystery surrounding him and the emotions—fear, nostalgia, childish wonder and rage—seemed to have dissipated. Lying in front of me was an empty shell of a man who lived under many layers of unknown pain.

"I figured as much," Kuber Bhairab's voice, accompanied by rapid breathing, came from inside the temple. "Everybody thought Babu's actions were arbitrary, but I always knew that everything he did had a reason. He wouldn't release a convict from the district-prison just for the sake of his chaotic entertainment. He did it—"

He paused to put in one last burst of energy to pull a large jute-made sack full of clattering contents out of the temple with his right hand, while using the staff to leverage himself with his left. Leaning on the wall near the door to catch his breath, he glanced at Arup Sai with a tired smile. "He did it to get into Babaji's head."

Seeing Kuber Bhairab come out of the temple, Biruda started hastily towards him. But Kuber Bhairab raised his hand and stopped our muscled protector in his tracks.

"I can do this myself, Biruda. You've done enough," Kuber Bhairab said. "Don't exacerbate your injury any further. Just roll the cart over here."

Biruda followed his instructions. Kuber Bhairab looked at Arup Sai and smiled.

"I knew that Subaji must be connected somehow to Bishnu and Pipali." Kuber Bhairab gazed at Suba Kashem's body. He then looked meaningfully at Arup Sai. "And most importantly, to you. I'm guessing 'Suba Kashem' is a name Babu made up to give him anonymity. That didn't help him in the end, though, did it? He had to face the inevitable."

"I never saw him after he left Pipali and Shormi in my hands and disappeared. Pipali was an infant and has no memory of him," Arup Sai said. "I…I don't even know how he ended up in jail."

"I guess we'll never know," Kuber Bhairab said. "His story dies with him. Perhaps that's fitting. Sometimes, a little mystery provides the dignity a person deserves while making the journey from this dunya to whatever lies thereafter."

Arup Sai came forward and put his hand on Abir's motionless body. "Lord, what have they done to him?"

"What Bhairabs usually do when someone defies them," Kuber Bhairab replied instantly. "They dispatched him into nothingness. But don't worry, we're taking him on our boats as well so that you get a chance to give him a proper burial."

Kuber Bhairab rested his staff against the wall and with all the strength his body could muster, he picked up the sack full of dry bones. Biruda took a hesitant step forward, but despite Kuber Bhairab's jittery, thin legs stepping haphazardly in various directions at first, they did eventually manage to propel Kuber Bhairab towards the cart. Biruda lowered the cart slightly to help Kuber Bhairab, who placed the clattering sack near Suba Kashem's body.

Kuber Bhairab, breathing heavily, looked at me and smiled. "Don't worry about me, my dear guest. The sack isn't as heavy as it looks. Dry bones lose a lot of weight as they age."

"You're going to take them with you?" I asked. Kuber Bhairab nodded. "Why?"

"What do you mean, 'why'?" Kuber Bhairab said with a chuckle. "To spread them on the pyre, so that these poor souls can finally have the send-off they deserve."

And so, he did. Ponditji arranged the pyre near Arup Sai's hut, the same way he had for Babaji. The base. The three layers of clothing in three colors. The hay. The butter. The smooth wooden cylinder in the mouth. The only differences were that we were in an empty, barren moor instead of the cozy, green backyard of Meghab Bhairab's house and the sky was red behind our back with the melting sun of dusk, instead of that of dawn.

Kuber Bhairab came forward and, with help from Ponditji, spread the dry bones from the sack all over the top. First, they were white as a sheet of paper. Then they started to darken. The last few bones came out in small black pieces, accompanied by grey dust.

Kuber Bhairab then neatly put the jute-sack on top of everything like a blanket. He looked back at the pujaris and they came forward to put another layer of hay on top. Kuber Bhairab then took the flame from Ponditji, circled the pyre a few times and started the fire, which immediately began to eat away at Babu Bhairab's skin and the flesh of his face. Yet somehow, the scene didn't feel unnerving the way Babaji's funeral had. Rather, it looked peaceful as Arup Sai's hut flickered in the distance.

I was startled by the loud pops when the fire reached the wooden foundation.

"That's the fire hitting air pockets within the hollow bark," came Arup Sai's voice from behind. "Biru did well in creating that foundation, but the wood in here is not as solid. We put more in there than usual. It will do." He nodded.

"This is about the same spot where we cremated Shormi," he went on. "He was this tall back then." He held his palm at the level of his knees. "I wasn't allowed to get too close to my own wife's funeral. But, no one forced Babu to stay away, yet he kept his distance. I saw his little, red lips trembling as he looked on, rubbing his tiny elbows over his eyes.

"Suddenly, he turned back and took off into the forest. I was worried and tried to alert the people, but everyone was intentionally avoiding me. I decided to let it go. I decided that he needed to have his own journey before he could make peace with what he was suffering from." He looked ahead and sighed deeply. "If I knew his journey would eventually bring him here, then perhaps I would have intervened."

"Perhaps," I said. "Or perhaps your intervention wouldn't have mattered. Perhaps he had already been set on his path by then. Perhaps it was necessary for his journey to his Nirvana."

Arup Sai looked at me with admiration.

"I got some wisdom from Ponditji during your brother's funeral." I chuckled. "Don't take me too seriously."

Arup Sai nodded and looked on. "Did he die in peace?" the old man asked.

"No, he didn't." I spoke the truth. "He found peace for a while, but it was forced away from him, along with his life. He died in profound pain, knowing that the people he was determined to protect were still in danger."

"Well, they are no longer in danger, so his soul must be in peace." He glanced at me with a dry smile, pointing towards the pyre of Babu Bhairab. "What do you think he will be reborn as?"

I took a deep breath. "Perhaps a tree. A giant banyan tree. Seems fitting."

"I guess. Well, it can't be here. Nothing grows in this place anymore." Arup Sai said.

"It will, or Babu's sacrifice will be in vain." Kuber Bhairab joined our conversation. Nituda and Nondi stood beside him. "I'm closing down the factory and will be investing in restoring this place back to its old glory." He looked at Arup Sai, nodding confidently. "You might not be alive to see it, but it will happen."

"I don't need to be," Arup Sai replied. "I think I've seen enough for one lifetime."

"The treasure chest will be used to help the Hizrapara community," Kuber Bhairab continued nodding at Nituda, who nodded back. "That is, if you take me there for a visit. "Babu told many stories about your people. I need to see you all with my own eyes."

"I would have taken you there anyway," Nituda said, smiling.

Kuber Bhairab nodded before turning to Arup Sai. "I have a request for you, Arupji,"

"Go on," said Arup Sai.

"You need to come back to the Bhairab estate."

"I would never—"

"I am not asking this of you to dishonor you, but merely as a necessity. You see, you don't know everything. You think your flutes give you the financial means to get through your days. But it doesn't. Bishnu keeps them with him. Every single one of them. He would never tell you, but he confided in me. The money he gives you is the money he gets from fishing and his fix-jobs."

The old man's eyes widened in confoundment.

"He has been providing for you all his life after you ran out of forest to make your medicines with. But doing that would be difficult for him now that he will have more mouths to feed. And he won't put all this financial burden on Dadima. I know him." Kuber Bhairab smiled subtly. "I know you love your craft and you have lived your life crusading against people who wanted to take it away from you. But you have to finally give in, not as a defeat, but as a father. Can you do that?"

Arup Sai brought his head down and nodded.

"Now, then," Kuber Bhairab said and drew a deep breath. "If the adults are happy, we, the young ones, would like to have our own little huddle." Kuber Bhairab nodded and then looked at Nondi and me. "Come now, friends. Let's pay our fisherman friend a visit."

He pointed his staff towards the pyre, where a couple of lone silhouettes stood closer to the flames, their shapes rippling in the fiery background of the evening—Bishnu, with Pipali resting on his shoulder.

"What's on your mind, my friend?" Kuber Bhairab asked as we got close to them.

"What do you think?" replied Bishnu. "I am thinking of Babuda."

"What in particular are you thinking of?"

Bishnu gave a dry chuckle. "He was my best friend. But all my life, I always thought that he was a spoiled brat. I thought if the day came when he needed to do the unthinkable to get what he wants, he would do it. Yet, on the night when he helped us escape from the island, he had the chance to impale that wretched whoreson, but he didn't. He didn't have it in him to take a life, even when it was necessary. He paid for that mistake dearly."

"Yet you had it in you when it was your turn."

"I did. I had to do it to protect my sister."

"How does all this qualify the two of you?" asked Kuber Bhairab. "Good? Evil? Right? Wrong? Can you tell?"

Bishnu looked ahead and sighed. "Don't know. It's a messy business."

"Buji." Pipali's whisper was the only thing that filled the silence that followed.

"I have a confession to share with you," Bishnu said, finally.

"You know you can tell me anything, Bishnu," Kuber Bhairab responded.

"You might not like me very much afterward."

"Let me decide how I feel. Go on."

Bishnu stared ahead. The fire had started to cover more and more of the pyre.

"I could have saved him," Bishnu murmured.

"Saved Babu? How?"

"Babaji sent me to the mainland on the day he gave away the winter harvest. He wanted me to go to my father and bring him to the island. He promised me that he could make Meghabda understand and manage a safe passage for Pipali and me. But I couldn't do it out of fear. Instead, I decided to prepare myself to provide my sister protection if she needed it. If I had just listened to Babaji—"

"If you had listened to him, there would have been an even bigger disaster than what we experienced. Trust me," Kuber Bhairab interjected. "My father was wise, but he had his weaknesses when it came to his children. He never realized what Meghabda was actually capable of. He was too proud to see what he'd created."

He put a hand on Bishnu's shoulder. "You think you had a choice, Bishnu, but you really didn't." He looked towards the pyre. His red lips trembled. "I loved my little brother more than anything else. He was too pure for this world. He was my happiness. But deep in my gut, I always knew that the path he had taken would one day lead here."

He paused to catch his breath, vigorously wiping away tears with his hand. "And I also knew that he couldn't be stopped. So, if I have to blame anyone, I would blame the people who put him on this path in the first place.

I would not blame anyone else. Especially not you or anybody who helped him cope with his own suffering. So, instead, I thank you for the friendship and belonging you gave him. I thank you for being one of the few rare people in his life who kept him in touch with his own humanity."

Kuber Bhairab looked at Bishnu and smiled, with visible pain. A tear fell from Kuber Bhairab's left eye and this time, he didn't wipe it away. It traveled down his pale face, shining with a burning aura in the warm light of the pyre.

"Well, even as we mourn for the dead, we must plan for the living," Kuber Bhairab said, after settling himself.

He took a couple of steps back, helped by his staff, to stand side by side with Nondi. He put a hand lightly on her arm.

"I have decided to let Nondi go. Since the population at the Bhairab household is dwindling, Biruda and Ponditji will be enough to look after it. As the head of the Bhairabs, I will eventually have to take a wife and start a family. Then I might require a housemaid. But that can wait and Nondi no longer needs to be a part of any of it. I think she has served the Bhairabs long enough and it's time she moves on. You can take care of her, right, Bishnu?"

"I can, if she agrees," Bishnu said, looking sideways at Nondi.

"I do," Nondi said, giving Bishnu the same dry grin, she always gave him when she expected him to be better. "Besides, I think you need somebody other than yourself if you want to take care of Pipali."

"If you say so," said Bishnu.

We looked on. The fire had engulfed the pyre fully by now. Thus, the flame was at its peak. In the prevailing darkness of the still summer night, thick smoke from the pyre rose up in various streams that made their own pathways into the starry evening sky.

60 A PROMISE OF REBIRTH

"Tell me about yourself, then," Arup Sai said, while we were taking a walk through the dead forest in the gusty morning after the Kalboishakhi Jhor. "Who are you and why don't you want to go back?"

"You really want to know?"

"I do."

"Does it matter who I am or what my past is? I think it's more important to know what I want to be and what I want to do."

"Yes, but please tell me anyway, since I feel curious."

I chuckled. "I am nobody important. Just a capital dweller like any other. I am young and I have parents at home who are worried."

"Why are they worried?"

"Because I am running away from something."

"What are you running away from?"

I gave a deep, exasperated sigh. "From death. Misery. Loss and destruction. Only to come here and find more of the same."

"So, you are disappointed?"

"I was at the beginning, yes. But over time, I've become inspired."

"Inspired?"

"Yes."

"How so?"

"Because here, in the midst of all this death, misery and loss, people have taken actions to remedy it. Actions that weren't all thought-out and executed with the intended consequences, but actions that, nevertheless, have made progress in restoring the damage and decay.

"You see, I came here from the capital because I had seen people's lives being bought and paid for in factories as they tried to make ends meet and to exist in this miserably cruel world. I've seen the lives of these people perspire into dust and smoke as they struggle to breathe under the rubble, without consequence, without remedy. But here, the deaths and sacrifices are meaningful. It inspires courage, maturity and the will to rebuild and repair.

"I came here because I wanted to run away from what I thought I couldn't change. I thought, no matter what actions I took, I wouldn't achieve anything. But I realize, now, that actions don't always yield perfect results, but no progress is made through inaction. So, after all this is over, I will go back and take the actions that I think are right. But before that, I need to help the people I have grown to care for—the people who inspired me."

The wind had finally started to die down. The morning of a brand-new summer was upon us—a season of hope.

The End

CHILDREN OF DECAY

CHILDREN OF DECAY

i A Bangla expression for grandmother

ii A common street food made with potatoes wrapped and baked in pastry

iii The highest-quality rice, sought after by people who are looking to cook luxurious meals

iv A common, skirt-like leg-wear for men. When people have to work in the fields, they fold it up above their knees for flexibility.

v A human incarnation of a God from Hindu Mythology

vi A silky scarf that girls wear with their kameez

vii An elaborate white loincloth, which is a standard leg-wear for the Hindus

viii A respectful word for 'father'

ix A part of typical dressing for women, which is a piece of long cloth that wraps around the body, covering the garments underneath

x Women, particularly of (but not limited to) lower social standing, often wear shari without a blouse in warmer seasons

xi An expression for grandfather

xii A curved, metal long knife that farmers use to collect harvest from the field; also used for cutting up fruit and light carpentry

xiii A type of waterlily—national flower of Bangladesh

xiv The tuber of shaplas that are eaten as fruits or vegetables

xv A call from the mosques for the late afternoon prayer

xvi Houses with tin-shed roofs tend to bring in the heat or coldness from the outside. Therefore, a thin, flat covering made of bamboo and wood goes under the tin-shed roof to absorb the temperature impact from outside.

xvii A weekly Muslim communal prayer

xviii Morning prayer time for the Muslims

xix An affectionate expression for grandson

xx Member of the society of wise, old people that provides guidance to the community

xxi A widely-practiced treatment for fever

xxii An alcoholic drink produced through fermenting rice

xxiii A popular dessert—a ball of solidified milk and dough in thick syrup

xxiv The religious leaders of Muslim community; they usually play the role of orators and lead in communal prayers

xxv Islamic concept of heaven

xxvi Instant verbal divorce that husbands could enforce on their wives in the old times

xxvii A long skirt women wear under their shari

xxviii A wise Hindu scholar who usually takes care of and conducts the affairs of a Hindu temple

xxix A traditional male attire

xxx Home-made baked and/or roasted edibles made from in-season fruits, fruit-extracts and harvested crops—mostly sweet, but also sometimes savoury

xxxi The chorus-group led by podits in religious ceremonies

xxxii A small wooden tool that varies from being a quarter of a foot to a full foot tall—typically used in the kitchen

xxxiii Cutting implement used in kitchens of rural areas of Bangladesh that requires you to sit in front of it on the ground

xxxiv Betel leaves, wrapped around areca nuts and slaked lime paste that becomes blood-red in the mouth when chewed

xxxv A streak of vermilion red that runs across the parting hairline of married Hindu women

xxxvi A type of small potato that becomes extra tender when cooked

xxxvii A special wok-pot used for cooking with high heat

xxxviii A curry made of leafy vegetables; the potent juice from leaves that grow in the tropical weather flavours the curry

xxxix Literal meaning is 'big father'—term used to denote great grandfathers

xl An arrangement of a heavy slab of stones used to grind spices into paste

xli A term for 'household' that people use when they are putting emotional emphasis on it

xlii Rice cooked with aromatic oil and spices for special occasions

xliii A spicy, sticky curry made with offcuts, legs, heart, head and liver of chickens, with potato

xliv A cage made with complex arrangements of thin bamboo slicers designed to confuse small fish after they enter it, not letting them escape; they are sunk overnight in shallow water, to be extracted in the morning

xlv The war of independence (1971)

xlvi Brainwashed native Muslim spies and betrayers who worked for the occupying Pakistani army, giving them information on freedom fighters and refugees hiding/fleeing from oppression

xlvii A religious dress with intricate designs

xlviii Sacred Hindu verses

xlix An add-on villagers use to names when they call out someone in deep pain and/or desperation

l An affectionate word for 'sister'; can be used to denote someone who carries sisterly respect or love or influence, but is not actually a sibling

li Older brother's wife

lii Child of a God—a word used to describe children who look exceptionally beautiful

[liii] A casual expression for big brother

[liv] 'The noblest of all creation'—a term used to describe humans in Koran

[lv] A word that literally translates to 'world', but has a deeper meaning when used in conversation, such as, 'reality', 'existence' or 'observable universe', etc.

[lvi] Islamic word for 'Angels'

[lvii] Light blankets, hand-made with layers of old clothing (or new clothing if it is to be used as a gift), held together by needle work of intricate design. When it is given as a gift, it is considered a gesture of affection.

[lviii] An affectionate name elders call young people by; literal meaning is 'father'. In Bangla, affection for the young is sometimes expressed through irony. Someone older would call someone younger with the same expression the younger person is supposed to use in that context. It is a showcase of high affection. The sentiment behind it is, "I love you so much that I return the respect and reverence you give me."

[lix] A term used to describe people who don't have the ability to put together coherent speech

[lx] The expression 'my boin' is used to affectionately address female siblings. It's different from the expression, 'Boinji', which can be used to denote *anyone* who receives sisterly respect and love

[lxi] Couple of small drums, played by striking them in different areas with varied intensity to create a complex beat

[lxii] A single-stringed musical instrument

[lxiii] Transvestite women

[lxiv] People with severe deformity

[lxv] Literal Bangla meaning is 'horse', but in this context, he is the middle-man who organizes transport of brides through palkis

[lxvi] *Komla* literally means the orange colour, or the fruit, mandarin

[lxvii] Islamic idea of God's blessings

[lxviii] A pendant full of beads, used to count ritualistic religious chants, usually after prayer

[lxix] An affectionate word older men call their wives with; literal meaning is 'little girl'

[lxx] Islamic concept of judgement day

[lxxi] Little niece

[lxxii] An affectionate word for father among common people

[lxxiii] An affectionate word for mother among common people

[lxxiv] Just like 'baba', older people use the word 'maa' to show deep affection

[lxxv] Ornamented anklets worn by dancers to create pleasant tunes

[lxxvi] Little nephew

[lxxvii] Literal meaning is 'The Black Storm of Boishakh (First month of Summer)'

CPSIA information can be obtained
at www.ICGtesting.com
Printed in the USA
BVHW082059030223
657845BV00003B/63